About the author:

After studying Politics and Economics at Ruskin College, Oxford, and International Relations at the London School of Economics, R J Fielding embarked on a career in higher education. He worked as a lecturer in International Relations at Lanchester Polytechnic (now Coventry University), and was Dean of the Faculty of Modern Studies at Trent Polytechnic (now Trent University, Nottingham). He has contributed to academic journals and radio discussions on the topic of British foreign policy. He lives in Coventry and has been a visiting academic at Warwick University.

TO HAVE A CHANCE

R J Fielding

Book Guild Publishing
Sussex, England

First published in Great Britain in 2014 by
The Book Guild Ltd
The Werks
45 Church Road
Hove, BN3 2BE

Typesetting in Sabon by
YHT Ltd, London

Printed and bound in Great Britain by
CPI Group (UK) Ltd, Croydon, CR0 4YY

A catalogue record for this book is available from
The British Library.

ISBN 978 1 909716 00 1

To the memory of Marjorie

Introduction

John Burren walked out of the railway station and looked for a café. After his journey he needed to relax over a cup of tea before going on his way. He could have called in at the station buffet but he told himself that such places were for the traveller waiting to catch a train rather than for when a journey had ended.

Satisfied with his own logic and looking around he spotted a café directly across from the station entrance. He headed for it. Once inside the café and having ordered tea he settled down to continue with the novel he had been reading on the train. The café was surprisingly empty with only one other occupant, a bespectacled man whom Burren reckoned in an abstracted way to be in his fifties and most probably a travelling salesman. And there his interest in the man ceased. He returned to the novel and read:

> 'But why in the world should I complain, Stephen? I have such an enviable life, there's so much to do and see and know, and people are so good to me.'
>
> 'I wish you could teach me to live like that.'
>
> 'I don't think it's something that one person can teach another. Each of us has such different problems.'

But he was restless and could not concentrate. The book did not hold his attention. This troubled him because normally he enjoyed reading whilst having a cup of tea on his own. He looked up and saw the woman serving behind the counter looking at him. She smiled and he returned a weak, non-attentive smile.

Again he attempted to become interested in the book: 'You'll find your own way, Stephen. Whatever you do, wherever you go, in the end it'll be all right.' But the words were being lost in a cloud of intruding thoughts. Thoughts of the past and the life he was leaving behind increasingly gained control of the conscious part of his mind. He smiled inwardly and turned his attention back to the novel. He wanted at least to try and finish the chapter he was reading when he left the train. He now read on: ' "I don't understand. How do you know?" "I just know," Sarah told me, smiling. "Believe me." ' Yet again however his mind wandered off beyond the words on the page.

Something about the title of the novel had intrigued him when he had read a review of the book in the *Observer* newspaper, which had also carried a profile of the author. At the time, this had opened up a completely new avenue for him to explore. Now his mind kept returning to what he could expect in the immediate future.

The café had now begun to fill up with groups of schoolchildren on their way home from school. They were busily swapping yarns, snatches of which drifted across to him. It made him recall his own school days, and the memory of this made him feel good. His thoughts floated between the children's conversation, the novel he had intended to read, and his home village and the family and friends that he was leaving behind. He knew that they would not be part of his life from now on in the same way as before.

'Would you like another cup of tea?'

He looked up and saw the friendly face of the waitress. She was now standing at his table.

'Yes please.' He smiled.

The woman quickly returned with the cup of tea.

'Thank you.'

Glancing at his luggage the woman asked, 'Going somewhere nice?'

'I very much hope so,' he replied.

The woman looked puzzled and made her way back to the counter.

He was 'going up', though not in any conspicuous way. There were no piles of luggage bursting from the boot of a sports car with which to make a ceremonious entry. No room in college that his father had occupied back in the twenties. And no porter at the lodge gate to acknowledge him obsequiously as 'sir'. But then this was the 1950s and he was not 'going up' in the conventional sense. He was going to an adult residential college, which he had been told was the most prestigious of its kind. He collected the novel from the table, wryly noting how inapposite its title, *The World in the Evening*, was to his own present position, gathered up his luggage and walked out of the café to catch a bus. He was excited – nervously excited – and very happy.

1

Morton was a well-established college and had been in existence since the 1920s. Its principal aim was to provide an opportunity to those who had missed out on a good secondary education. It was a place that offered a second chance. Its emphasis was upon political and economic studies for those students with a trade union background. In fact the great majority of its students were drawn from amongst trade unionists, or from people who had experience of and held office in the Labour Party.

It had a fine reputation of achievement and had seen a number of its students move on to occupy prominent positions in public life; not only in the trade union world, but in the public services as well as in local and national politics. Whilst it was anxious not to conflate its educational objectives with promotion to senior positions in society, it was naturally not averse to welcoming such success.

The college existed in two parts. The main, original building was located in an unglamorous part of the city, but near to the centre and to many of the constituent colleges of the university. It was obviously the senior half; the Principal had his main office there together with the college administration, and the second-year students were resident there.

The other part of the college was based in a large country house, which students referred to simply as the House, set in its own grounds 3 miles from the centre of the city. The house had been adapted and extended to accommodate first-year students, some 50 of them. This was a later development that had taken place after the college governors, with sufficient sponsorship, had decided to double the number of total students in the college. The setting in which the house was located was idyllic, and whether it formed part of some grand scheme on the part of the trustees or not, it had nonetheless charmed, captivated and enticed numerous students into the ambience of learning.

Burren made his way down the broad staircase that led directly into the main entrance hall. Leading off from the hall to the right was a large room in which the evening's introductory meeting was to take place. From the letter that each newcomer had received the idea appeared to be that it was an occasion for them to meet one another, together with a small group of second-year students. A buffet supper was provided and the intention was to create an informal atmosphere in which people would circulate and meet with as many others as possible. The Principal was going to be there and would deliver a short welcome.

As he entered the room Burren saw lapel name-holders set out on a table and quickly spotted his own. There were several still uncollected. As he started to fix the name-holder on to his sweater a woman came up and said hello.

'I'm Maureen.'

He looked at her name-holder and saw her full name as Maureen Styles.

He smiled. 'Hello, I'm John. John Burren, as will be clear once I've fixed this holder without stabbing myself.'

She laughed. 'Yes, they can be a bit tricky.'

'Have you just arrived?' he asked.

'Yes,' she said, 'In fact I arrived earlier than I needed to. I wanted to make a good impression, or something.' She gave a slightly nervous laugh.

'Well, I suppose I too arrived in plenty of time, but I stopped off and had a cup of tea first.'

'Very sensible,' she said.

They moved further into the room where most of the others were already clustered in groups. The room took up at least half of the front of the house. It had two broad bay windows, whilst set into the far wall were French windows leading out to a garden, he assumed, but it was now dark outside.

'My word,' Maureen exclaimed as she looked around the room, 'isn't it lovely? And so spacious. What must it have been like to live here?'

'Expansive. Expensive,' he suggested.

She gave a small giggly laugh. 'Larger than your place?' he asked with mock seriousness.

She caught his smile. 'No, much the same size,' she replied.

'I thought it might be.'

They looked around the room again; this would now be part of their lives for the coming year. There were several groups of people talking animatedly, and a little nervously, to each other as they made introductory conversation, meeting for the first time. Friendship forged from a sense of common purpose seemed already to percolate the room. John noticed that on the inner wall opposite the bay windows there was a large, exquisitely detailed brick fireplace in which there was a log fire. He drew Maureen's attention to it.

'That really is welcoming,' she said, and indicating the buffet supper laid out on tables in one corner of the room she added, 'That is quite some supper. You don't suppose we're to be lured into thinking that is how we'll eat here all the time?'

'I would like to think so,' he said with a chuckle.

He had taken an instant liking to this slightly plumpish young woman with pale blue eyes and very open expression. She appeared to be very much at ease, as if she knew about the set-up. He was curious to know more about her. 'Which part of the country are you from?' he asked.

'I live in Manchester,' she replied. 'And you? No, wait. Let me guess.' She thought awhile. 'I'd say West Country-ish, probably Dorset.'

'No, you are a bit too far west,' he said.

'Well?' she raised her eyebrows questioningly.

'Sussex,' he said, fearing that he had let himself in for some obvious comment.

She had a broad smile on her face as she said, 'So you are from the soft south. Isn't that where some prominent left-wingers have their country cottages?' She went on teasingly, 'You know, those rich lawyer types, writers, and so on.' She looked at him with a quizzical smile.

He thought he might as well play her game. 'Yes, there are a few. Some of them live quite near to me. You see, they like the peace and the beauty of the countryside to help create the right frame of mind for revolutionary thoughts. You know,' he affected a conspiratorial air, 'people like Guy Burgess holding forth at weekend parties, and always concluding by saying that the local population would be spared come the revolution.'

'Really!' she exclaimed with mock horror. 'I always thought they were up to no good.'

They were interrupted in their jesting by a shortish man, brandishing a pile of leaflets.

'I'm Tom Evans from the second year.'

He was wearing several badges in the lapels of his jacket. Burren assumed they were emblems of good causes.

'I assume both of you are new?' he said, peering to look at their name holders.

'I'm John Burren and this is Maureen.'

'Styles,' she added quickly.

'I thought I would just say hello and welcome you to Morton. There are a number of us from the second year here to welcome you ...' He turned on an avuncular smile and added, 'And to make you feel at home. Not that you could feel other than at home here. I much prefer it to the place in the city. It is wonderful here at this time of the year with the mellowness of autumn, and come the spring, well!' The expression on his face was all that was required to show the full measure of his enjoyment of the past year.

Burren turned to Maureen. 'It looks as though we've done the right thing.' And of Tom Evans he asked, 'Do we have any reason to go to the city part of the college during our first year?'

'Occasionally, yes. The lecture programme is carried out here, but there are talks by outside speakers in the city that you may wish to go to. You have those here too, but different speakers of course. So we go to one another's events, including the social ones, the dances for example. They are always a great success.'

'Sounds a good arrangement,' said Burren.

'Are you taking the politics and economics course?' enquired Maureen.

'Yes I am, and I'm taking the special course in industrial relations.'

'You are a trade union official?'

Tom Evans smiled self-approvingly, 'Yes, that's right.'

'Which union?' she asked.

'The T&GWU.'

'The same union as myself,' said Burren rather pleased by the fact.

'You!' she exclaimed, and then quickly checked herself.

Burren smiled benignly and thought she had been about to make some comment about the south again, though perhaps it was that she simply shared the image-prejudice held by many of the T&GWU.

'And what are you two going to study?' asked Tom Evans.

'I'm taking the politics and economics course,' said Burren, 'but I'm not sure about the special option yet.'

'Plenty of time for that,' said Tom Evans.

Maureen said that she was to take the one-year course in social studies.

'Does that mean you are a social worker?' asked Burren.

'No, as I am not qualified I cannot be a proper social worker, but I have been working as an assistant in a social work department. I'm here to try and qualify on a social studies diploma course.'

They could hear someone announcing that the buffet supper was now available.

Tom Evans started to head towards the food. On leaving them he quickly said, 'If I can be of any help do let me know. Room 23 in the main building.'

Burren enquired about the leaflets he was carrying.

'They are about the numerous societies and activities that are available to us,' he said, looking back over his shoulder. 'Anything you want to know, just get in touch.'

Burren and Maureen Styles began to move towards the buffet. As they walked across he saw that a group of students had gathered around the Principal by the fireplace. As they waited in the queue that had formed by the buffet Maureen said, after looking around, that she was going to move to one of the window seats to eat.

Having served themselves with food they moved towards the centre of the room and Maureen Styles spotted someone whom she recognised. 'Oh, there is Frank,' she said. 'I knew he was coming here.' She called out to attract his attention.

A tall man with dark hair saw her and came across. 'I was expecting to see you here, and I looked out for you when I first arrived.'

'Obviously you know one another,' said Burren.

'Oh yes,' said Maureen, 'we're old friends. But you haven't met Frank.'

The two men shook hands and introduced themselves.

She looked at Burren and then turned to Frank Bainwell, 'He tells me that he is from Sussex. You know, that hotbed of revolutionary zeal.'

'Don't take any notice of Maureen's little snipes.' He put a friendly arm round her and said to Burren, 'I don't suppose she has told you that there are very few revolutionaries in her posh part of Manchester.'

Burren laughed, 'No, she seemed to forget to mention that bit.'

They moved towards the seating beneath the bay windows.

'I'll leave you to chat together and see you later,' said Burren. He moved over to the group around the Principal, Robert Wilcox, who was explaining some of the background of the house in which they were gathered. The Principal must have talked about the house on numerous occasions, indeed had probably repeated the performance that evening as different people moved in and out of the circle around him. If that were true, then by his appearance he remained remarkably fresh and patient.

'But tell me,' asked an American from within their midst, in the confident tone that Americans have irrespective of the subject being discussed, 'who was the capitalist who searched his conscience and gave this place to Morton?'

There were chuckles of laughter from others in the group, but Robert Wilcox was used to being asked this kind of question, though perhaps not always expressed in the forthright manner of the American.

'The house did originally belong to a capitalist, as you put it. He had been a city merchant banker, though the family money goes back to the old East India Company. In later life he became profoundly interested in the ideas of Robert Owen, and decided that on his death the house should be in trust to be used to offer educational opportunities to those who, for one reason or another, had missed having a good secondary education.' Robert Wilcox gestured with his arms outstretched to take in the room and the house. 'When he died, the house was made over by the terms of his will to a trust.'

Those gathered around him listened intently to this; the generosity and idealism of the rich benefactor bearing in on them as they viewed the room, and thought of the house.

He continued, 'Naturally we have tried to keep as much to the original design of the house as possible in adding on the two separate wings that are now the student quarters.

'Is this the room where the lectures are held?' one of them asked.

'Yes, it is,' replied the Principal. 'It is not especially suitable for that purpose. Too comfortable.' He laughed. 'Although we do discourage people from using the soft chairs at lectures, and as you can see there are more suitable chairs over there.' He pointed to a corner of the room where chairs were stacked. 'We didn't want to spoil the effect of the house by building on a special lecture room. You'll notice the same principle at work when you use the library. What we have done there is to convert a long room that is similar in shape to this one. It does not entirely work, but we felt it was the best thing to do. There is something about the house that bestows an atmosphere of learning and we have tried to retain that.'

There were nods of agreement, though clearly they had not yet put the atmosphere to the test. Burren formed the impression that Robert Wilcox had spoken as though he had been party to these changes, but in fact he could have been Principal for only just over two years.

The Principal turned towards the supper table and suggested they take coffee. As they moved away he recognised Burren and drew close by him.

'Hello. John Burren, isn't it?'

'Yes,' replied Burren, 'though I'm surprised you should remember me amongst this sea of faces.'

Robert Wilcox smiled. 'I do not interview everyone who comes here but I am on the Reed Committee, and anyhow you reminded me unintentionally at that interview of my old constituency.'

Burren groaned an apology, and added, 'I thought I had blown it when I quoted your adversary during the interview.'

Robert Wilcox said, 'No, not at all. But it was interesting because you touched upon an aspect of my old political rival that made me think of him again.'

The group helped themselves to coffee and some of them

moved back to their position by the fireplace. The American who had previously spoken was rejoining the group too, and Burren overheard a snatch of his conversation.

'Yes, Adlai Stevenson was a great candidate but he was too much of an egghead, you know. The average American is not overly interested in ideas. Taxes their mind too much. They are more concerned about the size of the fin on the car.'

Robert Wilcox overheard the comment too and smiled in a way he reserved for these occasions. He encouraged his students to feel they were smart in talking politics.

Burren was aware of a tallish man of about his own age with long fair hair and clear, intent blue eyes standing nearby and looking towards him. The man made a point of introducing himself. 'I'm Chris Megson.'

'John Burren,' he responded.

'You must be another Reed scholar.'

Burren, surprised, smiled slowly. 'Yes I am, but how did you know?'

'I overheard part of your conversation with the Principal, and as he interviews very few of the applicants I guessed that you were more than likely a fellow Reed scholar.'

'How very clever,' said Burren. 'And you are of course one too.'

Chris Megson gave a self-satisfied smile. 'Yes.'

They both laughed. It was the shared laugh of confidence in their mutual achievement.

'But you must have made quite an impression,' Chris added.

Burren laughed, 'Yes, perhaps so, but not in the way I intended. At the time I thought I had probably ruined my chances. I waxed a bit too much on the Tory "One Nation" group, and in particular I talked of Maurice Watkins. As you probably know, he overturned Wilcox's majority at the last general election.'

'Yes, I see what you mean.'

They were now within earshot of the Principal and both fell

quiet. Robert Wilcox turned towards Burren, 'I should just add that we are the best of friends. Not all political adversaries dislike one another you know. Maurice Watkins is unquestionably one of the finest brains in the present day Conservative Party, and he could go right to the top.' He looked around as if to see who may be listening and then returned to Burren. 'If he doesn't self-destruct first.' He smiled thoughtfully and added, 'He is perhaps a little too clever for his own good.' He looked at Burren. 'So, you see, you triggered off quite a recollection as a result of your comment at the interview.'

This in turn set Burren thinking about Robert Wilcox himself. He wondered if there had been any regrets by him about leaving political life, parliament and office, he had after all been a junior minister at the home office. Admittedly, it was only junior office but he was more than likely set on moving upward on the ministerial ladder, if and when Labour were returned to office. He had however been swept away in the landslide against Labour in the general election. There were no outward signs now in the Principal's demeanour to suggest disappointment. In fact he looked like a man very much on top of his job and enjoying it.

A woman in the middle of the group commented on the large picture hanging above the fireplace. 'Isn't it just marvellous,' she said. 'Look at the detail. Where is it? I mean, does anyone know where that clump of trees is?'

Heads turned in the direction of the picture.

'It is Chanctonbury Ring,' volunteered Burren. 'I haven't seen the painting before but I'm sure it is Chanctonbury Ring.'

He felt very proud, and was instantly embarrassed too at himself for feeling that way.

Robert Wilcox was ready to explain. 'You are right. It is Paul Nash's masterly painting. The owner of this house knew Nash, and the two became close friends, though the owner was of a different generation to Paul Nash. There were several examples of his work here at one time I understand, though none as well known as the one on the wall here.'

As they continued to talk a young attractive woman, slim and of medium height with short golden-coloured hair came from behind Robert Wilcox and gently tapped him on the shoulder and whispered, 'I think you should start soon', just within earshot of those standing close by.

The Principal moved back a step, and those standing close to him similarly moved back a little.

He began, 'I want to say a few words of welcome to those of you coming here for the first time this year. You have a great opportunity ahead of you, and a splendid environment in which to bring it to fruition.' His eyes swept the room to express his point. He dwelt briefly on the history of the college and some of the past figures who had contributed to its development, and then went on to list some of the recent achievements of the college, including its links with colleges overseas. He thanked the second-year students for welcoming the newcomers, and concluded, 'I wish each of you every success in the year ahead.'

The golden-haired young woman joined him at his side and as they left the room together he discreetly cupped his hand round her elbow.

Although it had been brief and to the point, Burren thought there was just a touch of the politician about Robert Wilcox's welcome. The assurance and self-awareness, the sense of timing for effect, and the fitting of words together like building blocks, made it a cameo of the politician's art of drawing upon a repertoire of set pieces to match many different occasions. He turned to Chris Megson standing by his side and conveyed these thoughts.

'Yes, I agree. I suppose that once you acquire the style, it is natural and stays with you.'

'Do you think he hankers after the political life? Once that particular bug bites it must be difficult to be rid of it.'

'Well, even if that is the case, he isn't going to get very far is he?' said Chris Megson. 'We're in the middle of a parliament with a Conservative government and no guarantee that Labour will win the next general election. No, whilst I agree that he still has very much the style of the politician, I think he is enjoying his present job.'

They walked across the room to where Maureen Styles and Frank Bainwell were still in conversation. Frank Bainwell and Chris Megson introduced themselves to each other.

'I noticed that you were well cloistered with the power base,' quipped Maureen Styles, turning to Burren.

'How perceptive you are. I can see I shall have to be wary of you.'

'This reception has been most worthwhile. It is good to meet one another at the outset in this way,' said Chris Megson, looking to the others for affirmation.

The others agreed, with Frank Bainwell adding that it was well to sort out enemies and friends as early as possible. 'Just being facetious,' he grinned.

The conversation quickly turned to asking one another about their respective programmes of study, and if they knew whom their tutors were to be. Chris Megson said that he was taking economics with Jack Edell, as was Frank Bainwell. He seemed knowledgeable on the subject and revealed that he had written on the economic management of the nationalised industries in his application essay. Frank Bainwell was less well informed, and indicated that he was hoping to be able to relate each of his subjects to his basic interest in trade unions.

Neither Chris Megson nor Frank Bainwell admitted to having much knowledge of microeconomics, much to the relief of Burren who feared his own weakness in this area, and acknowledged it.

'I'm told by Tom Evans, a second-year guy – did any of you meet him? – not to expect too much from Jack Edell,' said Burren. 'According to him, Edell is a pretty hopeless case, quite unable, or disinclined, to communicate the diagrammatic material into words.'

The other two men groaned.

16

Maureen Styles said she was taking politics with Robert Wilcox who, apparently in contrast to Edell, dealt with his subject very much in the manner of an ex-practitioner.

'That is good – it is useful to have an insider's account,' said Burren.

Frank Bainwell was not so sure. He said that he had met Robert Wilcox at a summer school, and whilst Wilcox was speaking in that context on the practical aspects of government, he was not so sure he could cover politics in a conceptual way.

Chris Megson disagreed. He said that in fact it was useful to have this approach from Wilcox, as Timothy Framley, the other politics tutor, dealt with the conceptual aspect of the subject.

Maureen Styles was not to be deterred by any such considerations. 'I am very much looking forward to his lectures. I want a practical approach for my work. In social work it is important to keep your feet on the ground, and not to have too much airy-fairy stuff.'

Frank Bainwell laughed. 'Well, there'll be no fear of that.'

They allowed the matter to rest, and went on to comment on the second-year students they had met. They formed the collective view from what they had been told that they were in for a most enjoyable year ahead. There was a cornucopia of activities that they could become involved with if they wished, though each of them was guarded about dispersing their interests too widely.

Maureen Styles excused herself, saying that she was going to make a phone call home and then go to her room, as she felt tired after the day's travelling and the evening event. Frank Bainwell said that he too should make a phone call to his wife. They both went off to find phones.

Once in her room Maureen Styles reflected on the day's events. She had wondered just what she had let herself in for as she set out from Piccadilly station earlier in the day. Her husband Jack, and her 12-year-old daughter Susan, had been there to wave her off and say goodbye. The farewell had been a bit tearful on her part, and Susan had looked mournful at her departure.

'You will write, Mummy, won't you? As soon as you are settled in,' she pleaded. Jack had looked on, uncertain what to say. He had been very supportive, and had told her she should take the one-year course to enable her to become a social worker, which she so much wanted to do. He knew that she wanted, and needed, a new outlet to fulfil herself. Susan was an only child and soon she would be a teenager and wishing to create her own life. Maureen felt she must have something new to work at.

At the same time, standing on the station platform waiting for the train to arrive, faced with the reality of leaving, she realised she was going to be away from Jack and Susan, and her home, and she knew how much she was going to miss them. She nearly changed her mind. But they had discussed it at length. They had agreed it this way. She was going to try and come home for a weekend every third week, and on that basis she thought it would be workable.

Frank Bainwell had made his phone call home and felt he had done his duty. He was in his late thirties, though he looked older, and his wife had told him that at the pace of life he maintained he would soon look 50 and more. His wife, Dorothy, was not wholehearted in her support of him going to Morton. She thought he had already spent too much time away at conferences, weekend schools and speaking engagements, quite apart from his other Labour Party activities as chairman of his constituency party.

Dorothy was not overly interested in politics and he knew that she did not understand his need to be part of something larger than himself. To him, this was almost essential to his being; it was what gave him his drive. Only within some cause that demanded faith and conviction did he feel the significance of his own actions. He loved Dorothy, but she was not enough.

He needed a Movement on which to lavish his attention, and that Movement was the Labour Party. There was a lot still to be done to complete the Labour programme of 1945 and that meant putting Labour back into power. He wanted very much to be part of that.

He was a Bevanite and believed passionately in all that Aneurin Bevan and his followers espoused. He saw no point in having a Labour government unless it was committed to transforming society. He knew from the moment he arrived at Morton that he was going to enjoy what he saw as an extended weekend school. He could feel it in his bones, and he was determined to do justice to this feeling within himself.

Burren and Chris Megson continued to talk and exchange information about their lives and what it was that had drawn them both to Morton. Chris Megson told Burren how much the place at Morton meant to him. He had worked very hard to obtain a Reed scholarship in much the same way as Burren had, though from a rather different background. He had been to a minor public school but had been forced to leave on the death of his father, though he did not disclose this part of his life story to Burren. Only later did Burren learn of this.

On his father's death Chris Megson had to transfer to another school and very soon was out earning a living to help pay his way at home. Morton was for him his big chance and he was going to make sure he succeeded. He had made a vow to himself and for the sake of his mother. He would join clubs within the university. He had already joined the Labour Club, this very evening, after being approached by a young woman from the second year who had introduced herself simply as Jean, Morton's Labour Club representative.

In many ways Chris Megson and Burren, two young men in their mid-twenties, were contrasting figures. Chris Megson was from Newcastle, a man from a big city with the confidence that comes from identifying with its power and pride. He was confident too in what he wanted, and where he stood in the spectrum of loyalty within the Labour Party.

Burren was from a rural community but did not identify with rural life and positively disliked its insularity and suspicion of all things big. He saw himself as beyond all this, and as outward-looking. He too was confident, but his confidence came from a deep belief in himself.

And here they both were – about to share an experience that might cement a new-found friendship; or they might be destined to intense rivalry.

Most people were now beginning to leave the reception and Burren and Chris Megson began to make their way out too. As they moved towards the doorway, a young man of about their own age approached them, and spoke to Burren.

'Hello,' he said. 'Have you had a good evening? These get-togethers are a good idea, aren't they? People do seem to enjoy them.' He smiled. 'It was just the same last year.'

'Yes,' said Burren rather disinterestedly, and not wishing to become further involved in the evening's event.

The other man sensed his mood and said, 'I can see you are leaving, so I won't hold you up.' But he made no attempt to move.

Chris Megson excused himself and bade them goodnight.

The other man now continued, 'I've been trying to have a word with you since I overheard some of the conversation between the Principal and yourself.'

Burren was becoming irritated by this man's intrusion but nevertheless found himself drawn to him – there was something about his manner that was appealing.

He was speaking again. 'You are a Reed scholar, aren't you?' he enquired.

'Yes, I am,' replied Burren.

'I am also a Reed scholar.' He smiled and extended his hand. 'Paul Jenkins.'

He looked at Burren in a confidential way. 'And that is why I should like to have a chat with you. But now is not the moment, I can see ...' he trailed off.

Burren waited for him to continue.

'Look, will you be coming to Morton City early in the week to meet with your tutor?'

Burren had already learned that this was the insider name used to refer to the other part of the college. 'Yes. I'm in on Tuesday at 10 am,' said Burren.

'Excellent. Call to see me in my room.' He was already moving away towards the main door. He called out, 'Top floor – right at the very top – you cannot mistake it.'

Burren was intrigued. He decided he would call to see Paul Jenkins.

2

Burren reflected on the evening's event. The fellow students he had met had each in their different way a clear motivation, it seemed to him, for coming to Morton. And what of himself?

He thought back to when he first set his sights in a different direction from his workplace. From the time that he finished secondary modern school he had been dissatisfied with the course of his life and had felt that he must do something different from what he saw had happened to his schoolmates. Most of them had ended up working on the land, in shops, or in one of the few small industries that existed in the area. Opportunities were very limited and hence any ambition became quickly thwarted.

He had become a trainee motor mechanic on leaving school, and to obtain even a craft qualification in motor engineering involved a round trip of 50 miles three evenings a week to the nearest technical college. He had done this, so he knew just what it entailed.

Once set upon his new course of action he read as much as he could. As he read one book, be it politics or economics, history or literature, he came across the names of writers that he had seen referred to elsewhere, and in this way one thing led to another. He was impressed by the way in which his knowledge became extended in this manner.

At the same time, it made him recognise that in his present state of learning, each little bit more seemed only to emphasise the widening area of unknown knowledge. He had read somewhere that knowledge was like the circumference of a circle, which as it expanded enlarged the circumference of the unknown. He acknowledged this as a challenge, though a daunting one.

Where he lived was a beautiful part of the country and its rural grandeur rubbed off on the inhabitants. He too was part of this; to live in this idyllic part of the world in which nature bestowed all her gifts made people feel good and proud, even though they were described as the rural poor. He had nevertheless long come to the conclusion that for working people to be content with this close association with nature was to delude themselves, and it prevented them from wanting to improve their lot. The grandeur of the area had in large part contributed to its continued feudal social structure.

Sociologically the area consisted of three social strata. There were the very rich landowners, living in large country houses surrounded by large acreages of land, reposing amongst tall, graceful trees and shrouded by rhododendrons. This was a secret, self-contained world. The only time that such people ventured forth and were seen by the local people was when they opened the local fête or other event, or were required to lend their patronage to some local celebration. Of course they travelled up to the city, to London, for business meetings, and to their clubs. He had glimpsed this world from time to time when he had been summoned to come and start a faulty car engine or attend to some other piece of machinery. He had quickly realised that this was a totally different world from his own, and one which he could never be part of. It was, in his view, an anachronism: a medieval element residing in the midst of an otherwise twentieth-century industrial democracy.

What he disapproved of most was that this social segment of the countryside depended upon the local working people to maintain the grandeur of its existence, and that such labour was not properly rewarded with decent wages. He had had many an argument with his Labour Party colleagues on this issue; they had been for a quiet time, he for agitation.

There was also the increasing number of middle-class, mainly professional, migrants in the area. Again living in substantial houses – mock Tudor seemed a favourite amongst these people

pendent in varying ways on employing local
ore manual tasks. In the main, they were
s, those who worked in the city in finance of
ther. It was always difficult to tell precisely
w.. le did for a living. Rumour abounded, usually
from among the women who came closest to the money-
makers as a result of doing domestic work for them, such as
cleaning and sometimes cooking. So that 'engaged in finance'
could mean anything from actually working in the city as a
broker, to the more tenuous and dubious connection of import-
export trade.

Such people made the countryside a dormitory of city finance.
In Burren's view they contributed nothing to the quality of rural
life, they were neither part of it in a cultural sense, nor did they
play a part in public life by participating in local government, or
very rarely was this so. They were the leeches on the countryside, extracting what they wanted and giving nothing back.

Burren was able to work up most resentment for these people. Not only did he disapprove of them as a social entity, he
resented their intrusion at a personal level. He had seen them
shopping in the local village, pushing forward to be served and
brushing aside the local people, their braying voices suggesting
a military command structure. They had authoritatively pushed
his own mother aside whilst shopping and it made him angry
that she never asserted herself.

The rural workers at the bottom of the pile completed the
picture. They still retained many of the attributes of the pea-
santry. Their lot had unquestionably improved since the war, in
fact emanating from the war itself, with the establishment of the
war agricultural planning: 'War Ags' as the committees became
known. Nevertheless, doffing of the cap and showing due
deference towards their betters still marked the rural worker.
Perhaps most of all they irritated him because they did not
display any independence of mind, no critical thought. They
simply accepted their lot as ordained, as part of the natural

order of things, in the same way as the countryside itself which surrounded them.

They were not to be moved by any objective clarification, or definition, of their position. To them, such thoughts belonged to troublemakers; an alien breed that had no rightful place in village life. Their passivity was at one with the tranquil nature of the landscape. It was this very acceptance of their position within the rural social structure that completed the feudal picture.

At one time, he had desperately wanted to change all this. He was no longer so sure. There had been too many setbacks. Not just the opposition of the rural workers; that would in itself at least have been a positive gesture. No, rather it was their total indifference, their lethargy, that he found difficult to accept. But more than this, it was the attitudes that he encountered amongst his fellow Labour Party colleagues that depressed him.

Time and time again, whatever the subject under discussion at local Party meetings, there would be a reference to the apathy of the rural workers towards changing their subservient status in society. This was often by himself. He frequently referred to the need to be seen to be doing more for the rural workers, even if they were not prepared to help themselves. His colleagues however tended to mirror the outlook of the local community, and they would argue that this made them more representative of local opinion than himself. It was difficult to argue against this, because fundamentally it was true.

At the same time he was not sure that his disagreement with his colleagues was solely due to this. It was true that there were ideological differences, though on reflection he acknowledged to himself that this was not the real reason. He found that few of his colleagues were able to sustain a well-thought-out position on any of the major issues of the day. He felt that for most of them, supporting the Labour Party was an almost instinctive thing, or something handed down to them by parents or others from the past. It was not something that had to be thought about or be questioned, so that there could be a reasoned case made for any aspect of policy.

Another difference he found was that the urge to shy away from discussion of major policy was tied up with the need to discuss Party business. Endless hours were spent on the minutiae of Party business, points of order, keeping to the rules with frequent reference to the constitution; anything at all, it seemed, to avoid the actual interchange of ideas in discussion. So the big issues of the day – the Korean War, German Rearmament, the United Nations and the Welfare State – were never thoroughly debated.

There was, as he knew, a more personal aspect to the differences. He felt unable to relate to his local Party colleagues. Both he and they seemed to have so little in common. They rubbed along well enough on social occasions and he made a special effort to be warm and friendly, but outside of Party business and social events related to the Party, he had little contact with Party members. There was the odd exception, as with a trade union friend, Fred Oddle, with whom he used to travel around the constituency sharing a speaking platform at meetings. They were both on the constituency executive committee of the Party. He enjoyed the company of this man with the ginger-coloured frizzled hair and high-pitched voice who liked to give the impression that he was a political sage. After being at meetings together they had quite often dropped in at one of the local pubs for a pint and gossip.

Fred was a full-time regional official of NUPE, had a fund of experience to draw upon and was a well-developed raconteur. There was very little related to the constituency that Fred did not know, as his work had naturally taken him extensively across the whole area. He had also been the Labour Party's stock candidate over a number of years in the thankless task of standing for seats that could never be won in that part of the country. He was, Burren reckoned, cynical by nature, but certainly experience had made him the more so. Fred liked him and in turn Burren liked Fred, though he recognised that the friendship was not always helpful in relation to the Party as Fred was seem more widely as a not altogether constructive influence. Nevertheless, his voice had been listened to when he advanced Burren's name for the constituency executive committee.

'I told you they would listen,' he said. 'They know talent when they see it.' He gave his usual accompanying conspiratorial chuckle.

It was Fred who first told him that he should seek to move on in the Party beyond the constituency. 'Aim to get on the regional committee,' he had said, 'and try to get your name on the Party list for parliamentary nomination.' Burren had been grateful for the confidence shown in him and said so, but he was not sure that was how he wanted to develop at that stage. The fact was, he was in a very unsettled frame of mind and not at all clear about what he wanted in terms of a career. He knew only that he wanted to know more about subjects that were increasingly absorbing him, such as history, politics and economics.

Matters in relation to his local Party colleagues had truly come to a head during recent local government elections. The local Party had made one nomination for the district council and that was the Party chairman, Bill Holden. Burren was to carry out his usual organising role as agent, and he had arranged for a public meeting in the local school at which Holden would speak. To try and boost the campaign and to give Holden a lift he had arranged for one of the Party's councillors from a nearby borough council to come and speak in support of Holden. He knew the councillor quite well as a fellow member of the constituency executive committee, and Burren knew that he would deliver a powerful, uplifting address.

On the night of the meeting, which was well attended, the councillor spoke for the best part of 45 minutes. He spoke of the reasons for the lack of Labour representation on councils in the area, which in his view was not entirely due to the voting habits of the region. He showed how the selection of good candidates – the more likely to be elected, of course – could then affect policy in a very real way because of the laziness, inability or sheer arrogance of Conservative councillors to inform themselves adequately about the detail of council business and procedure. It had been a good, well-argued performance and just the right introduction for Holden to follow.

Holden rose in his ponderous way, pulled a piece of crumpled paper from his pocket and began, 'Ladies and gentlemen . . .' He meandered on for roughly five minutes from his piece of paper, and then sat down.

Burren could see the barely suppressed annoyance on the councillor's face. The councillor did not wait to hear what may follow: he quickly offered his excuses and hurried out. Burren stormed up to Holden after the meeting broke up and told him that he, Burren, had gone to great trouble to secure the speaker, and was pleased when the councillor had agreed as a personal favour to him. Holden's only response was that he felt the audience had already had enough of being talked to about politics. Burren, beside himself with anger, quickly walked away.

Not long after this incident he had become involved in a further row with his local Party colleagues, which led him to resign his position as secretary. The row had arisen over a letter that he had written to the local newspaper in which he had criticised the council's refusal to purchase a strip of land for council house building. Bill Holden had immediately requested that he call a meeting of the Party's executive committee.

At the meeting Burren was accused of going against Party policy and he was criticised for not consulting the committee before going into print. He had been asked to write a further letter to the newspaper pointing out that he was mistaken in his view as this was not official Party policy. He had pointed out that the policy may not have accorded with the views of the local Party, but it was in line with the Labour Party's policy of maximum council house provision. He said that he had no intention of writing such a letter.

He offered his resignation as secretary and left the meeting. This was the culmination of long-standing differences between himself and the others in the Party. Reflecting on the matter, he knew that it had been bound to happen sooner rather than later. It only served to reinforce him in his intention to move his life forward in a different direction.

He realised that his involvement in politics, whatever disenchantment may have followed, had given him an abiding interest in current affairs, and he wanted to know more about the background to events. He knew that this meant looking at history, at how government worked in the overall context of politics, as well as informing himself adequately on the intricacies of economics. The more he examined his motivation, the more he concluded that his interest went back, right back, into his childhood.

He recalled hearing his father talk about the coming war and how much his father hated and feared this prospect, having been a soldier and prisoner in the First World War. He remembered newspaper headlines at the time of Mussolini's invasion of Abyssinia, and a Salvation Army woman calling at the door in aid of the victims of the Spanish Civil War, as well as newsreels of German troops marching into the Sudetenland.

These were the experiences that helped form his political consciousness. The curious thing was that although his father talked endlessly about political matters of the day, he did not get actively involved in politics until quite a while later, when he became a parish councillor. This puzzled him, for he asked himself how anyone could be so interested in political affairs, as his father unquestionably was, and yet not commit himself to action. The thought disturbed him as he began to realise the implications of the apparent dichotomy.

Although he continued to work with the Labour Party at constituency level, he became only a passive member of his local Party. He found Party activity at the constituency level very satisfying and decided to enrol for the political agent postal course, organised by the Labour Party through its educational department at head office. This increased his interest in political work, but more importantly it led him on to reading material that was more directly associated with the British political system.

The local library could not begin to satisfy his needs and he looked around to purchase cheap second-hand books. To his delight he discovered a second-hand bookshop in the nearby seaside town. It was very well stocked, or it seemed so to him. He supposed it served the seaside tourist with a 'good read' on a wet and blustery day. Anyhow, it certainly helped to supply his need in the early stages of his self-imposed learning. He read voraciously, slowly at first as he was unused to the building up of a theoretical argument in the written word, but as he became familiar with the material he was able to speed up his reading. It became almost like a drug as it took hold of his whole being. The different dimensions of human activity unfolded before him like some huge drama. It was exciting. He did not know how to describe the feeling, except to express it as like being in love.

He concluded that he needed to place his reading in some form of structured learning and he decided to enrol for evening classes with the Workers' Educational Association (the WEA). One class was on the British economy and the other was on post-war Europe. He felt confident on the basis of his reading, though he soon became still further aware of what he didn't know. It was a daunting task but he was determined to stick at it and complete the programme. He readily volunteered to write the essays required on the courses, and he was generally pleased with the comments he received back from the tutors. It was clear, he was told, that he had a feel for these subjects.

The economics tutor went on to say – with the utmost

reluctance in view of Burren's enthusiasm – that his critical awareness had to be sharpened. His writing style also had to be improved so that the meaning of an argument could be more precisely conveyed. He ploughed on, determined to succeed and not allow any criticism to deter him. He accepted the comments of the tutors and worked harder.

On the last evening of the economics course, all the adult students joined Philip Todd, the tutor, for a drink in the Wheatsheaf, the nearby pub. They chatted generally and made jokes about the British economy – not too difficult to do – and had an enjoyable time. People eventually began to drift away as the evening drew on, and Burren was left chatting with Philip Todd.

'Well, John, you certainly seem to have got a lot out of the course.' And then jokingly he added, 'The depressive aspects appeal to you, do they?'

Burren laughed. 'Yes, that most of all! But seriously, I have enjoyed it immensely.'

This was true. The course had dealt with many aspects of the British economy. Before taking this course he had not known the extent to which Britain had used up her investments over-seas in fighting the two world wars, to the point where after 1945 she had to pay for all imports from her export earnings; the first time this was so in well over half a century. This explained the 'export or die' phrase he had heard quoted so much in the post-war years. After this course and the Post-War Europe study, he knew he must take things further.

Philip Todd asked him what he did for a living. Burren told him, and to his surprise found himself saying that he was going to change his job. The idea of changing his job had certainly been forming in his mind for some time but he had not spoken of it to anyone until now.

His intention was to join an old friend in a building firm owned by a socialist of the old inter-war 'things will only get better after they have got worse' school of thought. A view

31

which Burren dismissed as total rubbish. Despite his socialist inclinations however, the owner of the firm was by no means a philanthropist. In fact, although Burren did not know him well, he knew enough to convince him that the builder did not allow his socialism to interfere with his role as an employer. His friend Tom had told him that the builder would offer him a job assisting Tom as a painter. He had protested that he had not painted before and that Tom knew he was a mechanic. Tom had told him not to worry and reassured him that he would soon acquire the skill under his tutelage. Burren knew that Tom had a cavalier approach to most things, including work. In any case, Burren would be a bit of an odd-job man, maintaining vehicles as well as painting. Burren explained to Philip Todd that he wanted the job because it would pay more and enable him to buy more books, as well as give him the freedom and time to think about his reading in preparation for an application to an adult college.

'Do you think I have a chance?' he asked a little nervously.

'Most certainly you do.' Philip Todd looked a little surprised at the question. 'I have watched you over the year and have seen your enthusiasm and commitment. You have every chance.'

Burren thanked him and tentatively asked, 'Would you be willing to support me?'

Philip Todd smiled. 'Of course I will. Of course.'

He was as good as his word. Burren's appetite for reading did not fall away. He set himself a punishing schedule and at the expense of his social life. He applied to two colleges. He heard quickly from one of them and was invited for an interview. He borrowed a friend's car and drove up to the Midlands for the interview. It went well. He was interviewed by the Principal and offered a place there and then. On his way back he took careful note of the university city that he had passed through on his way up, and in which the second college he had applied to was located. He had made up his mind that if he was granted an interview and offered a place at this college he would accept it.

It was the first time he had seen this city and he instantly liked it and knew it was where he wanted to go.

He waited anxiously to hear from the second college. He knew that if he was to be interviewed, it would be in London at the Labour Party headquarters, for he had applied for one of the prestigious scholarships awarded under a trust fund bestowed by a generous supporter of the ideals of the Labour movement and administered by the education department of the Party.

Eventually he heard. He was to be interviewed. He was thrilled at his achievement, so much so that it was as if he had already been offered a place. The celebratory mood was soon tempered by reality. There were four scholarship places offered each year and he knew from his own enquiries that the competition for these was intense. He had no idea if he would be successful. All he knew was that he had to prepare in the only way he knew, to read more and make himself as well informed in relevant subjects as possible. He demanded more of himself, working late into the night. He had chosen to be tested and would be judged, he hoped, on his personal qualities. He was confident in his own ability, and at the same time nervous about the interview.

The interview had been arranged for 12.30. He calculated that the 'for and against' arguments for this timing were about equally balanced. In favour was the fact that the interviewing panel may be keen to get away for lunch, and therefore perhaps be less persistent with questions. Against was the fact that after a morning of interviewing the panel may feel jaded and probably irritable. In this respect, so much hinged on unknown factors. He could only wait and see and try and discern on the day which way the balance appeared to tilt. By which time, he reflected with a little irony, it would be too late anyhow.

It was a warm spring morning, as he made his way from the railway station and walked towards Smith Square. Crocuses were in full bloom in the small garden areas between buildings, their carpets of blue, yellow and white greeting the day. Daffodils too stood proud in their brief stay. On arrival, he was told where to report for the interview and directed to the lift. This particular apparatus had the appearance – and, as he discovered, the performance – of perfectly matching the popular image of the Transport and General Workers' Union. The heavy cage-like inner door creaked shut and the lift slowly but remorselessly made its journey upward. He left the lift at the fifth floor and entered a long, empty corridor. He noticed that the cream-coloured walls were badly stained and in need of redecoration. He smiled to himself at the critical eye he had now developed towards the painting of buildings, on the inside and outside.

The interview room was, he had been told, halfway along the corridor. He entered a small room and was ushered to a seat by a very efficient-looking secretary who smiled politely and explained that the interview panel was running a little late. He glanced at his watch; it showed 12.25. At 12.40 he was called in.

'Please sit there,' said the chairman of the panel.

There were five members on the interview side, and he quickly took in their faces. The chairman was introducing them by name, organisation and status. Burren did not catch all the detail. The chairman, who had introduced himself as Jim Thompson, Deputy General-Secretary of the National Union of Mineworkers, smiled and made a few introductory remarks: pleased that Burren was here . . . sorry he had been made to wait . . . wanted him to relax . . . interview was to be more of a conversation to get to know one another. That sort of thing. He then moved on quickly and invited the Principal of the college, Robert Wilcox, to begin the questioning. 'Why do you want to come to Morton College?' he asked.

Burren had expected this rather obvious and direct question and gave what he regarded as a suitable reply. He spoke of his high regard for the college, its reputation and record of achievement, and he said he would like to be part of this.

The chairman cut in and asked, 'Have you applied to any other colleges?'

Burren noticed a thin smile pass across the Principal's face. 'Yes I have,' he replied, 'but I can say that I would prefer to go to Morton, and I have chosen to compete for a scholarship place.' He hesitated briefly, and then continued, 'I know that is what you would expect me to say, but I can only tell you that it is genuine.'

The Principal muttered, 'Of course', and resumed his questioning by asking, 'Why are you so intent on securing one of the scholarship places?'

'Because I want to prove something to myself,' said Burren, a little too self-importantly he immediately realised. The Principal seemed satisfied however.

The chairman turned next to the Trust member. He was in fact the chairman of the Trust, though Burren did not realise this at the time. He was a sharp-featured man, with thick-lensed glasses. He turned his gaze directly upon Burren and held a steady, knowing kind of expression on his face, almost a sneer but not quite. Burren found it most disconcerting.

'Well now,' he said, 'you have chosen to apply for one of the scholarships. They are highly valued by us. We think of them as supplying the future thinking capacity of the Party. The philosophers, if you like.' A pale smile appeared. There was clearly going to be a statement here, intended no doubt to deflate Burren a little. 'They are the theoreticians,' he continued. 'There is a history of quite distinguished holders of these scholarships, a very high standard to live up to and maintain.'

Burren quickly got the message and started thinking about how he should respond. The chairman of the Trust was now looking at him, as were the other members of the panel. His attention returned fully in time to hear the questioner ask, 'And so why do you think you are qualified for one of these scholarships, and how would you endeavour to live up to its high and established standard?'

Of all the possible questions to be asked, he had not anticipated the question in this form. He began by saying that he
liked exploring the theoretical aspects of socialism. That he had
read Richard Crossman's *Introduction to the New Fabian
Essays* and John Strachey's *Theory and Practice of Socialism.*
He realised too late that having read this work by Strachey
might not commend him to the members of the panel, and
certainly not to the questioner. He ended on a rather facetious
note, 'I do not claim to be a future Michael Young' – at this
there was open laughter around the table, including the questioner – 'but there is always a risk in these matters. I can only
tell you that I should feel highly privileged to have one of these
scholarships and I would do my best to fulfil my potential in its
name.'

There were a few more desultory questions before someone at
the far end of the table asked him what he would do if he was
unsuccessful in his application.

'Keep on trying until I'm too old,' he replied.

There was more laughter around the table.

At this point the chairman brought the interview to an end.
He thanked Burren for answering their questions so openly and
told him that he would hear from them by letter very soon.

The waiting made him desperately anxious. The days dragged
on in an endless routine of painting window frame after window frame, the monotony broken only by replacing it with the
monotony of painting door after door. His workmate Tom kept
his distance; he knew that Burren had applied to college, and he
asked from time to time but made no attempt to enquire about
the interview itself. Burren was pleased about that, for he too
had no wish to engage in a postmortem.

On returning one evening from work there was a letter; the
one he had been waiting for. He had been offered a place and
had won a scholarship. He instantly felt a whole mixture of
emotions, but none more than one of immense satisfaction and
achievement. After that he suddenly felt very empty and humble.

The news was soon around the locality back at home, with the anticipated responses. Some people told him that it was a great opportunity and not to be missed. There were others whose adverse comments were along the lines of, 'Who does he think he is? He always did think he was different from us. Why even at school I remember . . .' This troubled him for he was not sure himself. Was he in fact different?

Socialist friends, particularly his intellectual friends, emphasised repeatedly that class loyalty is stronger than any barriers created by education. And in any case the ability to overcome the barriers is the real test of conviction. But were they right? If he was not different, then why was it that so few of his own class wished for the education that he craved, and which he believed was everyone's right? Again his educated friends would say it was simply that the circumstances were different. Nevertheless, the question of difference troubled him.

His local Labour Party colleagues, he was told, simply stated that they knew it was his aim all along, and that they together with the Party had been the vehicle for him to promote himself. He was not too bothered by this expected reaction, though he inwardly acknowledged that there could be some truth in it.

3

He awoke early and being unable to return to sleep he decided
to explore the grounds. Looking out of the window he saw that
there was a damp mist hugging the ground. He told himself it
was not a good idea to go outside at this hour of the morning,
but at the same time decided that is what he would do. In the
distance and not so far away, he thought, he could hear the
muffled and continuous rumble of traffic. He closed the window
and quickly washed, shaved and dressed, and walked out into
the grounds.

The mist was patchy and there was a cold damp air on this
October morning. He determined however not to be put off his
grand tour by any of nature's dispiriting moods. Beneath his
feet lay drifts of wet leaves spread out like giant cornflakes. He
walked round to the rear of the house, where to his right he
could see an apple orchard with other trees nearby. Continuing
on the path at the back of the house there was a walled vegetable garden. It looked as though there had been vegetables
grown there very recently, which he assumed helped to supply
the needs of the college.

He walked on round the side of the house alongside the
French windows of the room in which the reception of the
previous evening had been held. He could now see that these
doors gave access on to a large area of lawn, contained within a
perimeter of shrubs. Carrying on along this path took him to
the front of the house.

A short driveway led from the front of the house to the
boundary of the grounds, where large iron gates were set in
a stone wall that ran the whole length of the front of the
grounds. He walked up the gently inclining drive to the gates

so that he might look down on the house and view it in its setting.

The house looked settled and comfortable, as though every inch of the Cotswold stonework belonged to its surroundings. To one side of the front porch there was a gable below which was a curved bay window. To the other side of the porch above the ground floor was a balcony with a balustrade. Above that and extending along the whole of the front of the house were a number of garret-type windows. He stood for a time absorbing the scene, taking in what it must have meant to generations of students. Without being exactly beautiful the whole appearance of the house expressed charm and character, and belonging.

On both sides of the drive there were tall trees standing tall and elegant, and beyond these were horse chestnuts, the remaining leaves of which were mellowing from bronze colour to golden brown. A large stretch of finely mown lawn went down one side of the drive. Immediately to his left and adjacent to the wall were converted barns that now provided additional student quarters. These were better than the average student room, he had been told, as well as providing family accommodation with self-catering facilities.

He remained at the gates for a little time, taking in the stillness and grandeur at this quiet hour of the morning. He felt proud and especially fortunate to be at this college, and a feeling of communion with nature took hold of him. He recalled the words of the Principal the night before and realised even at this early stage the possible truth expressed in them.

The chill of the morning suddenly reached him and he walked quickly down the drive and entered the warmth of the common room, planning to have a brief look at the newspapers before breakfast. Several other students were already reading the dailies, and looking round the room confirmed that he was not going to get hold of a newspaper before breakfast.

'Good morning,' said a voice from behind a newspaper.

He turned and saw that it was Frank Bainwell.

'Good morning.' He slid into the chair alongside Frank.

'Are you off into the city to meet your tutor this morning?'

'Yes, I'm seeing the Principal and then I move on to see Mike Dawson, my subject tutor,' said Burren.

Frank mentioned that he was on the same routine and suggested they meet up for a lunchtime drink in the Rose & Crown. He assumed, rightly, that Burren didn't know where it was and went on to explain. 'It is roughly halfway along the very wide road, which I think is called The High, and is the main road leading out of the city to the north. You can't miss it. There is a narrow alleyway leading off the road and it has a sign pointing to the Rose & Crown. Say one o'clock.'

'Fine,' replied Burren.

They went in to breakfast together.

Later in the morning he walked along the corridor on the second floor of the main building towards the Principal's office. He stopped by the door marked 'Principal's Secretary', knocked on the door and entered when a bright-sounding voice said, 'Come in.'

Inside the office the secretary was seated at a very unpretentious desk, barely adequate to the task required of it, he thought. She smiled. 'Hello. I'll let the Principal know you are here.'

He did not at first recognise her as the young woman who had accompanied the Principal at the reception. She was now wearing glasses which gave her a distant manner and a touch of severity. He noticed again how attractive she was. She also looked younger, and he found himself speculating on her age.

'You are John Burren, aren't you?' she said.

'Yes,' he said rather puzzled by this.

She caught his expression and quickly added, 'The Principal likes me to check the name in the diary before he meets people for the first time.'

'Yes, I see,' he said, still a little puzzled.

'Please go in,' she said, nodding her head towards the door of the Principal's office.

He knocked the door and entered. He noticed straight away how small the office was and how the Principal seemed cramped behind his desk, which was placed at an angle to two walls so that he sat, as it were, in a corner. The Principal was busily turning over sheets of paper and stopping now and again to write in some comment.

'Have a seat, John,' he said, pointing to the chair on the other side of the desk. He did not look up. He carried on working through the papers and Burren noticed that he was using a pencil rather than a pen to make his amendments or comments.

At last the Principal tidied the papers and looked up. 'You've done well to get here, John.' There was a slight pause, and then he continued 'Do you feel that yourself?'

'Yes, I suppose ...'

Before he could finish the Principal went on, 'People come here from many different backgrounds. Oh I know it is supposed to be a college for people who have missed out the first time round, but there can be many different reasons for that.' He stopped and waited as if he half expected Burren to respond. He then went on, 'The fact is, we act as if you all have the same background which simply isn't the case, and we haven't the time or the resources to find out what implications this has for the education we provide, or should provide. I suppose what I am saying is that we rely on you as individual students to remind us of any problems you may have.' He paused again, leaving the impression that he was checking some list or other in his mind.

Burren saw how alert his eyes were, and how they appeared to dart in response to different points that he made. The Principal now enquired, 'Everything fine so far?'

'Yes,' replied Burren.

'Good. I think you can do very well.' Again a pause. 'Anything you wish to raise with me at this stage? You know your tutor for this term, I believe.'

Burren muttered agreement.

'Fine. Well you know where I am if you wish to see me for whatever reason.'

Burren proceeded towards the door.

'By the way, I run a public speaking class if you are interested.' The Principal was looking enquiringly at him.

'I am very interested,' he replied.

He went back along the corridor towards the staircase in a very thoughtful mood. He did not know quite what to make of Robert Wilcox. He had not formed a clear picture of what the Principal thought. He felt that the Principal's technique, if it was a technique, was to make you feel good, but not quite as good as you first thought. He found it rather disconcerting, yet intriguing. He continued to think that there was still a strong element of the politician in Robert Wilcox.

He checked his watch. He had an appointment with his political theory tutor at 10.30. There was no time for coffee. He returned to the secretary's office and asked where Mr Dawson's room was. It was now her turn to look puzzled. She told him that he must have passed it, as it was only three doors back along the corridor. She gave a little laugh. He smiled sheepishly.

Mike Dawson was searching for a book from one of his shelves and finding it difficult because of a large pile of books, magazines and newspapers rising from the floor and thus making movement immediately beneath the shelf precarious, the more so as Mike Dawson was a big man.

'You see,' he was saying, 'some people think there is a strong fascist element in Plato.'

He turned to look at Burren as if for confirmation but Burren was in no way equipped to reply knowledgeably. In any case he was still distracted at this point by the sheer chaos of the room.

'Ah yes, here it is,' said Mike Dawson. '*The Open Society and Its Enemies*. You'll need to look at this book by Karl Popper. It is important to our discussion. But you see, although we are concerned primarily with concepts in political theory we have also to be aware of the historical period, and what was happening at the time of the writing. So we have to be wary of injecting the thoughts and ideas of the present day into the distant past.' And referring to what he had previously said, he now added, 'and therefore we must be careful of using terms such as "fascism", which is essentially twentieth century, to understand the past. Do you follow me?'

Burren nodded.

As if following Burren's train of thought, Mike Dawson cast his eye round his room. 'I must sort this room out.' And then by way of explanation, he added, 'I've only just moved in here. There was some organisational upheaval over the summer and as a result I was relocated.' He shrugged resignedly. 'And I've been away all summer in the States.' He paused, and then continued, 'Right, now let us talk about you and this term's work. You'll be with me for one term and we have to try and cover political thought from Plato to the present day – that is quite some task and inevitably there are significant gaps. But we have to do what we can, and so ...' He interrupted his own train of thought. 'Have you studied any political thought before?'

'No,' replied Burren but quickly added, 'I have looked at a kind of history of political thought, but that is all.'

'Yes?' pressed Mike Dawson.

'It was *The History of Western Philosophy*, by Bertrand Russell.'

'Wow!' exclaimed Mike Dawson whilst exploding in laughter before immediately checking himself.

Burren looked uneasy.

'You do go in at the deep end, don't you?' said Mike Dawson, looking kindly upon him. 'It is a good starting point in a way, if you were able to follow him that is. Personally, I thought him a bit difficult, as though he had his mind on other things when he wrote it. However you do need a general reference text to refer to continuously. There are a number of these. You might try Sabine. And be sure to get hold of the latest edition. It was revised recently.'

Mike Dawson turned to look at something on his desk before continuing, 'We start with Plato and Aristotle and then move straight on to the Contract Theorists: Hobbes, Locke and Rousseau. We include the Utilitarians but place them in the context of the development of nineteenth-century thought, including the Idealists, and Marx obviously. I like then to conclude with a session on Social Democracy. Now as you can see that is quite a hefty programme. Of course I hope you'll find my lectures useful too … ' a wry grin spread across his face, 'though not everyone does!'

He looked at Burren for a moment and then asked, 'How did you get here?'

'I was awarded a Reed scholarship.'

'Were you!' he nodded, impressed. 'You should be able to cope all right then. The point is that there is always a bit of a problem to know where to start political thought: should it go at the beginning of the year's study, or towards the end after some other subjects have been digested? But that should not be a problem for you, even though as you say you haven't studied the subject before, except for reading Russell that is.' He gave a small chuckle.

Burren began to see the amusing side of this, or thought he did. He also began to realise some of the significance of the Principal's comments. Mike Dawson was speaking again, 'So, your first task will be Plato's *Republic*, and I want you to appraise his ideas of good government.' He then went on to list some reading for Burren and indicated how he thought the reading should be approached, pointing out that books he recommended could not be satisfactorily substituted by some other text but in fact each added to an evaluation of the topic. He raised himself from his chair and came to Burren's side of the desk. He was a big man, as Burren had already observed and taller than his own height of nearly 6 feet. He patted Burren on the shoulder and said with a huge smile, 'Be prepared for some rigorous discussion.'

Burren paused outside the door. Mike Dawson had immediately impressed him and he wondered if he would be able to match the demands being made of him. When he took both the Principal's and Mike Dawson's comments together, he could see the size of the task, and doubt began to creep in. Was he up to it? In this anxious frame of mind he felt inclined to go straight to the library and immerse himself in the reading for his first essay. Second thoughts prevailed, however. He decided he had time to take coffee before meeting Paul Jenkins as arranged and then to meet later with Frank in the Rose & Crown.

He found the common room and went across to the coffee trolley. There were several people sitting reading or chatting, but whilst he recognised some faces from the first evening he hadn't met any of those present. Having collected his coffee he went and sat down by a low table scattered with newspapers and magazines. He glanced at some of the headlines. Most of them were taken up with the Labour Party Conference that had recently been held in Brighton. Each of the headlines reflected in their own way Labour's continuing attempt to bridge the ideological gap which lay at the heart of the Party.

He picked up the *New Statesman* and turned to the Profile; a regular feature of the journal which portrayed a leading public figure, and which he enthusiastically read each week. This particular number of the *New Statesman* featured Ian Mikardo. He had met Mikardo at a Fabian Summer School, and he much admired this man, whose speech was slow and deliberate but whose mind was one of the best organised – almost machine-like, that he knew. The anonymous writer of the Profile expressed most of his own view of Mikardo, including the conclusion that he was the apparatchik of the left.

He looked again at his watch and decided he should go and see Paul Jenkins.

On entering his room Burren immediately noted the great

number of books on the shelves. Paul Jenkins, together with another man, was leaning over a desk looking at various scattered papers.

'Come in,' said Paul Jenkins. 'We are just looking at some articles for *The New Age*.' And gesturing towards the short man at his side, he said, 'This is David Smith.'

Burren gave a nod and a smile.

'I met John at the reception the other evening.'

The three of them talked generalities for a few minutes before David Smith said that he had to leave and moved towards the door. 'I'll be in touch, Paul, for us to go through the articles again.'

'Fine,' said Paul, 'I'd particularly like to discuss the one on "Power and the Trade Unions", David.'

'Yes, sure.'

Paul Jenkins and Burren sat down in the two chairs in the room.

'I'm quite intrigued,' said Burren, recalling their encounter on the first evening.

Paul Jenkins smiled. 'Yes, it was rather an elliptical ending,' he said. 'To come straight to the matter now, John. I'm chairman of the Socialist Society this term, and I wondered if you would agree to have your name put forward for the executive committee of the Society.' He looked enquiringly at Burren and waited.

'I haven't thought too much about clubs and societies yet,' said Burren. 'In any case, why me? You don't really know me.'

'Look, I probably haven't handled this too well, but I'm really keen that you should join us in the Society. You see I am most anxious that there is a continuous representation of Morton people to help manage the Society, and if you were to agree, I had in mind that you would become Secretary sometime during the year.' He smiled charmingly. 'And then you would have established yourself ready to become Chairman in your second year, as I am now.'

'You do seem to have it all well planned,' said Burren, 'and it is all very flattering, but again I would ask, why me? When you do not know anything about me apart from the fact that, like you, I am a Reed scholar.'

Paul smiled. 'I know a bit more than you think perhaps,' he said. There was something politely insinuating about his manner that was capturing Burren.

Paul Jenkins carried on, 'Jasmine can be very helpful in these matters, and she told me that you were a Reed scholar, and she also told me the subject of your application essay: "Britain and West European Cooperation after 1945".'

'Who is Jasmine?' He was becoming alarmed that Paul Jenkins should know so much about him.

'Jasmine is Robert Wilcox's secretary.'

'I see,' Burren spoke slowly, half to himself, not at all sure that he did really see. He went on, 'Well, she is certainly very attractive . . .'

Paul Jenkins cut him short. 'No, no, do not misunderstand me. There is nothing improper in any of this. Jasmine does not discuss anything she should not. She has a strong sense of propriety. It is quite simply an agreed thing within the college that office holders, as it were, may enquire about the new intake of students. As for Jasmine being attractive, yes she is, but I strongly advise you not to pursue that too far.' He looked at Burren with an expression that implied there was more unsaid here than said.

'All right,' said Burren, 'I take your point. But if I agree to be nominated, won't other members with a longer membership in the Society be resentful?'

'I don't think so. You see they much admire us in this college and they think, rightly or wrongly – wrongly in my view – that we all have administrative abilities, are worldly and have lots of contacts.' He laughed softly. 'All of this they see as good for the Society. And also, don't forget they have their fair share of offices. So you see it suits all parties.'

47

He now became quite earnest and continued, 'Look, I don't know how much you know about this place but take my word for it, Morton is a very competitive environment. Many people have already graphed their future career before they come here, and their time here is used to promote that career graph. The politicos join the Labour Club with the view that it will help them in their search for political preferment, parliamentary or otherwise, or will push them forward in the trade union movement.

'Now the Socialist Society is a different kettle of fish. It is essentially an ideas outfit in which we explore both domestic and international affairs, without any constraint, or feeling compelled to come to any fixed position. I'll be absolutely frank with you, it will not necessarily advance any career plans that you may have, but at the same time it won't in any way harm them either.'

Burren interjected, 'You say that the Labour Club is the route for political advancement but doesn't that mean it has the approval of the establishment here? Robert Wilcox for example?'

Paul Jenkins smiled knowingly. 'Not at all. Robert Wilcox is a political animal to his fingertips. He is also a very sophisticated animal. He knows all that is going on, and is able to discriminate between motives. I have always found him to be absolutely straight on these matters. He knows that I am chairman of the Socialist Society, he knows that I lean towards Marxism, but it has made no difference to my relationship with him, and he has been supportive of my plans for the future.'

He leant forward in his chair. 'Look, John, you must tell me if I am wrong but I think the Society will appeal to you. It is the catholic approach to ideas which I think you will find attractive. And make no mistake about it, you will find it intellectually enlivening because it does not limit itself to politics, it also takes in literature and the arts generally.'

He now switched his approach in his effort to recruit Burren. 'You've just come from meeting Mike Dawson, haven't you?'

'Yes.'

'Well, he supports us, and you couldn't get a stronger Social Democrat than Mike.'

Burren laughed. 'Which variety?' he quipped.

'I know what you mean. No, he is not in the European mode. Very much an Atlanticist in fact.'

Burren had made up his mind. 'Thank you for asking me, Paul. I'll accept nomination and I look forward to being on the committee.'

Paul Jenkins was enthusiastic. 'I'm very pleased, John. We should be able to work well together. I'll let you have the programme as soon as we have printed it, and you'll see that we normally meet on a Tuesday – speaker meetings in the evening, and our own discussions of a lunchtime.'

Burren was ready to leave and they both made their way to the door. He turned, 'Quite a collection of books you've got here.'

With pride Paul Jenkins told him that they belonged to his father, and were strictly on loan. 'He said to me that if I was set on coming here, about which incidentally he had reservations, I should be fully equipped, and hence the library. It was quite a job transporting them here.'

'You are a lucky man,' said Burren as he made his way out.

He hurried, not certain yet of his way around the city. He had forgotten to ask Paul Jenkins where the Rose & Crown was in relation to the college. He had a vague idea of its location from his chat with Frank Bainwell and he now headed in the direction where he believed the High to be. At the end of the road he turned left and found the street. He could now see the sign pointing to the Rose & Crown some way along on the other side. The city was crowded with late sightseers coming in for an autumn visit to view the colleges and gardens, as well as with returning students.

He pushed open the door of the saloon bar and looked around for Frank. He could not see him amidst the groups close by the bar. There were lots of students here, it was quite easy to see, for apart from their age and dress, the snatches of conversation were of people resuming friendships broken off by the summer vacation, or the more callow, excited talk of those just embarking on student life. Billows of cigarette and pipe smoke filled the air. He pushed his way through the crowd and at last spotted Frank at a table. Chris Megson was with him. He greeted them both.

'What'll you have to drink, John?' asked Frank, already on his feet and moving towards the bar. 'Will you have another, Chris?' he called.

'I'll have half a bitter,' said Burren.

'I'll have the same again,' said Chris.

Burren and Chris chatted idly about their first impression of the city, and both agreed that there was a buzz about the place.

Frank returned with the drinks.

'We were talking about the city,' said Chris. 'We reckon we'll enjoy it here.'

'No doubt about that,' said Frank. 'Though I reckon it has changed since the immediate post-war years.'

The other two looked at him enquiringly.

'Standing at the bar waiting to be served I looked around at all those young faces,' Frank said. 'They are no age at all.'

'But that has always been so, surely,' said Burren.

'No, it was different in the period just after the war,' Frank took a long swig of his beer. 'In those years there were a lot of adult students about the place. Servicemen returning from the war; many had had their studies interrupted by the war and they were resuming places to complete their degrees.' He looked at the other two, suddenly realising that they too were young men compared to himself.

'Was it more political then?' asked Chris.

'It must have been. After all, many of those returning had received a political education in the forces through what was known as the Army Bureau for Current Affairs as part of the good democratic citizen programme. I was here in 1947 for a short course and it included university students. It was quite an eye-opener. Politics seemed to pervade everything.'

He leaned forward a little more intently. 'There were two things coming together; this politically aware group of men at university and the social change being brought about by Attlee's government.' He chuckled enthusiastically. 'That makes for a powerful mix!' He took another long drink of his beer and continued nostalgically,

'That must have been a great time to have been here.'

Both Megson and Burren indulged the picture sketched in by Frank.

Burren was the first to speak. 'We'll just have to recreate that atmosphere,' he said optimistically.

'Yes, maybe,' said Frank, but the enthusiasm had now gone.

Chris changed the subject by asking Burren how he got on during the morning.

'Quite a morning,' said Burren. 'First meeting with the Principal – don't quite know what to make of him. Then I met Mike Dawson for my introductory tutorial. He insists he be called Mike. That was really quite a session. He is so enthusiastic about his subject, and lively. Also daunting.' He suddenly recalled the amount of reading he had to do. 'I then met up with Paul Jenkins from the second year.' He turned to Chris. 'He was the chap who came up to us at the end of the reception on the first evening. He wants to nominate me for the executive committee of the Socialist Society, and I've agreed.' He was quite excited about this.

Both Frank and Chris looked at him. 'Isn't that a Marxist group?' Frank enquired.

'I gather that some of them are,' he replied dismissively.

'But are you?'

'No,' he said wearing a broad grin, 'but I do want to hear all views and according to Paul that is exactly what they are interested in.'

They both looked at him doubtfully.

'I've joined the Labour Club,' said Chris.

'So have I,' said Frank.

There seemed to be a tacit consensus that the implications of each of their actions should not be explored further, and they fell silent. Eventually Burren declared that he must be off to the library.

4

Burren found that his life as a student soon established its own routine. There was the weekly round of lectures, most of which were held in the mornings – the university even offered some on a Saturday too. He did not find all the lectures helpful and supposed that was not unusual. It was especially unhelpful when the lecturer did not give clear advance signals of where he (they were all male) was going with his lecture. He thought that a brief outline of objectives at the outset would be useful. As this did not happen he found it difficult to know which points were important to note down. He had not yet found the best form of note-taking. Short of reproducing the whole lecture in note form, what was significant in the context of the subject, and what was less so, he had yet to discover.

He had discussed this with others, including Chris Megson and Frank Bainwell. Neither of them appeared to have the same problem, or at least did not recognise it as such. Frank had attended many conferences and numerous weekend schools, as he was fond of telling anyone who would listen, and perhaps that meant he had acquired the experience of how to note significant points. Though Burren doubted this.

With Chris it was different. Whenever they had discussed this, Chris in his inimitable way indicated that he did not see it as a problem. But then he found Chris a bit of an enigma, and he could not explain to himself the other man's confidence in respect to learning at this level.

Presumably none of them at Morton had received a first-rate secondary education, so how was it that Chris seemed not to show any of the anxieties over learning shown by some of the others?

Maureen Styles was quite open about her deficiencies. She had a fair share of anxiety on the subject of learning. He had not specifically discussed note-taking with her, but from time to time they talked of other matters related to their courses, such as the extent of the reading required and their need to speed up their reading. Maureen, invariably having a puzzled expression on her face (he had already learned to interpret that look), would come and sit beside him in the common room after supper and talk through some of the problems of the day related to study.

He found the tutorials with Mike Dawson exhilarating. Admittedly they were hard going and Mike Dawson did not let up; no leniency was shown or excuses accepted. The comment about rigorous discussion that he had made at their first encounter, Burren found to be deadly accurate. Mike Dawson pursued the discussion of particular points relentlessly and Burren discovered that his own thinking and oral expression were becoming more disciplined as a result of having to discuss ideas in a strictly analytical way.

As he walked along the street he recalled the session held with Mike Dawson the week before. It had been on the contract theorists and he had found it particularly difficult to compare and evaluate the three theorists. After they had agreed, or more accurately after Mike Dawson had established, that Rousseau's General Will concept was subtle but vague and rather woolly, though ultimately did express an intuitive residual core of truth perhaps, Mike Dawson had gone on to convince him of the Contract Theorists' importance in the development of political thought.

'You see,' he said, 'they are, each of them, starting with Hobbes, seeking to establish the principles which legitimise government. They are the first guys to do this in the wake of questioning the divine right to rule.' He added with emphasis,

'That is their importance.'

The crisp cold air of the November day made him pull his

camel-coloured duffle coat together to secure the toggles. He disliked November. But he liked the university city, as he knew he would. Walking along past the shops intermingled with the entrances to colleges made him feel that he belonged; that he was part of the centre of this place, combining its academic distinction casually with the ordinary activity of a city, and in more recent times incorporating a major industrial side.

He had just come from the college library where he had spent the morning reading Plamenatz on the Utilitarian philosophers. This was part of the subject of his next tutorial with Mike Dawson. As he entered the alleyway leading to the Rose & Crown he could see that it was already very busy with students at lunchtime. Frank and Chris had agreed to meet him at the pub after they had finished their committee meeting of the Labour Club. Both of them had now become assiduous participants in the affairs of the Club.

Looking around the saloon bar he could not see either of them and so he went ahead and ordered himself a beer. He sat at a corner table and waited. He reckoned that their committee meeting would be a lively affair. He had read that the Parliamentary Labour Party was meeting on this day to discuss and determine its position on the question of German rearmament. Or to put it another way, they were having to decide on the position they would adopt in respect to a German contribution to Western European Union; the proposal that Eden was putting forward as a British initiative. Eden was hoping to secure the agreement of the West Europeans to his proposal, following the collapse of the European Defence Community as a result of the failure of the French to ratify the treaty.

He recalled reading the account of that memorable hot summer night back in August when after an all-night sitting and much anguish the French Assembly had failed to rally behind their Prime Minister, Mendes France. The French were torn apart as they contemplated the past all over again. The British Labour Party was split too on the issue as well as much of the rest of Western Europe. There surely could be no more divisive issue so soon after the war as the prospect of the Germans with arms again.

Lost in these thoughts he had failed to notice that Frank and Chris had now arrived. They were now approaching him, each clasping a glass of beer. 'Sorry we are late,' said Frank, 'the meeting went on a bit, pointlessly in fact as we had already agreed our view.'

'It was not as simple as that,' said Chris.

'I thought it was,' said Frank sharply.

It was clear that feelings had been running high.

Burren asked, with an innocent air, 'What has been the trouble?'

'What do you think?' said Chris, finding it difficult to check the annoyance in his tone.

'It was the question of German rearmament again.' Turning towards Frank he went on, 'I cannot see why you will not accept the inevitable. Come what may, whatever you and others say or do, Germany will take her take place in the defence of Western Europe.'

'You may think it is inevitable ...'

The words trailed away from Burren's attention. He was attending his own Socialist Society's committee meeting later in the afternoon. They were going to seek a speaker of national reputation on the subject, and as members they too were divided, just like everyone else. Should they go for a speaker on behalf of the pro-German arms argument, someone who was against, or should they seek to have one from each side of the debate?

His thoughts had now drifted far away from the argument going on between Frank and Chris, though his mind was on the same topic. He was aware that Paul Jenkins was probably going to need his support, and he was not sure that he could give it. The acceptance of his nomination to the committee had gone through smoothly, as Paul had told him it would. But in relation to the current issue this could make for further anxiety. It brought into focus the question of loyalty; loyalty to individuals as against loyalty to principle. He had not always found it easy to reconcile the two, and he feared it may become an issue between himself and Paul.

He had rehearsed most of the arguments to himself over the German case but he still had serious doubts about the right course. He came back to the argument between Frank and Chris, as he heard his name. 'Don't you think so, John?'

He turned towards Chris.

'Sorry, Chris, I wasn't listening at that point.'

'Frank was saying that German rearmament is seen as necessary to push economic recovery forward throughout Western Europe, and I say that is nonsense,' repeated Chris impatiently.

Before Burren could respond, Chris was speaking again. 'It's utter nonsense to say that the rest of Western Europe fear German industrial capacity, after all she is now much reduced in size.'

'I am not so sure about that argument,' said Burren. 'Even without the Eastern half, West Germany is still sizeable and has immense industrial muscle. It is in fact in the Western half that most of the industry exists.'

'You bet it is,' said Frank. 'And to say that the others in Western Europe do not fear this, is to deny all the lessons of recent history.'

It was obvious that Frank was in a bellicose mood.

Burren intervened by saying, 'Look, why don't we take this up again sometime and talk it through thoroughly? In fact, it might be a good idea to mention it to Robert Wilcox as one of the topics to be debated in his public speaking group.'

The other two were not so sure that was a good idea.

'Anyhow I have to go now as I have a meeting of my own – the executive committee of the Socialist Society.'

'They've put you on the committee, then,' said Chris, seemingly surprised.

'Yes.' And turning to Frank he said, 'I think you would find the Socialist Society shares your view, though I am not so sure I share it – why not come along to one of our meetings?'

With that open invitation he left them both, sure that they would continue to wrangle over the subject of Germany and the Labour Party.

As Burren made his way towards Paul Jenkins's room he mused on college life and how groups had formed within it.

Not all of them from their group shared meals together, for example. Three of them ate together whilst he sat at another table with a group which became known as the apparatchiks, mainly because each member of the group, apart from himself, held some position or other in the Labour Party's organisation. Others referred to them as the Insiders as they seemed only to talk of Party matters. In fact they talked a lot of shop at mealtimes too, but as he had taken a Labour Party agent's course himself, he was both able and interested to participate in their insider conversation.

The Maureen Group as they became known met for coffee in the morning if they were together in the city. But more especially they would meet in Maureen's room after lunch over a cup of tea. These occasions had quickly developed into free-ranging discussions. A quite casual remark could spark off extended pursuit of related ideas.

He could recall some point about Catholicism raised in one of Mike Dawson's lectures leading to heated talk in the group about Catholic societies, birth control and economic development. He smiled to himself in recollection of the detail of that rather acrimonious session. Curiously enough, although they hadn't known one another for very long, apart from Maureen and Frank, there seemed to be an immediate understanding between them which set the parameters for discussion and prevented any rupture of friendship.

Maureen was a little less attached than the others, despite the meetings in her room. Her different programme of study meant that she spent some of her time at the Social Studies Centre in the city. Burren also thought that she perhaps felt more alone than the others and missed being with her husband and daughter. He had asked her to join him in going to the cinema and she had seemed pleased about that. He liked her, liked her puckish humour and accepted her motherly approach towards him.

He admired her decision to come to Morton. It could not have been easy for her to leave the security of home, and the love of a husband and daughter. She had told him how she and John, her husband, had made a deal in which John came to Morton two years earlier and that she would go later when their daughter Susan was a little older. She had set her heart on social work. That was the plan, and now to fulfil it she was having to work very hard.

Burren climbed the stairs towards Paul's room at the top of the building, and as he turned into the corridor on the second floor he encountered Timothy Framley, his year tutor.

'Hello,' said Framley in an almost friendly manner.

He had met Framley only once before and had not been overjoyed by the experience. Framley had not once referred to him by name on that occasion and Burren did not like his cold, seemingly dismissive manner. He had asked Burren nothing about his life before coming to Morton, and he seemed even less interested in what he was studying now. The only comment about himself that Burren could recall was Framley saying, 'I see you are a Reed Scholar. I suppose that gives you some status.'

To which he had replied, 'Yes, I suppose it does.'

He now stood directly in Burren's path. 'What are you doing here?' he asked.

'I've called to see Paul Jenkins,' Burren responded, resenting Framley's question.

'Ah!' exclaimed Framley. 'Paul has been casting his net wide. Would you please remind him that I am waiting for him to arrange a meeting of *The New Age* editorial board.' Whereupon he turned and walked on down the corridor.

'Framley asked me to remind you about a meeting of the editorial board of *The New Age*,' Burren said as soon as he entered Paul's room.

'He is an old fusspot,' said Paul with mild irritation in his voice. 'There is plenty of time. All the articles are in and we don't go to press for another month. But he likes everything tied up weeks before. It is his fastidious way. Wait until you have him as a tutor.'

'He is already my tutor,' groaned Burren.

'Poor you.'

'I gather you play some significant part in *The New Age*.'

'I am the editor this term,' Paul tried to sound casual.

'And Framley?'

Paul smiled. It was the smile that gradually enthused his face as he imparted information he thought to be secretive. 'Timothy is Robert Wilcox's acolyte – some might say agent. He is the Principal's right arm, extending into all corners of the college, hence his presence on our editorial board. He is there to advise us.' He gave a small chuckle.

Burren was interested in how well Paul himself was meshed into the system and said as much.

'Aha. Well let's say I am operating at maximum at present,' he laughed,

'"Stretched", I think is the expression.' He became pensive. 'I shall have to think about scaling back soon to prepare for the exam.' He quickly returned to buoyant mood. 'Anyhow, I've no intention of allowing you just to cruise along, you know. We shall be looking to you for an article next term.'

'I don't know about that,' said Burren.

'We'll have no excuses. Work upon your Reed essay and scale it down suitably,' Paul smiled, 'There. You see. It's already done.'

One of the things he liked about Paul was that he made him feel good. His quiet, assured air enfolded Burren and helped him feel that way too.

'Now to business, I suppose,' said Paul. 'What line are we going to take on the question of German rearmament?'

'It is tricky,' said Burren. 'The whole issue is becoming oversimplified into an anti-German prejudice. I can understand the emotive side of the matter but I want us to try and clarify aspects of the question. So if we go for one speaker, let us aim for someone who is a bit of an expert on the subject. Can be a politician, but it should be one whose interest is foreign affairs and who knows something about the whole European dimension.'

'Brown is the man,' said Paul enthusiastically.

Brown was Labour's shadow Foreign Secretary.

'Yes, maybe. The rest of the committee are likely to be anti a German contribution, aren't they?'

'I think so,' said Paul. 'And I lean that way myself.'

'I don't think I can just say flatly yes to German rearmament,' said Burren, 'but that is why I want all aspects of it discussed. For example, if German rearmament was to be the first step towards their inclusion in a larger European family in which there is a genuine collective effort, political and economic, as well as military, then I think the whole thing takes on a quite different complexion.'

'That is what they were aiming at with the Coal and Steel Community and the EDC,' said Paul, 'but yes, I agree with you entirely.'

'Of course the bit that is lacking is the political dimension,' said Burren.

Paul quickly added, 'And that of course is the most important aspect.'

'Absolutely.' Burren was pleased that they agreed. 'So we can go to the committee now.'

'Sure.'

They both enjoyed these chats prior to the formal committee meetings, and which they referred to between themselves as the 'caucus'. They walked out of college together and headed in the direction of Dipanker's rooms where the committee meeting was to be held.

Later the same day the common room radiated a comfortable feeling of warmth, and the flicker from the log fire made strange and beautiful dancing shapes on a wall. Maureen Styles sat quietly sipping her coffee. The sound of jazz – of Chris Barber, and the voice of Ottilie Patterson – drifted across from the record player in the far corner of the room.

After coming out from supper people sat around and talked, some played cards or chess, whilst others completed newspaper reading or consulted weekly journals. Quiet thought and reflection on the day or on wider matters was the mood of some. Maureen was one of these. She liked to relax in the reposeful mood of the common room at this hour and let her mind meander across the day, to her home in the comfortable southern outskirts of Manchester, or simply on the general matters of the day.

She realised now why her husband Jack had talked so enthusiastically about Morton, and had wanted her to spend a weekend with him whilst he was there. Her excuse for not doing so had been Susan, their daughter, but she knew that was only part of the reason. She had not wanted to go at that time because she realised that she might herself want to go and study at the same place, and at that point the comfort and security of her home with Jack meant everything to her. She had been unfair to him in not trying, and not wanting, to understand what he was doing. She understood that now, and determined to tell him so.

Burren came and sat down beside her.

'How are you?' he asked.

She smiled a radiant, creasy smile, 'Fine, John.'

'You were looking very pensive, very reflective,' he said, offering her a cigarette.

'Thanks. I was just idling, letting my mind wander where it may. I sometimes do that at the end of a day. Well, it hasn't ended yet, but you know what I mean.'

'Yes, I know what you mean.'

He lit their cigarettes and inhaled deeply on his own. Maureen, he noticed, more or less blew the smoke straight back out. She watched him twirl his cigarette between his fingers.

'What have you been doing?' she asked.

'I have been with Paul Jenkins and we went on to a meeting of the executive committee of the Socialist Society. Do you know Paul?'

'No. Who is he?'

'Paul is a second-year student and is chairman of the Socialist Society. Charming man.' He thought awhile and then said rather ominously, 'We have been discussing German rearmament.'

'Oh, not you too,' protested Maureen. 'I had to listen to Chris and Frank arguing over that at supper.'

'They were doing the same thing when I met them at midday in the Rose & Crown.'

'I do believe it is affecting them,' said Maureen looking to him appealingly. She fell silent as they both looked around the emptying room and then returned to the subject. 'I wondered if you might try and talk some sense into them, John. I know that sounds alarmist, but I'm concerned, especially for Frank. He is more vulnerable than he appears.'

'I don't know that I can do that,' he said. 'I too have views you know.'

'Yes I know, John, but you are ...'

The rest remained unsaid, as he cut in.

'We'll see,' he said reassuringly.

The common room had now emptied apart from them. He walked across the room and put a record on the player. As the soft music wafted out he danced back to where Maureen was sitting. They sat listening to the music each occupied with their own thoughts.

Suddenly he said, 'What are you doing this evening?'

She looked at him, puzzled, and asked, 'Why? Um, I have some reading to complete.'

'How about coming to the cinema?' he sounded enthusiastic.

She hesitated. 'What is on?'

'Your all-time favourite, Mrs Styles.'

She laughed.

'I'm really not sure but I think they are still showing *The Odd Man Out* at the Classic. Oh come on, you'll enjoy it.' He looked at her appealingly. 'Please don't tell me you've seen it.'

'No, I haven't seen it,' she smiled.

'Well there you are then.'

She was not sure. She ought to finish the reading, but she found it difficult to resist his enthusiasm and he was good for her morale. She relented.

'Good,' he said, putting his arm round her shoulder, 'we've just time if we hurry.'

They were lucky. That rare gem of a thriller was still showing. He had been to the Classic a number of times and he made a point of looking at their weekly programme. It was a small cinema not far from the city part of the college. It showed old films that had passed into the category of classics, as well as French and Italian films.

They were lucky too, as the cinema was not full he was told as he paid for the tickets. Maureen insisted on paying her share. Once inside the darkness enveloped them and despite the usherette's efforts they still had to grope their way along the aisles.

They watched an apparently pointless B film about two teenagers who eloped. The couple then spent the rest of their time wondering if total strangers knew of their sinful behaviour. The lights went up between this showing and the main film and two disinterested-looking women paraded the aisles with heavily stacked trays of sweets and ice creams. Burren thought about how different they looked from the enticingly piquant-looking women in the advertisements. He said as much to Maureen and she playfully teased him on the subject.

The lights dimmed again and a short newsreel came on the screen, a large part of it taken up with the issue of West European defence and the turmoil this was causing inside the Labour Party.

Burren whispered to Maureen, 'This is going to be with us for quite some time.'

She groaned agreement.

He thought balefully of his own efforts over the past two weeks to try and instil more balance into the discussion of the issues at stake. Within the Labour Party nationally however it was a different story, and he knew it was going to be a long and bruising business inside the Party.

The screen was now showing forthcoming attractions. And then at last the opening credits for the film they had come to see. They watched whilst the 'odd man' was hunted down by the police. The fascination with intrigue, the grimness of life in Ireland at that time, and the passion spent in fighting for a cause, all communicated itself to them with a deep intensity.

They came out of the cinema onto the dank pavements of a November night, with the outpouring of traffic from cinemas, theatres and clubs oozing its way past them. He was thinking of the film they had just seen. Of the brave and noble Irishmen who gave so much of themselves in the cause of independence during the Troubles, and reflected sadly that it should not have been necessary.

Maureen bustled along beside him. 'Thank you, John, for asking me. I enjoyed it.' She laughed. 'Well, you know what I mean.' She then added, 'But please don't feel that you have to ask me out.'

'I enjoy your company,' he said, smiling in the dark.

'That is very sweet of you.' She linked her arm in his.

The following morning Burren heard the raised voices of Chris Megson and Frank Bainwell at breakfast on the next but one table from himself. He wasn't sure what they were talking about but a shrewd guess told him that it was the continuing issue of German rearmament. When they left to go into the common room, he followed and overheard Chris saying something that suggested there had been a rather bitter discussion at the committee meeting of the Labour Club the previous day. He greeted both of them as he entered the common room.

'Hello John,' said Frank with a rueful smile.

Chris was his normal, cheerful self.

'You were both going it a bit in there over breakfast,' Burren said.

'Well, something sparked off the German question again and we just cannot agree on that.' Chris smiled in his dismissive way.

'No we can't,' said Frank, 'and what is more we do not agree about the Party either.' He went on, 'Anyone with two eyes in his head can see that it was not a democratic decision at the Annual Conference. The block vote as usual ensured victory for the leadership.'

'The block vote, that is always the old standby,' said Chris.

'But on this occasion it is certainly the case Chris,' said Burren. 'A majority of the constituencies were against it.'

'And they of course are the soul of the Party, reflecting the genuine socialist base,' said Frank with some feeling.

'And I suppose you'll say that this college is also the true repository of socialism,' Chris replied sarcastically.

'Well, true repository, or not, I believe you'll be in the minority,' said Burren.

'Of course I will, because most of you are still guided by sentimental nonsense. In some strange way you think that to believe, to believe strongly enough, is in itself to be right. Well I tell you it is not as simple as that.'

Although they were of the same age, Burren saw how young Chris looked when filled with intense earnestness, as now.

Frank was saying, 'Your trouble, Chris, is that you don't feel your politics. There is no deep involvement inside you. Your brand of socialism is expressed in figures: production figures, exports, percentages of those passing the Eleven Plus examination, and the proportion of people in social class, whatever it is. Anything, other than being genuinely about human beings. That is the way social democracy is going now.'

'Hey, steady on,' said Burren smiling, 'I may be amongst those.'

They were not to be put off by any such flippant remark.

'Sentiment hasn't yet made a society,' said Chris.

'It may not have made a society, but it would be a pretty poor specimen without any sentiment,' Frank retorted, and then went on, 'And your failure to understand that tells me a lot about how you see human beings in relation to socialism.'

Burren tried once again to be conciliatory. 'I think both of you are now taking up rather fixed positions,' he said. 'Part of the problem inside the Party is obviously linked to the issue of German rearmament. Now we've arranged for a thorough discussion of this subject in the Socialist Society – I may have mentioned this to you before. In my view we are adopting the sensible approach. The subject has to be seen from all angles. Not just from the British standpoint, not just from within the Labour Party – which in any case is not the government – but within the context of Europe. We need to try and obtain a convergence of view between ourselves and Western Europe on the broad issues at stake.'

This seemed to bring an effective end to the current argument, though whether it brought Chris and Frank any nearer to reaching agreement was another matter.

Burren said that he was going into the city for a tutorial and Frank readily joined him.

They chatted as the bus made its way circuitously around the industrial part of the city.

'Thank you, John, for your intervention. I know I get a bit emotional about these things but to me it is human beings that matter. We have always to think of our fellow beings, or we are lost.' Frank added sadly, 'Chris seems to me to have lost sight of that.'

'I know what you mean, Frank, and fundamentally I share your feeling of the need to be close to the people.' He looked directly at the older man. 'But it is going to happen, Frank; we'll not stop German rearmament, and therefore it seems to me that it is better to try and ensure that it is harnessed to some wider European interest rather than German nationalism.'

The bus stopped near the college and they both alighted to go their separate ways.

Burren knocked on Mike Dawson's door and discovered that he was still occupied with another tutorial.

'Just wait for a bit, John, I shall not be long.'

Burren closed the door and waited in the corridor. The man with Mike Dawson was Stephen Brill, a third Reed scholar. Chris Megson had tracked the other two Reed students early on in the term, with the intention of the four of them getting together. However, nothing much had come of the idea. They had met as a group a couple of times but somehow once together the means which had brought them to the college – the Reed scholarship – proved insubstantial. Their relationships worked well enough however on an individual basis. For example, Burren knew that Chris Megson and Stephen Brill were good friends. Both of them were members of the Labour Club, and both had recruited themselves into one of the local football clubs.

Burren had not struck up the same kind of friendship with Stephen Brill. He did not find Brill's self-righteous form of Methodism attractive and so was not drawn to his company. Brill was much the same age as Burren and Chris Megson but always appeared to act as though he were older, with the burden of his previous job as assistant manager in a large Co-operative store in the Midlands still weighing upon him.

The other Reed scholar, Tom Croft, Burren liked. He was a full-time official of ASSET. He had previously worked in local government and had been a Labour candidate at the last general election. It was a marginal constituency and he had been readopted, which if the national electoral tide moved in Labour's direction should take him into parliament at the next election.

He was a tallish man in his early thirties who on first acquaintance gave the impression of being a bank clerk: in physical appearance, dress, and in the anonymous persona he seemed to want to project. But as he came to know Tom Croft, Burren was aware that this was not the case at all. He was a keen and talented musician and played the saxophone in a band back home in north London. Before he became a parliamentary candidate he had also been a member of his local dramatic society.

He could be very amusing on the subject of amateur dramatics; retailing accounts of staging very elitist plays by Christopher Fry and T.S. Eliot, to rather highbrow audiences in Canonbury. He and Burren got on well together and enjoyed having after-supper chats in the common room.

The door of the Principal's secretary's office opened and Jasmine emerged. He watched her starting to head down the corridor. Suddenly she turned and saw him.

He smiled. 'Good morning.'

She allowed a smile gradually to lighten up her face. 'Good morning.'

As she turned and quickly carried on along the corridor he considered how successful she must be in projecting a favour-able image of the college; a considerable asset to Robert Wilcox.

Stephen Brill now came out from Mike Dawson's room and briefly exchanged a word with Burren before leaving.

'Come in, John.' It was the beckoning voice of Mike Dawson. 'Sorry I've kept you waiting. It is a bit like a doctor's surgery this morning. I'm running progressively late with my tutorials.' He frowned at this worrying trend in himself, and then beamed his usual friendly welcome. 'Right. Let's get started. It is Social Democracy today, isn't it?'

'Yes,' replied Burren.

'Did you like the topic? Just remind me; you were having to show what it is that differentiates Social Democracy from other forms of socialism, and then evaluate its primary characteristics.'

'Yes, that is right,' replied Burren, acutely aware that this was Mike Dawson's specialist area.

Burren talked from his essay, which later had to be handed in for marking. He indicated how he saw Social Democracy, other than in its European form, as less institutional than other forms of socialism, with not the same emphasis upon organisation and structure in the quest for power. He went on to state that he saw Social Democracy as not so much prescribing a set of policies as if they were an inviolate code, but rather as a set of values to be implemented, with the means for implementing them remaining flexible. It was the end that had to be kept in sight, with the means suitably adapted to circumstances in order to achieve the end. In other words, he went on, Social Democracy was very much concerned with process rather than structure. After making several points, he reached the end of his essay and now waited for Mike Dawson to comment.

'You've clearly done a lot of work on this, John, and I like what you say; it does get to the essence of Social Democracy.'

There was a pause, and then he asked Burren, ' Are they deluding themselves, these Social Democrat thinkers, when they state that the institutional aspect is unimportant, or less important?'

'Yes, I think they are,' said Burren. 'In fact when confronted with the need to organise power into decision-taking the institutional aspect becomes important.' He was pleased with himself and went on to say, 'It may be that the European form of the theory have got that part of it right.'

'Good point,' said Mike Dawson, quite well aware of this aspect all the time. He liked to encourage his students and make them feel they had discovered things.

The tutorial continued in this vein and it was clear that Burren's assessment of social democracy met with approval.

At the end Mike Dawson said, 'Well that concludes the course in political theory, John. How do you feel you've performed in this subject?'

He hesitated before replying. 'I've liked the subject very much. I've worked hard and I think I have a fair grasp of the development of political thought.' He gave a short laugh. 'I certainly know more than when I started.'

He did not admit to how difficult he had found it at times. Only to himself did he acknowledge just how much he had struggled with the conceptual nature of the subject.

Mike Dawson smiled benignly, 'You can be reasonably satisfied with your work. In my view you have worked hard, and I have watched your progress. More importantly, I have seen how generally your ability to analyse and weigh evidence has improved.' He glanced at his notes, and then resumed, 'I have just a few points to make to help you with your work.' He went on to cover areas where Burren needed to improve and then turned his head with its mass of dark, curly hair, to look directly at Burren.

'Remember what I said at the outset. The political philosophers are seeking to provide you with their view of the good society; of what it would contain and how it would be organised. In other words, how it would be governed and reflect the best society. You have to apply two tests in assessing them: (a) How well does each of their models of society match reality as

71

you see it? And (b) How far does the moral basis of their model satisfy the concepts of government, order, law, justice, rights, etcetera? In fact the same concerns in many ways that Plato expressed all those years ago. One final point. Again, as I mentioned at the outset of this course, our coverage of the field of political theory is incomplete.' He laughed to himself. 'That is the understatement of the day. You therefore have to fill in the blanks.'

They shook hands and Burren prepared to leave. At the door Mike Dawson said, 'I believe you are the next secretary of the Socialist Society.'

'Yes, that's right.' He wondered what was coming next.

'Should you want to use me in connection with the Society, or to chat about affairs in general, well, I'm here.'

The end-of-term social events were under way. There was a festive supper followed by a dance. Frank Bainwell's social committee – Frank had quickly installed himself as chairman back at the beginning of the session – had organised the supper and dance to round off the term.

Everyone agreed that Frank had made a great success of the supper. It was a munificent occasion; the food was excellent, with the kitchen staff producing the usual Christmas menu of turkey, Christmas pudding, mince pies, cheeses, etcetera. The social committee together with others had decorated the dining hall to give it a truly festive atmosphere. People expressed their thanks with several spontaneous speeches during supper.

Burren was placed next to his Russian tutor, Mrs Grey, an ageing lady of still quite remarkable beauty, now a widow. She had been with her parents in the flight of White Russians during the civil war following the revolution. They had settled in Britain, and after an unexplained period of years that he did not care to probe into, she had married an English academic and ended up at the university. He believed she had a son who lived in the city, but he was not sure of that. She now taught Russian and lived in a two-room dwelling in one of the poorer parts of the city. Her much reduced circumstances were a mystery to him.

She liked him. He knew that. For what other reason would she continue to accept his excuses, underpreparation and appalling inability to pronounce anything correctly in the language that she so dearly loved? To him, her life was mystifying, and part of her fascination was that he knew so little about her. Either she lived, as he sometimes imagined, in a recreated world of pre-revolutionary Russian grandeur, or she lived a life of the most dreadful emptiness.

He had made so little progress with the language that he was thinking of giving it up, if only because he felt it was unfair to her. He was overstretching himself. He had taken on more than he should have alongside his course subjects, and realised now that he should never have tried to learn Russian. It was some romantic idea of visiting Moscow that had inspired him. He told himself that he was crazy to continue with the language. He had no natural facility in foreign languages. The almost totally different alphabet, the different cases that had to be mastered, the acquisition of the vocabulary; his failure in each of these meant that he was near to being a hopeless case. He conveyed these doubts to her over the intimacy of the supper table. She implored him to stay, saying that things would become easier once he fully mastered the alphabet.

'You try so hard,' she said, trying to make him feel better, yet only confirming his inadequacy.

She turned her head slightly and he could see how attractive she must have been as a young woman. She still is attractive, he told himself. Her high cheekbones, slightly hooded eyes and silver-grey hair, seen now in the shadowy light of the burning candles, sent fantasies of an old Russia flooding through his mind. His mind jumped to her as a young woman. Where had she lived in Russia. Moscow? He knew not, and thought it better not to enquire. Suddenly he felt sorry for her. He knew that she needed the money from her tuition.

73

He had already given way to her charm and he now suc-
cumbed, telling her that he would continue until at least the end
of the year.

She was satisfied with this, gently gripping his arm and
whispering, 'We will speak Russian together.'

He could see the mischief playing at the corners of her mouth.
They continued their supper with a light conversation about
earlier days in the university, about which she was both well
informed and interesting.

Later the same evening the end of term dance was to take
place. Apparently it was customary to hold this event at the
House. He looked in on the final arrangements being made
before going off to The Bear inn for a drink. The social committee together with numerous helpers had made a splendid job
of transforming the large room at the front of the House into a
space suitable for dancing and making it colourful; it was now
festooned with lights, balloons and Chinese lanterns, and in one
corner stood a Christmas tree, sparkling goodwill.

The Bear was crowded with plenty of Morton students having a drink of good cheer before going to the dance. This was
the local inn serving the locality, including the students of the
house. He had used it a little himself but was not yet seen as a
regular.

Paul spotted him and came across to where he was standing.

'Hello John, I thought I might see you here.' He looked
around and took in the galaxy of people enjoying themselves.
'These events are usually great fun.'

Burren took a sip of his beer. 'Dipankar tells me that the two
of you met to formalise the programme of the Socialist Society.'

'That's right. It is essentially the same as you and I agreed – so
it should be good!'

They both laughed.

'By the way, Paul, I said to Dipankar that I thought you
should be included in our meetings that settle business – it will
help to give a touch of continuity to things. He agreed.'

Paul looked pleased.

They looked around at the familiar faces, all probably talking shop.

'I'm leaving in a minute,' said Burren, taking a gulp of his beer. 'The dance must be well under way by now.'

'Yes, sure, but let's have another before we go.'

Eventually the two of them went to the dance. As they entered the hallway couples could be seen languidly cruising round the dance floor to the music of 'Slow Boat to China'. Burren saw Maureen Styles sitting on the other side of the room and went across to ask her to dance.

Maureen began chatting animatedly. She commented upon the supper, and then the dance, and then tailed off into a summary of the term before asking him, 'Have you enjoyed the term, John?'

'Yes,' he replied, 'and I hope you have too.'

'I have John, I have.' Her happiness showed.

He thought her effervescent party mood probably expressed her excitement at going home to her family the following day. The music stopped and they walked back to the side of the floor. Maureen was quickly seized for the next dance and Burren walked round the edge of the room where he met Frank Bainwell, basking in the limelight of the evening's success with a glass of beer in his hand and looking every bit the genial host.

'Superb evening, Frank. You and your social gang have done a marvellous job.'

Frank beamed goodwill. 'Pity I can't organise the Labour Club as well.'

Burren laughed. 'Plenty of time yet.'

They parted and Burren turned and saw Jasmine at the far end of the room. Robert Wilcox was standing talking to Framley and Jasmine was seated next to them.

He decided to go across and ask her to dance. Just as he arrived the music stopped and the voice of singer Frankie Lane faded out. He stood in front of Jasmine and smiled a little foolishly. 'I was about to ask you to dance when the music stopped.'

Jasmine laughed quietly to herself.

The music started up again and Jasmine got to her feet. They glided into the dance, or rather Jasmine did. His own effort was rather more laboured. The freshness of her golden hair caught his nostrils. He could feel her body against his though she danced so airily it was almost as if she were on her own.

He asked with mock seriousness, 'Do you come here often?'

She looked at him and responded in kind with a faint smile. 'About once a term.'

He laughed inwardly as they continued dancing.

He made another attempt. 'How long have you worked here?'

'I have been here nearly two years now,' she replied.

He noted that was roughly the period of time that Robert Wilcox had been Principal. Again he noticed how her hair shone under the different coloured lights.

'Do you like working for the Principal?'

She now looked at him as if he were a naughty boy, and said admonishingly, 'The rules.'

He looked at her, initially puzzled by this response, and fell silent, but then realised what she meant.

Jasmine asked, 'Have you enjoyed your first term?'

'Very much so,' he said with real enthusiasm.

'And how do you get on with the tutors?' she asked.

'The rules,' he replied mockingly.

Jasmine smiled with amusement. 'Touché,' she said. 'Touché.'

They were beginning to know one another.

5

He made slow progress in walking to Dipankar's rooms. There was already a carpet of snow on the ground and it continued to fall heavily.

Dipankar was an Indian postgraduate student at the university and had followed Paul Jenkins as chairman of the Socialist Society. He was a confident, forceful young man of strong convictions. Burren had noticed in the first term when Dipankar was secretary of the Society that by force of argument and persuasion he more often than not got what he wanted. His assurance of manner suggested to Burren that he was used to having his way.

He observed also that Dipankar revealed a characteristic that he had seen in other people from lands that had previously been British colonial territories: they acted as though the class structure of former times in Britain still existed, where servants performed the more menial everyday tasks. In fact, of course, whilst British society still displayed many symptoms of its old class structure, the panoply of servants was not one of them.

By any standard, even without Dipankar's presumption about the British class system, his own family, Burren reckoned, would be regarded as rich. So that in his own society, he had more than likely been used to having servants do things for him. Burren knew that his father was a judge at state level in Bengal, and he believed there was substantial inherited wealth in the family.

He had now reached Dipankar's rooms. He knocked on the door and heard Dipankar's voice call, 'Come in.'

'Hello, John. How are you? Good to see you back. Have you had a good holiday?' The words came tumbling out with staccato speed.

Burren wished him a Happy New Year.

'And you too, John.'

'Did you go away?' enquired Burren. 'To stay with relatives or friends?'

'Yes I did, and got back yesterday. Travel from London was difficult because of this.' He pointed to the snow outside the window, which was continuing to fall rapidly.

'It must have been good to be amongst relatives for the vacation,' said Burren.

'Well ... it was I suppose . Yes, of course it was. But there are always lots of questions. Am I doing this? Am I doing that?' He laughed. 'A lot of fuss too. You know what Indian families are like. I'm the youngest son and my mother still refers to me as the baby of the family. Ugh.' He shrugged.

They continued to chat, until Burren said, 'Well, to business then. The programme is as we agreed it last term.'

Dipankar looked at it quickly. 'It is good you know. It is a full programme, and we have a number of outside speakers. Well done, John. I'm sure we are going to be a good team.'

'I'm sure too. Oh, and by the way I've allowed for any additional speakers that we might want to have, and for specific events that might crop up and for which we might like to have a last minute outside speaker.' He looked pleased with himself. 'And, I believe I've managed to hook Maurice Watkins. He has recently been promoted to the Treasury team, you know, and I think it could be useful to hear what he has to say.'

He knew that Dipankar was not overly interested in British domestic politics, and that his interest was much more directed towards the movement for colonial freedom. He therefore tried to express his own enthusiasm for the speaker in muted language.

'Good,' said Dipankar in a flat voice.

Burren was in fact overjoyed at the prospect of securing Maurice Watkins. He was not absolutely sure that Watkins would agree, and he had yet to confirm, but he was apparently going to be in the area for another engagement at the beginning of May and was prepared to fit in other events around this. Burren was hoping that he might arrange for Maurice Watkins to meet with Robert Wilcox over supper with the officers of the Society.

'Let's go across for tea on this dreary afternoon,' said Dipankar. Burren readily agreed.

Most of Morton had now returned from the vacation and the common room was abnormally crowded this morning. As he looked around he could see there was little prospect of getting hold of a newspaper. He spotted Maureen Styles and started to go over to her.

'Good morning, John. And a Happy New Year.'

He turned and saw it was Tom Croft. 'Best wishes to you too, Tom.' And he continued across towards Maureen.

'It is good to see you back, Maureen. I hope it hasn't been too difficult to return,' he smiled enquiringly and looked to see if she was anxious. 'I tried to catch you yesterday but I was tied up a great deal of the time at the city end, and then there was the problem with the weather.' He nodded towards the snow that still lay thickly outside.

'It is good to see you again, John.' She forced a smile.

'Everything all right?' he asked.

'Well, being just back is not the best of times, and there is the snow too.'

The snow continued to fall. It was dry snow and was now drifting in the high wind. It was a quite remarkably apt scene for the time of the year – as though it had been designed for Christmas cards.

'I'm supposed to go to the city today,' he said, 'but I doubt if the buses are running.'

'I don't intend to move from my room,' said Maureen.

Frank Bainwell came and sat down beside them. They exchanged seasonal greetings.

'We're besieged,' said Frank as if enjoying the prospect of war conditions. 'Iron rations too, most likely,' he joked.

'Oh do shut up, Frank,' said Maureen. She had listened to him in much the same vein coming down on the train from Manchester the day before.

The weather conditions were unquestionably very bad. The catering staff, drawn from the nearby housing estate, had said with enthusiastic pessimism that on their way in to the college there had been stranded vehicles on the main road, abandoned overnight. The morning news on the radio had confirmed that weather conditions were bad across the whole of the country, with forecasts of yet more snow as well as freezing fog.

There was nothing for it but to accept the conditions and get down to as much reading as possible. Burren settled into his room and continued with the reading of Joan Robinson's *Imperfect Competition*. He had been advised to look at this book, which he understood would be required for the subject tutorial in economics with Edell. It was exceptionally hard going, and for Burren with little previous experience of the more detailed diagrammatic representation of microeconomics, it strained his ability to concentrate to the utmost.

He looked out of the window at the grey day outside with the snow continuing to fall on the hard layer already formed on the ground. His room was at the rear of the house and the window faced directly on to the vegetable garden, beyond which was a meadow and then a further meadow that ran alongside the by-pass. There was no longer the continuous sound of traffic. The picture presented was of one long rolled-out carpet of snow extending out as far as the eye could see.

His thoughts idly drifted away from the reading in front of him to the college and the group of people that now formed the community in which he lived. Once he started to think about them, he realised how few he knew really well. Amongst the whole community there were only five women, including Maureen Styles. Two of these were American and he knew very little about either of them. Together with Al Krause, the other American, they were in college less than the other students. They spent a lot of their time going to London and other parts of the country to meet with politicians and representatives of public bodies, including local authorities. As each of them was from a trade union they were also keen to develop links with their counterparts in Britain. From this information Burren concluded that their main interest was in industrial relations.

The other two women, apart from Maureen, Burren knew only vaguely. One of them, Joan Symonds, was a trade union officer with USDAW, and he reckoned she was a bit older than Maureen Styles. The other, Sylvia Thurston, was an office worker from Hull. He had spoken to her from time to time, and formed the impression that she had little time for the frivolities of life, included amongst which were probably men. She was well set apparently on her ambition to become an MP, having already been adopted for a safe seat in the North East.

Politically, the community of students divided into a number of distinct groupings. There were the supporters of Aneurin Bevan – Bevanites – amongst whom was Frank Bainwell, and emotionally Burren included himself in that group. There were the great majority who considered themselves centrists and loyal to the existing philosophy and policies of the Labour Party. Chris Megson would most certainly wish to be thought of as one of these, he told himself. There were then a minority of very left-wing socialists, together with a handful of Marxists. They would sometimes close ranks when confronted by the others but left to themselves they were anxious to display the distinctiveness of their credentials.

Overlapping these groupings and existing within them were the Christian Socialists, mainly Methodists, who were always anxious, he found, to interpret any and all social phenomena, however trivial, in a religious context. If truth be told, he had to admit to himself, these were the people for whom he had least respect. It seemed to him that they were hypocritical and offended most in hiding reality behind their religious posturing. They were the least able to accept the complexities surrounding social issues and expose them to analysis. Always, it seemed, they had an answer in the smug embrace of their faith. He and Frank Bainwell, when talking of this group, referred to them as 'burst seamers' because the moral seam of Methodism was frequently close to bursting apart in righteous indignation.

He was jolted out of this musing by a knock on his door. It was Chris Megson.

'Are you busy, John?' He indicated the Robinson book propped in a reading position on Burren's desk.

'It depends if you call reading this busy. It is certainly painful,' Burren groaned.

'You took Economics last term, didn't you? How did you react to *Imperfect Competition* of the Robinson kind?'

'It is heavy going,' admitted Chris. 'You have to plod on, I'm afraid. It does become easier.'

'Good. I'm pleased to hear you say that.' Though he was not entirely convinced.

'Have a seat.' He gestured towards the one soft chair that he had in his room. Chris slipped into place. 'Cigarette?' He offered the packet to Chris before taking one himself.

'No thanks, I'll smoke my pipe,' Chris said, fondling the pipe in his pocket.

A contemplative mood enveloped them as they smoked. At last Burren said, 'Did you call just to share my company on this wretched day, Chris, or is there something you specifically want to talk about?'

'Yes there is.' He hesitated, not quite sure how to broach the subject. 'How can I best put this? I was wondering if we might work more closely together ...' he hesitated. 'You know, draw up a plan of campaign.' He stopped and gave a quick nervous laugh. 'That sounds rather portentous, and isn't quite what I mean.'

Burren looked at Chris with a quizzical smile. 'This is most unlike you, Chris. You usually say exactly what you mean.'

'I know. I know. Let me start again. What I thought we might do is have a common scheme of work in which we pool our knowledge and thus supplement each other's work. For example, you've told me some of the more important points you discussed with Mike Dawson, and as you know he is my tutor this term. And I have tried to keep you in touch with Edell's brand of economics, which you'll understand isn't easy.' He chuckled. 'But in this way we could work together and maximise our resources.'

'A good economic principle,' quipped Burren. 'It sounds a good idea.'

'I thought it would help as well when the time comes for us to apply for a place at the university.'

'University!' exclaimed Burren.

'Yes of course.'

'I haven't thought of university at this stage,' he said.

'But there is no reason not to start.' Chris gave a disbelieving and dismissive laugh.

'But ...'

Chris looked at him, genuinely puzzled.

'What exactly do you want from this place, John?'

'I'm not sure. I really haven't thought about it in that way.' He thought awhile whilst Chris looked at him closely.

'I suppose I want to study subjects that interest me. No particular aim beyond that at the moment. You understand? Just what I'm interested in,' he repeated as if to himself.

Chris shifted position and swung his long legs over the side of his chair.

'But what about later?' he asked.

'I haven't thought that far ahead. I'm too busy with what I am doing at present.'

'For Christ's sake, John, what a muddler you are. You have to make plans for university early on you know; certainly during your first year here. It's the only thing. To go on. No future otherwise. As it is, the job market is filling up all the time with graduates.' He got to his feet.

'You mean you've already started planning for university?' said Burren, not entirely convinced by Chris's confidence.

'Yes I have, John. There is no time to waste.' There was an almost aggressive tone to his voice.

'Well well!' exclaimed Burren.

Chris moved towards the door and rested his hand on the handle. 'Thanks for the chat.' He was about to open the door and then turned. 'John, think it over and let me know.'

The door closed behind him and Burren was left with his own thoughts again. It had come as a bit of a surprise. It hadn't occurred to him that some of his fellow students, and obviously Chris in particular, were already thinking about what to do once they left the college. Chris was a smart operator. With his ambition he is going to forge ahead, Burren told himself. There is something just a bit different about Chris, he mused. There is something ... the thought trailed away, defying clarification. Did he himself want to go to university? He hadn't thought of it before, probably because it had been impossibly beyond his reach. But it was more likely that it simply had not formed part of his thinking. It certainly had never been talked about in his secondary modern world – it would have been a ridiculous idea. But now? He toyed with the idea

Slowly, but slowly, his mind returned to the reality of *Imperfect Competition*.

Eventually after two further days the snowfall abated and there began a slow thaw. The house occupants were able once again to make their way into the city and Burren was ready for his first session with John Edell. His room was the largest of the tutor's rooms, and more than rivalled that of Robert Wilcox. It was completely book-lined.

Edell's bass voice greeted him. 'Good to see you at last.' He spoke exactly as he did in his lectures. The fact that there was now only Burren present made no difference. He went on, 'We have to try and cover the more essential parts of the micro-system and extend into the macro ...' his voice trailed off as if he was communicating only with himself. Burren noticed that Edell did not face him directly, his eyes focussing on some other point in the room.

Burren's mind wandered to absorb the surroundings of the room. Edell had an impressively large desk which was also remarkably tidy. There was a telephone at one end, and at the other end a tray which contained the inward and outward mail. He saw that this too was without any accumulated correspondence. The book-lined shelves contained not only economics texts, though they abounded, but there was a substantial amount of fiction.

'So you see ...' Burren returned his attention in time to catch the last part of Edell's address, for that is what it was. '... economics is in essence about infinite elasticity of demand and inelastic supply, defined in a given period of time.'

Edell sat back and for the first time looked directly at Burren. 'So for your first tutorial I want you to look at the different conditions in which the competitive process of production takes place.'

'What should I read?' enquired Burren.

'Are you looking at Robinson? Joan, I mean.'

Burren nodded. 'Yes.'

Edell indicated supporting reading that he advised Burren to consult. Again he brought Burren within his focus as he said, 'I shall be most interested to see what you make of this eternal aspect of the study of the economic process.'

Burren left the room, thinking of his first meeting with Edell. He felt that he was in for either a very hard time, or an easy ride, and he wasn't at all sure which of these it would be. Either way he had serious doubts as to whether Edell was going to assist his understanding of economics. Now that he had met

Edell he thought he understood why it was that Robert Wilcox did not want him to be the Vice-Principal, and was actively looking at every means to circumvent his position.

He was now on his way to meet the man the Principal was using to fulfil the role that was rightly Edell's. He knocked on Framley's door and heard the voice – clear and precise, unmistakably that of Framley – say, 'Come in.'

He entered and waited.

'Please be seated,' said Framley looking up from his desk and permitting the thinnest of smiles to lighten his face. 'For some reason we were unable to meet at the end of last term, though it matters not. I understand that you got along well with Mike Dawson.'

Burren noticed how Framley managed to imbue the comment with added meaning. 'He has reported favourably on your work in political theory.'

'Yes, he told me as much.'

'Though he does go on to say that you indulge in rather too many generalisations without a sufficient background of evidence.'

Burren attempted some justification but Framley cut him short. 'And that your written work needs to be more precise. The points that have been made are worth attention if you wish to improve the quality of your work still further.' His manner softened. 'You've obviously some facility for writing …', he paused as if to correct his manner and then the normal Framley mode quickly returned. 'Let's not confuse enthusiasm with knowledge, however.' He paused again. 'I think that is about it. We'll meet again in a month's time unless you have need to see me before then.'

Burren moved towards the door. Once outside, he tried to put matters in perspective. Mike Dawson's comments had already been made to him by Mike himself, but put in a rather more positive way. It was Framley's manner that irritated him. Framley had an insufferably superior air and Burren invariably responded badly to such people. He determined to try not to do so, and not to allow Framley to get under his skin.

He walked quickly to the college library with the intention of putting in a morning's reading on the competitive process. He selected his books, which happily were still available on the shelves at this hour, and chose his favourite reading place, a window seat which looked out upon the garden of a neighbouring college.

He became increasingly fascinated by the models used to explain the different competitive situations, and what had not been clear from Edell's lectures now began to take shape in his mind. Indeed, so preoccupied was he that the morning passed without a break for coffee.

It was now midday. He looked across to the far end of the row of seats, where Frank Bainwell was sitting staring into space. Chris Megson was sitting close by and Burren went over to him to ask if he was going to the Rose & Crown. Frank seemed less keen on the idea, but after some thought he agreed.

The three of them walked the short distance to the pub. Inside they positioned themselves alongside the log fire with its warm glow.

'Had a good morning?' Burren asked.

'Yes,' said Chris. 'I've rather taken to Plato.'

'He was a fascist,' grunted Frank.

'You are together for tutorials again, aren't you? That should make for some argumentative sessions with Mike Dawson.' He laughed.

Frank and Chris acknowledged that even with economics the tutorials had been lively, and they were anticipating even livelier times in a subject like political theory.

'After all,' said Frank, 'if you can't disagree about political ideas there is not much hope left is there.'

Burren could see that the pair of them were in for still more interesting times with Mike Dawson, especially when it came to the discussion of social democracy.

'You have tutorials on your own with Edell, don't you?' Chris asked Burren.

'You've established a very privileged position for yourself,' said Frank.

Burren leapt in quickly. 'Hold on. It may seem that way to you and I suppose it is in a sense, but you have to work harder, I can assure you, and there is no one else to help you out.'

'We don't help one another out,' grinned Frank. 'We make it as difficult for each other as possible.'

He could see that Chris did not share Frank's light-hearted approach to the matter, and he realised that this partly explained why Chris had come to see him in his room a few days earlier. Chris now sought to move the conversation on by asking Burren if he had completed his programme for the Socialist Society. Burren said he had and that he was inviting Maurice Watkins along in early May.

'In fact I want to call in and see the Principal this afternoon to see if he would like to join us and the speaker for supper.' Both of the others now seemed very interested. 'Come along to hear Watkins if you want to; it will be an open meeting.'

A quickly taken sandwich with another half pint of beer and they were on their way back to the college; the other two for their tutorial with Mike Dawson and he to the library before going on to see the Principal. Later he had to meet with Paul for the Socialist Society meeting on German rearmament.

He worked on mastering the different degrees of imperfect competition as outlined by Joan Robinson. It was unquestionably dry stuff and she in no way made any concession to making it more palatable by enlivening the text. He had to admit however that gradually the sheer persistence with the detail had its own reward, and it began to take hold of him.

He left his reading to wander and browse along the shelves of the economics section. Suddenly his eye spotted the name of Maurice Watkins. Could it be the same one? He saw two titles: *The Free Market Economy* and *The Economics of Laissez-faire*.

He pulled the books from the shelf and began to look at them, telling himself that to be forewarned is to be forearmed. It was indeed the same Maurice Watkins. He scanned both texts quickly, searching for the main thrust of the argument. They were very well written and he could see instantly that they were not just straight political tracts. He had not known that Watkins was such an articulate exponent of the free market principle. He decided that if he had enough time he would look at both books more thoroughly before the meeting with Watkins.

After leaving the library he went up to Jasmine's office. She was sitting behind her desk. Now wearing reading glasses, she appeared to him to epitomise the efficient secretary with just the right touch of pleasantness of manner to make a visitor feel welcome. He noticed that her hair was arranged differently. It was a little shorter than before, with a bob effect. It suited her, he thought, and made her look younger. She turned her head to look at who had entered her office, and seeing him she glanced quickly and then averted her eyes.

'Hello.'

'Hello,' she said and looked at him enquiringly without posing any question.

He asked if the Principal was in his office.

She smiled. 'I'm afraid not. Is there anything I can do to help?'

'Yes. Could you give him a message, please. Tell him that the Socialist Society have invited Maurice Watkins for Tuesday 4th May, and ask him if he would care to have supper with the speaker and the officers of the Society.'

He went on to explain the further details, noting whilst he spoke that Jasmine had the disconcerting look of appraising him.

When he had finished speaking Jasmine said, 'Of course. I'll let him know.' She then asked, already knowing the answer he was sure, 'You are the Secretary now, aren't you?'

'Yes,' he replied, smiling broadly.

She looked at him with an expression that told him his time was up. 'Either I or the Principal himself will be in touch to let you know.'

'Thanks.'

He made his way to the venue for the meeting at which Geoff Brown was to speak. He wanted to ensure that he would be in time to greet the speaker as he arrived. Brown was now shadow Foreign Secretary, and very well informed on European affairs. Burren and Dipankar were indebted to Paul Jenkins for securing him for this meeting. Paul's father apparently knew Brown and had pulled the necessary strings. Not only was Brown well on top of the subject of German rearmament, but he was also a powerful and persuasive speaker.

The room was already beginning to fill up when Burren and Paul Jenkins arrived. They exchanged greetings with Dipankar and they waited for the speaker to arrive.

'I do hope it goes well,' said Dipankar. 'This is my first meeting as chairman and I want it to be a success.'

Burren patted him on the shoulder. 'It will be,' he said, with a comforting smile.

There was some nervous activity taking place: the rearranging of chairs on the platform, the checking of water in the water jug on the table for the speaker, and checking the drinking glasses to see that they were clean.

They were taken by surprise when Geoff Brown came in through the side door. Immediately Burren was impressed by his strong physical presence. Dipankar and Burren introduced themselves and welcomed him to the meeting and then turned to introduce Paul Jenkins, but Brown was already grasping Paul's hand and with an avuncular tone said, 'Not you again.'

'We really are very pleased that you are able to come and speak to this meeting,' said Dipankar. 'It is important to us to be seen to be leading the debate on this question.'

Brown smiled. 'I understand. I am myself dashing off after

this meeting to address a trade union conference in Durham on the same issue.' His expression told of the ominous nature of the occasion. 'And I shall be taking the same message as I'm hoping to convey here this evening.' There was a brief pause and then he said, 'But I wanted to come along and encourage all of you in your efforts.' He switched on his affable manner and turned to Dipankar, 'Okay, let's get started.'

He spoke for 40 minutes, in turn amusingly and coaxingly, whilst at the same time holding his central message to the fore. He argued cogently for a West German contribution to the defence of Western Europe, not from any anti-Soviet motive, but in order to help preserve the balance right at the centre of Europe between the huge Soviet empire and a Western Europe that was seeking to unite. He went on to justify the rearmament of Germany, even Germany itself was reluctant to undertake this, on the grounds that Germany was essential to the unifying process of Western Europe. In his view, she could not be asked to participate in the economic unification of Western Europe if she were denied a part in other aspects of the process. He concluded with a call to those who thought as he did to go out and argue the case as forcefully as possible.

There were questions, but unfortunately Dipankar had to limit this as Brown had to rush off to catch the train to Durham. There was little doubt however that Brown's speech had made a substantial impact on the meeting. Chatting afterwards, the three of them – Dipankar, Burren and Paul Jenkins – each agreed that Brown had been just the right speaker on the subject of German rearmament. The other two congratulated Dipankar on his skilful handling of the meeting and he was clearly very pleased that everything had gone off well.

As they walked briskly along pavements still covered in slush, Paul said, 'Geoff Brown really was very good.'

'I quite agree,' said Burren. 'He is a consummate performer.'

Paul continued, 'I felt that he made a case that could be defended without jeopardising any deeply held convictions about the Germans. As you know, I have doubts about rearming Germany, but he made a powerful argument in favour.'

He looked to his friend for agreement but continued, 'And if we want to see the unification of Western Europe then his argument becomes very persuasive.'

'That is exactly it,' said Burren.

The two of them continued in this vein of convincing themselves that Brown was right before Burren suddenly asked Paul, 'How did your father come to know Brown?'

'They knew each other from quite early days.' He turned towards Burren. 'I don't know whether you know or not, but Brown was a communist in his youth. So was my father.'

'Brown has certainly shifted his base since then,' said Burren.'Yes,' replied Paul, 'and so has my father.'

The matter was left there as they reached the point where they went their separate ways, Burren to get his bus back to the House, and Paul to go to the college.

The morning following the Brown meeting, Burren saw Frank Bainwell in the common room.

'We had a good meeting last night,' he said as he sat down beside Frank. 'You'll remember the meeting on German rearmament that I told you about a few weeks ago? I think you would have been impressed by Geoff Brown.'

'I was there.'

'Well?' asked Burren.

'As you know I'm totally opposed to German rearmament but I thought he made as good a case as can be made.' He sighed and looked at Burren. 'I am not convinced however.'

'But why not?'

He was cut short by Frank. 'Look, John, I'd like to talk about this with you but I have to go off to the city.' He got up from his chair and moved towards the door.

'I'm off to the city too,' said Burren, 'Just wait a minute and I'll join you.'

'You'll have to hurry.'

As the bus made its way into the city he asked Frank, 'Why are you not convinced?'

'For a number of reasons.' He saw the keen face of Burren and suddenly felt very tired of the old arguments, but continued, 'For one thing, I don't wish to see the Labour Party split itself apart on behalf of democracy, whilst the Tories play their trump card of loyalty and remain united.'

Burren acknowledged that Frank was right on this. He too did not see why the democratic process should take place only within the Labour Party.

'But,' he said, 'we have to do what we think is right and put a constructive view to the general public.'

Again Frank looked at him with the expression of a reluctant admonitory friend. 'John, one of the arguments deployed by Brown was that a German military contribution is necessary to the purpose of West European unification. But we have no guarantee it will succeed. We are being asked to take the huge gamble on Germany in the hope' – he gave a cynical smile – 'in the hope, mark you, that it will assist Western Europe in its wider objective. It is a big gamble, and if the rest of Western Europe does not draw together you are stuck with it. There is no going back. You can't then disarm Germany. Nothing will convince me that the decision to rearm Germany is right.' His tone carried the certainty of conviction.

Burren was impressed by the conviction of the older man. He could see that nothing, nothing at all, would shift Frank from his view, and part of him admired his friend for this. If only he could be as sure. If only. But already it was too late. The seed of questioning his own previous beliefs had taken root and was growing more strongly with every passing day. In himself he knew it would have to be, and yet his instinct told him otherwise.

'It will be interesting to see if either of us changes our mind over the period of time we have here,' he said, unconsciously acknowledging the learning process, but more directly seeking to strike an emollient note.

'You mean which of us cracks first, don't you?' Frank said with a broad grin.

They now went in different directions to meet with their tutors. Burren was about to have another session with Edell. This time it was to be on the factors affecting the elasticity of supply.

Edell wasted little time on social chat and was swiftly well into the subject.

'Remember,' he said, looking over the top of his glasses at Burren, 'what we were discussing earlier about the relative inability to substitute one factor of production for another in the short run.' He had now ceased to look at Burren and was in fact focussing again on some point on one of the far book shelves. 'And remember, too, that always we are concerned with the short run. In the long run, as Keynes so aptly observed, we are all dead.' He gave a little chortle of delight. 'So from the point of view of supply we are concerned with the elasticity of each individual factor of production.'

At moments like this Burren could not understand the criticism made of Edell. To him, Edell seemed to clarify and exemplify aspects of economics with skill and precision, once you could get him away from being entangled with the geometry of the subject to which he seemed compulsively drawn.

'To sum up, then: what we have been talking about leads on quite naturally to look at aggregate demand. Here I want you to look primarily at the master himself – Keynes and his General Theory. Some people say that he is difficult to follow because his argument is so sophisticated. But don't be put off. Persevere and I think you will find that your efforts will be well rewarded.' A rare indulgent smile passed over his face.

'Of course supplement him with other material, particularly those that are critical of parts of his theory. It is worth looking at Hayek for example.' He now trailed off into the vagaries of the Economics section of the library and appeared to enjoy a private joke. It was in these situations that Burren became irritated with him.

Burren decided to spend the rest of the day in the library with his lunch break at the usual place with Frank Bainwell and Chris Megson, and on this occasion Maureen Styles too. As he passed Paul Jenkin's room he saw that the door was ajar and decided to look in on Paul. As he did so Paul came up from behind him.

'Hello, John. I'm pleased I've seen you.' He put on his secretive air and drew close to Burren. 'You'll never guess ...' He paused to see if Burren would ask, but his friend continued to look at him expectantly.

'Rumour has it that Tim Framley has applied for a position in the university and is being interviewed. So there you are. We may be losing the agent!'

'Good-ee,' exclaimed Burren.

'Well don't jump for joy too soon. It may not be for the good.'

'There will be no disguise to this blessing, if it happens,' said Burren as he moved on down the corridor.

Paul called after him, 'I'd like to meet soon, John, to talk over your article for *The New Age*.'

Burren waved goodbye and said, 'Yes, of course.' He had already decided from his previous talk with Paul to submit something based upon the One Nation part of his Reed essay. He walked out of the college towards the university library.

He was putting the day in perspective as he casually made his way down the street; going over in his mind the reading that he had been doing for the next economics tutorial. He was finding economics of increasing interest and was fascinated by the way in which each topic that he had dealt with offered part explanation, but was itself dependent upon some other part of the subject for a complete interpretation. In other words, the whole began to appear to him as a large system which only functioned properly, like any piece of machinery, if the separate dependent components meshed satisfactorily with one another. Take any part away, or if any part is deficient, and the whole system is affected to a greater or less degree.

His contemplative mood matched the nature of the day at the turn of the seasons. Spring flowers: crocuses already in full bloom and daffodils just breaking bud, foretold the coming of spring. At this time of day, in the late afternoon, there was a chill in the air as the weak pale sun, in a cloudless sky, gradually descended. He felt good, and confident that he had employed his time well in the library.

He reached the end of the road and was about to turn the corner into the next street when his idle mood was broken. Suddenly and without warning he was brought up sharply. There at his feet was a tangled mess of bicycle, books, burst handbag, and a young woman fallen to the ground. He immediately bent down to help her, asking if she was hurt.

'No, I think I'm all right,' she said.

She took his hand and he helped her onto her feet. He looked at her closely to see if she was okay, and asked again if she had sprained a limb or felt that any part of her was broken.

'No, I'm quite fine, thanks,' she said, managing a pained smile.

She began scooping up the contents of her handbag which were spread across the road.

He uprighted the bicycle and examined it to see if it was still working.

'The wheels are still round,' he said with a smile.

She gave a little laugh.

He started collecting the books that had spilled and suggested that she was carrying rather a lot of luggage.

'Yes, yes,' she said, clearly embarrassed by the episode.

She was now replacing books in the front carrier of the bicycle and mounting it at the same time. He picked up the remaining books and placed them carefully in the carrier. The bicycle was obviously overloaded but before he could comment any further the young woman was off, calling out her thanks.

Her black-stockinged legs were thrusting down upon the pedals, her calf muscles flexing under the strain. He registered how shapely her legs were, and went on his way musing how strange things happen.

Back at the House there was a note for him on the notice-board. It was from Robert Wilcox saying that he would be very happy to accept the invitation to take supper with Maurice Watkins. He added that he would come to the meeting itself if possible. Burren glowed inwardly with satisfaction.

The following morning as Burren put his head round the door of the common room he heard the hubbub of excited conversation.

'What's it all about?' he asked Tom Croft, seated by one of the windows.

'Have you not heard? Churchill has at last made way for Eden.'

'At last!' exclaimed Burren. 'You'll have your big chance soon, Tom.'

The bell went for breakfast and they all made their way towards the dining room. At table the Labour Party insiders were speculating on the possible changes in Cabinet now that Eden was Prime Minister, and whether he would call an early election.

'The earlier the better,' someone said.

'I don't know about that,' said Bill Williams, a thick-set man with a perpetual no-nonsense air about him. 'Let him make a few mistakes of his own first.'

'Quite right,' chimed in a third voice.

Burren thoroughly enjoyed mealtimes with the Labourite insiders. Their conversation varied little. Always it would be on some aspect of the Labour Party, or politics as it affected the

Party. Just occasionally the contents of a letter from home for one or other of the group might become verbally distributed to the table at large, but little else seemed to occupy their minds; certainly not the college or their fellow students, unless such matters became a major point of news. Their sole purpose in life seemed to be the welfare of the Labour Party.

Unlike other dining tables where at mealtimes the conversation ranged widely, that of the Insiders made no conversational demands of anyone. If it was to be silence, then silence it was. Nor did anyone strike a note of controversy. There was an automatic unstated consensus – normally an echo of Bill Williams's known views on most matters – combined with certainty of argument, again emanating from Bill, who was unquestionably the self-appointed leader. This amused Burren, as did their apparent dismissal of the need to test the validity of an idea. In fact their relationship to an idea appeared to be total opposition or total acceptance, without the necessity for an intervening process of evaluation. At times Burren envied them this certainty and had to check himself to prevent sliding into their comfortable mental state.

Throughout the morning at work in the library he immersed himself in the *General Theory* of Keynes. He had already discovered the principal components in the reasoning of Keynes from another book, and he now used this alongside the *General Theory* itself. He had been warned of the erudite and difficult nature of Keynes's work. He was not finding it overly difficult, but worried that he might be missing some crucial element in the argument.

The more he read, the more impressed he became by the theory that was developed. It was not only the power of the logical argument that struck him, it was the way in which complex theory was expounded in very well-written English. It was this more than anything else that impressed him. Until now, although increasingly grasped by the subject of economics, he had nevertheless found much of the language of the subject difficult and full of jargon. Here, with Keynes, the web of ideas expounding a theory was expressed simply, lucidly and beautifully, just as with a creative artist. The symmetry of the work surely made it the poetry of economics. He was pleased with the thought.

The four – Bainwell, Megson, Burren and Maureen – were together in her room for an after-lunch cup of tea and inevitably the subject of Eden's premiership came up.

'Labour will need to get their act together now,' said Frank. 'Eden will take advantage of their disarray and call a snap election.'

They all agreed with that.

'Nevertheless,' said Burren, 'he'll have to give himself a bit of time to put his stamp on things.'

Chris nodded agreement.

'Will he be any good?' asked Maureen.

'It is difficult to say,' said Burren. 'We think we know him because he has been in the public eye so much, but in fact he has never held a domestic post in government.'

Maureen looked at him. 'I didn't know that.'

'Consummate in foreign affairs though,' said Chris. 'Helping to pull the American chestnuts out of the South-East Asia fire, for example. And his initiative in rescuing Western defence.'

'Some of us oppose that,' said Frank pointedly.

'Well I know you do,' snapped Chris.

'And rightly so,' added Frank, warming to the subject. 'It is going to have the most damaging effect on the Labour Party.'

'Only if people like you allow it to do so,' said Chris, becoming increasingly irritated by Frank's intransigence over German rearmament.

Burren looked at Maureen despairingly. This argument had been going on for weeks and neither Chris nor Frank had succeeded in changing the other's point of view. They were simply repeating old, well-known views.

Burren now sought to bring it to an end.

'I think we should call a halt to this,' he said. 'The argument has become circular and doesn't lead to any positive conclusion. All that happens is that both of you become more hostile and personal.'

There was a lapse into silence and Burren chose this moment to leave.

Maureen came to the door with him

'It is my turn now, John. How about coming to the cinema with me tonight.'

He smiled. 'What is on?'

'*For Whom the Bell Tolls*,' said Maureen.

'Yes, most certainly,' he enthused. 'I've wanted to see that film for a long, long time, and for some reason have always missed it.'

'And so have I. See you later then.'

He returned to the library and to Keynes and aggregate demand. As he read on he reflected more widely on Keynes and his earlier work, going back to the Peace Conference at the end of the First World War. During the inter-war period Keynes's advice had been ignored. German reparations, the world economy, the Great Depression and consequent unemployment: on each of these matters he had expressed positive views and been ignored. It seemed to Burren as it had to others at the time that Keynes had supplied many of the answers to the problems that beset the politicians of the time. Admittedly Keynes had not written the *General Theory* until the mid-1930s, but the bulk of his thinking that infused that work was already known. Lloyd George had advocated much the same thing in his election manifesto at the beginning of the decade.

He spent the afternoon with further reading on Keynesian economic theory, using the texts of other economists and filling his mind with the great man's work. It was truly a comprehensive 'General Theory'.

And in the evening he went on to the cinema with Maureen

Styles. More time for reflection here too. He had visited Spain two years before going to Morton. There had been something about the visit of a Salvation Army officer to his parents' home, on behalf of the victims of the civil war in Spain, that had set his young mind thinking about what was, to him, a distant land. The war had conjured up all kinds of images: of intense fighting at close quarters, of outstanding bravery, and of comradeship. Much of these early impressions of Spain were self-acquired. Certainly none had come from the lazy, one-sided teaching of contemporary history at school. Anyway, that had been solely British history.

His Spain had been a romantic picture. Later, the picture was coloured by what he discovered from the writers and left-wing intellectuals of the period, several of whom had participated in the war on the Republican side, or had observed the war as correspondents. People such as Stephen Spender, Auden, Orwell and, very much his hero figure, Arthur Koestler. He had also read Tom Wintringham in *Picture Post* during the Second World War without knowing at the time of Wintringham's communist background and participation in the civil war.

His holiday, or more accurately perhaps his 'experience', in Spain had taken place against this backdrop of vicarious information. He had travelled widely across Spain by train: from San Sebastian to Seville via Madrid, and back up through the capital to Barcelona. He had seen much poverty alongside quite spontaneous hospitality, with local Spanish people sharing their food with him on trains. He had seen the influence of the Catholic Church. The magnificent terrain with its harshness and desert-like stillness was so well described by V.S. Pritchett in his autobiography as:

> unlike any other in Western Europe, monotonous yet bizarre landscape of flat-topped mesas that proceed like geometry the bleached yellow soil, sometimes changing to metallic pinks and cindery greys; the curious associations

of desert harshness and serenity, especially of desert-like space and of distances that ended in wilderness of rock

Both he and Maureen agreed as they left the cinema that the film was an excellent portrayal of one single incident during the course of the civil war. By showing one event, and the detailed preparation involved in blowing up a bridge, the film captured Hemingway's depiction of the isolation of one individual, and of one group, from the main struggle.

It had been a great cause and it had failed. Yet it so nearly triumphed, and probably would have done but for the pusilla-nimous response of the principal democracies, Britain and France. Burren wanted very much to meet with Paul Jenkins's father, as he now knew that he had fought on the Republican side in the civil war.

The following evening he returned to his room after supper to start writing the essay on the factors affecting aggregate demand. He had a plan for the essay in mind, and sat at his desk with a sheet of paper in front of him. He lit a cigarette. The torment of the weekly essay was upon him. Everything was in place, yet he fingered the objects on his desk. The reading lamp threw out a focus of light upon the surface of the desk, showing that the ashtray was near, spare pens and pencils at hand, and books that he would need to construct his argument. He found the act of starting to write an essay one of the most difficult things he was required to do. The task itself had become a little easier over time and with more practice, but still it was agony to get started. He supposed it was the same for most of the others too, but found that small comfort.

He picked up a sheet of paper and made a start. The first few lines of writing appeared on the page. He read it through, didn't like it and crossed it through. He referred again to his plan of the main elements that he had to analyse: level of savings, rate of interest, extent of disposal income, confidence factor, etcetera. He decided to write the essay in sections, conforming to the plan, before connecting them in a continuous thread. This time his efforts were more rewarding. He wrote a page and read it through. He was satisfied and continued writing, stopping only to light a cigarette. The more he wrote the easier it became.

He checked the time and saw that it was 11.30 pm. He made himself a cup of tea, lit another cigarette and continued with the writing until he had finished. He told himself that it was not quite as good as Keynes's work, but nevertheless he was pleased with what he had written, and hoped that Edell would be similarly impressed. It was 12.45am. He went to bed and to contented sleep.

The morning was bright, and Edell greeted Burren with a friendly 'Good morning.'

Burren reciprocated with a mildly enthusiastic 'Good morning'.

'Now,' said Edell once Burren had seated himself, 'We're looking at Keynes's *General Theory*, and in particular aggregate demand?' He spoke as if asking Burren a question.

'Yes, that is right.'

'Well, what do you make of it?'

Burren said how impressed he was at the completeness of Keynes's theory and how convincingly it explained how the whole economy could be viewed as a system with a number of variable dependents within it. In that way the concepts underpinning the work related to each other to form a coherent entity. He said that he didn't think any previous economist had done this before in quite the same way. He knew that he sounded enthusiastic about Keynes's work.

'That is a good introduction,' said Edell. 'Now carry on and let's see how thoroughly you have evaluated the *General Theory*.'

Burren began to read from his essay and was surprised at how much he had written and how well his own argument was constructed.

Edell let him read the whole of his essay without interruption and when he had finished he said, 'Not bad, not bad at all. I think you have a clear grasp of Keynes.' And with an ironic smile said, 'Helped no doubt by your obvious enthusiasm for his ideas.'

'Well, I do think he is exceptional,' said Burren. 'I find it quite remarkable that anyone can write about economics as he does. It contrasts so much with the work of other economists. Complex ideas are expressed in a form that can be understood.' He quickly realised that by implication he was including Edell amongst the other economists and tried to readjust his comment, but before he was able to do so Edell had cut in.

'Perhaps the one criticism I would make of your essay is that you have not given enough attention to his critics.' And then with an admonitory finger he added, 'There were some, you know, though you have not included their views.'

'Well ... ' again he was cut short by Edell.

'Keynes was a quite outstanding figure of course. He stood head and shoulders above his contemporaries.' He paused and stared into space as was his wont. 'Just don't succumb too readily to hero-worship. You have done well on this part of the subject. We have now to turn our attention to fiscal matters: to public finance, deficit budgeting, financing the public sector including the nationalised industries, and trade.' He smiled. 'There is still plenty to keep us occupied.' He peered at Burren above his glasses. 'That is all for now.'

6

There was already warmth in the air from a sun high in the sky which was rapidly replacing the chill of the early morning. It was going to be a good day, he could tell. There was blossom on the cherry trees on both sides of Broadway, and daffodils, though now departing, together with tulips could be seen in the borders adjoining the pavements on either side of the road.

Walking in the city on an early summer morning made him feel at one with the freshness of nature all around him. He was making his way to the Coffee House to meet Dipankar Shastri and Paul Jenkins to ensure that arrangements for the evening meeting of the Socialist Society, at which Maurice Jenkins was speaking, were all in place. The Coffee House was busy at mid-morning but the three of them managed to grab a table.

'Let us go through my list of things for tonight,' said Burren. Turning to Dipankar he asked, 'Is everything arranged for the lecture hall and have we arranged for it to be open on time and will the posters be on display outside the main building?'

Dipankar reassured him 'Everything is taken care of, John. Ken Murray is looking after these details as part of his campaign to take over from you as secretary!'

Paul laughed at Dipanker's wry humour.

'I told you not to worry, John. Now can we discuss something that may well be referred to this evening and that is, what is the government up to in Cyprus?'

'Hold on, Paul. I've not finished yet.'

Paul uttered a short groan.

Turning again to Dipankar, Burren asked, 'Will there be a duty watch on the hall? I know the Minister will have his own security officer but I just want to check this with you.'

'Yes,' replied Dipankar. 'Armed of course!' He gave a quiet laugh.

'He is on good form this morning,' laughed Paul, and added, 'They'll probably need to be.'

Burren now informed them of the arrangements he had made. 'The speaker will arrive either by ministerial car, or by train and taxi, depending on his other commitments. Either way he will be making his own way to the hall.'

Paul cut in, 'He'll know his way. It is his old college.'

Burren continued, 'We'll dine after the meeting, and this has been arranged for the dining hall in Dipankar's college ...' – Dipankar nodded agreement – 'for 8 pm. We have of course invited ourselves as officers and I've included you, Paul,' he added with relish. 'Didn't think you would want to miss the opportunity of supper with Watkins.'

'You bet not.'

'And I asked Robert Wilcox if he would like to join us as he knows Watkins quite well.'

Both Burren and Paul laughed with gusto.

Then, turning to Dipankar, Burren asked if he knew Robert Wilcox.

'I think I may have met him. I'm not really sure.'

'Well, you see, Watkins displaced him at the last general election and so you see ...'

Dipankar smiled, knowing the other's sense of fun.

'Anyhow,' continued Burren, 'Robert Wilcox can join us for supper and may come to the meeting.' As an afterthought he said, 'Have either of you met the Minister before?'

'No,' they said in unison.

'Now about the Cyprus business ...' asked Paul yet again, but Burren's mind was still on the meeting.

'I can see we will have to discuss this some other time,' said Paul. 'But we should have an open meeting on the subject, you know.'

'I know, I know,' said Burren.

Dipankar came in with a proposal of his own. 'I've heard from Okebe,' he said.

'He is going to be in this country after the summer and I should like to invite him to come and speak.' Realising that the others may not have heard of Okebe, he said, 'He is the General Secretary of the Movement for Colonial Freedom, you know.'

Burren and Paul nodded agreement. 'Good idea.'

'I must now leave you,' said Dipankar. 'I'll see you this evening, say 5.30, John?'

'Yes of course.'

Burren and Paul remained a little longer, finishing off their coffee. On leaving Paul asked Burren how his article was coming along. Burren said it was well under way.

'Don't forget, I shall want it in about a fortnight,' said Paul as he walked off in the opposite direction to Burren.

'And you shall have it,' said Burren, sounding more confident than he felt. For although he had made good progress and had used the time away from college in writing up the research he had done, he was finding it difficult to comply with the pre-scribed length. He wanted more space in *The New Age* than was allowed. He had asked for some concession but Paul and the editorial board were adamant.

Apart from a quickly grabbed sandwich at midday he spent his time in the library reading about trade and comparative costs. He arrived at the lecture hall to find Dipankar and Ken Murray already there.

'Anyone arrived yet?' he asked, though it was still quite early. He checked his watch; it showed 5.40 pm.

'You'd be surprised,' said Dipankar. 'The hall is already nearly half full.'

There was a steady stream of people arriving.

Ken Murray said, 'I think it will be packed. Watkins has after all been promoted and his brand of Conservatism is highly controversial. And he is a good speaker.'

'What can we do to accommodate more, if we have to?' Burren asked.

Dipankar laughed and said, 'Pack them in.'

They continued to chat for a while and then they went to inspect the hall. It was now full and people were continuing to arrive. Burren invited them to sit on the floor immediately in front of the platform, and then to fill the two aisles, leaving just enough space to walk through.

'I hope we're not breaking any safety regulations,' Burren confided to the others.

Paul Jenkins had by now arrived and reassured him, 'We have done it before. It is quite all right provided there are clear walkways.'

Maurice Watkins had now arrived. Dipankar and Burren moved forward to welcome him.

'We are very pleased you were able to come. I am Dipankar Shastri, the chairman of the Society and this is John Burren, the secretary.'

The Minister looked at each of them in turn, cast his eye around the hall, smiled slowly, and said, 'I am pleased to be back.'

Burren explained the arrangements for the evening and Dipankar then led the Minister to the platform. The hall was full and still more people were standing around the sides of the hall and by the rear door which Burren had requested be left open. After some flattering introductory comments, which Burren was sure he did not believe, Dipankar invited Maurice Watkins to speak.

Maurice Watkins made it clear at the outset that he was speaking outside of his role as a minister and would not be referring to the government, or its policies. He said he wanted to focus entirely on the theory of economic development in its political context, as outlined by him in his One Nation contribution. He kept to his theme, speaking not so much eloquently as relentlessly, as someone engaged in expounding a complete theory, the theory that world trade as a whole bene-fited most from a completely free market in capital and labour. It was clear to Burren that Maurice Watkins regarded himself as an authority on this subject and not only as a politician.

He was in his middle to late forties, well groomed, and had superlative confidence, granted only to those who at that age think, indeed know, they are within reach of the next stage of their career and will succeed. He spoke for 45 minutes and said he was prepared to take a few questions.

Burren saw to his surprise that Frank Bainwell was on his feet and asking a question. 'How can you be so confident that your ideas will work, when all the evidence and historical record suggests otherwise?'

Looking around the audience whilst Frank put his question, Burren saw that Robert Wilcox had arrived and was standing at the main doorway. Jasmine too was nearby and he noticed several students from Morton.

Maurice Watkins was replying to Frank. The case of Britain on which he assumed the question had been based was a poor example, he said. Britain had never been able fully to implement free trade because of her imperial obligations, and the impact of the First World War had been calamitous for Britain. Though he added with emphasis that he thought the British experience exemplified important aspects of the theory.

There were several more questions critical of the speaker's view and stressing the merits of the planned economy. Burren was struck by the inflexibility of Watkins. He appeared not to be willing to accept any modification of his view, let alone acknowledge any cracks in the edifice of his theory.

Dipankar brought the meeting to a close and thanked Maurice Watkins. People began to leave the hall and Robert Wilcox could be seen making a path towards the platform against this human tide.

'Hello Robert,' called Watkins. 'So good to see you.'

Wilcox returned the greeting and conveyed his congratulations to Watkins on his promotion.

Burren heard Watkins say in an aside, 'Bit of a dogsbody of a job actually. But you have to do it if you want to climb the ladder, as you will know.'

Wilcox nodded agreement.

They continued to exchange pleasantries and enquired about one another's families before Dipankar politely stepped in and suggested they make their way through to the dining hall for drinks and dinner.

Talking of Dipankar and turning to the others, Watkins said, 'He handled the meeting well, didn't he?' He laughed, 'Even when the questioning became a bit rough. You should become a politician.'

Dipankar glowed at the praise.

At supper Robert Wilcox, sitting beside Watkins, said, 'This young man,' pointing to Burren, 'is writing an article which is going to examine your ideas.' And then provocatively, and looking at Burren with a wink, he added, 'He hopes to straighten out one or two of your more extreme views!'

Watkins looked up from his food and directed his gaze at Burren, 'You had better send me a copy,' he said. 'Better still, let me have a look beforehand to see if it is all right.' There was just a hint of a smile accompanying this.

Burren gave a slightly embarrassed laugh and looked directly at Robert Wilcox who returned a mischievous expression. He then said to Maurice Watkins that he preferred to write without an editor on this occasion. Robert Wilcox chortled heartily and the others quickly joined in, including Maurice Watkins.

After that politics played no further part in the conversation. Both Watkins and Wilcox seemed to prefer to talk football, and particularly of Woolerton United, the First Division club in Watkin's constituency. He said to Wilcox that he felt he had to attend a number of matches for obvious reasons, though he didn't think they were a very good side. Certainly their position in the table indicated that fact.

Paul turned to Burren and asked him if he was going to the dance the following evening. He replied that he was but would be late as he and Dipankar had some Society business to discuss. Dipankar looked up and nodded, though he appeared to be absorbed with the conversation taking place between Watkins and Wilcox.

The supper came to an end and Watkins indicated that he had to hurry off to another engagement. He thanked Dipankar Shastri and left with Robert Wilcox.

Burren and Paul Jenkins lingered a little longer, chatting to Dipankar and Ken Murray before they too made their way down the Broadway. This part of the city had at this hour of the evening an alluring charm. It was now dusk and the evening's darkness descended to meet with the refulgent glow of the streets lamps standing each side of the road. When looked at in line the black lamp-posts topped with a yellowy-red glow gave the appearance of rows of sentries standing to attention. As a backdrop to this scene, lights began to appear in the leaded windows of the colleges.

The two young men sauntered along, hands in pockets, sharing the magical charm of the tableau bestowed by centuries of power and privilege.

Burren was the first to communicate his mood. 'Isn't it just wonderful to be here at this time?' he spread out his arms in an arc to encompass the whole scene. 'Not only to share this but to be fully aware of it and to feel its subtle affect.'

Paul agreed, but added, 'Let us not forget why we are here.'

There was a short silence between them before Burren asked, 'What do you intend doing after you finish here, Paul?'

Paul looked at him and a serious expression came over his face. 'I am not sure. I have been accepted here to study for a degree over two years, but my father would like me to go to the London School of Economics.'

Burren was surprised. 'Why?' he asked.

'There are several reasons, but mainly it is because he thinks this place is old-fashioned and out of touch.' He turned to Burren. 'But most especially, he thinks it corrupts the intelligence. Or rather, he sees it as corrupting in that it inculcates a mindset through which everything is assimilated and interpreted.' He gave a short, self-deprecatory laugh. 'Does that sound rather pompous?'

'Well ...' the rest remained unsaid. Instead he asked, 'What do you wish to study?'

'Well that is it, you see. I want to follow my father in the practice of industrial law, and that brings in his second reason against studying here. He is convinced that London is a better place for the purpose of industrial law.'

'Where did your father study?' asked Burren.

'Where do you think?' said Paul with a chuckle. 'My father studied for a law degree part-time at LSE.'

They had now reached the point where they had to go their separate ways.

'You'll soon have to decide,' said Burren.

'I will indeed,' said Paul moving off with a farewell wave.

Later, in the quiet of his room, Burren's thoughts drifted back to the conversation that had taken place with Chris Megson. And now here was Paul going on to one university or another. Obviously some Morton people had a very clear view as to their future and kept it in the frame all the time. He began to think seriously about his own future for the first time.

The next morning he met Frank Bainwell in the common room.

'I was pleased to see you at the Watkins meeting last night.' He gave Frank a friendly prod. 'And your question set Watkins back a bit.'

Frank grinned. 'That was the moderate form of the question. I would have liked to tackle him afterwards.' Then, guessing that Burren had spent some time with Watkins after the meeting, he asked, 'Did you nail him?'

'No, not really. You know how it is on social occasions, mustn't be a bore, etcetera. But Robert Wilcox did tell him that I am writing an article about his One Nation ideas.'

'And how did he react?' Frank was keen to know.

'Curiously, he seemed flattered, I thought, and went on to make a joke about letting him vet it first. At least I think it was a joke.'

'He is an odious creature,' said Frank.

'I don't know about that,' said Burren, 'but he does lack warmth.'

'I must go, John. I have a meeting in the city but I should like to talk further about this.'

'Sure.'

Burren looked across and saw that Denis Greenfell was at the far end of the room.

Greenfell looked up from his newspaper and acknowledged Burren's presence but neither exchanged words. Burren wondered if Greenfell ever left the common room, for whenever he himself went in there Greenfell was always behind some newspaper or other. He must be the best-informed person here on current matters, Burren thought.

He turned his own attention to the news on Cyprus leading most of the newspapers on that day. '20 People Killed in Clashes as Fresh Violence Breaks Out'. What a mess the government are in over this, he thought. They will have public opinion against them shortly, particularly as a result of their decision to send out National Servicemen. As he left to go to the library he concluded that Paul Jenkins was right: the Socialist Society would have to try and fit in a meeting on the subject of Cyprus before the end of the summer term.

Once in the library he selected Maurice Watkins's work and read selectively for the material he needed to complete his article. He agreed with Watkins that there were important qualifications to be made in using British experience for the purpose of free trade theory. At the same time he thought that Watkins did not pay enough attention to social cost in looking at the factors of production. More specifically, he was convinced that the basic weakness in Watkins's work was his failure to differentiate sufficiently between the inherent qualities of the different factors of production. Labour was equated with capital in plain cost terms.

In Burren's view this did not provide a satisfactory argument. It was not realistic to regard capital and labour as substitutable in respect to identical outcomes. Leaving aside the moral implications – quite a concession! – the consequences of deploying capital were relatively predictable but the same could not be said of labour. He now re-read the major points he was making in his article and was pleased with the result.

After taking lunch in college, and the usual session in Maureen's room over a cup of tea, he returned to his own room to finish off the article for *The New Age*. He decided he would then deliver it to Paul Jenkins on his way to meet with Dipankar. After spending some time writing he made himself a cup of coffee in the kitchen serving the rooms on his floor and bumped into Denis Greenfell again. This reminded him with amusement that this was the one other place in college where Greenfell took up regular occupancy.

He limited conversation to a brief comment on the weather as he made his drink. Strangely, Greenfell too seemed not to want to prolong conversation. He returned to his room. It was not that he disliked Greenfell. In fact, he rather enjoyed talking economics with him as this was a subject in which Greenfell was very well informed. He had to admit that he also liked drawing upon the man's stock of college gossip.

He took a sip of tea, lit a cigarette and looked again at what he had written. He had only the conclusion of his article to complete now. Once he had finished he was quickly on his way to catch the bus into the city.

Paul Jenkins was alone in his room as Burren arrived in triumphant mood, brandishing his article.

'Here it is,' he said. 'My article on Watkins's theory of free trade.'

' Excellent,' said Paul, 'We'll be able to include it in the next number due out at the beginning of the month.' He grinned. 'Assuming the board agree it.'

Burren suddenly looked crestfallen. 'Is there any doubt?' he asked.

Paul continued to tease. 'You never can tell.' And then quickly added, grinning again, 'In this case I shouldn't think there is much doubt.'

'It is handwritten,' said Burren, 'and my writing is a bit difficult to read. Is there any chance of someone here typing it up for me, do you think?'

'Try Jasmine's office, you'll like that.'

'It'll be a pleasure.'

Jasmine was not in her office and he was a little disappointed that she would not now know of his article. Her assistant, Joan Ridge, said she would type it for him and would let him know when it was ready.

It was early evening as Burren walked to Dipankar Shastri's room. Ken Murray was already there, and Burren knew that Paul Jenkins would have to miss the meeting as he was preparing for his final exams. Dipankar dealt with the matter of the election of officers for the next session and expressed the hope that Burren would be elected chairman unopposed. He added that anyone was free to stand but that he was confident Burren would be the next chairman, saying, 'You deserve it anyhow, John, after all the effort you have put in. The Society is stronger than ever.'

They turned to Ken Murray. He was from the same college as Dipankar and in his first year. He was a confident young man, well organised and very committed to the left wing of the Labour Party. He came from the same part of the country as

Burren, a large seaside town with a very cosmopolitan air about it. He shared with Burren the frustration of always seeing a Conservative returned at a general election. They joked about what it would take to have the area go Labour: the rest of the country being communist!

He was a tallish fellow with a crop of hair that refused tidiness, or appeared that way, and one rather sensed from his intense eyes and his posture that he had immense energy. Without any hesitation Burren said that he wanted Ken to be secretary, if he himself became chairman. With a friendly smile in his direction he said, 'We'll need someone to keep a tight rein on the business.'

Dipankar chimed in, 'He is your man for that.'

Ken Murray smiled, a little shyly for him, and said that he would welcome the chance.

Turning to Dipankar, Burren said, 'As with Paul Jenkins, I hope if I become chairman, you'll continue to help us by attending the caucus.'

Ken Murray agreed, and Dipankar said that he would be very happy to help.

'Let us cement all this solidarity with a drink in the Rose & Crown.'

They continued to talk of the Socialist Society for a while and how they could best ensure that it continued to flourish. And then quite unexpectedly Dipankar turned the conversation round to life in college. Dipankar was completing postgraduate work on colonialism. He talked of the poor quality of some of the tuition, including some of the lectures he attended, and turned to Ken Murray for his view. Ken as a current under-graduate was a little more cautious. They both told some interesting tales about their college. They talked of the anti-quated dining practices in hall, and the still more out-of-date facilities in students' rooms.

All of this was a bit of a revelation to Burren. Knowing little of the inside life of the university, he was genuinely shocked.

That a university with a worldwide reputation, and which was much admired for its academic standing, should have in many of its colleges the same basic facilities that had existed a century ago was poor to say the least. It was, he assumed, premised on the same principle that prevailed in the public schools: that young men benefited from spartan conditions. In a previous age it was thought to be necessary as part of the cultural conditioning for leadership, and fitted young men for the role of administering the empire. It reinforced him in his view that alongside whatever else it may do, it made for an elite aware of itself as such, and expressed in self-satisfaction.

He left Dipankar and Ken outside the Rose & Crown as they went back to their college and he went on to the dance at the House. It was late when he arrived and a check of his watch told him that there was just over half an hour of dancing left. The room was packed, with people standing around the edges of the dance floor, and the dance floor itself was a solid mass of bodies moving slowly to the music of 'Unchained Melody'. It was an excuse-me dance and he moved quickly to relieve Maureen Styles of a plump man, whom Burren was sure was from the city end of Morton.

'Hello, John, I didn't think you were coming,' said Maureen as they moved slowly around the floor. 'We looked for you earlier and neither Frank nor Chris knew where you were.' She smiled at him, 'You are a bit of a mystery man at times, aren't you?' She liked to prompt him in this way.

'It is useful to have a certain air of mystery,' he said with a smile.

'Well you certainly have that.'

The music stopped and quickly restarted with a different tune.

'These dances really are a great success, aren't they?' said Maureen. 'And have you noticed how we attract all the young nurses from the local hospitals?'

A slow smile spread across his face. 'You are worse than my mother.'

117

'Well I have to look after these things for you,' she said.

'I expect you have said exactly the same thing to Chris, haven't you?'

'Well ...' she laughed.

'Yes, I know. It is not part of your social work training to set up a marriage bureau for Morton males,' he grinned.

The music stopped and Maureen patted him affectionately as they walked off the dance floor and she moved away to sit with Joan Symonds.

He progressed around the edge of the dance floor and spotted Jasmine sitting near to where Robert Wilcox was standing, talking yet again to Timothy Framley.

He waited for the music to restart and then went and asked Jasmine to dance.

Once on the floor he said facetiously, 'You obviously do come here often – at least once a term.' Jasmine laughed her short, bright laugh, almost a giggle. 'I saw you at the meeting of the Socialist Society the other evening, standing in the doorway. I didn't know you went to those meetings. Did you enjoy it?'

'I do go sometimes, especially if they have a big speaker such as Maurice Watkins. And yes, I did enjoy it.' And then the small laugh again. 'Or at least as much as I saw and heard. I arrived rather late, you see.'

She danced superbly. He was looking closely at her, admiring her features. She really was very attractive, he affirmed to himself. 'I am pleased you enjoyed it. As you will have seen, it was very well attended and it was a great success.'

'Yes,' she said. 'I noticed that you looked every bit the budding politician sitting alongside Maurice on the platform.'

He immediately registered her use of Watkins's first name. There was a lot he didn't know about this woman. It made him wary.

'I have to be convincing,' he said, trying to sound as nonchalant as possible.

118

He suddenly remembered his article and that he wanted to check on its progress. He asked her if she had seen it, and if it had been typed.

She looked at him and said, 'Yes, Joan showed it to me. She told me that you had handed it to her as though it were treasure.' There was the smile again. 'I assume it is important.'

He gave her a thin smile.

As the music came to an end he saw Chris Megson talking to a young woman amidst a circle of people. Something made him look again. He was not sure. Although he could only see the back of her head, because Chris blocked his view, he was sure that he had seen her before.

He returned Jasmine to her place beside Wilcox. He caught Wilcox's eye and smiled, though his attention had now drifted elsewhere. Jasmine thanked him. He edged back through the crowded dance room towards where Chris was standing.

As he drew near Chris called him, 'Hello, John, we haven't seen you all evening.'

The woman turned her head too. She had brown eyes. He responded to Chris with only half his attention.

'I had to finish something in the city.'

He now knew.

'Well, well. Hello again.'

She smiled.

Chris looked surprised. 'Do you two know one another?' he asked.

'Yes and no,' he laughed.

He asked her to dance and they moved away towards the dance floor.

'Meeting you again is a great surprise,' he smiled. 'And I'm so pleased.'

They danced briefly in silence.

'You haven't fallen off your bicycle again, have you?' he said with an expression of mock pain.

'No,' she laughed. 'But I have been very careful. You see, you haven't been around to pick up the pieces.'

He liked the way she laughed and how it lit up her face.

'I haven't seen you here before, have I?'

'No. I haven't been to a dance here before this evening. Christopher phoned me and said how good these events were, and he asked me if I would like to come.'

She had a low voice and it seemed to him to be without a strong accent apart from the occasional vowel which she pronounced a little hard. He was unable to place the dialect geographically.

'So you know Chris?'

'Yes I do, but not over well.' She smiled, seemingly unaware that he was probing for more information. He was at the same time trying to place her in relation to the different groups of women who were invited to the dances. She did not help him by disclosing anything more.

The music stopped, and he realised how much he liked the tune they had just danced to, but he was unable to name it. He took her back to the group she had been with and was about to start a conversation when he was waylaid by Paul Jenkins, who wanted to talk to him about his article. She was whisked away by someone to dance again. Paul was saying that David Smith wanted Burren to modify the section of his article that dealt with social cost. He was paying only part attention to what Paul was saying, as his eyes were on the young woman as she danced with Chris Megson.

He heard enough of Paul's comment however to respond negatively. 'No, Paul. I'm not prepared to change any of the content. I have read it thoroughly and I want it to stand as it is. It is an important argument that I am making.'

'I know, I know,' said Paul seeking to be conciliatory. 'But I have to tell contributors what members of the board have said.' He looked appealingly at Burren, whose attention was again drawn towards the woman on the dance floor. 'Well, John, is that your final answer on the matter?'

'Yes Paul, it is.'

He wanted to escape at this moment and dance again with the young woman. She was now dancing with Framley. With Framley! Whatever next!

He turned to face Paul. 'I don't mind altering the piece to accommodate comments on style, or wording, but I am not going to change any content.' He sought compromise and added, 'I'll meet with David if that will help.'

'That would be fine, John.' Paul sensed that Burren's mind was not entirely focused on their conversation.

Burren looked at his watch. 'Hell!' he exclaimed, 'It is 11.15.' The dance finished at 11.30 to allow the bus to return the different women's groups to their accommodation before midnight.

'Excuse me, Paul.' He gave a confidential wink. 'I want particularly to dance with that woman over there.' He pointed in her direction.

Paul grinned. 'I quite understand.'

Frank Bainwell was making one or two announcements before the evening closed. Burren rushed across to where she was standing, brushing aside anyone in his path in his haste to get to her before anyone else asked her to dance. As he approached he saw her smile.

On the crowded dance floor she said, 'Did you know how terribly fierce you looked as you came across just now?'

He tried to recover his composure. 'I suppose I knew that I had a sense of mission.'

He wanted her to laugh, and she did.

'I simply had to dance with you again before the end of the evening. Our meeting again is so strange.' He looked directly at her. 'Don't you think so? Almost as if ...' He left it uncompleted, though his meaning was clear.

She looked at him with slightly raised eyebrows. 'Is that perhaps a little dramatic?'

The music was slow and mellifluous and the dancers were moving dreamily to the last waltz of the evening. He had seen when watching her dance how light and skilful she seemed, moulding her dancing effortlessly to her partner. She did the same with him, though he was conscious of the fact that she had to work harder with his unskilled movements.

'You did rather shoot off quickly when we last met.'

She frowned ever so slightly. 'Well, I was embarrassed.'

He saw that her very dark hair was done differently from before. It was now shorter and cropped to the shape of her head. She also appeared taller than he remembered from their previously brief meeting. He thought how very self-possessed she seemed.

The music stopped again and Frank announced the last waltz. There were sighs of disappointment.

He looked at her and smiled warmly. 'It is good to have met you again like this.'

She returned the warmth of the smile. He drew her closer to him and she complied. The smell of her hair came to him and he could feel her breathing. He was sure their chance meeting spelled more than just that. He knew that he wanted to see her again, and suddenly he felt ridiculously nervous.

He had to act quickly, for once the dance was ended she would presumably have to catch the special bus back to wherever. He realised that he knew so little about her. They had met in the most accidental of ways ... he laughed inwardly at the Freudian thought. He did not know what she did, whether she was a nurse, being trained as a teacher, or was a student at the university. He calculated it was the latter.

'Do you catch the special bus?' he asked.

'Yes, I do,' was the reply, with nothing more than that.

The music had now stopped.

As they walked off the dance floor, he said, 'I should very much like to see you again.'

'I thought you might,' she said, with a hint of flirtation in her voice.

'But I don't know your name,' he said.

'Jane. Jane Dayton,' she said, looking at him with some amusement.

'And I am ...'

'I know who you are,' she said.

'You know? But ...'

'Yes. I'll explain later.' She gave a little laugh.

He hurriedly explained. 'This college is in two halves, here and in the city. I'm going to be in the city on Tuesday. Can you meet me for coffee, at say 10.45 in the Coffee House in Broadway?'

'Yes, all right.'

There was something in her manner that was at one and the same time friendly, yet slightly remote. She conveyed a kind of recondite air.

He helped her slip on a coat, gently enveloping the collar around her neck. 'Goodnight,' he said.

'Goodnight.'

The Four were talking after lunch in Maureen Styles's room and a heated discussion of Aneurin Bevan had developed. He was again in the news because of his attitude over nuclear weapons. He was by now a cult figure amongst the left of the Labour Party, and together with his loyal band of parliamentary followers, as well as sizeable support within the constituency parties, he was a divisive element within the Party as a whole.

Frank Bainwell was stating the Bevanite position and quoting in support, practically verbatim, from Bevan's book, *In Place of Fear*. Burren knew that Frank was quoting the man accurately for he too had read the book with meticulous care and in adulation, regarding Bevan as the natural and rightful exponent of the socialist cause.

'But it is doubtful if he is as important as you say,' said Chris Megson, his unlit pipe in his hand.

'How can you say that? Bevan and his followers have completely captured the intellectual territory of the Labour Party. Do you want me to list the policies?' said Frank.

Maureen quickly added that her MP was a Bevanite.

Chris continued, 'Well I grant you that the Bevanites have command over ideas at the moment but that does not necessarily mean that what they advocate is good for the Labour Party, or is practical.'

Burren joined in and said that he thought Bevan had been consistent in his view of foreign policy ever since his wartime interventions with Churchill, and that he might well be proved right in respect to US policy towards Western Europe.

'I am with you all the way there, John,' said Frank.

'It is too early to say,' said Chris, 'but surely no one is going to deny the valuable role that the US has played in supporting Western Europe since 1945.'

'I think that misses the point,' said Burren. 'Bevan is saying that there is no automatic coincidence of interest between the US and ourselves. Whereas the orthodox view is that there is a special relationship between us based upon insoluble shared interests.'

'Hear, hear,' echoed Frank

Completely turning the subject, Maureen asked Burren what special option he was going to take. He was puzzled by Maureen's question and could see that Frank and Chris were puzzled too. 'It is just that you seem to like talking more about foreign affairs than domestic matters, such as the trade unions for example and so I wondered what you will be taking as your special option.'

'You are probably right. I'm really not sure at the moment, though it won't be industrial relations.'

'Most people do choose that option,' said Frank.

'That is true,' agreed Chris.

124

'I am more interested in foreign affairs than anything else,' said Burren. And then flippantly he added, 'It must be the influence of those toy soldiers I played with as a boy.'

Maureen looked at him. She knew there was more to it than that but left it alone. 'Goodness me,' she said, 'I have to go to a class on social structure at the Delegacy. Sorry boys, it's time to go.'

The three men left Maureen's room and slowly meandered down the corridor.

Chris turned to Burren and said, 'I saw you being very friendly with Jane at the dance. I rather gathered that you already knew one another.'

Burren related the incident of the bicycle.

'That would be Jane,' said Chris. 'Drifting and yet ... with it too. She is very unpredictable, I think. One minute you think you know her and the next you do not.'

He shrugged.

Some of what Chris said seemed to coincide with his own brief impression of her. But he didn't trust Chris on this matter. He asked him how well he knew her.

'Not over well. We were in the Newcastle League of Youth together at one stage. I liked her.' He thought for a moment. 'But she always seemed to want to keep her other life to herself.' He gave a short dismissive laugh.

On his way to meet with Edell, Burren reflected on what Chris Megson had told him about Jane Dayton. On but a brief acquaintance he had himself felt that distant quality in her – a kind of sudden withdrawal into herself. He quickly dismissed it as foolish. First impressions were often unreliable, especially where emotion was involved. In any case, he reassured himself, Chris's view was probably biased.

Having dismissed the matter from his mind he continued untroubled on his way for the last-but-one meeting with Edell. The subject was to be the factors affecting the balance of trade.

Edell conducted the tutorial in the same way as he had each

of the others. Burren had quickly perceived the formula. Invite him to talk on his essay, during which Edell would take an occasional note, but not interrupt the delivery, and he would focus his gaze on some point amongst the bookshelves as if searching for and reminding himself of a hidden argument.

Once Burren had finished talking, Edell would continue to gaze afar whilst asking him to expand further on certain parts of the argument. Edell would then ask him to recount the reading he had consulted from the list he, Edell, had recommended. And from that Burren was expected to evaluate the reading in relation to the argument he propounded. Only occasionally would Edell turn his head and bring his focus to bear upon Burren. When that happened he was acutely aware that Edell was not so much addressing any point in his argument, so much as weighing him up as a person. It could be a very disconcerting experience.

Having encountered Edell's tuition in both micro- and macroeconomics he felt that whilst Edell might not be judged a great economist he was not as bad as others had made him appear. It was true that he was not a particularly effective lecturer, and especially not so in the micro part of the subject where he tended to become obsessed with the diagrams. Nevertheless, if the conventional educational process was reversed and he the student was judging the tutor, he would award Edell a good grade.

He had enjoyed the subject, which at one time, knowing very little about it, he did not think possible. And this he could largely attribute to Edell's tuition. Without appearing over-enthusiastic or making great claims for the subject, Edell had achieved a major success with him. Burren was sure that this approach was most effective in maintaining the interest of those unfamiliar with the complexities of the subject.

The strange thing was that he knew so little about the man himself. At a personal level he probably knew no more about Edell now than when he first met him. He hadn't seen him outside of tutorials and lectures. He did not go along to any of the social events and was not seen conversing with students, or anyone else, in the corridor or the common room. He did not think this was because Edell was by nature unsocial. There had to be some other explanation, and it was probably linked to Edell's current position and his relationship with Robert Wilcox.

Edell did not seem unhappy. In fact the more Burren thought about the matter the less he felt able to make any kind of assessment of Edell as a person. He was nothing but completely professional in his work; nothing but the subject at hand came into the dialogue. He was on all counts a mysterious figure. Burren liked and respected him, and as far as he was concerned he was not going to be part of the general body of criticism of him that he knew existed amongst others at the House. He would ask Paul Jenkins if he knew more about this curious figure.

7

Burren had agreed to meet Jane Dayton mid-morning. After looking in at the common room of the city part of college and reading an article on the Cyprus question, he had headed for the Coffee House in Broadway. He chose a seat in one of the bay windows looking out onto the street. He had already ordered coffee when he saw her arrive.

He watched her cross the floor and come towards him. She was wearing a full, cream-coloured dress with red flowers printed on it, in contrast to the close-fitting dress she had worn at the dance a few days ago. The dress had the effect of making her look a little less slim and she now appeared shorter in stature because of her flat shoes. She saw him and smiled broadly.

'I'm not late am I?' she asked.

'Not at all,' he said, offering her a seat.

'Only you seemed so settled there with your magazines and smoking your cigarette.'

He ordered her coffee according to her taste and requested a choice of cakes.

'Not for me, thank you,' she said, 'though I would like a chocolate biscuit. Plain chocolate, please.'

He noted her precise choice.

'It is good to see you again,' he said, looking directly at her in an appreciative way.

'It hasn't been very long since we last met,' she said, placing a mild brake on his enthusiasm.

'I know, but I needed to see you again,' he said with an eagerness in his voice. There is a lot I don't know and you seem to know so much more about me.' She gave him a quizzical look. 'Are you a student? I rather guess you are.'

'I am very much a student.'

She gave him a quick smile. She cast her eyes around the room.

'This is quite a place,' she said, as if it was unfamiliar to her. 'Is it a regular hideout of yours?'

He was aware of the teasing, provocative note in her voice. He smiled, 'You make it sound as though I am some kind of conspirator.'

'Well?' she waited.

He switched the conversation to the questions that were in his mind. 'Now,' he said leaning forward across the table and looking directly at her. 'How did you know of me, including my name, since the only time we had met before was when you fell off your bicycle at my feet. And then, you shot off without so much as a goodbye.'

She gave a small tinkly laugh. 'I knew your name because I was at the meeting of the Socialist Society when you sat prominently alongside the speaker living vicariously the ministerial role.'

He laughed at her mocking tone. 'Well, well. I see you've been around a little.'

'A little.'

'I don't think I've seen you at Socialist meetings before.' He was curious. 'Do you go to many of the meetings? Are you a member?' She was becoming more and more interesting to him.

'Not so fast,' she said.

She took a sip of her coffee and then told him that she was a member but not a very active one. She went on to say that whilst the Society corresponded with her political outlook she was more actively engaged in the university's Literary Society.

He smiled and said, 'Well I do hope that now we've properly met you'll come along to more meetings.' He went on to tell her that he was going to be the chairman in the coming year and that he and the secretary were working on a very interesting programme of speakers and discussion sessions.

129

'How do you know that I'll be here?' she said with a smile.
'Well ...'

She laughed. 'I was only teasing you. I very much hope to be
coming back for my final year – of course there is the small
matter of exams.'

He was surprised by his own feelings. He now experienced
unabashed relief at what she had said. He looked at her and
caught her doing the same to him. They laughed at each other's
embarrassment. When she smiled or laughed as she did now,
the flesh on the lower part of her cheeks creased onto her high
cheekbones, lending fun to her whole face. He thought it very
attractive. He watched her face now return to composure and
saw that there was an underlying seriousness there as well as
fun.

He lit a cigarette and exhaled the smoke, and decided to
return to the dance where they had last met.

'I nearly gave the dance last Saturday a miss as I was late
returning from the city.' He smiled. 'I am pleased that I changed
my mind. I hadn't seen you there before – did Chris invite you?'

She looked at him, intending to disconcert him slightly.
'Quite the interrogator, aren't you?' she said.

'I'm sorry, it was just ...' his words trailed off. He realised
that he was becoming far too inquisitive.

She put him at ease. 'You are right, I haven't been to one of
your dances before. I'm sure you understand that we – I'm
talking of women students – do not get invited too often to
dances. Christopher knew that I was at university here, and
when he arrived he made contact. He had invited me several
times before but I always made some excuse; this time when he
asked me I agreed.' She smiled enigmatically. 'Interesting, isn't
it?'

She waited to see if he wanted to respond but as he didn't, she
continued, 'I knew Christopher. We were both in the Labour
League of Youth back in Newcastle.' She gave a tinkly laugh.
'We argued quite a lot. You see, we have very different views

about the Labour Party. Christopher doesn't let much get in his way. He is very ambitious.'

It was as if she felt that she had to say this. He wasn't sure why. And then realising that what she had said was incomplete, she added, 'I enjoyed the dance.'

'I am very pleased and I hope I had some part in that.'

She turned her head from side to side in a 'so-so' manner and smiled broadly.

They were becoming aware that they enjoyed one another's company, and continued mutually to explore aspects of each other's life before leaving the Coffee House. As they walked along Broadway he took her hand.

The grounds of the House were munificent with flower in the early weeks of summer. Rhododendrons and azaleas were already in full bloom and at the front of the House one border alongside the lawn was full of perennials, including delphiniums, lupins and phlox, whilst on the other side were bush roses of various colours. Immediately in front of the House the gardener was setting out his herbaceous plants of Sweet Williams, verbenas, stocks, marigolds and pansies. The gardener loved his flowers. The scent of the roses wafted up to the rooms occupied by the students.

Such beauty and tranquillity was infectious and made for a contemplative mood. Burren was ensorcelled by this power of nature as he walked the grounds after lunch. He was suddenly interrupted by Chris Megson coming towards him.

'I thought I might see you doing the same thing,' said Chris. 'It helps to put thoughts together, doesn't it?'

'Yes it does,' he responded, his mood not entirely broken.

'Edell always walks the grounds before he gives his lectures – whatever the weather.'

Burren laughed. 'I'm not sure that helps him.'

'I agree,' said Chris, laughing too. 'I'm going in to the city in a few minutes to have my last meeting of the year with the man.'

Burren looked puzzled. 'The man?'

'Yes. Edell is my year tutor.'

'I see. I'm going in too, for the same reason. I was just walking the garden to clear one or two things in my mind before I meet with Framley.'

The thought of Framley reminded him that he had not heard anything more from Paul about Framley's job prospect with the university. As several weeks had now gone by since Paul mentioned it, he assumed Framley had not been successful.

The two young men walked to catch the bus to the city.

'Have you thought any more about our conversation of a few weeks ago?' asked Chris.

'If you mean applying to the university, no I haven't, though I think your other idea is a good one for next year. Of course we are, I suppose, going to be taking different options, but that needn't stop us working together on other subjects.'

'Good. But you know, it will be foolish not to apply to the university.' He turned to look directly at Burren. 'Are you sure you are not just leading me on? You've probably already applied. You're a bit secretive, aren't you?'

'That's as maybe,' he replied. 'But I assure you I haven't done anything yet. I want to use the summer away from here to consolidate my thoughts.'

'Well, I wouldn't leave it too long after you return. As I said before, you have to act quickly.'

They headed off to meet with their tutors.

Framley seemed in uncharacteristically buoyant mood, and although not actually referring to Burren by name, he was unusually warm in his welcome. Maybe he had been successful after all with the university job, Burren speculated.

'Now let us look over the year,' said Framley, looking down at some notes on his desk. 'You must have hit it off well with John Edell. He thinks you've done well.'

He paused to look again at the sheet of paper in front of him, and then continued, 'Had you taken economics before?'

'Only a course on the British economy post-1945,' he replied.

'Well it seems that both Mike Dawson and John Edell think well of you.'

Did he imagine Framley's disappointment that his scrutiny of the sheet of paper in front of him offered so little basis for criticism? Why did he mistrust Framley so, even when, as now, his comments were favourable? He saw that there was a copy of the new issue of *The New Age* on Framley's desk. He hadn't yet seen it himself and the sight of it now set his pulse going faster. To see his name in print for the first time had been a keenly anticipated pleasure.

Framley now turned his attention to Burren's article. 'I see you have an article,' he said, lifting the magazine from his desk.

Burren made no reply but looked pleased.

'You've obviously looked closely at Maurice Watkins's work. 'I've read your article and it is impressive.'

'Thank you,' said Burren glowing inwardly.

'You do seem to have alighted on some fundamental weakness in Watkins's argument.'

'I hope so,' replied Burren, who by now was feeling very satisfied with his achievement.

Framley now mentioned that this may be the last meeting with him as his personal tutor.

He has got it, thought Burren. He is going to the university. Framley was already continuing, 'But of course you will have part of the Government course with me, and part with Robert.' He smiled slightly.

The session now came to an end and Burren decided to drop by Paul Jenkins's room before meeting Jane for afternoon tea. Paul was in and was surrounded by books stacked on his desk.

'Hello, Paul, working hard?' he said, grinning broadly.

'Yes. Yes, I am,' groaned Paul. 'Examinations next week.'

'I thought I would drop by and collect a copy of *The New Age*.' He could not suppress his excitement. 'Framley has just complimented me on my article.'

'Well done,' said Paul, tossing a copy of the magazine across to him.

He looked at it and saw his name in print: John Burren. It was really there. At this moment he was extremely grateful to his friend for cajoling him into writing a piece for *The New Age* and he thanked him.

'Think nothing of it,' said Paul. 'Your other copies will be waiting for you at the House.'

Burren's expression registered surprise.

'Contributors each receive six complimentary copies.' Paul smiled. 'To distribute to influential people, you understand.'

'Of course.' He knew at once that he would send a copy to Maurice Watkins.

'And we expect our writers to sell a few copies,' said Paul, pointing a finger at his friend.

'Will you be able to meet demand once the news of my article gets around?' Burren grinned.

'Heigh-ho, time to return to my work.' Paul waved him away. As a parting shot he said, 'Beware your friend. He wishes to become editor next year.'

He left Paul to his books and examination fever. As he approached the Coffee House he saw Jane coming towards him. He noticed her unstockinged legs and her light flat shoes. He registered this detail quickly as she approached him, her dress fitting her lissom figure well. They smiled at each other, held hands, and went into the Coffee House.

Once inside they picked up the threads of their conversation from before as they drank tea and ate biscuits. It was a continuation of exploring one another's lives and sharing the enjoyment of being together. He wanted to communicate his pleasure at seeing his own article, and he deliberately placed *The New Age* magazine on the table between them. At first Jane just kept chatting and did not notice it. Then quite casually she picked it up and began idly thumbing through the pages as she continued to chat.

Suddenly she saw his name and her face creased into a smile. 'I see,' she said, 'it was left there for me to see.' She laughed. 'It must have been agony having to wait for me to notice it.' She laughed again and he joined in.

'It looks terribly portentous,' she said.

'I should like to know what you think of it,' he said, adding hastily, 'I mean whether it is well written.'

'Oh, I see. I'm not expected to comment on the content.'

'Well ...' he hesitated, and then struggled. 'I didn't mean ...'

She cut in laughingly, 'I'm to be your literary critic, is that the idea?'

'Umm ...' he mused.

There was something about her that released feelings in him; a freedom and a sense of joy that he had not before experienced with anyone else. He wanted it to last, and he knew at this moment that he wanted to be with her more and more.

He realised that he hadn't asked her what she had been doing over the past few days. He quickly sought to put this right and smilingly asked her, 'What have you been doing since we last met?'

She looked at him, amused. 'I have had my hair trimmed.' She patted it lightly.

In his self-absorption he hadn't noticed, but could now see that her hair was a little different. He liked it and he told her how good it looked.

She smiled briefly and continued, 'I have been to a tutorial. I played netball for college,' she added enthusiastically, 'and we won.' She looked at him enquiringly. 'Do you play any games?'

'Yes a little – football and cricket rather badly.'

'And then,' she added, 'I have been in the library re-reading the ballads of Wordsworth. So there you are – a week in the life of Jane Dayton.'

'You pack a lot in,' he said.

'So do you, don't you?'

135

They both acknowledged they should return to the world of learning and left the Coffee House hand in hand.

In the course of the next few days he was surprised at the very positive response to his article in *The New Age*. He had already dispatched a copy of the magazine to Maurice Watkins accompanied by a letter. In this, he wrote that although his article was critical of aspects of the free market theory, he hoped that Maurice Watkins would find the time to return some comments.

He received back the most gracious letter. Watkins said that he had read the article and whilst not agreeing with Burren, he acknowledged there were circumstances in which the theory could not take root and flourish. He did not agree with the argument made in respect to the comparison of labour with capital, but went on to say that if they should meet he would like to talk about this. He expressed the hope that Burren would go on to write more, and he extended an open invitation to have lunch with him whenever Burren was next in London. Burren was very happy to receive this response and was still more encouraged when Robert Wilcox, having also received a note from Maurice Watkins, offered him his own congratulations.

A further response to his article was an invitation to speak at one of the Labour Club's discussion meetings early in the new term. The most curious thing that happened, however, was an invitation from the student Conservative Association. This had amused him, as he never, ever, anticipated being asked to discuss anything with a group of Conservatives; he was not sure whether to accept. This was not because he felt uneasy about the matter of talking to Conservatives but he thought it would leave him open to much taunting from fellow students at his own college.

He confided as much at one of the post-lunch tea sessions in Maureen Styles's room.

'Keeping your parliamentary options open are you, John?' quipped Frank Bainwell.

'I hadn't thought of it that way.' And then laughingly he said, 'But now that you mention it I suppose it could be useful.' He went on to say, 'I see that you have a piece too in *The New Age*, Chris, something about the future of the Labour Party, though I've not had a chance to read it yet. What line are you taking?'

Chris Megson seemed a little reluctant at first, but then said, 'I'm trying to restate the case for the centre ground in the Party, which I happen to believe is the best hope for the future.'

Burren more or less knew that Chris would take this line. At this stage each of them knew one another's basic position along the spectrum of socialism. He also knew that it would be well written and that its quiet orthodoxy would put Chris firmly in favour with the current leadership. What he didn't know, because he had not yet read the article, was whether the case was argued and analysed in a framework of values as done by Antony Crosland.

Frank remained silent and apparently uninterested.

Chris now said that he hoped *The New Age* would become more of a vehicle for advancing the cause of democratic socialism.

Burren interjected and said that a house journal should find space for arguments expressing different views.

'That is all very well, John, but the editorial line I think should have firm direction.'

Suddenly Burren realised the significance of Paul Jenkins's recent comment to him.

Maureen broke in by saying that she could see the coming year as being very interesting politically at Morton, and that she was going to miss all of this. 'Sometimes I quite envy you,' she said, referring to the rest of the group. 'The trouble is, the Principal was right when he said that the House bestows an atmosphere of learning, and this in its own subtle way does begin to affect you. I shall miss it more than I care to say.'

The men could see that she was becoming maudlin and Burren put his arm round her and said, 'You must come and visit us next year. There is the hospitality room in the main building and you and Jack could come and stay for a weekend.'

'That's right,' said Frank. 'Make sure it coincides with one of our dances.' He got up from his chair and started singing and jiving.

Maureen brightened up a little. They each knew that with the coming end of the session there were not many more days of tea after lunch.

Frank expressed their collective thoughts. 'I suppose that when you are brought together in a group such as we are, and live in the luscious setting of this House with its charm, and philosophise all day' – they laughed their approval at this – 'you have a pretty potent mix that is going to disturb a settled way of life.'

They each knew this was so and that it might be even more of a breach in a year's time. But now there was work to be done, and the men made their way to the door.

Outside in the corridor Burren turned to Frank and said, 'Along with the other invitations, I've now been asked to speak to the local Women's Institute.'

Frank roared with laughter. 'That is a different kettle of fish altogether. You'll become very versatile,' he chortled.

'I couldn't very well refuse once Mrs Charnley had asked me.' He shrugged. 'It is a social duty.'

'Of course,' said Frank mockingly. 'I quite agree. You could not have refused. Remember however that they do not like anything too heavy. Spoils their cup of tea.'

The invitation had come about in a rather strange way. He had got into the habit of rescuing some of the newspapers of the previous day from the common room to read in his own room after breakfast. Later he returned them for collection. Mrs Charnley, the cleaner, had told him to read the newspapers in the common room, as the rooms were to be left empty for cleaning at this time of the morning. He had persisted however, and the battle between Mrs Charnley's cleaning and his reading habits had continued.

He knew he had won when Mrs Charnley no longer uttered her old refrain, though she still made her point by knocking her broom against his chair whilst he was reading the papers.

One morning very recently, Mrs Charnley had set about cleaning his room as usual. He had watched her dusting in an apparently absent-minded way, repeating the operation over the same area. She finally stopped to say, 'I was wondering, Mr Burren ...'

What is she wondering? he thought, before asking, 'Yes, Mrs Charnley?'

'Well, I was wondering Mr Burren if you would come and give us a small talk.'

'A small talk?' His voice was disbelieving.

'Yes, nothing too grand, you see there are just a few of us in the local WI.'

He questioned in his mind what the WI did. What was its purpose? He had little idea.

Mrs Charnley continued, 'We usually have a small talk by someone or other and then we end with a cup of tea and a biscuit, or a slice of cake.' Her voice had the tone of someone who knew every idiosyncrasy of his taste.

'It is very cosy,' she smiled.

'But why me, Mrs Charnley?'

'Well I thought you ...' she hesitated. 'I know we disagreed a bit at the beginning of the year over the newspapers – of course I was right, but we soon settled into a good arrangement – but I know that all our members would like to hear you.'

He noticed that the 'few' had now become 'all'.

He suddenly felt ridiculously boyish. She had him on a tender spot. He was susceptible to this kind of flattery.

'Yes of course I'll come, Mrs Charnley. It will be a great pleasure to meet your fellow members. But there isn't much time left now.' And as an afterthought he added, 'Do please call me John.'

'Oh, thank you very much Mr – um – John. We had thought,

the committee that is, of next Tuesday, at 2 pm in the Community Centre.'

He could see that Mrs Charnley's committee had already got it all planned. He responded positively. 'Yes, that will be fine,' he said, melting away before her guileless charm.

He had given a full account of his encounter with Mrs Charnley to Maureen Styles as they sat together in the common room after supper.

'I can see you speaking to those ladies,' said Maureen. She could visualise his young, ruggedly handsome face charming the timorous hearts of the old ladies. 'You watch it,' she said, giving her giggly laugh, 'some of those old ladies can be dangerous.'

He gave a broad grin. 'Some of them are not so old, I've heard.'

'Oh really? Then that can be even more dangerous.' She gave a wicked smile.

Later, after he had spoken at Mrs Charnley's WI meeting, he recalled the occasion for Maureen's benefit.

'It was really very funny. Throughout the afternoon Mrs Charnley sat with an expression of proprietorial pride on her face. Then at the end she came up to me and said, "The members loved it, John", without having spoken to any of them to find out.'

'She is a dear old soul,' said Maureen. 'We always have a gossip of a morning. You'd be surprised what she knows.'

He looked at her, suddenly wary, as if she perhaps possessed some secret information about him as well as others.

She caught his glance. 'Now you are all curious,' she said teasingly.

'Well it's unfair – after all.'

He seemed very boyish, she thought. 'Oh don't be silly.'

It was the last full day before they went off for the summer. He and Jane planned to spend a lazy afternoon by the river. They edged their way along the path that followed the winding course of the water. They were not alone, for others too had the same idea, much to his annoyance. He wanted the two of them to be alone – to have the whole world to themselves on this particular day.

'Let's go on a bit further,' he said, 'and try to get away from some of these people.'

Jane gave him an affectionate prod. 'Not too far. Remember we have to walk back.'

They went on to where there was a bend in the river and the path ceased to follow its route so closely. This left an area of grass shaded by tall trees.

'Here we are,' he said, turning to Jane. 'This will do fine, won't it?'

Jane nodded approval.

They were grateful for the shade. It was a gorgeously warm day with the sun at its highest point. They sat down beneath weeping willows, forming a canopy of lamentation above, and began to eat a late lunch, silently happy in each other's company. Boats drifted lazily by, apparently aimlessly moving upstream, their occupants equally lazily enjoying the summer afternoon.

There was nothing disturbing the tranquillity of the day, and it was as though the rest of the world was still at this moment. A moment when all the happiness possible seems to be concentrated in oneself; a privileged moment, whilst strangely lonely too.

The world of work was not part of this world; it did not intrude. Yet simultaneous with the quietude of this moment was the world of factories, docks, mines and building sites; of offices with the cogs of commerce smoothly engaging with ever-increasing speed; and with shoppers bustling around in pursuit of everyday goods.

The business of finance and of government went their own way. World affairs, with one crisis inevitably following another, ingressed only vaguely in the mind. It was the plain simple stillness of the countryside on a summer afternoon.

The reality of the thought brought forth guilt. Did he owe all those anonymous people in that other world an obligation? The obligation to work at learning and to devote that learning to the common good? Had he worked hard? And was he going to use his knowledge and skill for the common good? He didn't know. He knew only the feeling that in some way he had been offered a chance.

They lay back on the grass amongst the daisies, welcoming the warmth of the sun on their faces, arms and legs. Jane pulled her skirt well above her knees to feel more of the sun. He could now see the length and shape of her legs and began thinking about the rest of her body. He saw the shape of her breasts beneath her dress, a little flattened as she lay back, and he looked at her face in profile; saw the soft texture of her skin and the roundness of her lips. He examined her face for a long time. She had her eyes closed against the sun. At last he leant across and kissed her softly on the lips. A gentle, contented smile radiated across her face. He kissed her again, and then they started to communicate in language.

'Isn't this just heavenly,' said Jane.

'Umm,' he mumbled agreement.

'We are so lucky to be here,' she said, 'I should like this to last for ever.'

He thought he caught her meaning accurately, and replied, 'So would I. We'll have another year.'

She replied, 'That is not what I meant. I mean this particular day, this very moment. Don't you ever feel that way? That you want a particular moment to freeze in time and last for ever?'

He did not respond in words but leant over and kissed her again. They continued their exploratory love.

The final event of the year was under way. The front lounge had been cleared and the chairs pushed back against the walls to make an area large enough for dancing. Frank Bainwell and his social committee had arranged for a special licence to serve drinks, and he was now checking the sound system by playing the one record that expressed the period after supper in the common room more than any other: 'The Cannon Ball Train'.

Burren said, 'How we played it all the time until we made ourselves tire of it!' He paused, thinking over the past few months, and then said, half to himself, 'And recently we've started playing it again as if we were anticipating this evening.'

Chris Megson was at his elbow and overheard. 'I think you are being a little overdramatic,' he said grinning maliciously.

Tom Croft now joined them together with Bill Williams.

'Let's make this a good old Labour Party do,' said Bill.

The others agreed and looked at him indulgently, knowing just what he meant.

Burren asked Tom if he was coming back next year.

Tom put his hand on Burren's shoulder. 'Yes, provided there is not a general election called for the autumn.'

The first year at college had drawn quickly to a close, or so it seemed to Maureen Styles as she completed her rather unsystematic packing. She was nervously excited at the prospect of returning home. Yet she also felt the tug of nostalgia for the past year. She sat down and surveyed her little room; the room which had depressed her so much when she had first arrived the previous autumn. She looked at the Van Gogh self-portrait print that she had hung on the wall opposite her desk. The compelling eyes held her in a hypnotic spell, making her look at them whilst the memories of the year took hold. Eventually she took it off the wall and carefully placed it in her case alongside the photograph of her husband and daughter.

She continued to drift between the past year and the present, which made her forget what she had already packed away. She remembered the day not long after she had arrived when John

Burren had caught her in tears in her room, and he had returned shortly afterwards with some flowers. Chris Megson had also been solicitous, fetching coffee for her after supper and asking her about her day.

Frank Bainwell had been good to her too in his own way. He had of course experience that the two younger men lacked, a depth of understanding of the problems which marriage and life at college entailed, and it had been good to know that he was there. She had derived confidence and security from that. She smiled to herself at the thought of how he ragged John Burren and Chris Megson about their bachelor status.

She had experienced difficulty with her studies; great difficulty at times. But she consoled herself with the thought that she had persevered and seen it through. She had beamed like a little girl who had been complimented on her dress when the Principal reported favourably on her year's work, but she had felt oddly embarrassed too. She now made ready to go to the last dance.

More people were drifting into the hall and Frank Bainwell was ready to start the evening's entertainment. The bus bringing the young women, the student nurses, the trainee teachers, and those from the university, would soon be arriving.

Burren waited for Jane. Timothy Framley, wearing a light blue suit and with his usual air of slight boredom, had arrived together with Mike Dawson, who contrasted with Framley in every way. Mike was dressed in an open-necked checked shirt and corduroy trousers, his hair resembling a large ball of tangled knitting wool.

The music began and several couples moved onto the dance floor. Burren saw Maureen Styles on the far side of the room sitting with Joan Symonds, and he went across to ask her to dance. They moved unskilfully to the rhythm.

She said, 'Do you remember our first meeting in this room, on that introductory evening?'

'How could I forget, after you made fun of my part of the country?'

She looked at him and saw the familiar grin.

The music was coming to an end. 'Be sure and save a later dance for me,' he said.

Jane had now appeared. As she walked towards him Chris Megson came up to her. 'Hello Jane, how good to see you again. You must like our dances.' He kissed her lightly on the cheek. 'Be sure and save a dance for me.'

She looked at Burren and made a face. He took her hand and led her towards the dance floor. It was a foxtrot to the tune of 'Slow Boat to China' – a dance in which he was least accomplished. Jane made up for his deficiency and steered him through the movements.

'What would I do without you?' he smiled, acknowledging her skill.

She replied by making a skilful movement more difficult and saying, 'It is no excuse for being lazy.'

He drew her closer to him and they danced in silence.

As the dance ended and they came off the dance floor, they passed close by Timothy Framley.

'Hello,' he said, turning his attention to Jane. The music had restarted. 'Would you care to dance?'

Burren was sure that Framley had deliberately chosen his moment. He briefly watched them dance together, and saw how animated Framley became in conversation with Jane.

Robert Wilcox and Jasmine were dancing together in a very slow, rhythmic way, with fixed smiles on their faces. At the far end of the floor David Smith was dancing with Maureen and quite obviously amusing her. It seemed that most of the House students were there, with many from the city end as well.

The music stopped and Framley led Jane back to where Burren was standing. As he released her arm he acknowledged Burren with a thin smile.

'He seems very pleasant,' Jane said. 'He was telling me that he is a tutor here.'

'Yes. Unfortunately he has been my year tutor as well.'

'Oh dear, you do seem down suddenly,' she said laughing lightly. 'You must tell me about it.'

'It is too boring,' he said. 'Maybe someday.' And quickly retrieving his party mood he said, 'Let's go and get a drink.'

They walked across to the bar where Denis Greenfell, festooned with badges in the lapels of his jacket, including that of the Labour Party, was dispensing drinks.

'What do you wish to have, John?' he asked whilst casting an eye on Jane.

Burren ordered their drinks and he and Jane then began to head towards the French windows leading to the garden.

'Hello John, I knew I would find you here.'

It was Paul Jenkins.

Turning to Jane, Burren said, 'This is Paul – probably my best friend here.'

'Only probably,' laughed Paul.

Jane smiled as Paul ostentatiously took her hand and kissed it. 'I believe I have seen you at Socialist Society meetings,' he said.

'Maybe,' said Jane.

Burren bought Paul a drink and the three of them then headed back towards the French windows. They were greeted by warm evening air with the scent of roses.

'Isn't this a wonderful evening for us all to be together?' said Paul.

'Yes,' said Burren. 'The charm is working, just as we were told it would.'

'It is beautifully still, and aromatic,' said Jane.

'Perfect,' exclaimed Paul.

Burren turned to Jane. 'You haven't seen the grounds, have you?'

'No,' she said, taking his hand.

'Right, well let's take a stroll.'

'I'll leave you to walk together,' said Paul.

They both looked at him, 'No, do join us,' they both insisted.

They meandered round the grounds, taking in the beauty of the garden and the whole setting, feeling the joy of the occasion. Others too were taking the evening air. Jane sensed the feelings of the two men as they shared their privilege of having studied here, of having learned together and forming their political beliefs anew. And most of all, of having a second chance. She linked arms with them both and they lingered with their own thoughts in the setting sun before returning to the melody and movement of the dance.

Jane was soon whisked away by Chris Megson. Jasmine was sitting in her usual place next to Robert Wilcox, who was yet again busily engaged in conversation with Framley. Burren went across and asked her to dance. She looked as attractive as ever, wearing a dark red dress.

She looked at him with her clear blue eyes. 'Have you enjoyed your year with us?' she asked with mild amusement.

'Do the rules permit me to reply?' he asked with an indulgent smile.

'You like the teasing game, don't you?' she said.

He responded with a shrug.

'I enjoyed reading your article. And I understand it has given you quite a name.'

'Well, I don't know ...'

'Now you are being modest,' she said. 'It doesn't suit you.'

The music suited her, however, and he noticed as before her skilful sense of rhythm. Again he experienced the feeling that it was as if she was dancing on her own.

'I see you have a friend with you this evening.' She looked directly at him in a questioning way.

'Yes. You've noticed her?'

'But of course'

'Her name is Jane.'

'She is very attractive.'

The music stopped. He led Jasmine back to where Robert Wilcox was sitting, and still talking to Framley.

The Principal turned his head in their direction as they arrived. 'Hello John, I hope you are enjoying yourself. You've made quite an impact this year.'

Burren caught sight of Framley's expression as the Principal said this.

'Thank you,' said Burren, 'I've enjoyed the past year.' And he turned and thanked Jasmine for the dance.

The dance room was very crowded as more people had returned from the garden, and at first he could not see Jane. Then he saw her and Paul talking enthusiastically to each other as they danced together. He headed back towards the bar and saw Maureen. It was time to have that last dance with her.

She was very nostalgic and close to tears. She said, 'I'm going to miss being here. I thought I had prepared myself for the leaving bit but this place does take hold of you, and I've met so many very good people.' And looking at him through damp eyes she said, 'Thank you, John, for lifting my spirits when I felt down.'

He smiled. 'I've enjoyed your company.' And he added teasingly, 'And your tea wasn't bad.'

She gave him an affectionate prod.

As Framley and Jasmine passed them on the dance floor Framley smiled at Maureen in a leave-taking way.

Burren continued, 'And remember what we said the other day – be sure to come and visit us poor slaves staying on!'

Maureen produced a smile and cheered up a bit.

The dance came to an end and he steered Maureen in the direction of Jane. As they approached, Maureen whispered, 'I think she is very pretty.'

'I am so very pleased you think that,' he said giving her arm an affectionate squeeze.

He turned to Jane, 'I see you've been kept busy on the dance floor. This is Maureen. She is leaving us.' And with a sly smile, he added, 'And we, her tea partners, are going to miss her.'

Maureen forced a smile.

Jane chatted to her for a minute and then he said, 'Now, don't forget, come back to see us. And write and let me know how you get on outside!' He put his arm round her and they hugged. As they parted he kissed her warmly on the cheek.

Frank Bainwell had now put on the music of 'My Foolish Heart' and Burren and Jane danced together.

He said to her, 'We seem to have been apart a lot this evening, with you being in such demand.'

'Well, we have the last dance together, and that is the important one, isn't it?' she smiled with her sense of fun.

They danced on in silence and then Jane asked, 'Who is the very attractive woman you were dancing with earlier?'

'Which one?'' he asked, feigning innocence.

Jane gave him a prod. 'I think you know very well which one! The one with the golden hair – and there is only one of those here.'

'Ah, now I see,' he said. 'That is Jasmine, she is the Principal's secretary.

'Well she certainly likes you.'

'I think that is exaggerating a bit,' he grinned. 'Just a bit.'

'Really?'

He drew her closer to him as the popular tune began to have its effect on their mood and Jane rested her head on his shoulder. They continued dancing in happiness until Frank Bainwell's voice could be heard bidding everyone goodnight, best wishes for the summer, and a welcome return in the autumn. Burren and Jane were met by Paul Jenkins as they left the dance floor. 'I'm going to miss having you around, John. Do come and spend some time with me in north London where I live.' And turning to Jane with a smile, he said, 'You too of course, Jane.'

'Well, that is very kind of you.' He hesitated briefly.

'Jane is off to Greece, you know, for part of the summer.'

'Lucky you,' said Paul.

'I don't know what my plans are yet, Paul, but I should like to meet at some point during the summer.'

'Fine. Look, I shall be to-ing and fro-ing between here and London so let's keep in touch.' Jane left to collect her coat.

'You are a lucky man John. Jane is lively and intelligent.' Paul nodded his approval. 'Attractive too.'

Burren placed his arm affectionately on his friend's shoulder. 'I do believe it's love, Paul.'

Jane returned and they bade Paul goodnight.

'Enjoy Greece,' Paul said, as he kissed Jane affectionately on the cheek.

'I shall,' Jane smiled.

The following morning they were together on the platform, waiting for Jane's train. They stood awkwardly together, waiting, not knowing what to say to reassure each other. Yesterday they had been as happy together as they were ever likely to be, and now they were about to go their separate ways, if only for a short time.

'You will write to me?'

'And you write too. Let me know all about Greece.'

The train drew alongside the platform and they kissed one another goodbye. Jane settled into a compartment, finding herself a window seat, and the train began to draw away.

They waved until they were lost to each other's view.

8

The scaffold surrounding the fifth floor of the vast block of flats resembled a huge observation platform in a prison camp. At the far end of the block the arms of the bricklayers moved rhythmically as they placed brick beside brick in building the wall of the final storey, their naked backs bronzed beneath the mid-July sun. Burren leant back against the scaffold railing and yelped with pain as the hot metal touched his bare skin. He quickly put his shirt back on. His back was already sore with overexposure to the sun. He had not known a summer like this for a very long time. The sun had shone unremittingly from an unclouded sky since he had returned from college.

He ran his hand self-pityingly across his back and felt the soreness and sighed deeply. It was no good. There must be easier ways of earning a living. Of course he knew there were easier ways, but that did not help him now. There were many good reasons why he was here and he was well aware of them all. He needed money and this was the best-paid manual job he could get. It was also the old firm he had worked for before going to Morton, and he knew that would make things easier for him. He laughed out loud at the thought now – if this was easy, what was hard work like? And he had to admit to himself that he had been too lazy to look around for anything else.

So that was why he was here, and here he would be for another eight weeks. He sat down and prepared to light a cigarette.

'Hey up, John.' The voice was unmistakably Tom's. 'I've been looking all over the place for you, where've you been?'

He looked ruefully at Tom Warren. 'I've been trying to

escape your clutches. And just when I thought I had, you push your ugly face before me and say, "I've been looking for you".'

Tom grinned broadly. 'It's a bit different from college, eh, John?'

'And if I hear that again I'll ...'

Tom placed a restraining hand on his shoulder and gave him a significant wink. 'The old man is about,' he whispered.

Burren raised his aching body. 'All right, lead me to the work, you slave driver.'

Tom clamped a cheery hand upon his back. 'That's my man.'

Burren groaned in agony.

They walked back along the scaffolding together. 'Now what we must do' – Tom gave a quick hitching-up of his trousers – 'is to prime all the window frames before the brickies are ready for them to be put into place.'

They worked away on the frames, steadily and methodically. The pink paint was quickly soaked up by the dry timber. From time to time Tom muttered upon this fact but it was not in his nature to do anything more about it. Burren worked on, his eyes following the course of the pink paint as he pursued the repetitive task of brush to paint, and paint to wood. Gradually his muscles began to pick up the old routine and he did not have consciously to apply himself to the work. It was this automatic aspect of the work, this separation of the conscious mind from the physical reflexes, that he had previously found so relaxing. He remembered how, whilst painting, he had carried on long philosophical discourses with himself, becoming quite oblivious to all around him. It was satisfying, too. He felt a sense of achievement when he finished painting, even when he knew it was only a door post for some coal shed.

He completed the frame he was working on and laid the paintbrush across the top of the paint kettle, then lit a cigarette. The smoke curled lethargically upwards to mix with the soporific haze above.

He watched Tom continuing to work. Dear Tom. He had

been a good friend. But for Tom, he probably wouldn't have applied to go to college. Always Tom had been there with an encouraging word at the right moment. At times he had felt he would not make it. The reading after long hours at work, the essay to obtain the Reed scholarship, and the application itself and the references to support it. And then the agony of waiting. He knew now just how morose he had been at the time, and how patiently Tom had sustained him.

He watched Tom continue to apply the paint to the window frame. It was curious to him why Tom had not tried for a better job. He was always talking about how soul-destroying this job was, and yet he did nothing about it. It wasn't as if it was too late. He didn't know Tom's exact age but he was sure that he was no older than middle forties. Of course he knew that Tom would not change. He was far too taken up with the idea of the dignity of labour to ever do that. Stupid fool, thought Burren, he is no more part of his fellow labourers than they are of him. He didn't even eat with them at meal breaks.

At last the lunch break came round and he welcomed the respite. He grabbed the holdall which served as his lunch bag and surprised himself at the speed with which he negotiated the ladder down from the scaffold. Once down he made his way to the back of the flats and found a shaded spot close by a wall.

'Over here, Tom,' he shouted as he saw his friend come round the corner of the third block of flats. Tom carefully picked his way through rubble and ill-stacked bricks, hitching his trousers as he did so.

'You were quick off the mark, weren't you?' he grinned at Burren.

'This time is precious,' he muttered from behind his newspaper whilst passing part of it to Tom, and for while they both sat in silence, engrossed in their different parts of the newspaper.

At last Tom spoke. 'Have you seen any members of the Party since you've been back?'

'No.' He hesitated. 'Well, I saw Jim Meeks last week for a few minutes as I was coming home from work.'

'You know that he is Secretary of the Party now?' said Tom.

'Yes, he told me.' He refused to show much interest.

'Did he tell you how he became Secretary?' There was no doubting that Tom was trying to arouse his curiosity.

'He said very little. He seemed in a great hurry. He simply asked me if I would give a talk to the Party whilst I was home.'

'And are you going to?' asked Tom.

'I said I would think about it and let him know.'

He knew that Tom was keen to open up the question of the local Party, but he had no wish to become involved in that subject. The local Party's political games struck him as futile. Tom had always backed up his views inside the Party, but what could two of them do against the rest? Anyway it didn't matter now, because he was no longer part of the local set-up.

The hooter announced the end of the lunch break and they both walked back to where the unpainted frames stood. They soon finished the frames and moved on to the top scaffold once again. The sun seared into their skin as they painted the facia board, making them both perspire heavily. The afternoon dragged on endlessly. Burren felt that his arms would drop off from the continuous upward stretching action of painting the facia board. He longed for the cool evening. He now knew what it was like to be back. He had quickly forgotten the seven to five daily grind amongst the charm of college life. Now that he was back amongst it all, he realised how fundamentally it enfeebled the spirit.

He continued painting round the far end of the block of four flats, and then rested before starting to paint the front of the block. He could see Tom painting at the other end of the block. The plan was for them to meet about halfway along the front of the building, but Tom was going to do more than his share on this particular afternoon, as Burren just could not keep pace with his colleague. Afterwards he continued painting: the top of a window frame, then down one side, along the bottom and finally the other side. It was exactly the same procedure for window after window. He looked at his watch; it showed 4.30 – half an hour to go. Wearily he resumed his painting.

After work he walked slowly home past the newly built semi-detached bungalows, each proudly sprouting its own TV aerial. The bungalows were depressing in their uniformity; one vast sprawl of mortar and brick. Well, this is what the great majority wanted, he reflected, and now they had got it. It seemed just, after all.

Now he was walking along Willow Lane past laburnum trees that were already shedding their chandelier-like blooms. The rich fragrance of mimosa filled the air. Willow Lane brought back memories of childhood, of long summer days spent exploring the nearby woods with his friends. The days seemed so much longer then and the summer holidays spread themselves out far into the future. He wondered what it was like for boys now.

He reached the end of Willow Lane and turned into the council estate. The thought of tea put a new vigour into his stride. He could visualise his mother fussing about, arranging the tea. His plate would be placed at the end of the table opposite his father and facing the kitchen dresser. Nothing had changed. Only he had changed.

When he had sat down to supper on his first night back from college he felt he had never been away, so meticulously did everything follow the previous pattern of life. Conversation had taken the form of episodes in a serial: a comment would be made by one or other of them, then their attention was held by something on television, and the next instalment of the conversation had to wait. He didn't mind this because he hadn't felt like talking. At that stage it would have required a controlled mental effort to jerk him out of his life at college and to think about being back at home. It was much easier simply to surrender the mind to television.

His father, working a 7.30 am to 5 pm shift at a local heating

ventilation factory, would already be at home. He could see his
father seated at the table, his body beginning to fatten now,
though up to two years ago his physique would have done any
athlete justice. His shirt sleeves would be rolled up, exposing his
long sinewy arms. He still thought he was in his manual prime
but Burren had seen him having to pause after digging a few
rows of soil in the garden. It was high time his father eased up a
bit, he told himself; he will be 60 next month. It was curious
how his father's generation of men clung to the idea of physical
prowess; a mark of independence, he supposed. Those poor law
commissioners did their job well, he reflected bitterly.

He had argued frequently with his father about politics
before going to Morton, but now the fiery passion seemed to
have gone out of their exchanges. They were both disposed now
to be more deferential to each other, as if trying to understand
the meaning of their different lives. It was a little embarrassing,
for it brought out a new shyness with each other. Yet he felt
that he knew his father better now. He no longer exacted such
an impossibly high standard but was ready to accept his father's
many hare-brained schemes for what they really were – the
perpetual dream, without which the working man's life is
nakedly revealed for what it is: a boring routine which eventually kills the mind before the body.

He unhooked the rusty latch on the gate, walked up the
cracked concrete path and let himself in by the back door. His
mother and father were seated at the kitchen table. He let his
holdall slip from his grasp to the floor, slumped into a chair and
sighed heavily.

His mother was already on her feet. 'Are you tired, John?,'
she asked solicitously. 'What will you have to eat? I've got some
nice steak pie in the oven.' Her brown eyes looked at him
concernedly.

'That's fine, Mum. But no hurry. I'll have a cigarette first.' He
disliked his mother fussing in this way.

'We've heard from Peter.' His father passed the letter across to him. 'He seems to be having a great time out there in the sand.' His father laughed.

His brother Peter was doing his National Service in the Canal Zone.

'He had better make the most of it, then, because he'll soon be out of there. And in a great hurry.'

'What do you mean?' his mother asked anxiously.

Why had he spoken? She was bound to worry now.

'What I mean is, he'll be evacuated.'

'You reckon so?' His father looked up from lighting his pipe.

'Yes, I do.'

'But why?' He could see that his mother was still troubled.

He tried to find some way of reassuring her but could not find the right words now that her fears had been aroused. He settled on, 'Because there are certain people who do not want us there.'

His mother became quiet while his father prodded away at his pipe. It was an opportune moment to go upstairs to bath and change his clothes.

After dinner, he sat back in a chair and lit a cigarette. What a difference. The heat, sweat, and aching muscles of the long day were past. It was quite amazing the difference a bath and a good meal made. He slipped lower into the chair; it was luxury, pure luxury. His father sat across from him, already absorbed in a programme on television. Normally he would have been critical of his father sitting and watching this mind-rotting nonsense. But not now; his father deserved these few precious hours of leisure, and they were his to do with as he wished.

From the kitchen he could hear his mother arranging her domestic domain. What did she manage to find to do? He had already helped her with washing and drying the dishes. He supposed that she was preparing something for lunch the following day for him and his father. Repeatedly he had told his mother that she needn't do this, that he could easily place some cheese, or other food, between two slices of bread and butter, but it made not the slightest difference.

157

Of course he knew that his mother's fussing was because to her he was still her boy. Every time she packed his lunch, it was for him going to school. The fact that he had already been away from home doing his National Service, and had now been away again for a year, learning and discovering new things, made little difference to her. He felt sure that his absence was seen by his mother as his having been away on a long holiday.

Jane had written to him before she went away on holiday. Her first letter after going back home from university had expressed mixed feelings. One part of her was naturally very pleased at seeing her parents again, but she said how much she missed him and she reminded him of their days together during the last term. He in turn had written and spoken of his love for her. He reminded her of how strange it had been to meet quite by chance through her falling off her bicycle. He told of life on the building site and how much he wanted to exchange it for life in the university city again, and to be with her.

Jane's latest letter from Greece had arrived that morning. Seeing it lying on the front door mat he had picked it up as he went to work, and had tried to read it as he walked. He had managed to read only part of it:

We arrived in Thessalonica on July 10, after a rough and not very pleasant early part of the voyage. There was thick sea mist combined with what we were told were very heavy seas in the Bay of Biscay – and it lasted for the best part of two days! One of the crew told us that it was the worst weather he had known for that time of the year.

It was now lunch break at work and he pulled Jane's letter from his pocket, telling himself that he was lucky that Tom had gone home at midday. If Tom had been there he would not have been able to read a sentence of the letter without interruption. He started to read again. She had gone to Greece with three friends from her college. Her letter began:

My Dear John,

As I have told you already in my other letters, I continue to miss you as much as ever, probably more so in fact here, for it would be so nice to share this with you. It will be so good when we can see one another again.

But Greece. It is enchanting. We have arrived back in Athens after a few days exploring the northern part of Greece. It is as though the hours of reading musty books in the old university library suddenly had come to life. It is here before one's eyes. Some of the villages appear to have remained transfixed in time. The life is pastoral and unhurried, and the people have an immense dignity as though conscious of their great ancestry. They are also very kind and friendly. We spent a day with a family in one of the villages and they gave us fruit, and cheese, and wine, for our return journey. I so wish you could be here, John.

He paused in his reading and nodded ruefully. He too wished he could be there. He read on: 'We are going to spend a bit more time in Athens and then start exploring two of the islands. What are you doing with yourself?'

What was he doing with himself? He looked at the block of flats enveloped in metal scaffolding and gave a short sardonic laugh. What about this for the good life?

The words of Framley came drifting back to him: 'Students should relax in the long vacation, escape to some tranquil, preferably ancient, environment so that they may meditate on their studies.' Well, perhaps, but he reckoned that Frank Bainwell was right when he said that Framley was unsuited to such a college. What was Framley doing as a tutor in an adult college? The nearest Framley had come to industry or a piece of machinery was when he lifted the bonnet of his car, if in fact he even did that. The fact was, he found it difficult to relate to the students and had little understanding of their problems.

He gazed absent-mindedly at the page of Jane's letter in his hand and dreamed wonderful thoughts of holidaying with her beneath a bright sun and surrounded by clear blue water. Finally he folded the letter and put it back in its envelope. What would he write back to her? Of his labouring under the burning sun from 7 am to 5 pm each day? Of his conversations with Tom, of his mother and father, of the talk to the local Labour Party? Of what should he write? Write and tell her what he was doing, of course.

A mood of self-pity took hold of him. It was all so unfair, he told himself. Here he was on a building site to earn enough money to supplement his grant. There was Jane, enjoying Greece. Jane wished he was there, and he wished he was there. It didn't make sense.

His mood was broken by the return of Tom. 'I've just seen Jim Meeks. He tells me you've agreed to come along and speak at the Party meeting.'

'That's right,' he said, looking down at a spot of white paint on his shoe and showing little interest.

'Good for you.' Tom sat down on an upturned bucket and looked amiably at his friend. 'It's best to let bygones be bygones, John.'

Burren muttered softly to himself.

At home that evening he replied to Jane's letter, which would probably be her last before returning to college. He started:

Darling Jane,

I received your letter and am most envious of the Greek experience. The only thing we have had in common these past few weeks is the sun [he had thought of crossing this bit out lest it be misunderstood, but he decided to leave it in]. I continue to miss you too and I am looking forward to the day when I will see you again. As much as anything, it is the thought of sharing my time with you again once back at college that has helped me through these monotonous days. I think it was that wonderful day by the riverside when I realised for the first time that I was opening my soul to you.

He did not finish the letter until after he had spoken to the local Labour Party a few days later, and he used part of his letter to describe that event. He concluded his letter: 'I love you Jane, and I want so much to be with you again.'

Through the kitchen window the evening September sun glowed in a red phosphorescent ball. On the kitchen table were the notes for his talk to the Labour Party that evening. A final glance through them, he assured himself, and he would be fully prepared. He poured himself a cool drink and took a long sip before sitting down at the table. The silence of the room made him realise how much he missed his parents.

His mother had fussed in her usual way before she and his father had left for their holiday by the sea. 'Make sure you have enough to eat. I've stocked up well, so you don't have to bother too much about buying food. And I've bought things that are easy to cook.' Her instructions had been endless. He smiled to himself. She had been so excited, almost like a girl going to her first party. By contrast, his father had been nonchalant, as though it were a frequent event. Yet it was the first holiday that he could remember his parents taking. They had always been too busy trying to make a week's earnings stretch to meet a fortnight's costs, to take a holiday.

As he read through his notes he reflected on the long hot summer that he had spent back in his local community that was now to culminate in his talk. Soon he would be back at college in a life that was so different from the past few weeks in a quiet village. He felt cheered at the prospect and turned his attention back to the notes with renewed purpose. He read quickly, smiling approvingly at his efforts. He intended to show them a thing or two. He knew they would take a lot of convincing and he was not sure he would succeed, but he was jolly well going to try.

The Labour Party met in one of the largest rooms in the new community centre. Why they chose such a large room baffled him. During his time with the Party he not known more than 20 people to attend, and that had been only when there had been a scandal concerning the social secretary. As it was, people usually spread themselves all over the room so that whoever was speaking frequently had to turn their head, like a spectator at a Wimbledon tennis match, in order to hold the interest of the audience.

He walked down the corridor to the large room at the end of the building and stopped by its half-open door. From the door a stiff cardboard notice was hanging rather forlornly. It read: 'Labour Party meeting'.

He could hear voices from within: 'I intend to raise the matter at the next constituency meeting.'

He entered the room and turned his head in the direction of the voice. It was John Tapsell, the only local tradesman of which the Party could boast. He owned a small tobacconist's shop in the High Street and was considered by the Party to be quite an authority on rates. Though his supposed expertise had never led him to put it to effect by becoming a councillor. His name had been put forward many times but he always excused himself by saying that it would jeopardise his business. 'I am willing to do my bit from the sidelines,' was his stock phrase, accompanied by a sickeningly ingratiating smile.

Burren watched him talking to a tall, grey-haired man whom he did not recognise. Tapsell up to his usual tricks, he thought. Big talk of what he will do at the constituency level.

He walked to the front of the room to where Jim Meeks was laying out the usual Party literature, and gave a cursory glance at the leaflets. They looked rather worn and well handled, he thought.

'Would you mind putting a few of these out as well, Jim,' he

162

asked, handing Jim Meeks some copies of *The New Age*. 'But people have to pay for this one.' He laughed. 'It is reasonably priced, however, and great value!'

Jim Meeks looked at the journal and saw Burren's name on the front cover amongst the listed contributors. 'Well, well, turning writer too are we, John?'

'Some members might be interested,' Burren said, doubting the truth of his own comment. 'Expecting many to turn up tonight?' he asked, opening up in the usual Party way.

Jim Meeks gave a thin smile, 'We hope so. I expect people to come along to hear what you have to say. And it is a very fine evening,' he added.

Burren gave a short embarrassed laugh. 'I'm not going to start a national revival, you know.'

'Ah, don't get me wrong.'

He noticed how Jim Meeks flexed his fingers, a sure sign that he was in earnest.

'You see, the Party is interested in you. They are watching your career.'

For a moment Burren thought he saw a smile beginning to enliven the bucolic face.

'With . . .' – Jim Meeks looked up at the ceiling, searching for the right word to give maximum effect – 'anticipation!' He smiled at the aptness of the word.

But Burren was distracted by the trivial. It was curious, he thought, how Party officers, however minor their rank in the Party structure, used the collective noun to clothe their personal remarks: 'the Party' this, and 'the Party' that.

Jim Meeks continued to lay out the Party literature on a table set to one side of the officers and speaker. A jug of water and drinking glasses gave the table that served as the speaker's rostrum a proprietorial air. Several more people had now drifted into the room; at a quick glance Burren reckoned they already numbered the statutory twelve.

A prompting of loyalty combined with curiosity made him ask about the political activity of the Party.

'Quite good really,' said Jim Meeks. He looked up from the table, and Burren waited for the implied qualification to be made explicit, as he knew it would be. 'But of course there is the usual problem of too few people willing to do the donkey work.'

Burren nodded agreement. 'It is the same all over.'

They continued their platitudes of Party talk. Meanwhile a few more people had trickled into the room. He could see Tom Warren standing near the doorway talking to John Tapsell. And next to them Mrs Brown, cigarette in mouth and hair precariously supported in a bun, sat writing. She was vintage, having founded the local Party back in the 1920s. She was content now to be an onlooker, though she continued to attend meetings with faultless regularity. Many a time her good sense had pulled the Party back onto the rails when it had become embroiled in fractious trivia.

The Chairman came bustling up to the table. 'Evening, Jim.' And turning towards Burren he said, 'So you are back with us.' There was a hint of malevolence in the remark.

Burren looked at the myopic eyes. He disliked Holden. 'I thought I should have a look at the old firm again,' he said facetiously.

'Before you turn to other things,' Holden flashed back.

Burren did not respond.

'Well come on, Jim. Let's get this meeting started. We don't want to be here all night.' Jim Meeks promptly took up his place.

Holden brusquely gestured to Burren to sit on his right. 'Don't talk for more than half an hour,' he grunted.

Burren suppressed his annoyance and sat down. He was already regretting that he had agreed to speak. Holden's unconcealed hostility brought back all his old misgivings.

He watched Holden asking the meeting to approve the

minutes of the last meeting. Jim Meeks sat toying with his pen. From the room came a murmur of approval. He could see Mrs Brown in the back row, still writing and giving off the impression of being oblivious to all that was going on. Loyalty that had become ingrained habit was all that brought her to these meetings, he was sure.

The meeting was now discussing plans for raising money to fight the local elections next April. They had candidates for each of the vacant seats. He was impressed. At least this was an improvement on the past. A member objected to spending so much money on elections for so little return. They currently had only two members on the district council. He could see that they were back to the same interminable discussion, with objections to any course of action being raised, hesitations and doubts expressed, and all the old excuses to avert action being aired. It convinced him that it was still the same.

Holden wearily wiped his glasses and replaced them, askew. He was clearly impatient with the way things were going. Something must be done to stop this political claptrap: Burren had yet to speak and he did not want to miss his favourite programme on television. He looked at his watch.

But John Tapsell was now on his feet and delivering himself in his usual prolix manner, 'I advise the Party under the guidance of the Chair, and having due regard to the circumstances, to refer the matter back.'

Holden acted promptly. 'Are you moving a motion?' he demanded.

Tapsell, not used to having himself cut short in this way, faltered. 'Well, no. I was simply advising the Party. I thought we were still discussing . . .'

Again Holden cut him short. 'Are you going to move a motion?' he repeated.

Tapsell's face flushed with annoyance. 'No, I am not,' he said.

Holden pleaded with the meeting. 'Comrades, we have

discussed this question thoroughly. Now will someone please move, so that we can make progress.'

Tom Warren raised his hand, 'I move that we accept the proposal of the Executive.'

'Will someone second?' asked Holden, his tone more conciliatory now.

A hand went up at the back of the room.

'Is everyone agreed?' Holden did not wait for confirmation. 'Good, that is settled.'

There were a few murmurs of protest but Holden ignored them.

Burren smiled inwardly. Reluctantly he had to admire Holden's handling of the meeting. He did not know of anyone so politically uncommitted, so uninterested in ideas, lacking belief and without conviction. Nevertheless, he had to acknowledge that Holden's toughness was a very suitable quality for Chairman of this local Labour Party.

Holden was now introducing him. He didn't waste any time. 'Our long absent comrade of course needs no introduction. We naturally claim some credit for his success. He is bound to have much to tell us.' He sat down and looked at Burren whilst at the same time surreptitiously pointing to his watch. Burren got the point.

'Comrades, this is a great pleasure for me.' He smiled at the faces in the front row but didn't feel any reciprocating warmth or response coming from the audience. He continued, 'Studying politics has taught me much, and perhaps the most important thing it has taught me is that we should not accept political ideas and values uncritically simply because they fit with our own predisposed views.'

He felt Holden stir uneasily beside him. In front of him faces were set in impassive expressions. He recalled the promise he had made to himself and thrust his hands deeply into the pockets of his jacket in self-conviction. He would show them.

'It is this that I should like to talk about tonight in relation to

166

Party policy. I want to try and show how this failure to examine thoroughly our own policies has led us to seriously under-estimate the change in our political opponents. There is no point in thinking we are a modern and dynamic Party if we cannot recognise this change. And let me remind you it was we who lost the last general election.' He turned to Holden and Meeks to bring them within the compass of his audience. Holden's face was sullen behind his glasses. Meeks doodled on a leaflet bearing the face of Attlee.

'The Tories have beavered away at the public about natio-nalisation to such an extent that it is now seen as an election loser for us. It doesn't have to be, however. We know amongst ourselves that the current form of nationalisation has weak-nesses. Let us not be dogmatic about it. Let us rethink the matter. The end goal of public ownership should remain a key objective, but let us be flexible about the means for securing that goal. It is possible to adopt methods of public ownership that are designed to suit the needs of particular industries.'

Burren caught sight of Tapsell in the audience vigorously nodding his approval, whilst by contrast Meeks's face had become set in disapproval. He felt confident in what he was saying. Inner conviction acted like whisky inside him. He sus-pected that most of them in the audience didn't like what he was saying, but he had to say it. Someone had to tell them. Beside him, Holden did not betray his feelings.

He went on, 'Let us acknowledge, for example, that between 1945 and 1951 we moved politics too far towards the state with not enough emphasis upon the individual citizen. It is admit-tedly a fine balance to secure within the socialist concept an optimum relationship between the state and the individual, but we should not allow the Tories always to claim individual freedom as their territory.' He appealed to the faces before him. 'At least let us not be afraid to discuss the matter.

'Finally, I should like to say a few words about foreign policy. For whilst it is said that foreign policy does not win elections, our security as individual citizens ultimately depends upon safeguarding our interests abroad. This evening I am able only to focus on what I regard as one of the main security issues for us, and that is German rearmament. In my view the German question in its broadest sense is going to continue to be the central issue for us. We must make our policy position absolutely clear here, and remember this is a field in which we can rightly claim to be the party of internationalism. But . . .' – he paused briefly for effect – 'but, only if we do not allow the subject of German rearmament to tear us apart. We must adopt a sensible approach to this question. I believe we can achieve that if all sides are prepared to be patient with one another and genuinely try to accommodate a German contribution.

'It seems to me that having established a democratic constitution for the Federal Republic we must allow them to run that democracy. And one of the responsibilities of a democracy is being able to manage its own defence effectively.'

He noticed one or two heads nodding agreement with this.

'I respect the feelings of that generation of servicemen who fought the war. But war, and victory in war, does not alter geographic fact. Germany occupies a strategic position in the centre of Europe and is pivotal to any security system for Europe. I believe that properly argued and fully explained, a policy of German rearmament will allow all sections of the Party to recognise that it is compatible with a socialist internationalist outlook.'

He looked at his watch lying on the table, and then at Holden. He had been speaking for 35 minutes. Better end it now he told himself. 'And so, comrades, our period in opposition, which let us hope will not be for much longer, can be good for us if we use the time productively and rethink some of our policies. The job of 1945 to 1951 is unfinished. There are exciting things still to be done, and if we are positive I am confident we can win next time.'

He sat down to a little clapping and looked fixedly at the

tumbler of water in front of him. Holden invited questions with the clear implication that he didn't want any to be asked. There were a few desultory questions and then Holden said a few words of thanks and brought the meeting to an end.

He turned to Burren. 'I suppose you'll be standing for parliament soon.'

He saw the knowing look in Holden's eyes and felt inexplicably guilty. So that is what he thinks I am up to. 'I haven't thought about it,' he replied.

People began to leave. Jim Meeks hurriedly went around assiduously collecting the Party literature. 'Don't forget the second Tuesday of next month,' he called out to those leaving the room. He grudgingly acknowledged that it was Burren who had brought them to the meeting. If 20 would stay and listen to that sort of intellectual nonsense, he told himself, then surely they as a Party could encourage more to come along and discuss facts. Facts were always Meeks's counter-thrust to intellectualism. He knew where he was with facts.

Burren pressed the clasp on his briefcase and walked towards the door.

John Tapsell came up to him. 'A very good talk, John.'

'Glad you liked it,' he said. From anyone else he would have been pleased at the compliment, but with Tapsell he suspected the motive.

'Shook some people too, I'll bet.' He gave Burren a confidential wink.

'I didn't so much want to shake people, as to make them think.'

Tapsell paid no heed. 'I know just how dogmatic some of these people can be. As a shopkeeper it is very difficult, you know. They come into the shop and because I am a member of the Party they think they can say what they like. It is embarrassing, I can tell you, particularly if I have some of my ...' he hesitated, and then in a whisper he said, '... influential customers in the shop.'

Burren looked at the man in front of him. Whatever had made this tobacco pedlar join the Labour Party?

Tapsell continued, 'And so you see, I wholeheartedly agree with what you said. We do need to make the Party more respectable.'

Burren felt the anger mounting inside him. This man hadn't understood one word he had said in his talk. Or had he? He looked again at the flaccid face. But of course, he had understood. He had deliberately chosen to misinterpret the talk in this way. Suddenly he felt hopelessly disappointed and empty. There was nothing more to be said to Tapsell. He stomped past him and walked quickly down the corridor and on to the street.

The buildings in the early morning light stood silhouetted against the nimbus sun. Workmen prepared for another day's labour. Planks were removed from standing ladders, the cement mixers made their first chugging protestations, hods were filled, and labourer's shovels gleaned in anticipation. Burren walked into the paint shed. For him it was the last day on the site before returning to college.

'Good morning, Tom,' he said brightly.

Tom looked out of the shed door at the sky. 'We'll make a start on the front doors before the sun gets round,' he said.

'Fine by me.'

Tom grinned. 'I expect it is. Anything is fine on your last day.'

'I've enjoyed every minute of it.' He pulled on his overalls and collected his paint brushes.

'Right then. Let's get going,' said Tom. 'Must make the most of you today.'

Tom started at one end of the block and Burren at the other. After he had finished a couple of doors he stood back from his work to appreciate the affect. The bright blue doors looked good against the brickwork and relieved the otherwise monotonous affect of the front of the block. A very pleasant change from the old standard green used by the council in the past, he thought. He ran his eye along the whole length of the block and then up to the top scaffold that was now being removed, and he recalled when he and Tom had painted the facia board under the blistering July sun. It had been a long two months since then. Tom strolled across to where he was standing.

'Not bad, are they,' said Burren, pointing to the painted doors.

Tom idly turned to face the doors. He had seen too much paint in his working day to enthuse over a couple of doors.

'What did you think of the meeting last night?' Tom asked.

'Much as I expected, I suppose. I don't think they liked what I had to say but then I didn't expect them to. They are far too settled in their ways for that.'

He looked to Tom for confirmation, but Tom remained silent and thoughtful.

'Tapsell came up to me after the meeting. He is a bigger hypocrite than even I realised. What is he doing in the Party?' he became quite angry. 'Hasn't anyone tried to have him thrown out?'

'He is just a fool,' said Tom.

'He is more than that, he is dangerous.'

'He is just a fool,' repeated Tom.

Burren shook his head.

'I'm more interested in what you had to say to the meeting,' said Tom settling down to the matter that had brought him across in the first place.

Burren looked puzzled. 'What do you mean?'

'Well, you don't really believe all that stuff that you put across, do you?'

Tom's approach was that of implied disbelief, though he knew that in fact Burren believed every word that he had said.

'Of course I believed it. I wouldn't have said it otherwise.' He turned a bewildered face to Tom. 'What are you trying to get at?'

'If you believe all of that, John, then you have changed more than I thought.'

171

'I just don't ...' he broke off. He didn't know what to say. Tom's comment was a surprise to him. He could not understand why Tom of all people should be critical of what he had said at the meeting.

Tom pulled a tin of tobacco from his pocket and carefully began to roll a cigarette, trimmed the ends, opened his box of matches and then stopped.

'Look, John,' his tone was friendly. 'What you said last night came straight from the top; from the research department, from the intellectuals.'

'But ...'

Tom cut him short. 'No, let me finish.' He lit his cigarette and looked at Burren through the smoke. 'I know what you are going to say – that I've dragged in the whipping horse of the intellectuals.'

Burren nodded in agreement.

Tom continued, 'Yes, but they are guilty. They talk as if things have changed. That we must adjust our image, etcetera.' He raised his voice in protest. 'But things have not changed and the trouble is that those fools cannot see that. They take no account of human feelings. To them, politics is all about power, manipulating opinion, and statistics. So if you swallow that lot you are bound to get people's backs up.

'And if they don't listen to hard truths, and you too,' he said peevishly, 'then their messy human feelings won't get them very far.'

Tom shook his head sadly.

'So you do really believe that stuff then?'

'Yes, I do,' he said adamantly.

'But you shouldn't dismiss people because they have prejudices. Remember those prejudices have grown out of a lifetime of bitter experience. Rational arguments and abstractions are not going to remove those prejudices overnight.'

'I thought you were different,' said Burren despairingly.

Tom gave an ironic laugh. 'But why should I be? I am no

172

different. Multiply my attitude enough times and you have the aggregate opinion of the Labour Party membership.'

The whine of the hooter signalled the lunch break. They both walked across to the shady spot where they habitually sat and ate their lunch. Burren walked a little behind Tom.

It is hopeless, he thought. Tom is the same as the rest of them. As soon as something is said which hits home at their prejudices then by some metamorphosis you become an intellectual. He kicked viciously at a pile of sand, dislodging a hardened lump at the top of the pile.

For a time they both sat in silence, each locked in their own thoughts. From time to time he looked apprehensively at Tom as though expecting some new onslaught of criticism. He felt there was something more behind Tom's remarks; something that he was slowly trying to get around to. He decided to broach the subject once more.

'What is it you are really trying to get at, Tom? I can't believe that it is because I've fallen for the intellectual line, as you put it.'

Tom looked out at the downland, rising above the building site and the nearby village, before turning to face him. He smiled wearily, 'Well it is, and it isn't.'

'Let's have it straight,' said Burren sharply.

'It is like this. I know I supported you in the Party in everything you did before you went away. I did that because your ideas were good and because others had to be shown a thing or two.' He bent forward, fixing his eyes on Burren's earnest young face. 'But I did it most of all because you needed a chance. I wanted to see you get on. To make a success of your life.'

Burren turned his eyes away.

Tom continued, 'Now you have your chance and it is up to you. But I didn't give it to you.' He gestured in the direction of the village. 'Those people who listened to you last night, they gave you the chance because it was through them that you expounded and developed your ideas. Now I am with them,' said Tom defiantly. 'I know some of them are pretty hopeless, they are weak and afraid to speak out' – he laughed briefly – 'and when they do, they talk a lot of rubbish. I know all about their faults. But still I am with them because for all their faults they are the people that matter.' He lowered his voice almost to a whisper. 'Don't separate yourself from them, John. Don't repeat clever intellectual phrases because it is fashionable, or the right thing to do. That isn't socialism. Working-class people have been let down too often by educated people within the Labour Party. That is why they have an almost instinctive mistrust of smart intellectuals, people who air their knowledge and talk down. For heaven's sake, don't fall into that glib political behaviour.'

Tom relit his cigarette and went on again, 'You see, the hopes of my generation were frustrated in the bitter struggles of the 1930s. In any case we were confused, no education. It was all too complicated for us. But you have a chance.'

He placed his hand on Burren's shoulder. 'Don't let us down, John.'

Burren didn't say anything in response. His first impulse was to dismiss Tom's admonition as pure sentimentalism and to leave it at that. But he couldn't rid himself of a feeling of guilt. He assured himself that it was stupid to think that way; that he didn't owe them anything. They hadn't even helped him get to college. Indeed, most of them had thought it just a little absurd. He catalogued all the reasons why he should not feel guilty and convinced himself that he was right. But still his conscience pulled at him.

As the afternoon wore on, Tom's remarks kept recurring in his mind. Had he let them down? He didn't think so. He certainly tried to get behind their prejudices. But then, what was education for if it wasn't for just that very purpose? Was he being too clever? Probably he was, but then it was difficult. You cannot always reduce complex ideas to the lowest common denominator, he convinced himself, and it seemed as if that was all they understood. They didn't even bother to try and understand. Anyway, he admitted ruefully, they are bound to win because ultimately to try and win them over, you have to express things in their terms.

He left the building site for the last time and was pleased that he would be returning to college.

9

The train drew into the station and Burren was among the passengers making their way along the platform towards the exit. He walked out of the station entrance and went across to the café, as he had done the year before. Inside he noticed that little had changed. There had observably been no redecorating of the interior of the café; it had the same faded cream-coloured walls. The same waitress was behind the counter, though naturally she had no reason to recognise the traveller of a year ago.

He had again decided to have a cup of tea before going on his way. He was going to meet his friend, Paul Jenkins. They had corresponded during the course of the summer and Paul had written to tell him of his decision to go to LSE. Burren was disappointed that he would not have the company and advice of his good friend in the coming year, but he acknowledged that Paul had made the right decision. Apart from its fine overall reputation, LSE was probably the best place to go to study the branch of law that Paul wanted to.

He had his travel reading with him – fiction as always, a novel that had been recommended to him by Mike Dawson: Lionel Trilling's *The Middle of the Journey*. Mike had said that it expressed one of the best accounts of the dilemma of the liberal conscience confronted with dogma and intransigence. He had suggested it to Burren in the context of the reading on social democracy. He was now at the denouement of the theme that had been simmering throughout the narrative. He read:

And so you and I stand opposed. For you – no responsi-bility for the individual but no forgiveness. For me –

176

ultimate, absolute responsibility for the individual, but mercy. Absolute responsibility: it is the only way that men can keep their value, can be thought of as other than mere things. These matters – social causes, environment, education – do you think they really make a difference between one human soul, and another?

These were the two alternative positions which confronted the liberal conscience. He read on:

Is it really a question. An absolute freedom from responsibility – that much of a child none of us can be. An absolute responsibility – that much of a divine or metaphysical essence none of us is – you put it very well. And you spoke up for something between. Call it the human being in maturity, at once responsible and conditioned.

This, as he knew, had been written during the McCarthy era in the US. He was pleased that Mike Dawson had recommended it. The philosophical underpinning of the novel left him pondering the dilemma of the liberal thinker: to stand eternally on the sidelines recognising the merits of all sides to an issue, or to commit and lose the freedom to acknowledge openly the fallibility of all causes. The central theme of the book, in a curious and interesting way, corresponded to his own position in relation to the learning process and personal integrity. He thought back to a year ago and the hopes that he had at that time. In many ways those hopes had been more than fulfilled, but of course he was only halfway there, and he intended to build upon the past year and vindicate those who had invested their hopes in his success.

He left the café and caught a bus into the city. He was going to the main part of the college where he had agreed to meet Paul, before he left for London. He was going to move into Paul's old room in college, and had decided to return a few days early to see Paul and to give himself some time to browse in the

bookshops. He especially wanted to visit the numerous sec-
ondhand bookshops where he hoped to pick up several reasonably priced books. He wanted also to give himself the time
to look around the city afresh and explore parts that he had not
had the time to look at during the past year. He wanted quite
simply to have the leisure and time to soak in the atmosphere of
the university city before getting down to the serious business of
study once again.

He climbed the stairs to Paul Jenkins's room and saw that the
door was open. He tapped on the door and entered. Paul raised
himself from where he had been collecting items from the floor.

'Hello John. It is good to see you.' He stood back and
examined Burren. 'My word, you look ridiculously fit!'

Burren grimaced in response.

'Have you had a good summer on that building site?'

'It is good to see you, Paul.' He placed an affectionate hand
on his friend's shoulder.

'It is good to be back. Tell me, what have you been doing
here?'

'The odd thing or two.' He swept his hand to take in the
room. 'Mostly this: sorting things out and packing.' He looked
at Burren. 'I should have done the same thing as you and made
myself fit and healthy.'

Burren cast his eye round the room. Apart from the desk and
a chair it was now almost bare. All the books had gone. He
moved towards the window to look out on the city. The room
was one of two attic rooms situated at the very top of the
building. As he looked out on the city he was pleasurably
captivated. Immediately below was the street at the front of the
college, and beyond the view widened out to embrace the whole
of the northern part of the city: rooftops, spires, and one or two
buildings with minaret-shaped towers. Although he had visited
Paul in his room many times, this was the first time that he had
seen the view from the window. It was now to be his, and
looking out over the city sent a whole mixture of emotions

surging within him. It was inspiring, and he was sure this was the right place to spend the next year. He stood awhile, indulging his mood, before turning and facing Paul Jenkins.

'No wonder you always appeared so uplifted last year,' he said with a grin, 'with a view like that you must have felt ...'

'On top of the world,' offered Paul.

They both roared with laughter.

'Look, why don't we have a drink together and some lunch perhaps, at the Rose & Crown, before you leave for London?'

'What a good idea,' agreed Paul.

They walked to the pub and entered the saloon bar. They ordered their drinks and lunch from the barman and went outside to the pub garden and found an empty table. It was pleasant on this late summer day, warm with a weakening sun, and in relaxed form the two young men chatted idly about how they had spent their long break in their different ways.

Paul asked about Jane, telling Burren yet again that he was a lucky man to have found someone like her. Paul had stayed on at college for a few weeks before going home to north London where he would now live with his father, while studying industrial law at LSE.

'So you are going to stay at home?'

'Yes,' said Paul. 'I might as well. I'll have complete freedom. There is only my father living there now and he is still going each day to his law practice in town.' A sudden shadow of sadness passed over his face. He continued, 'My sister was married a year ago and although she and her husband would have been quite happy to stay with my father, he was adamant that they should have their own independent way of life. It will be different for me. My father and I live quite separate lives, though we'll be together a bit at weekends, and he is of course pleased that I have chosen LSE. That is why I say again that you are always welcome to come and stay, and bring Jane.'

'Thank you, I should like that.'

He had not heard Paul talk about his family before and he

now realised that some event in Paul's life had saddened him greatly and that it was still painful to him. He decided not to probe but to allow his friend to confide further in his own time.

They ordered another drink and continued to talk about the past year: life in the university city, the Socialist Society, the life at Morton and the different lecturers. Burren turned the conversation particularly to Edell.

'I was on my own with Edell for economics and although I do not share the popular view of him, he is nevertheless still more or less a stranger to me. I don't think I know any more about him now than I did at the outset.'

'I share your unwillingness to go along with the popular condemnation of John Edell,' said Paul. 'As to the mystique surrounding him, I always felt that he was a very private man. He has been known however to have parties at his house for Mortonites, though I haven't been to one myself. I believe they've fallen off rather since Robert became Principal. I suppose much of his recent attitude has to be seen in the context of the poor relations between himself and the Principal.'

'Yes, I suppose you are right,' said Burren. 'Whilst on the subject of Morton and the Principal, I recall you telling me early on last year, when you warned me off Jasmine, that there was more to be told.'

Paul smiled and put on his confidential air. 'Well, if you are keen to know, it was before I came to Morton. Probably in Jasmine's first year here. A Morton student took a strong fancy to Jasmine and wanted to take her out on a regular basis. It was very quickly made clear to him, I understand, that he should not pursue Jasmine, but he ignored the warning and persisted.'

'What happened?'

'I gather that he was told that he should not stay on but should find some reason for leaving the college, which he did before the end of the year.'

'But why shouldn't the chap go out with Jasmine if that was the wish of them both?' asked Burren.

180

Paul laughed. 'Aren't you being a little naïve? Jasmine is almost certainly Robert's mistress.'

'Yes, well, I had supposed that, but she is a free agent presumably?' he looked directly at Paul. 'And may choose?'

Paul laughed again a shade derisively at the line being taken by his friend. 'I think she is pretty much in tow to Robert.'

Burren now said, 'When I was talking to her about the meeting of the Socialist Society at which Maurice Watkins spoke, which she came along to incidentally, I noticed that she referred to him by his first name. Is she well connected politically, or did she just take that from Robert Wilcox?'

'There was nothing incidental about her coming along to the Socialist Society meeting. She came along to many of these with me during my first year. She is very political. Her father was after all a junior minister in Attlee's government.'

'I didn't know that,' said Burren, realising in an instant the reason for her apparent, though largely undisclosed, political interest.

'She is completely wasted on Robert Wilcox,' said Paul with just a touch of feeling. 'Jasmine could be a political figure in her own right, and she is simply subordinating all of that to Robert's interests.'

Burren shrugged his shoulders. He would from now on view Jasmine rather differently.

'My word,' exclaimed Paul, looking at his watch. 'Come on, John, help me finish my packing. I must leave for London.'

Burren used the morning of his first full day back going round the shops – window shopping, he supposed it was – before buying the few texts he wanted and which had been recommended as useful for his coming studies. A few more books would also help give his room an air of learning, he assured himself, though he couldn't hope to emulate Paul Jenkins's book-lined walls in the previous year.

On going out from college he had briefly seen Jasmine. She

had expressed surprise at seeing him back so early – pleasantly surprised, he thought. He thanked her for whatever part she had played in securing Paul Jenkins's old room for him.

Jasmine's only reply had been facetious. 'We have to do these things for important people.'

He smiled and feigned the part.

Several days had now passed since his return, and second-year Morton students were coming back. He looked in at the Rose & Crown at midday to see if either Frank Bainwell or Chris Megson had yet returned, as he knew this was the most likely place to meet them. He pushed open the door of the saloon bar and looked around. Doris the barmaid was busily wiping a glass and talking to a young couple seated on bar stools.

As he walked towards the bar, a hand clasped his shoulder, 'Hello, John, welcome back.' He turned.

'Frank! It's good to see you.'

'What'll you have?' Frank gestured to the bar.

'The usual,' he said.

'Two pints, Doris, when you are ready.' He turned to Burren, 'It's good to be back, isn't it?'

'Indeed it is.'

Doris returned with the beer. 'Hello stranger,' she said to Burren.

He winked at Frank. 'Do you know, Frank, it was only the thought of sharing a drink here with Doris that kept me going during those long summer days.'

Doris gave her little giggle. 'Tell me another,' she said. 'I'll bet you were living it up in some Continental resort.'

'Of course he was,' said Frank, always ready to exchange banter.

Burren laughed. 'How I wish that were true.'

The two men went and sat at a table close to the door leading to the darts room. They talked of what each had been doing during the summer. Frank said that an old friend, a tutor with

182

the WEA, had arranged for Frank to work in their office arranging the programme for the autumn.

'Good for you. I could have done with something like that.'

But Frank played it down, and there was something in his low-key manner that suggested to Burren that one way and another, all had not been well. Frank quickly downed his beer and said, 'Drink up, and let's have another.'

Frank returned to the bar and Burren noticed that he seemed more animated once again, with Doris giving him a crinkly-eyed giggle.

'I told Doris you had been living it up in Nice,' said Frank, placing the beers on the table.

Burren lifted his glass and looked across the top of it to Frank. 'She'll probably believe it.'

He noticed how distant the expression was on Frank's face. Frank fell silent and Burren saw that he had already drained half his glass.

He enquired if Frank had seen Maureen whilst he was back in Manchester.

In an uninterested way Frank said that he had encountered her shopping in the city centre but that was all. The earlier bonhomie had now all but disappeared. Burren suggested they have another drink, and Frank readily agreed.

At the bar Burren asked Doris for two more beers, and as an afterthought he said, 'Make mine a half.'

Doris came to the end of the bar with the beer. 'I suppose you can't stomach too much English beer after Nice,' she said placing the half-pint glass down in front of him.

He smiled at her, 'I'll tell you all about that another time. Right now I want to ask you a question.'

'Really?' exclaimed Doris, pretending wide-eyed innocence.

'Yes. How long has Frank been here?'

'Almost as soon as we opened,' said Doris. 'I thought it odd that he should be drinking so much on his own.' Her pretty face became thoughtful. 'Domestic trouble if you ask me.'

183

'What makes you say that?' he asked.

'Well ...' Doris hesitated.

'Go on.'

'Nearly always is,' said Doris authoritatively, and shrugged her shoulders.

Burren picked up the glasses and began to walk away.

'Why? Are you worried?' Doris called after him.

He turned his head and signalled for her to be quiet.

'And what is worrying you?' asked Frank, eagerly grasping a full glass.

'Nothing. You know what Doris is like. Number one dramatist.'

Frank gave an ungoverned laugh and leaned forward heavily on the table.

It hadn't occurred to Burren when he first arrived that Frank had already been drinking for some time. He should have known. The signs were evident: the swing from jollity to sullenness, and being only half attentive. He could now see that the cumulative effect of the earlier drinking was taking hold. He felt that Frank wanted to confide something, yet couldn't. Frank sighed heavily. There was obviously something wrong. Any further speculation was now interrupted by the arrival of Chris Megson.

'I thought I would see one or other of you in here!' The fresh-faced Chris looked happy.

Frank made an effort to restore himself to an alert posture. He smiled wearily at Chris. 'Good to see you, my young adversary.'

Burren offered to buy Chris a drink and made off towards the bar. On his return Chris gave him a knowing wink.

'Here's to our success,' said Chris with the air of one who had already secured it.

They reminisced about the past year, or at least Chris and Burren did, and they talked of the year ahead. Frank played little part in all of this but appeared quietly content to allow the conversation to flow over him.

After some time Chris suddenly said, 'I've just remembered Maureen will not be returning.' He looked rueful. 'I shall miss her.'

Frank at last looked up. 'I expect she is back in her snug Manchester suburb,' he said with a tinge of cynicism.

Eventually they walked back to the college, with Chris alongside Burren and Frank sauntering detachedly behind.

'What are your plans for this year, John?' asked Chris.

'Much the same as last year, only better I hope. That is: do well on the course and continue to enjoy the life here.'

'Yes, yes, that goes without saying. But are you going to apply to the university?'

'Well I have given some thought to that over the summer and I'm going to discuss the matter with my special option tutor once I know who that is.'

'But that may be too late,' said Chris with irritation in his voice.

Burren turned to look at Chris striding confidently by his side. 'Why are you so keen for me, Chris?' He was curious why Chris should take such an interest in his future.

'I would have thought it was obvious. It would be good if we could both go to the university here at the same time.'

It was interesting, he thought, how Chris put on this guardian act. Probably it was quite genuine, but somehow he felt it was Chris's way of showing how he did things in the right way.

'I dropped in and had a word with Timothy Framley on my return this morning,' Chris said. 'And he said I should begin making approaches to colleges straightaway. He gave me one or two contacts.'

Chris knows what he wants all right, Burren told himself, and he said, 'I want to be clear about the area of political science that I am most interested in, and at the moment I'm not sure of that.'

Chris gave a dismissive shrug.

Burren, together with Frank Bainwell and Chris Megson and others from the same year, went along to the introductory session for the new group of first-year students. The event took much the same form as in the previous year. He met several of the first-year students and tried to get them interested in the clubs and societies, and especially he canvassed their interest in the Socialist Society. Most of the interest expressed, however, was directed towards the Labour Club – not much difference here from the year before, he mused.

One chap, a smallish man with thick glasses, did express interest in the Socialist Society, and Burren discovered that he was a fellow Reed scholar. The man, whose name was coincidentally Reed, had already discovered his Reed contemporaries and described them to Burren as best he could. Burren did not meet them, however, and had already concluded in any case that not everyone wanted to be associated with a group simply because they had been awarded the same scholarship.

He listened to Robert Wilcox give his welcome as he had done the year before, and again he speculated on whether the Principal hankered after the political life. He supposed it must be difficult to relinquish that kind of life: the closeness to where things happen, the big events, the contacts, the socialising and the gossip, even though you may still be removed from the point of power and decision-taking.

Jasmine was there too. He talked with her briefly and asked her if she knew that Paul Jenkins had gone to LSE. She said that she did know, and that she had encouraged him in that direction. Burren was a little surprised at this, but even more surprised when Jasmine told him that her own family lived near Paul's father in Muswell Hill. She gave him a secretive smile as she told him that Paul was one of the nicest young men she knew. The story was unfolding, and he was fascinated. He laughed quietly to himself. No wonder Paul knew so much, yet was discreet about disclosing anything.

The following day he went to meet Jane at the railway station. He had written to tell her that he would meet her and to say how much he was looking forward to seeing her again – and as he approached the station entrance he became more and more excited at the prospect. The station was very busy with students returning for the commencement of the new academic year. He enquired about Jane's train and was assured that it was running only a few minutes late. He checked the platform for the train's arrival and made his way in that direction.

He watched the trains entering and leaving the station in much the same way, he imagined, as a devoted trainspotter. The trains gave the appearance of long gigantic snakes, as the carriages curled and slithered slowly towards or away from platforms. At last he could see the train that Jane would be on approaching, slowly edging towards the platform and finally coming to a halt by the buffers. He looked for Jane amidst the rush of people pouring out from the train and through the tangled crowd he caught a glimpse of her slim figure lifting her case from the compartment. He rushed forward to greet her, and she turned, saw him and smiled broadly.

'Hello,' they said simultaneously.

He took her in his arms and held her tightly to him. Then quickly he released her and grinned affectionately.

She asked, 'Are you pleased to see me?'

He bent forward and kissed her softly on the cheek. 'Of course,' he said.

Her brown eyes communicated her pleasure.

They walked down the platform. Carrying her cases, he watched the neat lines of her figure, and passed his eye down to her slender legs. He'd almost forgotten how very attractive she was.

'When did you get back?' she asked.

He looked at her dark, closely cropped hair, and her high cheekbones with creases beneath as she smiled. The Mediterranean sun had lent a richness to her face.

She gave a small laugh. 'When did you get back?'

'You really look very good.' He was lost in her presence.

'When did you get back?' Jane laughingly persisted.

He suddenly realised she had spoken.

'Three days ago,' he said. 'I came back and saw Paul before he left for London. He is going to LSE, you know, and I've got his old room.'

They had now reached the station forecourt.

'Look, let's take a taxi to Morton. I can show you my room, and we can have tea before I take your luggage on to your college.'

Jane nodded agreement.

They entered his room and he led her across to the window. She stood awhile looking out, then turned and took in the interior of his room. As she stood framed in the dormer window he drew her towards him. She relaxed her body against his.

'Have you missed me?' she asked, resting her head on his shoulder.

Her could feel the softness of her hair on his cheek. 'But of course,' he whispered.

They moved their heads together slowly, exploring, finding one another again. He felt the gentle texture of her skin on his lips, until their mouths met in soft moist kisses. They moved towards the bed, swept books and clothes to the floor, and sat down. Eagerly they sought each other. He could feel her firm breasts, vibrant against his chest. They slid downwards on the bed, still holding one another.

'Tell me about the building site,' said Jane mischievously.

Later, as he made tea, Jane said, 'Now tell me about the building site.'

'There is nothing to tell. It was just a boring old building site. I told you any interesting bits in my letters.'

He handed her a cup of tea.

'Well, they were pretty dismal,' she said. 'What about Tom? He sounded quite a character.'

He had not mentioned anything in his last letter to her about Tom's disapproval of what he had said in his talk to the local Labour Party. He still had mixed feelings on that subject but didn't wish to discuss them now. Better for Jane to continue to think of Tom as a character.

'He is fine,' he said.

Jane sensed that something had changed but did not say anything. They both sat silently drinking their tea; she thinking about suitable tourist posters as decor for her room, he thumbing through the pages of the *New Statesman*. Jane was the first to break the silence by asking about his friends at college.

'They're back,' he said looking up from his journal. 'We, that is, Frank Bainwell and Chris Megson, had a drink together yesterday in the Rose & Crown. Quite a binge really.' He thought for a moment. 'Frank was odd, though.'

Jane was curious. 'In what way?' she asked.

He told her how Frank had been drinking heavily before he had arrived, and then continued in the same way until Chris came along. He went on to mention the odd remark that Frank had made before Chris had joined them.

'It could be anything,' said Jane, rather disappointed that it wasn't something more gossipy.

'No, there was something behind it. Of course I didn't want to ask him outright. It would have seemed like I was prying.'

'Which you would have been,' said Jane. 'That is what I would have done.'

'Well yes. But you know what I mean.'

She nodded.

'I feel sure he would have opened up and told me eventually but Chris joining us put an end to it.'

'I don't suppose it is very important,' said Jane dismissing the subject. 'Probably a domestic argument.'

He recalled Doris's self-same words in the bar the day before and smiled inwardly at the unity of their thought.

'You haven't asked me about my holiday,' said Jane, going over to her luggage.

'You told me about it in your letters,' he said defensively.

'You haven't seen these,' she said, thrusting a folder of photos in his hand.

She sat beside him and together they looked through the photos of her summer in Greece until it was time to leave.

Robert Wilcox was now telling Burren how his part of the subject would be handled, and which part would be covered by Timothy Framley. This was to be Burren's introduction to British politics and government.

'I shall handle the more formal aspects of British government. For example, Cabinet government, the executive versus the legislature, the constitutional aspects of law, select committees, delegated legislation, the nationalised industries in their relationship to parliament – that sort of thing.' His darting eyes came to focus on Burren. 'As you see, there is a lot of material here, and as I expect others have already told you in their subjects, we cannot hope to cover all aspects. You have to read up on omitted topics with necessary guidance.' He smiled at Burren and then hurried on. 'And of course that is only half of the subject, there is Timothy's part too: the principles of democratic government, the nature and function of political parties, the evolution of executive power, different electoral systems, etcetera.' He gave a small laugh. 'The more interesting bits, perhaps.'

He looked across his desk at Burren, his alert face searching as if for confirmation of his thoughts. 'You had a good year, John. Both Mike Dawson and John Edell reported well on your work and you did an article for the *New Age* which drew some favourable comment. Did you get any response from Maurice Watkins?'

'Yes,' replied Burren. 'He sent me quite a gracious letter given that I was highly critical of his argument. In fact he offered me a standing invitation to take lunch with him whenever I'm in London.'

'Can be quite charming,' said the Principal. With an impish grin he suddenly asked Burren, 'Not thinking of decamping, are you?'

Burren smiled. 'No, I think that is unlikely.'

The Principal changed tack. 'Well, this year we are looking for much the same from you and I hope you have a good year.' There was a pause, and then he asked, 'Are you going to write more?'

'I'm interested in looking at US policy towards Western Europe since 1945, if I have time. And I want to tackle it from the angle of socialist criticism.'

'That sounds quite ambitious.'

Burren acknowledged that he may not have the time to complete it.

'And what of your future plans?' He waited for Burren to respond.

Burren hesitated before replying. 'I have not definitely settled on anything yet.' And then he found himself telling Robert Wilcox how much he was looking forward to his special option course and how this may decide matters for him.

Robert Wilcox gave his knowing smile. 'That's fine. When you are ready, just let me know and we can talk about it.' He looked at a sheet of paper on his desk before continuing. 'Now, I should like to put you with Mike Dawson for second-year surveillance.' He gave a small chortle at his use of the word.

Burren accepted this with thanks. So, he was to be rid of Timothy Framley!

He left the Principal's office and went off to the university library to read for his first essay in British government. The subject: 'To what extent is Cabinet government the dominant feature of the British political system?' He expected Jane to be in the library.

He had already spoken to the Labour Club's discussion group on the subject of his article in the *New Age*, as he had agreed to do before the summer break. Chris Megson, now installed as the secretary of the Labour Club, had warned him of the dissenting element that existed in the Club and made reference to Frank Bainwell in this context as 'not always as helpful as he might be'. This was Chris's way of expressing Frank's dissent from his own orthodox views.

The discussion group meeting was well attended, and Morton students from both years were there in good numbers. He spoke for about half an hour and then the meeting held an open discussion. The subject was hardly likely to be controversial in itself before such a Labour group, and this proved to be very much the case. So much so in fact that the subject was turned upon its head.

Laissez-faire was thrown out of the window and the discussion centred upon the role of the state: state ownership of basic industries, and the particular form that ownership should take. He had argued that where some form of state control was agreed as necessary, the means should be flexible and very much adapted to the requirements of the particular organisation or industry being controlled. To him, nationalisation was not the be all and end all. This led to a stormy debate, with himself, Chris Megson and Tom Croft focusing the views of the flexible approach side of the argument, and Frank Bainwell and Bill Williams defending in every detail the nationalisation principle.

The discussion had so taken hold that it was followed up amongst many of them when they left the meeting and went into the Rose & Crown. Later, as Burren walked back to college, he confided to Chris Megson that the sharp difference of outlook between the two groups in the discussion was probably as much a matter of an age gap as anything else.

Frank Bainwell's generation – those who had helped spawn the Morrisonian nationalisation principle – saw it as an article of faith of the socialist creed, and were highly sceptical of anyone who wanted to introduce more flexibility into the concept of public ownership.

'It is the religious principle in politics,' said Chris, 'expressed with an absolute certainty and a total refusal to entertain anything seen as undermining the faith.'

They continued to talk about the socialist dilemma and discussed how pragmatism is, or is not, possible within a socialist view of politics, until they reached the college.

The meeting that he was invited to at the University Conservative Club was a very different event. On the evening of the meeting he went along and met the chairman and secretary. They were both dressed in dark three-piece suits and were formal in manner from the outset. He began to wonder if he had after all made a serious mistake in agreeing to speak.

After the officers of the Club had introduced themselves, he was told of the arrangements for the discussion, including how long the meeting was to be. He wanted to know of their own interest in key aspects of the free trade argument but was told that it was Maurice Watkins who principally interested them. When giving some thought to his talk to the young Conservatives, he had anticipated that perhaps they would be more interested in the overall position of Watkins rather than a narrow focus on free trade.

He told as much as he knew of Watkins and how he had received an open invitation to have lunch with him. The two Conservative officers then led him into the meeting. It was a packed meeting, and as Burren took his place beside the chairman he could tell that it was going to be a lively evening. He spoke for half an hour during which there were several interruptions from the audience, but he adhered strictly to his prepared script. He pointed to the lineage between Watkins and the nineteenth-century anti-Corn Law movement, and suggested that there was a hidden tension between modern Conservatism and this historical perspective.

There followed a short discussion in which there were ferocious exchanges between the pro-Watkins group and the antis. His presence was no longer required. He had not appreciated the extent of Watkins's popularity amongst this generation of Conservatives. This was all the more curious in a way as Watkin's views on economic matters were in marked contrast to the policy of the government of which he was a member.

As he was leaving the chairman and secretary apologised for the rowdiness of the meeting and thanked him more than was necessary. Their previous formality was quickly falling away, and he found them eager to discuss politics more broadly. They were keen to know more about Morton. He took the opportunity to broach the subject of possible exchanges between the Socialist Society and their Club. He explained that he would have to approach his own committee but that he anticipated their agreement. On a number of carefully selected topics, discussion between them might make for interesting and lively meetings.

Furthermore, as he pointed out, such meetings might well carry appeal to a wider student audience. The two Conservative Club officers were quite excited by the prospect and immediately started to suggest topics.

He felt pleased with his innovative idea. He was sure there was merit in having some exchange between the socialists and Conservatives, whereas he knew there was no prospect of this happening between the Labour Club and the Conservatives. He decided he would speak to Ken Murray and Dipankar about it.

Over breakfast the following morning he told others of his plan to have a few joint meetings between the Socialist Society and the Conservative Club. The group with whom he ate breakfast was composed of the same people as the year before, and hence the latent political assumptions underpinning any discussion were also the same as the year before. Nothing had changed. Whilst often not altogether sharing their view, he nevertheless enjoyed their company and quite often used them as a sounding board for the conventional Labour view.

Bill Williams offered him his advice: 'You want to avoid that sort of thing, John. They'll filch any good ideas and adapt them to their own purpose in exactly the same way as their seniors in government borrow anything good from the Opposition.'

Others at the table echoed agreement.

Burren winked at Bill Williams. 'Don't worry, Bill, I'll be sure to refer to you before agreeing to anything.'

As he was leaving the dining room he met Chris Megson.

'How did the meeting with the Conservatives go?' Chris was eager to know.

Burren smiled. 'I do believe it was by far the most interesting meeting I've been to,' he said as he continued on his way out of college.

'Well?' Chris was anxious for more.

'I've not got time now, I'm on my way to meet someone and I mustn't keep him waiting. But the meeting became embroiled in quite vicious exchanges between the pro- and anti- Watkins factions, and I tell you, Chris, the free marketeers were substantially in a majority. What is more, I do believe that the acceptance of the welfare state together with public ownership by the Conservative government will not last in the long term. The meeting last night was most revealing. The people I met are the next generation of politicians and they will prevail. In any case, I believe there is a deep, instinctive inclination towards the free market within conservatism.' He patted Chris's shoulder. 'And now I really must go.'

10

It seemed that the weeks were passing by at an alarming rate, as Burren prepared for another tutorial with Timothy Framley. He was near the end of the tutorials with Robert Wilcox and he reflected on these as he made his way to meet with Framley.

Overall they had been disappointing. The tutorials had been substantial enough in themselves and undoubtedly Robert Wilcox knew his subject well and was able to illustrate his points from personal experience and with personal anecdote.

That was not the problem. It was simply that he seemed less than interested, and yet Burren knew this was not in fact the case. The Principal was very interested in his subject. But he was unexciting as a tutor – he did not enthuse. He was at the same time very sound when it came to showing how government works in practice. All of this led Burren to speculate that perhaps despite their experience, practitioners of a subject – be it politics, law or whatever – do not necessarily have the inspirational element that makes for a good tutor.

'Sit down. I won't be long.' The voice had an edge of impatience to it.

He selected the red upholstered chair, opposite the one that Framley himself used when he came round from behind his desk. Unlike the other tutors, Framley had installed himself in an attic room outside college, overlooking the High Street.

Burren looked idly around the room at the book-lined walls and then to the dormer window where rain was gently dropping against the panes. The room was tastefully furnished, though its correctness of style also conveyed Framley's formality. He assumed that the room itself and in particular its location were all part of the academic image that Framley so successfully wove around himself.

The tutorials with Framley were in many ways as disappointing as those with Robert Wilcox. He simply could not establish contact with Framley. There was no sympathy of mind: they seemed forever to be at cross-purposes. It was not that Framley was altogether hostile, far from it, at times he was quite friendly. But the chemistry between them simply did not seem to work. Ennui seemed to settle naturally upon Framley.

He continued to read the typescript lying on his blotting folder, frowning occasionally at something in the print. Burren looked at his face more closely. He was undeniably handsome, a little too much so, perhaps. His was the kind of face that belonged to men in advertisements, usually offering women some brand of chocolate, or escorting them after they had bathed with a luxurious soap.

Framley placed the sheet he had been reading carefully on top of a pile of foolscap on his desk and then came round and sat opposite Burren.

'Right, read away,' he said in a voice that implied that it was Burren rather than himself who had delayed the proceedings.

Burren lifted his essay from its folder and began to read: 'The title is ...'

'I know the title,' said Framley. 'The function of second chambers, with special reference to Great Britain.' He smiled at his own thoroughness.

Burren began again, and settled into a steady pace of reading once he found that Framley did not interrupt as he normally did. As he read on he felt rather pleased with himself and thought it read well. He looked up and saw Framley appearing to look distractedly at a bookshelf. He assumed that a book was out of place, or askew – something which spoiled Framley's sense of symmetry.

He now turned to face Burren. 'Too wordy,' he said.

Burren looked surprised.

'Too wordy,' repeated Framley, turning his attention once again to his bookshelf. Burren continued to read and became less confident in what he had written. He became aware of his own voice; it sounded strangely detached from himself and hollow within the room. Points which carried the force of his argument he now failed to emphasise properly in his reading.

Framley let him continue without further interruption. When he finished reading Framley leant back in his chair with one leg dangled languidly over the side.

He looked at Burren and asked, 'Did this topic grip your interest?'

'Yes. I didn't think it would at first because some of the reading was not overly interesting. But then I found that the need to achieve balance in the representation of interests and reconciling that with checks on power became fascinating.'

Framley nodded as if confirming a private thought, then he said, 'Your enthusiasm comes through in your work, and I don't wish to be overcritical because as I say you communicate enthusiastically and there is not a lot wrong with the content of this essay.' He checked himself, and then continued, 'Though I would have liked to see you give a bit more attention to the role of second chambers in representing different interests and different constituencies within the state. But no, my criticism if criticism it be ...'

Oh dear, thought Burren, he is now re-entering his pedantic mode.

'... is that you write in a too journalistic a style.'

Before Burren could respond, Framley quickly added, leaning forward in a confidential manner, 'Don't get me wrong, that is what makes your work read well and it is appealing, but I believe you need to edit more thoroughly.'

Burren was genuinely surprised by this change of approach.

Framley got up and crossed to a shelf and rearranged a book. He turned and asked Burren what special option he was going to take.

'I am hoping to take international organisation.'

Framley thought for a moment before saying, 'Very interesting.'

Framley rarely brought matters to a formal end but Burren knew that this tutorial had now finished and he began to place his papers in his case.

'Hold on a minute, John,' Framley said, and paused as though not sure just how to put what he was going to say. He then said, 'I should like your advice on something.'

Burren was surprised.

'Do you think we should accept Frank Bainwell's article for the next issue of *The New Age*? I have of course already asked Chris Megson for his view, but I should like to have yours as well.'

Burren knew what Chris Megson's view would be. Chris had become editor of *The New Age* after Paul Jenkins, largely by bending the ear of Framley. Burren knew too that Paul had opposed Chris becoming editor, and had felt that it required a broader approach than Chris would give it. Framley was looking directly at Burren, awaiting a response.

'I would include it,' said Burren. 'I don't agree with Frank Bainwell's line on public ownership but that is hardly relevant.'

Framley continued to look at him and he was aware of being tested. But for what? He wasn't sure.

He continued, 'It does not fit my idea of the New Age. Frank's views are I think too rooted in a traditional approach and are rather inflexible. I think *The New Age* should be representing new thinking and new ideas, but having said that, I would include it. I know he has worked hard on it. There is scope for the occasional piece which reflects older thinking.' He laughed. 'We haven't too many of those.'

Framley smiled. 'No, we haven't.' He then asked Burren, 'How is your own article coming along?'

'All right I think.' He was not entirely confident that he could do the work required in the time.

'On foreign policy, isn't it? From what you have said about your choice of option, this would seem to be your field of interest.'

'Yes. I think my study of economics, and also the politics course, have helped to steer my interest towards foreign policy.'

'Well, your choice of option did not take me by surprise.'

As he left the office he pondered Framley's change in attitude. It seemed to Burren that Framley now wanted to bring him into the camp, for what reason he did now know, but it was not unwelcome.

He mused further on the subject of Frank Bainwell's article. He had known that there was some discussion taking place about the article between Framley and Chris Megson. One evening, about two weeks past when most of the college had gone off to hear Aneurin Bevan speak at the Labour Club, he had entered the common room to look through the weekly journals and had been waylaid by Denis Greenfell. In his well-known conspiratorial style, Greenfell asked him if he knew that Framley wanted to reject Frank Bainwell's article in favour of one by Peter Smytheson on industrial relations. At the time, he had been inclined to dismiss the story as part of Greenfell's inveterate pursuit of gossip.

It now seemed that Greenfell was right all the time, though the Smytheson part of the rumour had not been established. More interesting in light of his own discussion with Framley was the likelihood that there was some difference of view between Framley and Chris Megson. If that was correct then it was possible that Framley was now beginning to question his own earlier assessment of Chris Megson: of Chris's judgement and suitability as editor. That would almost certainly explain Framley's approach to himself for advice.

Burren considered the day ahead as he walked towards the library. There was the reading that he had to complete for the coming tutorial with Framley on the subject of 'The oligarchic nature of political parties'. And after that, and much later in the evening and into the night, he had to put the finishing touches to his article for *The New Age*. The subject of the article increasingly occupied his interest. He was sure that Aneurin Bevan's comments, in speeches that he made in the House of Commons during the Second World War on the US attitude towards Europe, remained valid in the present day. It raised in turn the position of the French. Their perception of Europe's interest did not coincide with that of the US. He felt that if the US relied on Britain to represent the European view they were making a big mistake. It was apparent, certainly in the eyes of the French, that Britain was seen as an extension of the American view rather than as a modifying influence on American policy. The subject absorbed him, but he found it very time-consuming because most of the material that he needed to consult was in journals.

He saw Jane seated in her usual place as he entered the reading room, well immersed in her reading, and went and sat next to her.

She looked up. 'How did the meeting go?,' she asked.

'Well it was one of the most interesting . . .'

Tut-tutting from nearby occupants silenced him.

He smiled, 'I'll tell you about it later.'

The rest of his day was spent in reading avidly the theory of oligarchy as developed by Robert Michels, whilst Jane worked away on literary criticism. As they left the library they walked hand in hand in the direction of the Okebe meeting at the Socialist Society. He was pleased with the way in which the Society had started off the new session. The membership had increased, largely due to the enthusiasm and energy of Ken Murray, and to Burren's surprise and pleasure more of the first-year Morton people had joined than in the previous year.

The programme of talks and discussion groups had been agreed and this included at least two major outside speakers: Bob Griffiths, the shadow spokesman on colonial affairs, and Kwame Okebe, the Secretary-General of the Movement for Colonial Freedom.

'I hope my first meeting as chairman is going to go well,' he said to Jane. 'We agreed to Dipankar's suggestion of Okebe, but I understand he can be very inflammatory at meetings.'

Jane was reassuring. 'You'll be able to handle it,' she said.

He nevertheless remained concerned because there had already been some disagreement about the exact nature of Okebe's talk. Okebe was Ghanaian and wished to promote the Ghanaian cause for independence, whereas Burren wanted him to talk more broadly about the issues related to independence for the colonial empire. He conveyed those fears to Jane.

She replied in as matter of fact a way as she could, 'I'm sure that whatever you say, he will say what he wants to say.'

He replied. 'I'm sure you are right.'

The hall was already well packed with overseas students, most of them from the colonies, wishing to promote their own national cause he assumed. Burren and Jane went to the front of the hall where Ken Murray and Dipankar were waiting. He introduced them to Jane and cast a nervous eye around the audience. He turned to Dipankar and asked if he knew anything more about Okebe. Dipankar tried to reassure him and said that he had been at a meeting in London at which Okebe had spoken, and everything had been fine. He added that Okebe was a most powerful speaker. Burren felt uneasy.

Okebe had now arrived, accompanied by two other men whom Burren assumed were his own security people. They shook hands with him as he looked each of them in the eye with a piercing gaze. With Jane he was at his most charming, saying how pleased he was to see a beautiful woman amongst the grey men. He accompanied this comment with a huge laugh. He had a massive presence and knew it. There was a calmness about him, though Burren felt this might well be the stillness of a dormant volcano. The meeting started, and Burren introduced Okebe as one of the outstanding leaders of the independence movement.

When Okebe addressed the meeting he played with his

audience as a skilled musician might play a cadenza in a symphony. Burren formed the impression that Okebe knew exactly how to evoke a specific emotional response from his audience, and how far to take it. It was a consummate performance in which Okebe gave an historical survey of British imperialism, and stated that independence was not something that was in the gift of a British government and its people to grant, or deny. It was, in his view, an absolute, fundamental right. Nor was it for the British to decide when they thought a particular colony was ready for independence. Again, he stated, this was a right to be addressed at once. He concluded by saying that it was up to the British people, and especially that privileged group that held influence, to put pressure on their government to grant independence.

The response to his speech was nothing short of ecstatic. Everyone wanted to talk and Burren had some difficulty controlling the questions and contributions from the floor in the time available. At the end, Okebe beamed and acknowledged the applause with hands held aloft.

He turned to Burren and said, 'If the decision was theirs I'd have independence tomorrow.'

Burren laughed and acknowledged the truth of that.

He awoke late the following morning. Work on his article for *The New Age* had continued well into the early hours of the morning; but he was satisfied that he had done as much as he could and thought the article was now suitable for publication.

He was too late for breakfast in college. He looked in the mirror, pulled a face and turned away, then walked across his room and flung open the window. The wintry morning air licked stringently at his face and it smelt fresh, despite the traffic that he could see in the street below. He gulped the air into his lungs in his morning practice of breathing exercises. That finished, he threw his dressing gown around himself, grabbed his washing bag and made off towards the bathroom. He looked at his watch and saw that it was 9 am. There would be time to phone Jane and arrange breakfast at the Union if he hurried.

He broke into a run. He liked doing things in the grand manner from time to time – it made him feel good. It would be the more so shared with Jane. He saw Mrs Charnley at the corner of the corridor going through her ritual of sorting out her brooms and other cleaning appurtenances in preparation for the daily round.

'Good morning, Mrs Charnley,' he called as he rushed past. 'Can't stop. Haven't yet had my breakfast.' Mrs Charnley good-naturedly shook her head. He rounded the corner, continuing to to call, 'Just leave my room, I'll do it myself later.'

Jane looked at him over an appetising plate of bacon and eggs. 'But I've already had my breakfast,' she pleaded.

'Just have the toast, then, and I'll eat the rest,' he grinned. 'What gratitude. I take you out for breakfast at the Union of one of the finest universities and all you can say is "But I've already had my breakfast"! Look around you. All the famous figures of history have dined here.' He laughed. 'Well, some of them, anyway. And they are bidding you to take breakfast in their historical presence. Where is your feeling? Your sense of occasion?'

Jane eyed him quizzically. 'And what famous event are we celebrating this morning?'

'This morning,' he said in laughing self-mockery, 'we are celebrating my article!' He feigned reverence. He looked and sounded ridiculous.

Jane burst out laughing. 'I hope that doesn't mean more literary review by me,' she groaned.

He smiled benignly.

'Really, you are a fool,' she said affectionately. 'And that is the only reason?'

'But of course.'

They fell silent and continued with their breakfast. At least he did. The exaggeratedly refined accents of two young men, talking that intense, self-absorbed conversation of under-graduates, came drifting across to them. A third young man sat alone reading *The Times*. It was the complete picture of young men in a chrysalis of hauteur; a microcosm of life in the older universities. Yet insidiously the mores of this life ingressed even upon those previously untouched by privilege, such as himself. The absurdity of it was tragi-comedy. A building site became transformed into a university Union and in doing so he became the toy of institutions. It was not that it was ostenta-tious that made its effect telling, it was that you could not help but be affected. It became part of you because you wanted to feel that it must be so. It must be important, for this was its justification – its sole rationale. To ignore it was to be an ico-noclast to a degree that only the old can afford to indulge. Everything is important to you when you are young, and in that lay the subtle strength of the British system of class and privilege.

He looked across at Jane in that moment of self-awareness. The pale morning sun glimmering through the long sash win-dow made a picture of her that stirred sublime emotions within him. And he wanted nothing more at this moment than to be with her in this idyllic self-creation, uncomplicated and per-fectly conceived.

Jane saw him lost in a world of thought. 'What are you thinking about?' she asked.

He thought before replying, then evaded the question by asking, 'What do you want from this place? The university, I mean.'

'What makes you ask?'

'Because I should like to know.' Jane was still puzzled. 'Because I should like to know,' he quietly repeated.

Jane looked thoughtfully down at her coffee and then said, 'I suppose I want what everyone tells me I should want.'

He leant forward, 'And what is that?'

205

Jane laughed self-consciously. 'Well ...' she drew imaginary lines on the tablecloth with a teaspoon, then looked up. 'That I should feel it has been one of the profound experiences in my life, if not *the* experience.'

'And has it been?'

Jane again gave a self-conscious laugh. 'You become a bit embarrassed about it after a while.' Her expression became serious as she continued, 'The point is that so much is expected of you if you had to struggle to get here, and if your parents have struggled too on your behalf. Your family, your friends it is they who impose the image upon you, and you have to act according to that image, or else you have let them down.' She looked at him. 'Do you know what I mean?'

'Yes, I certainly do,' he said.

'Well. That is it, you see. It is all right for your first year because you are still impressed by all the trappings, but after that, if you have any imagination at all, you rebel.' She frowned. 'It is then that you pay the price of both sides. You become unpopular here, and also at home. After all, you've been accorded an honour, therefore what right have you to criticise? That's how it goes.' She was smiling her impish smile again. 'Do you know, I haven't really talked about it to anyone before. Curious, isn't it?'

The beginnings of a collectively febrile state of mind was taking hold of the Morton community. The origins of that state of mind could not be precisely defined but there were discernible influences, the most obvious of which was the fact that a point had been reached in the academic cycle that pointed to impending examinations. They were five months away, but nevertheless the psychosis had already set in. Minds became seized of the knowledge that soon there would be a return to old jobs, unless other opportunities were explored. And there was the rub and the panic: how to pursue opportunities whilst focusing on examinations. Quite apart from the wish to do well on the course for its own sake, thriving ambition fostered the same objective. Everyone was affected.

Burren was not immune to these pressures and he had still not made up his mind about his future beyond Morton. He was sure of only one thing: he had no wish to return to a building site. He knew of only one person who seemed free of this anxiety and that was Chris Megson. He appeared calm and unaffected most of the time, but then he had already decided where he was going and seemed certain that it would happen.

The common room appeared empty as Burren put his head around the door, but too late he realised he was not on his own. Sitting at the far end was the unmistakeable figure of Denis Greenfell, his scrubbly brown head of hair visible above the back of the chair. He didn't wish to draw Greenfell's attention to himself, knowing that once that happened he would become captive to Greenfell's endless verbal outpourings. Yet he was also aware that if he chose to beat a retreat Greenfell would now call out. In any case it was now too late. Greenfell, who obviously had been dozing, had now awoken and seen him.

'Hello, John. I didn't at first hear you come in.'

Burren looked at Greenfell. Saw the plump, rather flushed face with spectacles halfway down his nose.

'I have something to tell you,' said Greenfell, already conveying a conspiratorial air.

Burren knew that this was but the opening move – a kind of verbal hors-d'oeuvre before the more succulent main course of political subterfuge. Greenfell looked at him through the web of intrigue that he had permanently spun around himself.

'Did you know that Frank Bainwell's name is going forward for House chairman?'

Burren tried not to show too much interest but was genuinely surprised at this, assuming it was true, and said, 'Well!'

'I thought you were going to stand, and as Frank is a friend of yours ...'

Burren cut him short. 'What gave you that idea I'm not?'

207

'Well, I ...' Greenfell was now unsure of himself. 'I thought you ...'

Why should Frank Bainwell decide quite suddenly to stand for House chairman? It simply wasn't like him. Even Greenfell's gossip machine had let him down here, Burren told himself. Frank had always disdained any desire for the job of House chairman, always protesting strongly whenever anyone suggested he stand that it prevented one from taking an independent line.

He asked Greenfell, 'Who told you this?'

To his great surprise, Greenfell replied, 'Chris Megson.'

If this was true, then Frank had certainly sprung a last-minute surprise, for the election was that very evening. Had Greenfell been told because he was a notorious intriguer and therefore likely to distribute the news, or had he found out by chance through his usual wheedling methods? Was it all simply a piece of gossip on Greenfell's part? He hadn't given the evening's business meeting much thought, but he now decided that he would go along to see if Frank was nominated.

Greenfell said that he must go, and Burren too now left the common room and made off to the university library deep in his own thoughts. He supposed that both Frank and Chris would already be in the library in their usual places. Both of them were now using the university library regularly in preference to the college, and they quite often joined Jane and himself for coffee at the Coffee House. This may offer a chance to talk about the House chairmanship, he thought.

He hurried up the library stairs, swung open the heavy wooden doors and heard them shut behind him with the faintest of creaks. The library was already full of students in the daily pursuit of learning. Stealthily he walked to the far bookshelf. Fortunately the book he wanted was still there, and selecting it he returned to where Jane had kept a seat for him. He grinned 'good morning' as he sat down beside her and then got down to the task of reading about Cabinet government. Parts of the book were dull and repetitive and made the task a painstaking one. He concluded that the book could be substantially reduced without affecting the argument. He looked at Jane from time to time – she worked in her usual relaxed way.

Promptly at 10.45 Chris Megson came and asked if they were ready to go for coffee. They nodded agreement. The four of them walked along to the Coffee House, commenting on the mildness of the winter's day. The Coffee House was busy in its usual way with students, but Jane spotted a free table and headed for it; the others followed.

'Well done,' said Frank. 'That was sharp action.'

Jane smiled and proceeded to talk to Frank about the film she had recently seen, *The Snows of Kilimanjaro*, showing at the Classic Cinema. Chris lit his pipe and started telling Burren about what was happening in the Labour Club. Burren looked across from Frank to Chris; there was nothing in the manner of either of them that gave a clue as to what they may have planned for the meeting that evening. He wanted to ask them outright but had no wish to drag Jane into the affair.

Very soon both Frank and Chris left to go back to the library. Frank was certainly keen on the bookwork recently, thought Burren. Not so long ago he would spend plenty of time chatting and gossiping over coffee; indeed it seemed to be one of his favourite pastimes.

Walking back to the library he mentioned what appeared to be yet another change in the behaviour of Frank to Jane. She said that she too had thought that both of them had left rather quickly. He went on to tell her of the coming election of House chairman and what Greenfell had told him.

'But why should he keep it secret?' she asked.

'That is what puzzles me,' he said.

Jane asked if the House chairman's job was important.

'It all depends. There has been much manoeuvring for it in the past. You make yourself known to the right people and that can be useful, I suppose, in relation to moving on. Often however, people are not keen at this stage because they think it will interfere with their academic work. At this stage you are either known, or you are not,' he said.

'Were you thinking of standing?' asked Jane.

'No, indeed not,' he said a little too emphatically.

She looked pleased, he thought, with his response, though he couldn't think why.

'I didn't realise he was interested in the job. He never indicated the least interest in it. In fact he was apt to make fun of it. I thought there was too much of the rebel about him for the task.' He was speaking as much to himself as to Jane.

'It is not important,' she said.

'I know it isn't, but it irritates me. After all he has said about it in the past. How hypocritical can you get?'

'You don't know it is true yet,' she said trying to be emollient.

'Maybe not,' he said, feeling quite sure it was true.

They entered the library and resumed their places. The question of the House chairman kept intruding into his reading on Cabinet government.

The common room was full as the House chairman and secretary prepared for the meeting. Burren positioned himself at the rear of the room. Greenfell slipped in beside him with a knowing wink. He saw that Chris Megson and Frank Bainwell were not sitting together.

Joan Symonds from the other side of him asked, 'Did you know that Frank Bainwell is standing for chairman?'

'Yes,' he said.

'Why don't you stand?' she asked. 'I'll nominate you.'

'I'm not interested in standing, but thanks all the same.'

The chairman brought the meeting to attention. Frank Bainwell, as social secretary, reported to the meeting. He was his usual effective and humorous self. He was popular with his fellow students, that was plain to see; Burren had known that for a long time. Slowly the meeting made its way through the agenda and at last reached the item: 'Election of officers'.

'The meeting is open to nominations for chairman,' declared the current Chairman.

Greenfell turned quickly to Burren. 'I'll nominate you, John.'

'No, I do not wish to stand,' replied Burren firmly.

Greenfell looked upset and annoyed, though Burren could not understand why.

In the meantime he had heard Frank Bainwell's name mentioned but could not hear who had nominated him. He turned to Greenfell and asked, 'Who nominated?'

'Chris Megson,' said Greenfell.

Frank's nomination was quickly seconded and he was elected unopposed.

Greenfell turned to Burren in disgust. 'You are a fool. Why didn't you allow me to nominate you? You stand outside of any grouping and that would have been good.'

'So do you,' Burren replied with a smile. 'I'm sorry if I've let you down but I really did not want to be considered and there is something odd about the whole business.'

He saw a smile pass across Greenfell's face.

He went to his room, lit a cigarette and looked out of the window across the top of the city. There was something inordinately comforting and reassuring in seeing old buildings illuminated by street lamps at night. He could not properly explain the business of Frank Bainwell and the chairmanship to himself, and this bothered him. He felt that Frank didn't really want the job but was driven by other considerations, and what these were he didn't know.

Had he really wanted the chairmanship for himself? He didn't think so, though he hadn't, apart from mentioning the matter to Jane, talked to anyone about it so the idea had not been tested. He mistrusted Greenfell's motives so that was no help. The competitive instinct is a strong driving force and motive is not best explained by an interested party, he told himself. Without knowing why, he found himself recalling his old friend Tom from the building site saying to him that to get to the top you have to sell so much of yourself, that once there you are everybody's property. He laughed to himself; Tom was obviously not speaking from experience.

The last meeting of the Socialist Society under Burren's chairmanship was about to take place. He and Ken Murray stood waiting for Bob Griffiths, the shadow Colonial Secretary, to arrive. The Executive Committee had just met prior to the evening's event at which Ken Murray was elected as the new chairman, and Peter Smytheson, a first-year Morton student, was to become secretary.

He was pleased that both of these names had gone through unopposed. Ken Murray would be a good chairman, he was sure of that. It was largely his drive and energetic pursuit of increasing the membership that had led to an all-time increase of members. He could be persuasive in discussion too, as Burren had found out. He was also pleased to see a fellow Morton student, in Peter Smytheson, continue the college's representation amongst the officers of the Society. Peter Smytheson was a trade union officer with the Electrical Trades Union and he had been active in the Society since he arrived at Morton. He had wanted to promote industrial subjects for discussion, such as the role of the trade unions both at a national level and within the international community. Burren thought this would be good for the Society as it would provide a balance between the political and the industrial side.

He saw Jasmine enter the hall on her own. Robert Wilcox had told him that he could not come as he would be in London. He drew Jane's attention to Jasmine and suggested they go and have a word with her.

After introducing the two women to one another he asked Jasmine if she knew Bob Griffiths.

'A little,' she said.

'Then do come and meet him before we start the meeting,' said Burren.

As they went back to the platform Bob Griffiths appeared. Burren knew him only from newspaper pictures and he was surprised to see that Griffiths was shorter than he expected. He was balding and wore a moustache. There was a military touch about him in appearance and manner. Burren and Ken Murray welcomed him to the meeting and they shook hands. Burren then introduced Jane and Jasmine. Griffiths kissed Jasmine on both cheeks and said how pleased he was to see her looking as beautiful as ever. She clearly knew him better than she had disclosed earlier.

Burren introduced Griffiths and began the meeting. Griffiths spoke for longer than he intended. Halfway through his talk he felt he had to explain, as he afterwards told Burren, and go into a caveat on the unforeseen legacy of colonial rule. He went on to tell his audience that this was significant in the case of Cyprus with its strategic position in the Eastern Mediterranean.

His talk was well received and he had no difficulty with the questions that followed, though it was interesting that when asked what an incoming Labour government would do in respect to Cyprus, he reverted to the standard response that it would depend upon the circumstances at the time.

After the meeting, Burren with Jane and others went to the Rose & Crown where they continued to talk about the situation in Cyprus and what should be done.

Burren was congratulated on his period as chairman by Ken Murray and Peter Smytheson, but Jane interjected by joking that they should not overinflate an already well-inflated ego. He was by now becoming used to Jane's tendency to bring him back down to earth with a bump. He looked at her with an indulgent smile whilst assuring the other two that despite a deflated ego he would continue to help the Society, just as Dipankar Shastri and Paul Jenkins had done before him.

He sat in the Principal's office and waited for the last session on politics whilst Robert Wilcox read over some letters before signing them. Outside the gloom of the day contrasted with the warmth of the office, emphasised by the intimate light cast by the reading lamp on the desk.

At last the Principal looked up. 'I am sorry about that, John. I just had to get these few pieces of correspondence to the post.'

He smiled the way he did with anyone first entering his office. He now excused himself again whilst he spoke on his internal phone to Jasmine in the adjoining office and asked her to come in and collect the mail. Jasmine entered and he passed her the letters. Burren noticed that Jasmine was wearing an autumn-coloured dress which he thought set off her appearance to best effect.

Robert Wilcox turned to him. 'Now, perhaps we can get down to business. This is the last of our tutorials together, I believe?'

'Yes, it is.'

'Right, so you are going to be talking about Cabinet government. Please go ahead.'

Burren proceeded to read selectively from his essay. There was no interruption from Robert Wilcox but when Burren had finished he asked him if he was impressed by Jennings' book on Cabinet government. The book, it was claimed in some quarters, was the authoritative work on the subject.

Burren hesitated a little and then said, 'I did a lot of work on Jennings and whilst it covered the subject comprehensively I felt that it did not provide much empirical evidence for the assumptions made about the working of the Cabinet. Is that fair criticism, do you think?' He looked to Robert Wilcox for confirmation.

'Yes, I think that is fair.'

Burren wanted some confirmation on the practical inner workings of the Cabinet and decided to ask, 'In your experience, does what a textbook such as Jennings says about the Cabinet reflect the way it works in reality?'

Robert Wilcox looked a little doubtful before replying. 'Well of course I only viewed it from the outside, but from what I gleaned during my period in the Attlee government, and the titbits that came down from on high' – he chortled – 'the account is pretty accurate. And don't forget, he had access to a number of people in government, not least Herbert Morrison. And I believe the account to be largely true irrespective of which political party is in office, or whoever is the Prime Minister. Though naturally each individual Prime Minister has his own particular style.'

Robert Wilcox lapsed into reflective mode. At last from the shadow behind the reading lamp he said, 'You have had a good session, John, with both myself and Timothy. You have every reason to feel pleased. For my part I have enjoyed our discussions and I like the way you have challenged some of the accepted orthodoxy in the subject.'

'I have enjoyed them too,' said Burren trying to sound genuine. In fact he still thought Robert Wilcox was uninspiring as a tutor, though he liked him in other respects.

The Principal was speaking again. 'You have been very active in recent weeks with chairing the Socialist Society. I understand that it is growing in popularity and you had a very successful meeting with Bob Griffiths, I hear.'

Jasmine has put in a good word, thought Burren.

'Bob Griffiths was excellent,' he said. 'He gave a first-rate analysis of the implications of colonial rule for the post-imperial situation.'

'Yes, he is good,' said Robert Wilcox. 'It could be seen when I was still in parliament that he was a rising star.'

Burren looked at the alert face of the Principal. Surely he must still miss the life. He was young enough to return, Burren thought.

Robert Wilcox returned to the subject of the Socialist Society and teasingly said to Burren, 'I wondered why you chose the Socialist Society in preference to the Labour Club.'

Burren smiled and said, 'The reason is very straightforward. I thought there would be more scope for independent thought in the Socialist Society. The Labour Club seems to me to be trapped in a conformity of ideas – to a tyranny of ideas if you like.' Robert Wilcox smiled at the phrase.

'That may sound a little paradoxical in view of the accepted contrast between a supposed Marxist Society and the Labour Club, but I believe it to be true.'

'Yes, I see,' said Robert Wilcox, giving nothing away.

And as an afterthought Burren said, 'And Paul Jenkins played some part – he helped persuade me.'

'Ah, did he,' said Robert Wilcox, chuckling to himself. 'He can be quite persuasive. He wants to follow his father, I believe.' Then as much to himself as to Burren he said, 'A very fine man.'

The Principal now changed tack. 'And of course you have written again for *The New Age*. When is the new issue due out?'

'It should be out in a few days,' said Burren.

'And you have written on the topic that you told me about?' he smiled enquiringly.

Burren was enthusiastic. 'Yes, I worked well into the early hours to complete it in time for inclusion.'

'I look forward to reading it. It seems to me that you have discovered an area of study that is attracting your interest more and more. In view of that have you decided on your option course?'

Burren again became enthusiastic. 'I want very much to take the international organisation option.'

'Well that seems logical,' said the Principal, giving a short laugh. 'Did you know that very few people choose that option, so much so that we have to negotiate for a tutor from within the university? I think you'll like him. His name is Sean Halloran. He is excellent and we were very lucky to get him. Very young and very bright.'

He looked directly at Burren. 'Any more thoughts about the future?'

He didn't want to be negative and disappoint Robert Wilcox, but in fact he couldn't really add to what he had said before. He found himself saying that he would like to discuss matters with the tutor for international organisation.

'Yes, well, that makes sense.' He gave Burren a thoughtful glance. 'No parliamentary ambitions? I thought you might be interested in a political career, hence my earlier question about the Socialist Society.'

'Yes, I thought perhaps that was the reason for your question.' He hesitated and thought before continuing. 'As a result of being here, the mental horizon expands enormously and similarly possible careers. I want to be sure, though. You raise the question of a political career. Well, whilst I am not pursuing that objective at the moment I feel I shouldn't rule anything out.'

The Principal smiled benignly. 'It takes us back to the initial interview, doesn't it?'

'Yes, I know. It does.'

'Look, John, come and discuss the subject with me whenever you feel the need.'

'Thank you,' Burren responded, genuinely appreciative of the Principal's interest.

11

There were many of them gathered in the saloon bar of the Rose & Crown. Most of the second-year students from Morton were there, and some staff too. Burren was with Jane and Chris Megson and Frank Bainwell. No one could recall what had brought them all together – what event it was that they were celebrating, if any. Nevertheless, there was a great atmosphere of bonhomie pervading the saloon bar. Timothy Framley was seen to come in with Jasmine and take up a place at the far end of the room.

Jane was talking to Chris Megson about the redevelopment that was going on in the centre of Newcastle, whilst Frank and Burren were saying to one another how each year of Morton students seemed different from the others, and how a group identity seems to emerge. They speculated on whether this communicated itself to staff, or if they viewed the matter quite differently.

Burren suddenly turned the conversation by asking Frank about his future plans.

Frank immediately became defensive. 'What makes you ask?' he said.

'Well, you seem to be conformist these days.' Burren smiled knowingly. 'And making the right moves.'

'Hold on a minute,' said Frank, becoming agitated.

Burren was not to be deterred however and said, 'You surely can't deny that you have changed, to say the least, from the man who arrived here last year full of notions about only wanting a liberal education.'

Frank became still more defensive. 'Things are not quite as simple as they seem when you first arrive.'

'Well that is very true,' said Burren, acknowledging the obvious truth of the comment. But he was curious and wanted to know more, and to discover what lay behind Frank's recent change and the bout of heavy drinking at the beginning of the year. He decided on the direct approach and asked Frank if his change in outlook was created by his need to justify his time at Morton to those back home.

Frank looked at him with an expression that amounted almost to pity. 'I don't believe you begin to understand,' he said. 'Or him,' he added, pointing towards Chris Megson.

'Well tell me more, then.'

Frank hesitated, undecided whether to continue with the conversation, but then looking up from his beer glass he said, 'You'll remember that occasion back at the beginning of the year in the Rose & Crown when we had just returned after the summer before Chris arrived. Well, I was on the point of telling you then but his enthusiasm combined with yours made it difficult and so I just closed up.' He looked straight at Burren. 'I had been drinking quite a bit before you arrived, you know.'

Burren laughed. 'I guessed that.'

'Oh yes, I had been drinking well before you arrived. I had quarrelled with Dorothy, you see. We had argued about me coming back here. She said two years away from home was too long, and then she said it was wasted time anyway because I wouldn't have anything to show for it. I tried to reason with her and told her it was something I had always wanted to do, but she wouldn't listen. She kept saying it wasn't fair. There was one almighty flare-up and finally I left to come back. But of course I was very unhappy about it.

'And so, you see, I have to be able to offer her something. In any case, the pressures from home are only part of it, and there are other things too, you know. We do have a conscience. Sacrifices have to be made and you feel in some way that you have to show it has all been worthwhile in some tangible form.' He took a swig of his beer. 'And then there is the internal crisis.'

He gave a resigned smile. 'You subject yourself to being tested and so you become correspondingly concerned about failure. You need to prove something to yourself.'

'I know,' said Burren.

By this time Jane's conversation with Chris had run its course and they were both listening to Frank. He looked at each of them in turn. 'Then something happens to you. One day you look inside yourself and realise you have changed; you are looking at things – everything – in a different way without having been conscious of it happening. Your reasoning has changed and with it your perceptions, and all that formed your previous self.'

The others were captivated by this revelation. Burren certainly was, because he thought he knew exactly what this man sitting beside him was saying beyond the words. He felt the others did too.

Suddenly Frank turned on Burren. 'You're a fine one to talk, anyhow. What are you going to do? And don't tell me that you are going to return to a building site.' He laughed scornfully at the idea.

Burren was on the spot and he was uncertain how to reply. Frank had stated the truth. He did not want to return to a building site. But he was still unsure about what he wanted.

He settled on saying, 'I share much of what you say, Frank, and you are quite right, I do not want to return to what I was doing before I came here. I don't know the answer, but I believe that somehow we have to try and retain some internal guidelines, or we are blown all over the place.'

'Hear, hear,' echoed Chris, before asking everyone what they were drinking and heading off to the bar.

Frank turned to Jane and smiled wearily. 'Alien to you, I suppose, most of this.'

Jane returned the smile but contented herself with simply saying, 'Not really.'

Burren had seen Mike Dawson arrive, and after passing a few

words with Timothy Framley and Jasmine and collecting a beer he came across.

'Hello, you things.' It was his usual form of greeting. He turned and smiled at Jane before sitting down beside Burren. 'We should have had a tutorial, John, after you finished with Robert and I'm sorry about that. It just wasn't possible because as you know I was in the States.' He gave a short burst of his normally loud laugh. 'I'm now allowed back in.'

'Was it a good trip?' asked Burren.

'Yes, very worthwhile.' He saw that the others were talking amongst themselves and turned back to Burren. 'I thought we might have a bit of a chat here, in these very congenial surroundings.'

'That is fine by me,' said Burren.

Mike Dawson took a long, slow drink of his beer before speaking. 'You have had a good session with both Robert and Timothy. They reported very favourably on your work. You must be very pleased.'

Burren tried not to appear smug. 'Well, yes, I'm quite pleased.'

'Come on, sound a bit more enthusiastic. By any standard you've done well and you have been a success with the Socialist Society, I gather.'

Must be Jasmine again, thought Burren. He told Mike Dawson that he was more than satisfied by the comments from Robert Wilcox and Timothy Framley.

Mike Dawson continued, 'And I hear from Robert that you are opting for international organisation. Your choice interests me. Do you have anything in mind for when you leave here?'

Burren sighed. 'Why does everything have to be linked to future plans?'

'Sore point is it, John?' Mike Dawson laughed loudly.

Burren had thought that at least Mike Dawson might be different in his approach to these matters, and would understand.

'Look at it this way,' Mike Dawson said. 'What you are going to take as your option is different from most of the others here, and so I naturally thought you had a further objective in mind – it is as simple as that.'

Burren found himself going over much of the previous conversation that had taken place with Frank Bainwell.

'I see,' said Mike. 'It looks as if I've touched a nerve end.'

Burren said wearily, 'I do get tired of continually being asked about future plans. The reason I chose international organisation is as much to do with not wanting the alternatives, especially industrial relations, as anything else.' He knew this was only part of the reason, in fact wasn't the real reason at all.

'I do have a very real interest in international affairs.' It was almost a confession. He thought for a moment before continuing, 'I'm no different from most of the others here. Now that I've been here I do not wish to return to my old job, but at the same time I am not at all clear about what I want to do and there is a certain sense of guilt surrounding this. I do think the college does not help in this respect. It tends to feed the idea that we must all want to change jobs, knowing that we have been through a kind of mental revolution, but it does not recognise the problems this causes some individuals, if not most.'

'Fair enough,' said Mike.

Burren was unhappy with this response. 'I'm afraid you do not see, Mike. This is a very real problem.' He was aware that he had probably pushed this too far. 'I'm sorry, Mike.' He smiled wanly. 'You must have seen this many, many, times before.'

Mike Dawson smiled indulgently. 'Just a few,' he said light-heartedly. He knew from hard experience that this was the stage in the academic year when everyone questioned the direction of their life and, he mused, the human condition in general. He looked around the bar at all the others apparently enjoying themselves and yet perhaps privately asking the same questions of themselves as Burren.

He turned to him and said, 'John, at the end of the day, you have to resolve this for yourself. I'll do what I can to help you in whatever you decide. But remember this, you are halfway there in recognising the nature of the problem. Let me just add this: you have a lot to contribute to whatever you choose to do.' He put a hand through his untidy hair before going on to say, 'I hope this doesn't sound too pompous but I believe we owe it to ourselves to use whatever talent we have to best effect.'

Burren thanked him and said that he would keep him informed. 'We'll meet again soon for a full tutorial in my room.' He gave Burren a friendly pat on the shoulder. 'And now I had better go and chat to a few others.'

Jane turned to Burren and said, 'He is another of your tutors, I suppose?'

'Yes, and that goes under the name of a pub tutorial.'

Jane looked at him. 'I couldn't help overhearing some of that and it seemed a little more serious to me.'

'It was nothing, really. I simply find it difficult to justify expectations sometimes, and people keep asking me what I am going on to do. It was odd really, following on so immediately from the conversation with Frank. I sometimes feel I am moving in an opposite direction to the accepted view, just to uphold some stupid principle.'

Jane smiled reassuringly and squeezed his arm. 'Don't worry,' she said, 'don't let the pressure get to you. The answers will come at the right time.'

He kissed her gently on the cheek and smiled. It was good to have her by his side. 'Let's have one more drink before we leave,' he said to the others.

At the bar, Doris the barmaid was busily at work serving a queue of waiting customers. He saw Jasmine on her own at the far end of the bar and went up to her. 'Are you enjoying the evening?' he asked. 'It seems we are all here, though no one quite knows why. Can you as our guardian angel tell me?'

Jasmine smiled serenely. 'You are obviously enjoying it.'

223

'Why not come across and join us?' indicating where they were sitting. 'Jane is there too.'

'Good, I shall come across.'

He returned with the drinks and Jasmine. She and Jane were soon talking animatedly together.

He sat and sipped his beer, reflecting on the conversations of the evening. He looked around at the different groups of Morton people. He thought of how random it was that they should have all been brought together in this way and would separate again and take separate routes. They had shared a common experience and each would leave with their own individual interpretation of that experience. There was nothing more to it than that, though some may take with them continuing friendships.

This musing was broken by the voice of Framley who had come across to join them.

'Hello. I thought I would join you for a few minutes before leaving.' He turned to Chris Megson and said, 'Congratulations, Christopher on *The New Age*. It looks good.' And to Burren and Frank Bainwell he added, 'Both of you have contributed to it as well. What success!'

Chris quickly added that the copies for Frank and Burren were now in his room.

Burren admitted to himself that Chris had put together a good edition of *The New Age* and he added his congratulations to those of Framley.

Framley himself was now talking to Jasmine and Jane and obviously enjoying himself. Burren had not heard him laugh as much before.

Shortly afterwards Framley and Jasmine said goodnight and left. The others left soon afterwards and went their separate ways: Frank and Chris going back to college whilst Burren walked Jane back to her college.

As she slipped her arm through his, Jane said, 'Did you know that Jasmine studied literature at London University?'

'No, I didn't.'

'And she did a year's postgraduate study in the States. She specialised on the novels of Scott Fitzgerald. What is she doing as secretary to your Principal?'

'I don't know,' he said. 'It is an odd business.'

He must ask Paul Jenkins more about this he decided when he next met him. He hadn't heard from Paul for a few weeks now. If he could find time he would drop him a note, but he supposed that Paul was as busy as himself. He did miss Paul, and being able to chat things over with him.

He heard Jane saying, 'She likes you a lot.'

'I'm sorry, I was a long way off. Who are you talking about?'

'Jasmine, of course. I am saying she likes you a lot.'

'So you keep telling me,' he said with an unseen smile in the darkness of the night.

'Well, it is true. And it will do you no harm in your dealings with your Principal.'

Further evidence of how Jane had her antennae extended on his behalf he told himself. 'Yes of course,' he said.

The Principal had told him the name of his tutor for his international organisation option, and his address had been given to him by Jasmine, but little else. When he had asked her for more information she simply smiled detachedly and told him that he would have to find out more for himself. Surprisingly, she had expressed interest in his choice of option, and confirmed that he would be the only Morton person studying with Sean Halloran.

His first meeting with Sean Halloran had been timed for 6.30 pm – an unusual time, Burren thought, for a tutorial. Most tutors held them during the morning. This was not the only thing that would be different with his new tutor, as he would soon find out.

The address he had been given was 84 Oldfield Road, which was in the northern part of the city. He took a Number 27 bus and got off, on the advice of the bus conductor, at a stop a few yards from the bottom of the road. He turned into the road and discovered that Number 84 was at the far end. It was a long, straight road with terraces of large three-storeyed houses on both sides, and with trees at regular intervals in the grass verge beside the pavement. There was a gradual incline to the far end of the road where Number 84 was located. He consoled himself with the thought that having to walk would be good for his physical condition – a much neglected feature in recent weeks.

He reached the house and mounted the three steps to the front door. There was a nameplate on the wall beside the front door with the names of the occupants and a press button beside each. It was difficult to make out the names, but after scanning them he saw the scrawled name of Sean Halloran. It looked as though his room was at the top of the house.

He pushed the button and heard a soft Irish voice say, 'Come to the top floor.' A further fitness test, he told himself as he climbed the rather shabby staircase. The paint on the walls of the stairwell was badly in need of renovation and there was a general air of neglect about the place. The paintwork of the door to Sean Halloran's apartment was similarly deteriorating. He knocked on the door and waited, and heard footsteps approaching the door from within.

The door opened and Sean Halloran stepped forward with outstretched hand, 'Come in, you must be John Burren,' he said, with a ready smile. 'That sounds a good, solid English name.'

Burren gave a slightly embarrassed laugh.

Sean Halloran offered him a seat and sat opposite him. The brown, intelligent eyes held Burren in a steady gaze. He was in no haste to make conversation but, it seemed, was allowing Burren to assimilate the room. It was a large room, well decorated with a deeply embossed paper on the walls and a cornice etched out in a plum-red colour. The furniture was stylish, modern and comfortable and arranged on a cream-coloured deep pile carpet. Burren sat back and was enveloped in the comfort of the chair.

'Tell me about yourself.'

Burren told him all that he thought he should know, con-centrating mostly on his recent activities since being at Morton.

'Most interesting,' said Halloran, 'You seem to have met some interesting and well-placed people through the Socialist Society. Now let me turn to what you have been doing by way of study. Politics and economics are very useful to this subject, and political thought too. The weakness I suspect is your lack of European history and knowledge of the United States in this century.' He looked enquiringly at Burren. 'Am I right?'

'I have done little in either field, I'm afraid, though I have looked recently at US policy towards Western Europe since 1945. In fact, I have written something on this for our House magazine.'

'Is that so?' said Halloran. 'You must let me see it.'

Now at his most enthusiastic, Burren said, 'I have a copy with me.' He reached into his briefcase and passed a copy across to Halloran. Halloran cast his eye over the magazine, assuring Burren that he would look at it before they met again.

He then said, 'I can see that you have a general interest in this field but what made you choose international organisation? It is not normally associated with your college, is it?'

Burren confirmed that this was so, and said that he had long been interested in world affairs in a general way. He went on to tell of how he had followed the course of the Second World War as a boy through the pages of *Picture Post*.

Halloran gave a soft laugh. 'That is quite something. I think you can make up the history deficiency if you are prepared to do some additional background reading. I would suggest A.J.P. Taylor's *Struggle for Mastery in Europe* to begin with.

'Now, as we are going to be meeting over the next few weeks, it is only fair to tell you something about myself.'

He told Burren that he was a history graduate of Trinity College, Dublin, and that he had done postgraduate work at the university on international organisation, specialising in the

League of Nations. He did some lecturing at Trinity and at the university, as well as consultancy work.

Whilst Sean Halloran was speaking Burren formed the impression that he was at the most only a few years older than himself, if that. His sharp facial features revealed a seriousness of purpose combined with open enthusiasm.

Having finished speaking about himself, he now turned to the subject itself. 'We'll have about six sessions in which we are going to try and cover the origins of international organisation towards the end of the nineteenth century, the Paris Peace Conference, and the establishment of the League of Nations, the workings of the League, and the United Nations. Phew!' He laughed. 'I can promise you that you are going to have to work fast and hard. Is that all right?'

'Yes,' replied Burren. 'I'm prepared to work as hard as is necessary.'

The phone rang and Halloran excused himself to take the call from his desk situated in the far corner of the room. The diversion gave Burren an opportunity to take in further features of the room. On the wall closest to him there were some attractive prints of city street scenes and on a farther wall there was a tapestry depicting a stained glass window. There were also some attractive pieces of sculpture in the room. The whole effect was of style and comfort.

He could hear the phone conversation, or at least Halloran's end of it, and he gathered that it related to some group of meetings with which Halloran was involved. He heard Halloran say that he was not available on a particular date as he would be in Geneva. The call came to an end and Halloran quickly scribbled a few notes before returning to Burren, and draping one leg languidly across the side of his chair. Burren doubted that he was quite as languid as the gesture suggested.

'Sorry about that,' said Halloran. 'One of the penalties of being accessible here whilst on short stays. People quite naturally try to arrange things whilst I'm here.' He paused briefly to regain the context of his previous comments before continuing, 'Now, as you can see, we have a vast field to cover and how well it goes will depend largely on you. We'll meet every ten days or so. I think you'll need that time to complete the reading for each topic and that will fit in with my own movements and periods of stay this side of the water. I have sometimes to move things at rather short notice. I hope you don't mind. Incidentally, I sometimes like to adjourn of an evening to a pub across the road at the corner, especially if I haven't eaten. It is quite congenial and you can usually find a quiet spot.'

Burren said that he was more than happy to go along with this arrangement.

A sudden thought prompted Halloran to ask, 'Do you look at a good weekly? *The Economist* for example? It is very good for our purpose, and of course I assume that you look at a good daily.' Without waiting for an answer, he went on, 'Try and make a point of doing this; it helps you keep in touch with the broad trend of affairs and there is also coverage of some topics in greater depth. You see the international system – of which I will say more another time – does not stand still. On the contrary there is a continuous process of change.'

He then asked Burren if he had any questions. Burren said that he hadn't, except to ask for advice about reading.

Halloran had been toying with a pencil and he now made a note on a pad and then carried on, 'Your first task then is to look at the factors that influenced the development of international organisation in the latter part of the nineteenth century and before the First World War. Now to the reading ...' He rattled off a few titles and handed Burren a general reading list.

Before Burren knew it he was being ushered to the door. 'See you on the seventeenth, same time. Best of luck.' Burren saw the charm in the smile.

He caught the bus back to the centre of the city and went back to college, stopping only to collect some of the recommended books from the library. He then made a start on the long haul of reading for this new subject.

He told Jane of his first meeting with Halloran, about how young he was, his sense of style, and the intellectually romantic life he seemed to live. Jane rather dampened his spirits by saying that Halloran's life seemed full of work. Nor was this the only dampener. The first topic that he was working on seemed rather uninspiring; the reading was dull and heavy going, and made frequent reference to wider considerations of an embryonic international community together with the principles which underpin such a community. He knew so little about this wider context.

Most of what was being said about emerging international organisation seemed to be predicated upon the reader already having some knowledge of what led to the conception of a community. Sean Halloran had assured him that A.J.P. Taylor's book was good for the European background of the nineteenth century, but it seemed to Burren to be so concerned with the thicket of the argument that he became lost in the detail, especially in the labyrinthine nature of the Austro-Hungarian Empire.

He hoped very much that the subject overall would become clearer in time, as at this stage he felt that industrial relations might by contrast be more revealing of the human condition. This was certainly the case if Frank Bainwell and Chris Megson were to be believed. They talked of little else. It seemed their whole world these days resided in the workings of the inner sanctum of some industrial tribunal or other. Jane too seemed more than content with what she was studying, and she was having numerous tête-à-têtes with Jasmine, presumably about literature.

A general election had been called and those at Morton became caught up in the fever of electioneering. Eden had decided to seek a renewal of the government's mandate and the battle lines were now drawn. Bill Williams proudly proclaimed at breakfast on the day of the announcement of the election that a Labour victory was now in sight.

Bill must have led the Gadarene Swine, thought Burren, but contented himself with the comment, 'Bill, your conviction is truly messianic!'

Everyone was mobilised for the great assault on the government. For four years the Labour Party had been in opposition. Four years that had seen the subtle dismantling of the nascent welfare state, and four years of cleverly restoring those things that accentuated class differences. For four long years Labour had waited for the chance to show just what the Tories had done, and to show that given the choice the people would once again revert to them. The people had been hoodwinked once by the materialist apostles of Toryism, but now they would respond to the great moral cause. And at Morton they were going to be in the vanguard of the attack.

In reality of course the political landscape was different. The prospects of regaining power for Labour were poor. The evidence was against them. The Tories had not in fact seriously undermined the welfare state – the 'One Nation' group of Tories under Rab Butler's influence had modernised the Conservative Party. It was Labour's misfortune that they had not recognised this. Furthermore, the Tories had relaxed a number of controls which had remained from the war under Labour; this had been popular with the people. A quite fortuitous factor had helped too: the terms of trade had improved – a problem that Labour had to wrestle with whilst in power.

And there was the tired image that Labour projected. The Party had not really thought how to build upon its significant creations during its post-war period of government. The leadership, Attlee and his senior colleagues, were worn out and had seen their day. Attlee had failed to bring into office a sufficient number of the young good brains from the 1945 intake into parliament, which meant there was now a lacuna of experience.

On the first evening after the announcement of the election there was a meeting of all those interested in supporting local candidates, under the leadership of Frank Bainwell as House chairman. A lengthy discussion ensued on the question of the right course to pursue. There were two constituencies near at hand in which they could lend a hand. One was perhaps winnable if everything went in Labour's favour but the candidate was unexciting, yet safe. The other constituency was mainly urban and included a large chunk of the city, and the Labour candidate was everything that the other candidate was not. The pessimists said that the seat was unwinnable whilst the optimists conceded that it would be a massive task to turn it around.

Greenfell stated his case in his usual obtuse way. They had to support the candidate whose views corresponded most closely with their own idea of socialism. In other words, he said, be true to your ideals and convictions. By now, however, most people who had any experience of Greenfell knew that he was not to be trusted, and that there was a deeper layer to him than showed on the surface. He was initially supported, unsurprisingly, by the burst-seamers who welcomed any opportunity to lend their support to a moral cause.

Chris Megson, sitting beside Burren, whispered, 'We must put a stop to this.'

'I fully agree,' replied Burren.

Together they acted quickly before loyalties became too dissipated by the pulls of different groups, arguing vigorously that they should all concentrate their support behind the candidate who at least had a chance of winning. After further discussion, which Frank Bainwell skilfully kept to a minimum, the majority were persuaded. All, that is, except Greenfell and a handful of others. In any case, Greenfell was too committed by now to change his mind.

So John Worlton was to be their man. Honest John Worlton – public school educated (though only a minor one), Oxford

University, and barrister, correctly dressed in pinstripe suit and waistcoat, and with well-oiled accent; here were all the appurtenances of the respectable bourgeois socialist.

Burren reflected on Worlton's prospects as he glanced through the local newspaper. On the centre page there was a full-sized photograph of Worlton smiling his well-rehearsed smile, and alongside there was an account of his connections. Burren ran his eye disdainfully down the list of public service: long-serving member of the regional hospital board, honorary president of two national charities, president of the local cricket club ... and so they continued down to honorary president of the village hall committee where Worlton lived.

He threw the newspaper down and walked out of the common room to meet with Frank Bainwell and Chris Megson for that evening's round of canvassing, but not quickly enough to avoid Greenfell coming through the door.

'Just the chap I wanted to see,' said Greenfell standing athwart the door and effectively barring Burren's exit.

'What is it?' Burren snapped, trying to dodge round Greenfell's bulky figure. 'What is it? I'm in a hurry.'

Greenfell was not to be hurried. He looked carefully at Burren, half through and half over his ill-positioned glasses. 'Going canvassing?' he asked. The asinine appearance of the glasses added to Burren's impatience.

'Yes I am. Now let me through.'

Greenfell continued to look at him. 'How about speaking in support of Varndell?'

Varndell was the Labour candidate for the other constituency and a prominent local trade union official. He was a strong candidate and a very forceful speaker. A little too forceful, perhaps, for it led him into indiscretions on the platform and undoubtedly had not endeared him to the leadership of the Party. Hence the reason for his fighting a constituency which he had no chance of winning, when his ability in fact spoke for something better.

For a second Burren was tempted, for he liked Varndell, but he checked himself. What was the point? It would simply be a waste of time.

'No,' he said emphatically. 'Varndell doesn't stand a chance, and you know it.' He tried to push on past Greenfell.

'Now wait a minute,' said Greenfell, his stance becoming more determined. 'What is this peculiar loyalty you feel for Worlton?'

Burren turned sharply on him. 'It is not loyalty to Worlton, as you well know. It is loyalty to a decision agreed at the meeting. Remember? And we reached that decision because Worlton is the one candidate with a chance of winning.'

'But we don't want his type to get in,' protested Greenfell.

Of course Burren didn't approve of Worlton as a candidate, but he wasn't going to be a martyr to Greenfell's principles by telling him so. He adopted the good Party worker approach.

'Perhaps you don't want Worlton to get in, but I'm not interested in political games, or political types. I am interested in seeing the Labour Party returned to power and a Worlton victory will be one more for the green benches.' He now thrust past Greenfell.

'You fool, John. You are letting others use you.'

Greenfell's words followed him through the door. You are the fool, he thought. Always taking up lost causes.

After he had presented his first piece of written work on international organisation, Sean Halloran commented that it was satisfactory, but Burren was left with the clear impression that he was not entirely happy with it.

Halloran now asked him, 'What did you think of the first topic?'

'I can see the importance of it,' he said without enthusiasm.

'But ...?' Halloran smiled. 'There is bound to be a but!'

'The difficulty for me is that the subject is located in ideas about an international community. And this in turn is based upon certain assumptions, or principles, and I don't know enough about these.'

'I know,' said Halloran. 'The problem is you are studying international organisation and it is out of context. You are right. The reading will make reference to the context in which such international organisations exist, and the question is raised as to whether that amounts to an embryonic international community. That in turn suggests that there are some organising principles which constitute an international community, or as we prefer to call it, an international system. And so it goes on.

'The last time we met, you'll recall that I referred to that international system. Well, that is very much what this whole subject is about and I want to talk more fully on this, but I should like you to be more advanced in your study first. Don't be discouraged. Trust me. I think you will see that things come right. I hope so.'

He asked Burren if he had any further questions at this point. Burren laughed and said that he was sure there would be more once he was in deeper.

Halloran pushed on, 'I am going to recommend a book which I think will help you in respect to the theoretical context, but remember that I cannot reduce the scale of the subject. I will give you an extended reading list with accompanying advisory notes and then it is up to you to do as much as you can.'

Halloran stopped and raised himself from his chair. 'How about a drink to help this heavy stuff along?'

'Yes, thank you.'

Halloran returned with the drinks and resumed talking. 'Right. We now turn to a topic that is either going to ignite your interest or, if it doesn't, I shall know that you have chosen the wrong subject and should go no further in studying international organisation. The topic is "The Peace Conference at Versailles and the setting up of the League of Nations", and I want you to evaluate the objectives of both.'

He sipped his sherry. 'Now I suggest that you look particularly at the following: Keynes, *The Economic Consequences of the Peace*; Nicholson, *Peacemaking 1919*; and Walters, *The League of Nations*. And I should like you to look at Carr, *The Twenty Years Crisis*. The last book I think will help you to understand theories about the emerging international community.' He smiled in his charming way. 'That is about it. Hope you can fit everything in.'

Burren hoped so too. As he walked down the road towards the bus stop he told himself that he would give the electioneering work a miss for that evening, and instead take a preliminary look at the reading he had been recommended. He was determined to cover as much of the reading as possible – he wanted to prove something to Sean Halloran.

What had he meant by saying, 'and should go no further'?

12

The constituency that John Worlton was fighting as Labour candidate flanked the western side of the city. It consisted of two highly contrasting social components; a heavily concentrated industrial pocket adjoining the city, and a sprawling rural area with several over-large villages which were no longer truly agrarian yet remained relatively untouched by their proximity to urban life.

This posed a problem for the campaign organisers. Their records told them that the vote was split evenly between the two main parties: the Conservatives taking the rural part, and Labour the industrial area. Most in the local Labour Party felt that if their own vote could be fully mobilised within their own area of support, the seat could be won. Others argued that this Labour solidarity could not be relied on, and that more effort had to be made to trawl the rural vote. At the centre of this equation was the time-old factor of the apathy of the Labour vote.

These were the thoughts that circulated in Burren's mind as he prepared to go out for an evening of campaigning. In the event, he concluded, they were the victim of their candidate, of his patriarchal appearance, brusqueness of manner and his profession. These qualities obviously did not commend themselves to an egalitarian, 'I am one of the people' approach. It had to be that of 'man of intellect with social conscience'. These last thoughts disturbed Burren when he recalled Greenfell's pleading on behalf of Varndell. But Worlton they had, and having got him the Party strategists decided it was best to play on his personal approach.

This evening Worlton had six helpers from Morton, including Frank Bainwell, Chris Megson and Burren, together with some local Party workers. Beneath an angry sky, with squally showers and prematurely dying daylight, they hurried to complete their canvassing. Burren walked up the path of the last house in the council estate allotted to him, taking in the privet hedge, neatly trimmed lawn, concrete path and blue front door. It reminded him that the estate he had worked on back in the summer would look the same as this in a few years' time.

He rang the front door bell and mechanically rehearsed his opening comments as he waited. Shortly, a plump, early-middle-aged woman appeared. The woman, seeing it was a stranger, put on a defensive expression. He could hear voices from behind the half-opened door. He spoke, or rather was aware that he was reciting, the set piece of electioneering strategy. The woman watched him with an air of exaggerated concentration, her eyes reading his face. He finished speaking and waited for her reply.

'No, I'm sorry, I can't say what we'll be doing.' She spoke the words automatically, it seemed, from either indifference or preoccupation.

The implication that he was extending an invitation to attend the poll amused him, but he suppressed this to ask, 'But you and your husband are free on polling day ? That is May 10th.'

The woman replied, 'Oh yes, we'll be here. I'm just not sure what we'll be doing on that day.'

He pressed on, 'Then can we take it that you'll give us your support?' He switched on a smile.

The woman gave a little embarrassed laugh. 'Oh, you'll need to talk to my husband. He knows all about politics.' Then she added more confidentially, 'You see, I don't get the time, what with the family.' She turned her head to glance back into the house and then returned her attention to Burren. 'Mind you, I would if I had the time. What with the bomb and all that.'

'But you are supporters of the Labour Party?'

Suddenly the harassed look became reproachful. 'Of course we are supporters. What else could we be in our position?'

He put on a Good Comrade smile and thanked her.

He walked back and found the others having already finished their canvassing waiting for him by Worlton's car.

'How did it go?' asked Worlton cheerfully.

'I have completed Midgeley Close,' said Burren.

'That is the estate completed, then,' said Chris. He smiled at Worlton. 'We'll have the whole canvas finished in good time.'

'Excellent,' clucked Worlton in his gratitude. 'You have all been absolutely splendid.'

Chris collected up the cards and leaflets and put them in the back of the car. Worlton thanked them again and waved cheerily goodbye as he moved off in his black limousine. They watched the car disappear round the bend in the road.

'Not once has he offered us a lift,' said Frank, continuing to look down the road.

'But he lives in the opposite direction to us,' said Chris.

'I know that,' said Frank. 'But he doesn't even make a gesture.'

'Let's have a drink,' suggested Burren.

The other two readily agreed

Burren took a long pull on his pint tankard and looked disconsolately at Frank and Chris. 'I can't see Worlton winning on tonight's showing,' he said. He turned to Chris. 'How did you get on?'

Chris ran his hands through his long fair hair and pursed his lips in hesitation. He did not reply directly but said, 'It is still too early yet. I reckon more support will swing our way once people get a more positive view of the Party nationally.'

Burren looked at him, genuinely surprised. He surely didn't seriously believe that. The Party continued to be divided and that division was publicly displayed for all to see in the conflicting speeches delivered by leading figures in the Party. Even a miracle of solidarity at this stage could not remove those very real differences. And anyway, Worlton did not dissent from what was supposedly the Party line, and so presumably the only

239

support he was losing from within the traditional area of Labour vote was on the left. It was difficult to see how Chris had reasoned his point. The fact was, Worlton was a poor candidate. Burren now said as much to Chris.

'No. I most emphatically disagree,' said Chris. 'Just because he doesn't strut around mouthing political slogans.' He then added rather bitterly, 'You are all against him.'

Burren retorted, 'I didn't say that.' He wanted to avoid becoming embroiled in the old left-wing versus right-wing fracas with Chris.

'But that is what is at the root of your objection to Worlton.'

'That is not so, Chris. The fact is that in a marginal seat of this sort we need someone with thrust, someone who feels sufficiently about political issues to make them come alive.'

Chris shrugged dismissively.

Frank had been unusually restrained. He now said, 'John is right. It is the first time Worlton has stood for parliament and he gets a marginal seat straight away. Whereas poor old Varndell, who has fought umpteen elections, is stuck with a hopeless seat.' He banged his tankard down upon the table. 'It's a racket. Give Worlton's constituency to Varndell and he would win it every time – even against the current tide.'

Burren turned to Frank. 'Greenfell is campaigning for Varndell. Did you know that?'

'Really?' Frank was interested.

'Yes, he asked me to speak in support of Varndell.'

'He is a political mendicant,' snapped Chris.

Frank ignored Chris's comment and went on to ask Burren, 'Well, you agreed, I assume?'

'No, I didn't. I said that we had all agreed, except him, to lend our support to Worlton and that is what I would continue to do.'

'Quite right too,' said Chris rather prissily.

'I wonder ...' said Burren ruefully, questioning his own decision. He turned to Chris. 'I know we all agreed, or at least the great majority of us did, to give our support to Worlton. It seemed the right thing to do, but now I wonder.'

Chris sighed.

Burren continued, 'It is ironic, really. We give our support to a candidate we disapproved of – well, except you of course – and deny it to someone with whom we are in sympathy.' Chris tried to interrupt but he carried on. 'And for what? So that we might get one person into parliament. But even if we succeed, what have we achieved? We don't agree with his views.'

'That is nonsense,' said Chris. 'He is a good candidate, and he'll make a splendid MP.'

Burren smiled at Chris, 'Well, it may be irrelevant.'

Frank laughed.

The consolidation of two years of academic study in preparation for the examinations which were now only a few weeks away kept Morton quiet, apart from the electioneering that some still tried to fit into their busy schedule. Burren had the additional demands of a new subject with its own very specific complexities. He wanted to do well in international organisation and was prepared to work extremely hard at it, but he was finding it difficult to balance the demands on his time.

The new subject was very demanding not only because it was an entirely new field to him but because it was situated in the context of the much wider study of international relations – and that field, as he was finding out, was a tangled web to the beginner. He had of necessity to know something about the layers of complex ideas without going too far. That was the problem: where to draw the line. And he found this difficult to control because it was so absorbing and enticed him into deeper exploration.

He had already experienced the thrill of discovery in reading Keynes's *General Theory* and the way that had expounded a comprehensive theory of the working of an economy as a system. He now found that Keynes was every bit as eloquent and profound in the case that he argued in *The Economic Consequences of the Peace*. The consequences prophesied by Keynes had proved tragically accurate, and this made a great impression on Burren.

The subsequent tutorial with Halloran was one of the most satisfying discussions Burren had engaged in, and led far beyond the original topic into the very nature of the sovereign state itself. Halloran suggested that he now look at the experience of the League of Nations during the inter-war years, and suggest reasons for its failure.

Halloran hinted that this would necessarily entail looking at different perceptions of an international community. He went on to say that *The Twenty Years Crisis* by E.H. Carr was important to an understanding of the conceptual approach in international relations. He spoke even more enthusiastically of the work of Hans Morgenthau, and told Burren to begin to look selectively at relevant parts of *Politics Among Nations*. He then added with a smile that both Carr and Morgenthau were known as 'realists'.

Burren told him that he had already begun to look at *The Twenty Years Crisis*.

'Yes, I know,' said Halloran, 'but don't get lost. Ideas are seductive.' He gave a snort of laughter. 'Ask any dictator! Be sure to keep your feet on the ground.' Again a quick laugh as he added, 'Avoid the Rousseau syndrome.'

Jane had taken to joining Burren in his attic room of an afternoon – she to do her final revision and he to continue to do as much reading as he could. The arrangement suited them both, as they could stop whenever they wished and meet others in the kitchen below whilst making a drink. They could chat to one another as well in the privacy of his room without being told to keep quiet as in the library.

Jane watched him out of the corner of her eye as he lay on the bed propped on one elbow, there being only one chair in the room. He looked comfortable and reassuring, she thought. The large light blue sweater he was wearing made him look more rotund than usual. Jane often joked about his waistline and he was aware that he had not taken enough exercise in recent weeks. He was sensitive on the issue. She continued to examine him and concluded that he was handsome in a non-conventional way. She recalled the bicycle incident when they had first met, and remembered how, though it was all very brief, she had noticed the light-coloured eyes beneath the thatched eyebrows.

He turned to see her looking at him with a smile playing on her face.

'What is amusing you?' he asked.

'You are becoming rather rotund, John,' she laughed.

'Ha ha. How would you like me to say that you are bosomless?'

'Oh John, you become so pompous when you are irritated.' She laughed again. 'I recognise your remark as a statement of fact,' she said, still playing with him. 'Anyhow, I'll have you know that it was fashionable to have small bosoms in the 1920s; nowadays large ones are all the rage but I'm endeavouring to set a new fashion.' After a pause she asked, 'Do you like women as portrayed in the twenties?'

Feigning not to know what she meant, he said, 'A bit too old.'

'You know what I mean!'

'I like everything about the twenties. The hedonism, the jazz, the Keystone Cops, the cloche hats, and the dimply baby doll faces that women seemed to have, judging from the photographs of the period. It must have been a great time. Despite the war and the flu epidemic, they seemed so innocent and optimistic.'

'Leaving aside the unemployment and the misery of poverty,' she added.

'Leaving that aside,' he acknowledged.

'So do you like the thirties? Apart from it ending in the last bit of course,' he asked her.

Jane looked thoughtful for a moment. 'Yes, very much,' she replied. 'I have happy childhood memories. But more generally I think there was something noble and brave about it. The political emancipation of women completed. Little Baby Austin cars and Morris tourers going through the countryside carrying brave, serious young people. Good universal causes to fight and die for. Auden and Isherwood and death.'

'I remember one Sunday morning, it must have been in the autumn of 1936,' he said, 'a Salvation Army woman officer came to our front door appealing for money to help the victims of the Spanish civil war. She talked of the brave people in Spain. My curiosity about the civil war and Spain dated from that moment. I suppose that it marked my first awareness that all was not right in the world.'

'And the forties?' Jane asked.

Instantly he said, 'Ration books, utility clothes, dried egg and no bananas. The gas masks, thankfully unused of course, and at the beginning of the war only half days at school.'

'You weren't evacuated?'

'No, of course not. We lived in the countryside. Children from London were evacuated to us, though in fact we lay right in the middle of the corridor used by German aircraft in the bombing of London. And much of the famous Battle of Britain was fought immediately above us.' And then with a gleam in the eye, 'Yes, I know – everything was run by women. Nearly all the teachers were women; we had a woman scoutmaster, and women ran the buses, the shops. It was a truly matriarchal society.' He laughed. 'And then everything returned to normal! And finally, much promiscuity,' he concluded.

'Really,' Jane said with mock surprise.

They sat for a moment reflecting on the 40 years they had just looked at.

Then Jane said, 'That only leaves us now.'

'A very difficult generation,' he said, feigning a serious tone. 'It will require both of us to assess this.'

They became serious in looking at their own times as he said, 'We are a bit torn apart, I suppose, between two generations that have different outlooks. The insecurity of our parents from the inter-war years has been handed on down to us, and at the same time we are being drawn towards the tastes and desires of today's youth very conscious of emerging wealth.'

Jane interjected, 'There was the war as well. Don't you think that has made us rather sentimental – a sort of precious attitude towards people and things?'

'Yes, I hadn't considered that,' he said thoughtfully.

'Politically we are confused, I think; or at least those of us on the left are. We are unable to understand what happened to the landslide of 1945, the idea that at long last socialism was here to stay – and then suddenly it is lost and we don't know how to recover it. We are left frustrated and angry.'

Suddenly he wanted to take Jane in his arms and hold her very close to him. He moved closer towards her. She anticipated his thoughts and laid her head on his shoulder. Their lips came slowly together.

'What about our generation?' asked Jane.

'We are the loving generation,' he said.

They both laughed.

Burren pressed the buzzer and heard a voice say, 'Come on up.'

As he entered the room Sean Halloran said, 'Good to see you. Would you care for a sherry?'

'Yes, thanks,' Burren replied.

Halloran passed Burren a glass of sherry and raised his own. 'I'm celebrating the publication of my book.' He cast his eye downward to the book lying on a small coffee table.

Burren lifted his glass and congratulated him. 'What is it about?' he asked.

'The League of Nations,' said Halloran.

'Oh dear,' groaned Burren. 'I had no idea.' And he added, 'I can expect a pretty rigorous session, then.'

Sean Halloran laughed and sat down, beckoning Burren to join him. 'Right, well, let us see what you have made of my own special subject.'

Burren referred to his essay but didn't read it as he developed his argument. Sean Halloran listened closely and jotted down an occasional note. He did not interrupt whilst Burren presented his argument. When he had finished Burren looked to Halloran a little apprehensively.

Halloran fixed him with a searching look for a moment before speaking, and then it was to ask him a question, but not about the topic in hand. 'What are you going to do when you leave here?'

He suddenly felt his morale slipping away and responded flatly, 'What makes you ask?' Halloran said, 'I'm interested. I'm interested to know if you are thinking of taking this subject, or rather international politics, any further.'

Burren was surprised, though he now realised what Sean Halloran had meant by his comment about 'taking the subject further'. He knew that he had vacillated for too long and he also knew that it was probably too late to be accepted for further study in the coming year. Yet he was still uncertain. If he was frank with himself, he would have acknowledged that the reason he had not taken a decision was because he was fearful of making the wrong decision. He also did not know enough about what he would be undertaking. The uncertainty was linked with lack of knowledge.

He made some attempt at a reply. 'I am very interested in this subject, and of what I understand of the wider study of international politics.'

Halloran said, 'Well, your enthusiasm for this subject is very apparent. I believe you have a flair for the wider field of international politics. I can tell. You have quickly grasped the right kind of critical and analytical approach. Your work on this last topic was first rate. Almost as if you had read my book,' he joked.

Burren laughed. He thought that he had done well, but it was important to have this confirmation from Halloran. He felt the subject. It was curious, and difficult to put into words. It was as though it was something that had always been there but had lain dormant and was now awakened. It was certainly what he had been searching for intellectually. It was exciting, it was significant, and it made him feel good.

Halloran said he had not eaten and suggested they go across the road to his local pub. Burren readily agreed. They entered the quiet bar and Halloran ordered food and beer for them both.

'The point is,' said Halloran, taking up the subject again, and knowing that he had touched something in Burren, 'you have reached a point where you are on the fringe of the systematic study of international politics, or international relations as the purists refer to it. The subject is still relatively new, having been established following the First World War in London University and in Wales at Aberystwyth.' He raised a forkful of shepherd's pie and munched away before continuing, 'It is still in its infancy and has not really taken off yet in many universities. The fact is, it has met with open criticism from the traditional disciplines. Government has probably seen it as a bit of a challenge to the traditional stronghold of diplomacy. And other academic disciplines – principally history – have opposed it on the ground that it is not a proper subject, it lacks precise focus, has inadequate methodology, etcetera. The same criticism was previously trotted out against economics, and sociology of course. There are always vested interests.

'Nevertheless, those who have inspired the study have been determined to provide for the scientific study of the international system. It is of course the most exciting thing to happen in the social sciences. To seek to understand how sovereign states relate to one another and to see how power and the need for security affects this relationship, and to see this in the context of the international system; to see that the system itself also impacts on the behaviour of states – that there is an inescapable aspect to this too, as states have to participate. That power is unevenly distributed throughout the system. The importance of how the state itself is organised: democratic or autocratic. So you see it is quite something. Had it not been for a short three month-stay at Chicago where Morgenthau is, I probably would not have explored this field at all. He was truly inspirational.

'It is a hybrid subject. It borrows heavily from other academic subjects – history, economics, sociology, law, but primarily it is politics based. The other subjects are used to substantiate the primacy of the political process. Aristotle would have been so pleased.' He laughed at his own comment.

He sat back and looked at Burren as if weighing what he had said. 'I think you may be unhappy intellectually if you do not take this study further.' He smiled benignly. 'Anyhow, I suggest you give it some thought. But you will have to act quickly if you are interested in trying to enter for the coming year. My advice would be to try for London.'

Burren knew that he had to make up his mind. Further delay would be foolish. Halloran's words reflected something stirring inside himself. He was receiving confirmation and he was grateful to Sean Halloran for that.

At last he said, 'I found *The Twenty Years Crisis* one of the most exhilarating books that I have read. In all that reading, you suddenly encounter a book which changes the way you see things, not just one thing but a whole range. It is a seismic shift in the whole mental outlook. It is as if the integrating of one's own personal position is taking place.'

'Very well put,' said Halloran. 'That is exactly what happens.'

As they left the pub Burren said, 'I believe I do know what I want now and I should like to talk with you about this before the next tutorial.'

'That is fine. Just phone me.'

Polling was in a few days and electioneering was almost complete. Several times Burren had been approached by Greenfell to speak in support of Varndell, and each time Greenfell had emphasised the contrast between Worlton and Varndell. But each time he had refused. Just why, he was no longer sure. He told himself that it was because victory was more important than the respective merits of individual candidates, but he knew this was an excuse rather than a reason.

As the campaign drew to an end it became increasingly evident that the Labour Party was going to lose, and incredibly, it seemed to want to lose. It continued to be wracked by internal dissension and contradictory statements issued from Party headquarters, but worst of all was the wanton political suicide by leading figures in the Party. There was an orgy of political self-indulgence which made a travesty of the trust and loyalty of thousands of anonymous Party workers in the constituencies – the manual labour of the Party who gave of their spare time in the naïve hope of a Labour victory.

Though with his rational self he knew that electoral failure would happen on Thursday, May 10th, he too shared these people's naïve hope, wanted desperately to feel that that they must win. Without that hope there was no meaning to what he was doing in the campaign. 'Don't separate yourself from them.' The words of his old friend Tom from the building site suddenly came to mind. There was something far deeper and more profound than reason that influenced political behaviour, and he was part of that too. He realised in an instant that without logically thinking it through, he had chosen sides in the great divide within the Party.

Several Morton people had chaired meetings that Worlton had addressed during the election campaign, including Frank Bainwell and Chris Megson, and for the last meeting it was to be Burren. Worlton finished his speech to a few desultory handclaps. Burren looked across at Worlton as he ceremoniously removed his reading glasses. At least his peroration had had a little more guts to it than in the earlier speeches of his campaign. But looking at the rows of passive faces whilst Worlton had been speaking convinced him that it would take more than a last-minute revival to enthuse these people.

He leaned across and caught Worlton's attention. 'Excellent conclusion to the campaign,' he said, smiling but feeling like a hypocrite.

Worlton smiled back, looking more than satisfied. 'Thank you,' he said, adding, 'I'm sure we've done enough to win.'

Burren did not reply to this. He could see Jane making her way towards the platform amongst the crowd heading for the exit. He collected his notes and turned to Worlton. 'Will we see you later?' he asked.

'Certainly,' Worlton nodded.

He took Jane's arm and steered her through the slowly dissipating crowd. Once clear of the doorway they walked quickly in the direction of the Eagle & Bear.

'Do you think he'll win?' Jane asked.

'It is most unlikely,' he said. 'There is a two per cent swing against us nationally and Worlton already has a marginal swing against him in the constituency. So there you are.' He shrugged resignedly.

'But he spoke well this evening,' she said, pulling out evidence in Worlton's favour.

Jane's knowledge of Worlton was limited to the one occasion of this evening. He decided not to disillusion her. 'Yes, he spoke well this evening.'

They saw Frank Bainwell and Chris Megson seated at the long table in the corner as they entered the oak-beamed saloon bar. Jane went across to join them whilst he went to the bar to order their drinks.

'Welcome to the pre-postmortem,' said Frank with a sardonic touch as Burren joined them.

'Oh no,' groaned Chris.

Burren took a long gulp of his beer. 'Worlton will be along later,' he said.

'That should be very interesting,' said Frank. 'The lawyer's last word before quietly slipping into oblivion.'

'Shut up,' snapped Chris.

Frank quickly moved to attack. ' Well, isn't that just fine. Until now you have been only too ready to defend every nuance of your pendulous lawyer friend. But now that you can see it is certain he will be defeated, you want it to be kept quiet.'

'That is not the point at all.'

Burren broke in, 'All right. Let's drop the subject. Worlton will be here soon.'

He was wearied of the whole business. Of course Worlton was a poor candidate. Of course he should not represent Labour in a marginal seat, but their interminable arguing over the same ground would not make any difference. It was much better to see the thing quietly through to the end.

'He is rather handsome,' said Jane, switching a disarming smile on Frank. 'That may be worth a few votes.'

But Frank had lost all sense of humour on this subject. 'Oh, he is that all right. He is one of those fellows whose intellect is in his smile and handsome charm.'

'Quiet,' snapped Chris, looking at Frank. 'Here he comes.'

They turned to see Worlton and his agent approaching their table.

'So here you are,' said Worlton cheerily. He introduced his agent, though he was already known to them, and went on to enthuse about how well the meeting had gone. Burren noticed that his agent looked markedly less happy.

'I suppose you are eagerly awaiting polling day now?' said Jane.

He replied smilingly with a mild correction, 'I am confidently awaiting.'

He actually believes it, thought Burren. He believes he is going to win. It isn't just an act for the benefit of his public and his immediate helpers. He is going to get the most almighty shock when the result is announced.

Chris was now ceremoniously raising his glass, 'Well, here's wishing you a resounding victory, John.'

The others limply responded in like fashion.

'Thank you,' said Worlton, holding his glass in both hands and swishing the whisky. Then he said, 'I should like to thank you all for your great efforts during the campaign. You've been a great encouragement to me.' He patted Burren on the shoulder. 'And you were a great support to me this evening on the platform.'

'It was a pleasure,' said Burren, feeling miserable.

'Where are the other people from your college who helped me during the campaign?' asked Worlton, looking around.

'They'll be here shortly,' said Chris.

'And so you are hoping to be swopping one sedentary occupation for another,' said Frank. 'Or should I say, swopping one green bench for another.'

Worlton, unaware of the underlying malice in the comment, or choosing to ignore it, laughed and said, 'I should hope to be a little more active than your comparison suggests.'

'Yes, well plenty of people enter parliament with big plans,' said Frank.

It was clear to each of them, apart from Worlton perhaps, that Frank intended to go for him.

Burren was wondering how best to rescue Worlton from the situation when Chris came up with the answer.

'I see some of the others are drinking at the bar, if you would care to join them with me,' he said to Worlton.

'Yes, let's do that,' said Worlton, and he and Chris walked over to the bar.

Jane asked Frank about the likely outcome of the dispute in the car industry and seemed genuinely interested in Frank's reply. Burren looked across to the group now gathered round Worlton at the bar. The mood was optimistic, judged by the way they were laughing with Worlton. He was playing up to the role of a 'jolly good fellow', accompanied by the clinking of glasses and bright repartee. Burren thought that maybe he was wrong after all and had misjudged the whole situation. There was nothing to do now but wait until the people in their wisdom, apathy or ignorance made their decision.

Burren stared idly at the walls of his room, unable to concentrate fully on the work he had to do for Sean Halloran. His attention drifted back to the election result declared the day before. A group of them had joined Frank Bainwell in his room and listened to the radio for the first all-important result; it was thought to be a pointer to the way things would go across the nation.

The first result came in around midnight. It had been a Labour-held seat with a reduced majority. It was an accurate portent of all that followed. By around 2 am they had heard enough to convince them that all hope of victory had gone. It had been a forlorn hope anyway – a hope that had only been sustained by their deep personal involvement in the campaign.

He selected a cigarette from the packet lying on his desk and toyed with it for a second before beginning to smoke. It was curious how, in the wake of all the eager anticipation of the previous evening, Worlton had been quite forgotten. The meetings and the canvassing, so important at the time, seemed now in the bitter taste of defeat to have been utterly futile, a kind of charade, devoid of any meaning. He had discovered from the newspaper that the previously marginal seat contested by Worlton had now become a safe Conservative stronghold. Poor Worlton.

In the immediate aftermath of disappointment at their defeat, a sense of bitterness had taken hold of many of them at Morton. It made some of them search vindictively for the cause within the Labour Party itself. Hence there was to be more fratricide. Burren's own loyalty was inevitably caught up in the maelstrom of political feelings which now pervaded all discussion on the subject.

A knock at his door and the entrance of Chris Megson jerked him out of his meditation.

'Are you busy, John?'

'Should be,' he said, 'but I can't get past the crass stupidity of our election campaign.'

'I can't either,' said Chris, moving across the room and slumping onto Burren's bed, 'but I suppose it is best now to forget the election.'

'It is still too close,' said Burren.

'Yes, but it is best to bury the disaster and work now for the future success of the Party.'

'Which party?' asked Burren.

Chris looked down the stem of his pipe. 'I know it seems pretty hopeless at the moment with the Party torn asunder between two factions, but we must try. Unless someone tries to do that, there will not be a Party at all.'

'But which party?' Burren persisted, looking hard at his friend, 'You see, Chris, what you are saying does not make sense. I'm sorry. But there are in effect two Parties at the moment or at least very much the potential for that. Remember? – "a Party within a Party". When you talk about working for the future success of the Party, do you mean working for the success of one of the existing groups? Or do you mean trying to establish a bridge between them? Or do you mean trying to create a new Party altogether?' He cut off Chris's protestations and went on, 'Now if you propose the latter then it is important who sets about doing it. If it is anyone, or group, who has previously been closely attached to either of the main groups inside the Party, then it will fail right at the start. So what do you suggest?'

'Well, for a start, why don't you join us in Socialist Spectrum?'

Burren laughed. 'How is that going to help?'

'Now wait a minute. Give me a chance to explain.'

'Okay, okay.'

'The point is,' Chris went on, 'the people who belong to Socialist Spectrum are moderate. They are not committed to dogmatic belief. Their only belief, if you can call it that, is that all ideas should be subjected to thorough examination.'

'A bit like the Socialist Society,' interjected Burren

Chris was not to be deterred, and went on enthusiastically, 'Now there is something upon which we could build the future of the Party – a Party that would be empirically progressive.'

Burren had not been to any Socialist Spectrum meetings but he had heard about them. Frank Bainwell was damning in his condemnation of them and whilst he didn't completely share Frank's view he did think they were too detached. The Spectrum consisted mainly of members from the professions, and overwhelmingly they were academics. The one thing it did not contain was any genuine working-class membership. He was sceptical, not only of its effectiveness as a ginger group within the Party, but of its authenticity as a repository of socialist ideas.

'Who would listen to such an uninfluential group?' he asked.

'But it is a nucleus,' said Chris earnestly.

'No, you are wrong. You won't establish the future of the Labour Party on the basis of Socialist Spectrum.' He laughed at the absurdity of the idea.

Chris's face flushed momentarily with annoyance.

Burren went on, 'For one thing there is already a too deeply rooted mistrust of intellectuals by the rank and file for Spectrum to have any influence outside of those it represents. And anyway, the future of the Labour Party will have to be worked out by those who possess political power within it.'

'Such as?' asked Chris.

'Oh come on, Chris. You know as well as I do: the trade unions, the Parliamentary Party, the constituency parties. Do I need to say any more?'

'Huh,' scoffed Chris.

'It is true. And you know it.'

Burren got up from his desk and went across to make a cup of coffee for them both.

'So you won't be joining Socialist Spectrum?'

Returning with the coffee and handing one of the mugs to Chris, he said with a smile, 'Of course not. Things have not reached such a sorry pass yet.'

He knew that to join Socialist Spectrum was the fashionable thing to do at the university and that was the reason Chris had joined, but to him it was too detached from the practical problems of politics and this was inevitably so with any organisation founded within such a narrow environment.

Chris shrugged resignedly. He knew there was nothing more to be said on that score. He stood up. 'With the Conservatives in for another five years it is going to be every man for himself. You have to look after your own interests, for nobody else will.'

Burren did not disagree with that.

13

Jane came south to visit Burren's home and family and she enthused about her first stay in that part of the country. He took her to the seaside nearby and they strolled across stretches of soft sand, with the pale blue of the sea reaching out into the distance where it merged with the darker blue of the sky. Inland from the seashore, the town itself nestled comfortably against the backcloth of gently sloping downland. This had been one of his favourite places to visit as a child, and held many happy memories.

On their first evening, after walking part of the downland he suggested they drop in to the Dragon's Head for a drink. This, as he explained to Jane, had been one of his favourite inns where he had often been in for a drink with his old Labour Party colleague, Fred Oddie, after Party meetings. He and Jane went outside and sat in the garden area at the rear of the inn.

There was stillness – the stillness of the closing of a summer's day, and they sat absorbed in their private thoughts. There was just the hint of a breeze that from time to time touched their faces as it came off the Downs. He dreamily looked out beyond the garden to the long sweeping fields, broken only by short hedgerows, ascending gradually to the foothills of the Downs which extended along the skyline as far as the eye could see.

The whole formed an enormous chiaroscuro effect with fields, hedgerows and the occasional cottage, as if etched in by an artist. It was a picture which at that hour of the day seemed to bring everything together. Jane must have caught this moment too as she quoted:

I have felt a presence that disturbs me with the joy
Of elevated thoughts; a sense sublime

And then said, 'This is truly beautiful. Would you not like to
return here to live?'

He laughed ironically and said, 'Yes, probably so, if I had the
money to have the lifestyle. What you see is the very obvious
beauty of this part of the country. It is different if you have to
live here, I mean, *have* to. Of course if you have money, or a
well-paid job in London or somewhere, then it is different. But
for those dependent on being here for their living it offers only
what you see.'

Being together here with Jane, with the beauty of the landscape and the charm of the evening had briefly taken hold and
pulled him back. But he knew it was not to be. Not now.
Perhaps never.

Jane viewed him with an affectionate but appraising look. 'I
believe you know what you want,' she said.

Now they were to go and visit Jane's home in Newcastle. As
they made their way to the railway station he plied her with
questions, but she was adamant. 'You will soon know,' was all
she would reply. He had to remain contented with the position
of a stranger. She stepped lightly beside him. He could feel the
suppressed excitement in her arm which was linked through his,
and seeing her out of the corner of his eye he knew that she was
pleased that he was going with her.

'You should have brought your coat,' she said.

He regarded her affectionately. 'Stop fussing.'

She giggled and pulled his arm towards her.

They passed through the barrier and walked on down the
platform, stopping at a confectionery stall to buy cigarettes and
newspapers for the journey. The train was ready for boarding.
They continued to walk along the platform looking for an

empty compartment. They found one and settled themselves in for the long journey.

A light rain was falling outside and the windows of the compartment had misted over. He wiped enough away to create a clear view. As far as the eye could see there were lines of carriages, the roofs shiny from the rain which spilled gently over the sides. At last the train began to draw slowly out of the station, like a long-distance runner preserving energy for the long stretch ahead. They both began to read.

They spoke little on the journey; just an odd comment or two passed between them as one or other of them looked up from their reading and commented on the scenery outside, or on something prompted by their reading. The train sped north-ward past fields and meadows bordered by neat hedgerows interspersed with tall sprawling oak and elm trees. It began to slow down only as it began to approach the industrial heart-land, as though in perverse mood it wished to make its pas-sengers look long and hard on the rows of dingy houses that backed onto the railway track, and beyond to long columns of smoke that reached up and were caught by the blanket of grey sky above. Then on to where the texture of the countryside became noticeably harsher, to the slated roofs and land encompassed by stone walls. The gentle rain continued to fall.

Eventually they reached the outskirts of Newcastle and the train crept slowly towards the station like some returning runaway from home. He saw the massive nineteenth-century stone buildings that had been built at the time of the Gothic revival, their surfaces black from soot and fumes.

'How far is your home from the station?' he asked.

'A threepenny ride,' replied Jane.

They crossed the road at the front of the station to the bus stop. As it was early afternoon they had little difficulty in finding a seat on the bus. The bus crawled slowly out of the city centre, past warehouses and up hills until it reached the plateau on the north side of the city.

'This is our stop,' said Jane, as the bus swung round into a road that was long and had terraced housing on both sides. Each house had a bay window on the ground and top floor with three concrete steps leading up to the front door. The houses, though old, looked well cared for.

'Our house is number forty-four. Just past that second lamp post,' Jane said, squeezing his arm.

He looked ahead and saw the house. The woodwork of the houses was painted alternately in brown and green. Jane's house was painted green. For some reason, he didn't quite know why, he was pleased about that. They waited on the steps whilst Jane fumbled for her key. He saw that that there were no net curtains at the windows and he was pleased about that too. Jane found her key and they stepped inside.

'Hello, Mum,' Jane called. 'We've arrived.' Jane's mother appeared in the passageway.

'Hello dear, how are you?' They kissed one another before Jane's mother turned to Burren and said, 'Jane has told me all about you, John.'

Mother and daughter laughed.

He stepped forward to shake hands. 'Glad to meet you, Mrs Dayton.'

'You are looking well, Mum,' said Jane.

'And why shouldn't I, my dear?' exclaimed Mrs Dayton, smiling at Burren as she spoke.

He saw that she smiled in the same way as Jane. That she had high cheekbones and creased her face. In fact physically they were very much alike, though Mrs Dayton was shorter than her daughter. He guessed that she must be in her mid-fifties, and she was still very trim.

'Well come along in, we don't want to stand about in the hallway. You must both be hungry after your long journey and certainly in need of a cup of tea.'

They followed her into the kitchen at the back of the house, with Jane looking back at him and grinning broadly.

'I'll get you something light now,' Mrs Dayton was saying, 'because we'll be having our main meal when your father comes home from work.'

'Has Dad got the job of supervisor yet?' asked Jane.

'Yes he has. It is much better for him now. He has a little office of his own and is able to take things easier. He even wears a white shirt.' Mrs Dayton gave a little shrug of pleasure.

Again he noticed the similarity between them. She seemed a cheerful person, he thought.

Jane's mother methodically fetched tea and sugar from one cupboard and crockery from another, deftly handling things like a craftsman, whilst Jane plied her mother with questions about her father, her sister Susan, who was at school, and her brother Michael, who was completing his National Service abroad. Jane was the eldest of the children. The tea was soon made and Mrs Dayton sat down and offered them homemade fruit cake.

'How are your studies, Jane? You are not worrying about your final exams, I hope.' And then to Burren, she asked, 'And what are you studying?'

'Politics and economics,' he replied.

Jane broke in quickly with, 'He is a political animal to his fingertips.' She looked at him and smiled.

Mrs Dayton laughed. 'You'll get on all right with Father, then, he is as interested in politics now as when he was a young man and we were courting. Many is the time I was asked to sacrifice an evening to attend a political meeting with him.'

At that moment the door opened and Jane's sister Susan entered. She smiled shyly.

'Hello, Jane, I didn't expect to see you at home yet.'

'Hello, Sue.' She turned towards Burren. 'This is John.'

Burren smiled and said hello. They shook hands rather formally. She was unlike Jane – still at the puppy-fat stage of development, she was going to be a larger woman than her sister.

Mrs Dayton now began to make preparations for the evening meal and Susan stayed to help her mother whilst Jane took Burren into the front room – known as the sitting room. Along one wall was a very large bookcase with glass doors. He saw that it was well stocked with books and a quick glance across the shelves revealed that there were books on politics and history as well as literature.

The room was comfortable-looking and cosy in a Sunday-ish sort of way – an impression about such rooms that went back to his own childhood. But like most working-class sitting rooms it was overfurnished and had far too much bric-a-brac in it.

He sat in a chair and watched Jane going round the room identifying familiar objects in their customary places, in the way that is done after absence from home. She then came and sat on the arm of his chair.

'What do you think of the old house?' she asked.

'Seems all right to me,' he said non-committally.

'Mum has wanted to move into one of the new council houses that have just been built in the Louthdon estate, but Dad is not keen. He sees no great advantage in that. He maintains that unless you can move into a different kind of house altogether there is no point in moving.' She put her nose up in the air in mock disdain. 'He also dislikes estates.'

He laughed. 'I think your father has got a point.'

'Yes, but Mum wants modern facilities, you see.'

He avoided a direct response by asking, 'How long have you lived in this house?'

'As long as I can remember. It has happy memories for me,' said Jane. She smiled. 'Lots of questions – the interrogator again!'

He laughed, though he realised that she was right. He continued with questions, asking her if she would want to return here to live.

'Why not?'

His questions were quite deliberate as he wanted to know

how attached Jane still was to her home. Since first meeting her he had been impressed by the natural way she behaved in different circumstances, as though completely unaware of such things as class, background or social values; though he knew this was not true. He now knew that it was not some psychological device to be deployed only in the rarefied atmosphere of university. She was, he believed, quite naturally classless.

'Well?' she asked.

'Nothing,' he said, surprised out of his meditation.

The door opened and Mr Dayton entered.

'Hello, Dad.' Jane went to embrace her father. 'I didn't hear you come in.'

After kissing his daughter, Mr Dayton held her at arm's length looking at her appreciatively. 'How are you, my darling?'

'This is John.' Jane grabbed his arm and brought him towards her father.

They stood chatting for a while before going into the kitchen where Mrs Dayton had the evening meal ready. Jane's mother had prepared an Irish stew that looked delicious as she set it down on the table. The helping which she placed before Burren was enormous: the working man's meal at the end of the day. He set about the task with determination.

Conversation at the dinner table was taken up with Jane's father asking her many of the same questions that her mother had asked earlier, with the occasional reference to Burren to bring him into things. Mrs Dayton, whilst joining in the conversation, also kept an eye on each of their plates to see that everyone was satisfied. They appeared a very happy and united family and he felt it was not just put on for his benefit; they quite naturally enjoyed being together. Their affection reached and embraced him too within the mesh of family life. He felt easy in their company.

Jane's father asked what she intended to show Burren over the weekend, and she replied that they were going to the art gallery, the Gala Field, and with a laugh she said, 'And of course the bridge!'

They all laughed and Susan said, 'That is very original, Jane.'

Her father told Jane to make sure that she showed Burren the Town Hall, which he said was one of the finest pieces of nineteenth-century architecture.

Mrs Dayton replenished her husband's plate and offered Burren more too. He weakly protested and Jane supported him by saying that they all ate too much at home. Her mother remained unrepentant however and said, 'Go on, John, there is so little left here.' He relented.

The following day passed quickly, with Jane and Burren going off to see the points of interest in the city. In the evening they all went to the cinema and saw *Rebel Without a Cause*, but it was not a film to bridge the generation gap. There was much lively discussion of the film later in the evening at home with predictable responses from the different age groups. Burren was surprised at how confident and articulate Jane's sister was in the discussion. She could be quite a success.

After a lazy beginning to the Sunday Mr Dayton invited Burren to join him for a drink at his local before lunch.

'I always visit the Crown & Anchor,' explained Mr Dayton as they walked round from the house. 'Well, you get to know people in one pub; it becomes your local. And anyway their bitter is much better than at the Flying Horse, the other nearby pub.'

They sat at a table close to the bar. Burren commented on how popular it seemed to be, with people coming and going and calling in for a midday drink before lunch.

'Aye, I suppose it is,' said Mr Dayton, 'but nothing like as busy as it used to be. Folks don't drink to the same extent now. Why, I can remember a time when you wouldn't have been able to move in this bar on a Sunday at midday, and all men.'

'But why has it fallen off?' asked Burren.

The older man looked at Burren with a slow smile filling his face. 'People are becoming more civilised,' he gave a knowing wink, 'more middle class, I believe is the expression. It is like everything else today. As soon as people discover themselves doing something that is considered very working class they immediately stop it.'

It was clear that this was something that Jane's father regretted.

'I suppose that higher wages have shown them new possibilities,' ventured Burren, feeling that he must defend them.

'But it is not a question of wages, it's a question of values. People don't have to change their values because they've got a few extra pence in their pockets.'

It is odd, thought Burren. Here he is criticising his own folk yet defending them at the same time. Loyalty is what it was. If I were to say that they let us down in the general election, I am sure he would find some way of coming to their defence.

'Drink up, we must have another pint to do justice to our Sunday lunch.'

Burren emptied his glass in one gulp. He watched Mr Dayton cross to the bar and stop to talk to two men sitting at a table. He admired Jane's father for the way he had worked to give his children a decent education, and because he did not boast about them, not even Jane. He admired him most because despite all the setbacks experienced by his generation he still held to some idealism or faith in people to do what is good.

Mr Dayton returned with the beer and asked Burren what he thought of its quality.

'Excellent and very strong,' he said.

Mr Dayton laughed with approval.

They returned home to devour Sunday lunch prepared by Mrs Dayton and Jane. Over the meal Mr Dayton wanted to talk about the recent general election, and proclaimed that much of what had been achieved by the post-war Labour government would now be progressively dismantled by the Conservatives.

Burren rose to the challenge. He said that he did not think the balance of views within the Conservative Party would favour that, and the One Nation group of Conservatives under Butler were still in the ascendancy. Given time however, he thought that Maurice Watkins's view would prevail.

Mr Dayton was delighted to have a political sparring partner and Mrs Dayton seemed pleased to see her husband enjoying his old pursuit.

Conservatives were much the same as they had always been, Mr Dayton said, and any supposed change in them was superficial, and only for electoral ends.

After lunch and with much opposition Jane persuaded him to go for a walk in the park. As they set out from the house he thought how much he would have preferred the comfort of a chair and the continued discussion with Mr Dayton. As they reached the park, however, he was pleased that he had agreed to go out. It was a warm afternoon and they both felt the pleasure of the freshness after being indoors.

He turned and said to Jane, 'You are lucky, you know.'

'Oh do tell me why,' she said mischievously.

'You come from a community that appreciates education and is prepared to make sacrifices to see that it is secured. And yet they accept you quite naturally as one of them, without putting you on a pedestal and treating you as someone different. No barrier is erected between you and them. And communication is still possible between you. But you know all this.'

'Are you talking about my family or the local community?' asked Jane.

'Well, I have assumed both.'

'Yes, I suppose that is right,' said Jane. 'I realised it soon after I went to university and talked to other girls from similar backgrounds – though there aren't too many of them of course.' She laughed. 'We are a special breed! They told me of some of the difficulties they experienced when they returned home, of feeling cut off and not being able to talk, almost strangers in their own home. Even so, it hasn't all been plain sailing for me either. There have been times when I've thought the gap is unbridgeable because we are too far apart and I know it won't narrow let alone close.' She looked at him closely, 'Well, I have told you about this already, haven't I?'

He recalled the occasion of their conversation over breakfast at the Union.

Jane continued, 'But I think I've come through it and there is an awareness by both my parents that I will be different.'

'I know the feeling,' he said.

'I hope that having had the experience with me they will be able to show the necessary understanding with Susan. Of course Dad, like a lot of other working men in the north, although self-taught is very well read. Even now he can catch me out on some author or other. Yet at the same time he is perfectly natural about it. It isn't anything special. Do you know what I mean?'

'I think so,' he said, 'Self-educated people often make no distinction between ordinary conversation and what might be termed intellectual conversation – it all flows in a stream.' He laughed at the thought. 'It is like a continuous weekend school.'

'That's right.' After some thought Jane then said, 'There is a difference of course. What I have, and they haven't, is that through education I have become more disciplined. You learn to control your emotions. Actually, although we get on well together this is the one thing upon which Dad and I disagree. Sometimes, especially if it is an issue on which he feels strongly, he approaches it with his emotions fully engaged – through a fixation with a belief, if you like. Whereas to me, that is unsatisfactory because I am aware of another aspect of truth. That, it seems to me, is the big difference that occurs once you become educated: you know when you are being intellectually dishonest.' She gave a self-deprecatory laugh. 'Doesn't mean that you are not dishonest, of course, but you know you are being so. Does that make sense?'

'Yes, I know what you mean,' he replied, impressed by what Jane had said.

They had now reached the park gates that led out on to the road from which they could catch a bus back. They walked silently together to the bus stop, holding hands.

On their return from visiting Jane's home, there was a note for Burren from Jasmine. The note said simply that the Principal would like to see him. The following day he called into Jasmine's office to ask if she knew what the Principal wished to see him about. Jasmine was vague on the matter except to say that it was something to do with Transport House. She said she would tell the Principal that he was here.

Robert Wilcox came into Jasmine's office and welcomed Burren. 'Come on in, John,' he said in his most avuncular manner. He settled himself behind his desk and invited Burren to take a seat. He wasted no time in letting Burren know the reason for asking him to call and see him.

'The Labour Party has been set back on its heels by the election defeat,' he said, 'and the leadership now recognises that there has to be a major review of policy to take account of possible developments over the coming decade. Part of that review is to look at issues of foreign policy with emphasis on major international questions such as the unification of Western Europe, Western defence, and the continuing role of the United Nations. The idea is, as I understand it, to have a strategic view of Britain's relations with the rest of the world. Could be very interesting, don't you think?'

'Yes indeed,' replied Burren, wondering however just why he was being told this.

Robert Wilcox continued, 'The Secretary of the International Department at Transport House has been in touch with me to ask if we have anyone here who could assist him on the foreign policy side of the Review.' He paused to observe how Burren was receiving this information, and then went on, 'Naturally I thought of you. With your strong interest in international affairs and given the piece that you have recently written for

The New Age I thought you might well be suited to help. It seems to me that this chimes in closely with something that was talked about at your initial interview. Do you remember?'

Burren was about to respond but Robert Wilcox quickly raised his hand to indicate that he had something else to say. He now asked, 'How are you getting on with Sean Halloran?' and then as much to himself as to Burren, he said, 'A very bright young man. I'm told he is being lined up for some role within the Secretary General's office at the UN.'

Burren had learned from his conversations with Robert Wilcox that the latter rather liked to talk in vague and general terms, as he had now done in relation to Sean Halloran. He now told the Principal that he was getting on fine with Sean Halloran and that he liked him. He said that Halloran thought he could do well in his option and that he had a flair for international politics: 'In fact I have decided on what I'm going to do. I shall apply to university to take international politics, or international relations as the purists liked to call it.' He hesitated. 'And I was hoping that you might support me.'

Robert Wilcox beamed. 'Of course I will. And I think you have reached the right decision.' Burren continued excitedly, 'I haven't yet made up my mind where I should apply, and I need to talk further with Sean Halloran about that. According to him, to study international relations in a conceptual, systematic way it is necessary to go somewhere that employs that approach rather than the historical method.' He stopped, conscious that he was probably taking too much of the Principal's time. 'I'm sorry, you are probably too busy to hear all this.'

Robert Wilcox smiled. 'No, carry on. I'm sure Sean knows what he is talking about.'

Burren lost no time. 'I have the impression that he thinks LSE is the place for this subject, whereas here the university adopts a more historical approach, and so you see I have to make up my own mind on the merits of these two approaches. Of course I may not be accepted.'

'I wouldn't worry too much on that score. But I am sure you are doing the right thing. I've entertained high hopes for you, and I believe you are moving in the right direction.'

He returned to his opening subject. 'Now what am I to say to Michael Jenkins?' He laughed. 'No, he is no relation of our mutual friend Paul.'

'I should like very much to help with the review of policy,' said Burren. 'And thank you for putting it my way. I am quite excited by the idea.'

Robert Wilcox came round from behind his desk and saw Burren to the door.

'I'll let Michael Jenkins have your name and he should then be in touch. Good luck, and let me know how things go.'

As he passed through Jasmine's office she looked up.

'My word,' she exclaimed, 'who looks like the proverbial cat with the cream?'

He was conscious of looking rather pleased with himself. 'You knew,' he said. 'You do like the world of secrecy, don't you?'

She smiled, 'Not really, but I am pleased for you.'

He hadn't told Jane yet of his plans to go on to university, nor had he had an opportunity to mention his conversation with the Principal. Together now in his room he approached the subject.

'There is something I should tell you,' he said.

'That sounds ominous,' said Jane, with a suitably neutral expression.

'I've already told you how much I like the international organisation subject and how interested I am in the wider context of international politics, and you know how uncertain I have been about my future.'

'I think I know what you are going to tell me,' said Jane. 'You are going to tell me that you want to go on to university.'

'Was it that obvious?'

'It was becoming increasingly clear to me that you were moving that way.'

'The problem is,' he said, 'I am not sure yet where I should apply. Sean Halloran thinks that I would benefit most from going to the LSE.'

He went on to explain the different approaches in the study of world politics, and said, 'As you probably know, because I must have bored you with it, I am captivated by the subject. Nothing before has so taken hold of my whole way of thinking about politics as this study on a world scale.'

'I know it has,' said Jane, 'and I am pleased for you because I think it is what you need.'

'I have something more to tell you,' he said.

Jane raised her eyebrows questioningly.

He now told her of the nature of his conversation with the Principal.

'Things have been happening,' said Jane. 'I can see that you must be feeling very good.'

He took her hand and drew her to him. 'I don't want anything to spoil what we have, Jane. You mean so much to me.' He continued with what was on his mind. 'If I go to LSE I shall probably stay with Paul Jenkins.' He hesitated, realising that he hadn't yet asked Paul. 'I think that will be possible.'

Jane said, 'I think you have made up your mind.'

He could see that he was assuming too much and looking too far ahead, which could change things at a time when the other important matter of their examinations loomed ever closer. He tried to reassure her.

'If I go to LSE, and it is still an if, you could come and stay for weekends at Paul's home – he has invited us both.'

'Of course, of course,' she said, seeming quite keen on the idea.

He held her close to him. 'I know you have little time to spare at the moment; we both have little time.' He shrugged. 'But I have to go down to London to meet Michael Jenkins, the head of the International Department at Transport House, and I have to do it more or less straightaway. I shall stay with Paul

271

overnight.' He looked at her appealingly. 'Will you come with me?'

'I'll try,' she said.

14

Having decided matters in his own mind about what he was going to do after Morton, he suddenly felt overwhelmingly empty. He was pleased, in fact had been elated at the prospect of researching aspects of foreign policy for the International Department of the Labour Party, yet it did not compensate for the emptiness he now felt. He ought to feel very good, he told himself, but he didn't, and he could not understand why.

In recent weeks he had seen less of Frank Bainwell and Chris Megson. The three of them no longer met for coffee at mid-morning as they were using the library at different times. The fact that they were taking different optional subjects meant that their patterns of study no longer coincided as they did previously. They were now caught up, as most of them at Morton were, with the imminent onset of the final examinations. His own consuming interest in his new subject also drew him away from the others. They were concentrating on British affairs, whilst he was combining this with his international study.

He felt an acute sense of being out on his own and this extended in part to his relations with Jane. He was not sure any more. They were becoming more immersed these days in their own thoughts as they looked not only to the immediate future, but beyond. He began to feel a sense of panic and inadequacy to the tasks in hand. What if he should fail? What then awaited him? Was it all worth the effort anyhow? His mind drifted back to the uncomplicated days before he went to Morton – the memory came back to him, quite erroneously, as pleasurable, undemanding days.

He found it difficult to check the mood that was descending upon him. He recalled the evening at the Dragon's Head with

Jane only a few weeks back; of seeing the beauty of the Downs as they both looked out beyond the fields and hedgerows. Jane's words on that evening came back to him. Was he doing the right thing in pushing on and forward? To what? New challenges, new setbacks. And would he be up to it anyhow? And what of his future with Jane? Did they have a future together? He knew that Jane was going to teach after having completed the postgraduate diploma at the university here. Jane would be a success, he was a confident of that. She was strong and resilient.

He made himself a cup of coffee with the intention of completing the reading on the United Nations but he could not concentrate. Reading about the obstacles in the way of founding the United Nations, and later the failed attempt to establish an international agency to control atomic energy, whilst important and interesting in itself seemed now to depress him. His head began to ache and his mind felt tired, very, very, tired. He drifted off into the world of sleep.

He awoke to find that his headache was still with him. He turned to look at his watch optimistically ticking away on his wrist. It showed 9.05 pm. He raised himself and stood up. His head felt as though it was forcing its way down into his chest. He decided that fresh air would clear his head and a walk would get his thoughts back on track for the reading.

He tried to put extra briskness into his stride, and breathed deeply, compelling the air into his nostrils and then forcing it out again quickly through his mouth as he had been taught as a child. It did not help. The air hung heavily as though suspended from the huge canvas of thunder clouds above.

As he walked on down The High he felt the presence of the massive walls of colleges on either side of the street reaching out to grip and crush him in their assertion of immortality. As he looked up at the stonework silhouetted against the billowing clouds the grave beauty of it all bore in upon him, giving sharp stabs at the ache inside and yet adding to his numbness. He came to the end of The High and turned down into Gosford Street carrying him in the direction of the Eagle & Fox. He knew that he would go into the pub, though he hadn't planned it when he left college. Something inexplicably drew him towards the pub. It was located in the poorer part of the city amongst the streets of small, terraced housing, and was popular with servicemen, especially American, and pretty, tartish women.

As he drew near to the pub he could hear the sounds of jazz music coming from the open windows. The music whorled its way into his head, creating a cacophony in his resonant sinuses. He put his hand to his head to protect it from the hurting sound. Yet still he knew he would go in.

He entered the saloon bar. It was crowded with people standing around in groups. He started elbowing his way through and in doing so awkwardly knocked a man's arm, causing him to spill some of his drink. The man glared and Burren apologised and moved on, nudging his way towards the bar, past uniformed servicemen, couples petting with not too furtive hands at play. He reached a space at the bar and ordered a pint of beer. He heard it rattle down his throat to the empty tank of a stomach below. It felt warm and tasted bitter. He drank quickly and pushed his glass forward for refilling.

In the far corner of the room to his right a trio of musicians continued to pour out a very improvised, rather poor form of off-beat jazz. People sitting close by around the trio were swaying their heads to the beat of the music in a weird mechanical way, their pale mask-like faces under the shaded light lending a further surreal element to the scene. After a time the musicians stopped playing, apparently to rest and have refreshments. Drinks were brought to them whilst they slumped back lethargically in their seats looking tired and bored.

Now that the music had ceased he could tell that his head was aching more than ever. It felt as though his head was performing concentric movements around his neck. He thought it would shortly break loose and drop to the floor. Then the pain would stop.

He laughed aloud at his own bizarre thoughts and saw that a young woman was looking at him quizzically from the other end of the bar. He grinned, feeling the pain as the flesh creased on his face. He turned his attention back to the bar and ordered another pint of beer. He took an enormous gulp of the beer and looked around the room. To him, it seemed to be full of happy people, enjoying the first evening of their weekend and making no demands other than to have a good time. He wanted to be part of this; not to have to think of anything in particular but simply to allow the senses to take over, and to forget that in just over two weeks he would be tested.

His thoughts began to drift between the setting of the test to come – of people sitting in rows of seats each with an occupant doing exactly the same as the person in the next seat; a room full of people engaged in a single activity yet each individual separate and alone performing in this great test, and the crowd in the saloon bar – not being tested in any way and free. The very nature of this entity was social; to belong in the warmth of human company. He finished his beer. Aristotle was right after all, he told himself, we are social beings. He laughed out loud again at his thoughts.

The barman came across as Burren caught his attention.

'Another pint of the same,' he said, as he suddenly became aware of the drink taking hold of him. He welcomed the feeling of becoming drunk. It made him feel warm and social.

The barman returned. 'She is very interested in you, you know,' he nodded in the direction of the young woman at the other end of the bar. Burren followed his direction and grinned inanely at the woman.

The young woman came across to his end of the bar. 'Are you all right, love?' she asked.

'Perfectly,' he grinned.

'Well, you don't look it. You are deathly pale and you keep laughing to yourself.'

He looked at her closely and smiled, 'Everything is funny, everything. That is why I am laughing so much.'

The young woman looked both puzzled and slightly anxious.

She impressed him, in his befuddled state, as a rather earnest woman, not much older than himself, he guessed. He focused on her as though doing so would determine her age for him, whilst continuing to grin at her. She was pretty with clear, blue eyes, and fair hair, nearly blonde, though his vision was not clear enough to make the distinction. He noticed that she was not drinking and he insisted on buying her a drink.

'Thanks.'

He was intrigued by the woman. He felt sure he had not seen her before in the Eagle & Fox. 'How did you come to be here on your own?' he asked, realising now that his words were becoming a bit slurred.

'That would be a long story,' she smiled.

He leaned precariously forward, resting one elbow on the bar counter, and again looked deeply into her face. 'I've got all evening,' he said. He tried to speak slowly so that his pronunciation would be correct, but it had only the effect of making him appear stupid. He reached out his hand to touch hers. She seemed pleased, he thought. 'What made you come over to me?' he asked. He could feel the beer increasingly having its effect and he was no longer attempting to hide the fact.

The woman looked concerned. 'You looked rather ill, and I thought you might need help.'

He laughed almost uncontrollably.

'Why do you laugh like that? Don't you believe me?'

'Believe, believe,' he repeated to himself. 'Yes, I believe you, and thank you.' He tried to smile but felt it was twisted. He went on, 'It is very important to believe what people tell us. Tell me, what do you believe in? And don't give me any nonsense about God.'

The woman looked at him disbelievingly. 'Are you at college, or something?' she asked, as though she had divined something that she didn't altogether like.

'Answer my question,' he insisted.

'I don't know,' the woman said, fearing that most probably she had got herself involved with some crazy fellow who was cracking up before his exams.

'I believed in people,' he said. 'Nice, straightforward thing like believing in people. But either my faith was weak, or I expected too much. I don't know which. It is all too much.' He sighed and then swallowed his beer.

The woman was clearly bewildered. She looked at him with equal degrees of fear and awe, not knowing how to reply. He saw her expression and despite his bibulous state, sensed her thoughts. He wanted to laugh but he knew that if he did it would upset his stomach and probably make him sick. He ordered more drinks.

The woman now seemed to him to be coming up very close to his face and then quickly receding. He rubbed his eyes but it did not alter the picture. He tried looking at other parts of the room and focusing on particular objects. He was unable to differentiate any clear lines on anything in the room, and colours and shapes blended into a continuous blur. He went to lift his glass of beer from the counter and found that his hand was stretching too far beyond the glass. He slowly drew it back until he felt his fingers safely around the glass.

The lights had now been dimmed and then returned to full, and the landlord was calling 'Time!' It occurred to him that he would have to leave the bar and he wondered what would happen when he started to walk. He tried to rehearse in his mind how he would reach the door, but he failed to complete the thought.

The woman was now speaking to him. 'Are you going to be all right?'

'Sho-or,' he said. 'I'll see you home.'

She laughed. 'It is more likely to be the other way about.'

He felt himself beginning to fall backwards and quickly grabbed at the bar counter.

The woman took his arm and he began his lurching journey towards the door – for journey it was, as the door seemed an infinite distance away to him. They reached the door safely and started the walk along the pavement. He could feel a solid wall on one side of him and he moved his hand along it for support, whilst the woman helped him on the other side. The air was now much cooler. He could feel it on his face and it made him aware of the fact that he was sweating profusely.

His stomach was churning like a huge cauldron, and now and again it reached his throat as if about to boil over. He lurched on, supported by the uncomplaining woman.

He wanted to thank her. To tell her that he was sorry he had spoilt her evening. He could not understand why she was still with him, but he was grateful for it. He knew that if he dared to speak too much, he would be sick. He did not want to be sick in front of her. The thought of it embarrassed him.

She asked him for the name of his college. He managed to mutter the answer. She was relieved that it wasn't very far.

He tried to think of what it had been like in the street when he had passed down it earlier in the evening, but it was too difficult to sustain continuous thought. He faltered and nearly fell. The woman encouraged him on. He looked up, as he had a sudden fear that the sky was coming down upon him. He felt trapped. He wanted to run, to escape from the street.

The churning in his stomach stopped suddenly. It now felt empty, though in fact it was full. The cool air was clearing his mind and he felt less drunk, yet sweat poured down his face in rivulets. The woman gripped his arm tightly, exhorting him on. He knew nothing more.

He blinked. He was slumped beside the short wall that ran alongside the pavement. The woman was leaning over him.

'Thank God for that,' she said.

He blinked again. 'What?'

'I was frightened when you passed out.'

'I'm very sorry,' he said.

He jumped to his feet and shook himself. 'I feel fine.'

'Are you sure?'

'Quite sure.' He tried a smile and succeeded. 'And now I will see you home.'

The following day he was his normal self and appeared to suffer no ill effects from the bizarre episode of the night before. He could not explain why it had happened. He told Jane about some of what had happened.

She was clearly puzzled. 'I have been concerned about you,' she said. 'You have been very self-absorbed.'

'I know,' he said.

'I hope now that you have taken some important decisions you will feel more at rest within yourself.' She reached out her hand.

He knew that she was right. Uncertainty about the future had troubled him more than he was prepared to acknowledge. He did feel more relaxed, though he still had to decide where he wanted to pursue further study. He leant across and softly kissed her.

'Thank you,' he whispered. 'And will you be able to come to London with me when I go to meet Michael Jenkins? We can visit Paul and stay overnight. I have checked with him and he says that he would love to see both of us.'

'Yes, I will come,' said Jane. She was keen to see Paul again and to see the Jenkins household in Muswell Hill.

His last tutorial with Sean Halloran was on the United Nations and how its founders sought to improve on the League of Nations. He had been asked to look at how well the organisation seemed designed for the conditions in the world following the Second World War.

This was a topic of immense interest, coinciding as it did with his own formative years. He had as a boy at the end of his schooldays read the newspapers on the explosion of the two atomic bombs in Japan, and he had kept a newspaper cuttings file on this as well as on the Nuremberg Trials. He had also read about the founding of the United Nations in San Francisco, without knowing the background to its creation or the reasons for the failure of the League of Nations.

The subject material of international organisation, especially when viewed in the wider context of the idea of an international community, gripped his interest in a way that no other intellectual enquiry had. It was perhaps its immense significance to his own generation, and to future generations, that appealed to him. But more than that it was because for the first time the political process was viewed as a system: of how sovereign states related to one another; how they pursued their own interests and worked with other states to this end through organisations and alliances; how economic and military power was distributed throughout the world and the significance of this; and how countries sought to establish international institutions to help create peace and security. Each of these components was interconnected and together they formed an intricate whole, in which each part affected the others to a greater or lesser degree. It was in fact a system.

It was this concept of a system that held him and made it a compelling intellectual study. And he was only at the foothills of the subject. The decision as to where he should follow this study further was in fact narrowing, whether he consciously recognised it or not.

'So you believe the veto power of the big five was an ingenious device?' asked Halloran.

'Yes,' Burren said. 'It seems to me that the veto is a clear indication by the founders that to do otherwise could entail action under the auspices of the Security Council against one or other superpower, and given the distribution of power in the

281

world at that time and still more so now perhaps, that could mean legitimising world war by the United Nations.'

Sean Halloran smiled in a way that Burren knew invited debate. 'I can see that Carr and the realist school have influenced your thinking. My point would be that you have not sufficiently examined the position from the standpoint of other views.' He grinned mischievously. 'And there were some!' He laughed softly. 'Remember that the veto power was included largely at the insistence of the Soviet Union: without it she would not have agreed to join the UN. So you ought not to read too much into it to support your conceptual argument.'

'Well . . .' Burren was about to protest.

'I can see,' said Halloran, 'that you will enjoy examining international relations in a conceptual setting, but do not get too carried away by the eloquence of certain writers. Realists are especially plausible, indeed persuasive, in this context.' He paused and then said, 'But you have a decision to make?'

'I believe I know what you are referring to, and yes, I do have to decide but I am clear about wishing to study further. I'm going to London this weekend and I'm staying with a friend who is studying law at LSE and so I hope that will help me decide. And I'm meeting with Michael Jenkins. I mentioned him to you, I believe.'

'Yes, you did.' He looked at Burren in an almost fatherly way. 'Well, I hope you find out what you want to know. As I've already told you, I can arrange for you to have interviews at a couple of colleges here if you want me to. Just let me know on your return from London.'

He nodded approvingly. 'I think you will enjoy working on the foreign policy. These things are always useful to have.'

Burren thanked him generously for opening up a new field of study. In a general sense he had always been interested in world affairs, but it had been Sean Halloran who had articulated this interest in him. He said he would be in touch after his London visit to let Halloran know what he had decided.

'Maybe we could have a drink together when I let you know,' suggested Burren.

'Yes, why not,' said Halloran. 'We can go across to my favourite haunt, or perhaps somewhere in the city centre. Anyhow, we can settle that when you get in touch.'

They shook hands and Burren left.

They emerged from Paddington station into the warmth of the summer day, made still warmer by the enclosed atmosphere of the London streets. Burren was going to meet Michael Jenkins and Jane said she would explore some of the attractions of London. They made plans to meet for lunch.

Entering Transport House, with its ramshackle lift and long uninspiring corridors, reminded Burren of his first visit to the building two years earlier when he had been interviewed. He recalled being told by the interview panel that Reed scholars were expected to be the thinkers of the Party, and now he was returning to pay – in part at least – his debt. At the same time he was hoping to benefit from the experience.

Michael Jenkins greeted him with a not altogether effusive welcome. 'So you are just finishing at Morton?'

'That's right,' said Burren.

'And then what?' Jenkins asked, without showing much interest in the answer.

'I am hoping to go on and undertake a full study of international relations now that I've completed a course in international organisation. Perhaps Robert Wilcox indicated that in his letter.'

'Yes, he did,' said Jenkins. 'In fact, he positively waxed about you.' He added flatly, 'You are going to have much to live up to.'

Burren did not respond. He had already concluded that it had not been Jenkins's decision to ask for assistance from Morton.

'Right, well, let us get down to business.' Jenkins went on to explain that there was resistance amongst a powerful and influential element in the Party to engage in any policy review, but that some of the younger members of the National Executive Committee had pushed Attlee into agreeing to it. It was therefore important to realise that it was a highly political exercise. Burren thought he knew what he meant. 'I read your article on the United States and Europe, from which I gather that West European unification is an interest of yours.'

'Yes, I am very interested in what is happening in Europe,' Burren replied enthusiastically.

'Okay. Well, in terms of division of work, I should like you to look at Labour policy towards Western Europe, bearing in mind the attitude of the Tories on this issue. And look at our approach towards the UN. Which probably means we are satisfied with it.'

Burren chose not to comment on this, but asked, 'Should I arrange to meet with members of the Party with responsibilities in relation to foreign policy – the Shadow Foreign Secretary, members of the Parliamentary Party with expertise or interest in foreign policy matters – that sort of thing?'

Jenkins laughed. 'That would mean the whole bunch of them! They all fancy themselves as experts. No, there is nothing to be gained by meeting anyone at this stage. Just concentrate on the policy, I suggest. We'll supply you with any existing policy statements that you may wish to have.'

He got up from behind his desk and started pacing the room whilst continuing to speak to Burren, 'After we have made some progress between us I suggest we meet to review matters. I will contact you, and of course I want us to keep in touch with one another on a regular basis. After we have reviewed matters we may then wish to meet with some of these self-appointed experts!' He laughed at his own comment. 'Anything else you want to know at this point?'

Burren said he was satisfied with his assignment and collected past policy papers before moving towards the door.

'Well, you know where I am now,' said Jenkins. 'Be sure to keep in touch.'

On his way to meet Jane, he reflected on the meeting with Michael Jenkins. He was keen to start the work on the policy review and calculated that he would probably be able to spend a lot of his time on this over the summer months, but he was not sure he was going to get on good terms with Jenkins. This youngish man, not much older than himself, Burren estimated, came across as a bureaucratic creature: wary and probably of limited vision. He also had Jenkins placed as highly political and likely to resist anything that did not fit his own particular ends. Time alone would tell if he was right in this assessment. Meanwhile he intended to take the review seriously and ensure that what he did was attributed to him.

He had now reached the place where he and Jane had agreed to meet. She was not yet there and he looked around for her. He scanned the rushing people crossing the busy road intersection and concluded that it had not been a wise choice of venue at which to meet.

Nevertheless, after a few minutes he caught sight of Jane making her way along one of the crowded streets. She was walking in his direction, though she hadn't yet seen him, in a relaxed purposeful way with head held upright. She looked happy, he thought.

'Have you had a good time?' he asked.

'It is such an exciting place, isn't it?' she said enthusiastically.

'This is where it all happens,' he said with a broad grin.

After they had lunched and chatted about each other's morning events, with Jane enthusing about the National Portrait Gallery, they made their way to Paul's home, following his instructions closely. Paul had said that it was only a short walk from the tube station and soon they saw the nameplate 'Clarissa' on the entrance wall to the drive and knew this must be the house.

They stopped momentarily at the drive entrance, from which they could see part of the house beyond the thick rhododendron foliage that followed the bend in the drive.

As they walked on and the house came into full view, Jane exclaimed, 'What a beautiful house. I rather thought it would be.'

He looked at her affectionately. 'Would you like a house like this?'

Jane screwed her face in mock doubt. 'Umm, well ...'

They both laughed.

The house most certainly did look attractive. It was a large house with a white stucco frontage and had windows with diagonally shaped leads on both levels, with a recessed front door and porch. An additional charming feature was the two dormer windows nestled beneath the eaves and slightly pro-jecting out with an eyebrow roof.

A ring at the front door brought Paul out to greet them.

'Hello Paul,' they said in unison.

Paul kissed Jane and turned to embrace his friend. 'It is so good to see both of you again.'

After unpacking their bags in the rooms set aside for them, they joined Paul downstairs. The room they entered was large yet intimate, and comfortably furnished with a conker-coloured carpet. There were books on open shelves around the room, and a black cat lay luxuriating on one of the soft chairs. On two of the white walls were reproduction pictures, and Burren imme-diately recognised William Robert's *Woman and a Cat*. The room conveyed warmth and fraternity.

'Now tell me all about what has been going on back at base,' said Paul, before checking himself by saying. 'No, let me first of all offer you both a drink.'

They clinked glasses to one another's future. 'Now tell me.'

Burren related all that had been happening: their campaign-ing efforts during the election, his own decision to go on and take a degree ...

Paul interrupted him. 'You are so right to do that, John. I was wondering if you had made up your mind.' He turned to Jane, 'He is right, don't you think so?'

'I am sure he is right.' And she added mischievously, 'Though he has already solved most of the world's problems.'

Paul laughed heartily. 'She is going to keep your feet firmly on the ground, my lad.'

Knowing by now Jane's way of bringing him down to earth, Burren was able to share the joke. He continued by telling Paul what he knew he would be keen to hear: that the Socialist Society had increased its membership, was doing well and in good hands with continued Morton representation.

'And what has been happening here in your life at LSE?' He looked at his friend with a broad grin. 'I gather you've not got involved with the Labour Club.'

Paul said that his life was very different now from the previous two years. He lived at home and therefore was not part of LSE in the same way as it was for others. The Labour Club? 'Well!' he laughed a little ruefully, 'it is not the Socialist Society. The Labour Club at LSE is very hard-headedly political. It is very institutional and not interested in political ideas or any other ideas. Very good for advancing a political career though.'

He turned to Jane and smiled, his old charming smile. 'What has your life been like, Jane? Apart from being with this fellow,' he glanced at his friend.

Jane related a few tales about the Literary Society, explained that she had encouraged Burren to come along, and she mentioned how she and Jasmine had exchanged thoughts and ideas about literature. She said with a smile that in the last few weeks, Wordsworth had made his presence felt.

Paul laughed merrily. 'I just love it. Jane has such style.'

Burren seized on the mention of Jasmine to say to Paul, 'I didn't know that you and Jasmine were so well known to one another. You really are a cunning old rascal. You kept that very quiet throughout the whole year.'

Paul laughed to himself whilst he refilled their glasses.

'I was simply being discreet and respecting Jasmine's position.'

He took a sip from his glass and then casually said, 'She did say she might pop round to join us for a drink.'

This slight turn in the conversation away from student affairs and towards home life led Paul to indicate the domestic arrangements for the evening. He said that his father would be joining them for dinner. Paul explained that Mrs Bornley, who was a family friend and who came in occasionally to help prepare a meal and make arrangements for his father when he was entertaining, was cooking the evening meal.

Paul returned to Burren's principal reason for coming to London by asking him,

'How did your meeting at Transport House go? You have done very well there, John.' And with a sly smile he added, 'I can see you as Foreign Secretary.'

They laughed at the make-believe world.

Burren went on to say that he had some reservations about Michael Jenkins, and mentioned that he was not sure the Labour Party was serious about the policy review.

'Well, we always wonder whether they are serious about reviewing things,' said Paul.

Burren asked if he might make a phone call as he wanted to check something with Michael Jenkins.

Left alone Paul and Jane continued to talk about their lives over the past year. Jane liked Paul and they talked easily together. Nevertheless, she felt that beneath the outward charm and assurance that Paul exuded there was unhappiness. On second thoughts, 'unhappiness' was perhaps not sufficient. She had noticed before that, when caught off guard, there was something more akin to an underlying sadness in Paul. She thought she saw that sadness again now.

The cat raised itself from the seat of the chair and after tidying its coat with a dampened paw walked majestically towards the door and out of the room. Jane commented on what a beautiful creature it was, and said that she supposed it was a family cat – everyone's favourite. Paul replied that was true, though it had been especially his mother's cat. There was a peculiar emptiness behind Paul's remark: dejection mixed with painful nostalgia. Something had caused this emptiness and Jane guessed at what it was.

She scanned the room and turned back to Paul. 'This must have been a delightful home for a boy. Did you grow up here?'

'Yes, I did. They were happy days. My mother always used to say that it was a happy family that made the house enjoyable.' Jane saw the anguish appear in Paul's face as he sought to cope with his emotion.

'I think I understand.'

He forced a smile. 'I still find it difficult to talk about my mother.'

Quietly she asked, 'Would you like to talk now that we are alone?' She waited. 'I can see that something has hurt you very deeply.'

He looked at Jane. 'Yes, my mother died here.'

She saw the infinite sadness in the eyes.

'Do you want to tell me?' she said softly.

Paul explained how close he had been to his mother. He was her only son. She had died after a long struggle throughout which he witnessed the slow deterioration of her mind as well as body. It had left him and his father utterly devastated. His sister had coped much better and had readjusted her life – marriage had helped her. But even after this lapse of time since his mother's death, he found it difficult to control the welling emotion taking hold of his voice. Jane spontaneously reached out and put her arms round him and hugged him tightly.

Then slowly releasing him she asked, 'When did she die?'

'It was a few months before I went to Morton. Her death left my father drained of life. She meant everything to him. She was his wife, confidant and friend, and lover – just everything. It left him crushed. So I didn't really want to leave him at that stage, but he insisted and told me that I must go, though he had no great love for Morton.'

He looked wistfully out into the room. 'I still miss her so. I tell myself that I shouldn't after this time, but I do. It left me feeling so hollow. I've not spoken about it much. I haven't told John.'

Again Jane held him close to her and whispered, 'It is no use my telling you that I know how you feel, because I don't. Both of my parents are still alive and I know that if either of them were to die I would be shattered, but I haven't experienced it.'

She looked into his face and gently smiled assurance. 'But you have good friends and John and I will be here for you. John admires you, you know that. He would want to help you mend.' She held his hand and stood back. 'Enjoy your home again, Paul, as your mother would want you to.'

Mrs Bornley came into the room and Paul quickly regained his composure. She said that she was now leaving. The meal was ready and had only to be served. That was to be Paul's job, she said with a broad smile towards Jane. Burren returned to the room and Paul quickly introduced both of them to Mrs Bornley before she left.

Not long afterwards, Paul's father joined them and introduced himself. He asked if Jasmine was coming. Paul looked at his watch and said that she hadn't phoned but he thought that it was now unlikely. Mr Jenkins expressed his regret at this, smiled benignly and helped himself to a drink, enquiring of the others if they wished to join him. He then went and sat in the chair previously occupied by the cat, and asked both Jane and Burren what they had been doing in London.

Burren said that he had been to a meeting at Transport House as he was now going to be involved in the review of Labour's foreign policy. Mr Jenkins was mildly interested but echoed what had already been said about the reluctance of the Labour Party to revise anything.

Then turning to Jane with a smile he said, 'But that wasn't very interesting for you perhaps.'

Jane explained that she hadn't been to the Labour Party but had visited places of interest, including the National Portrait Gallery.

'Good,' said Mr Jenkins, stroking the black cat that had returned to his lap seeking affection. 'It is always good to see people visiting our galleries.'

Jane assumed from this that Mr Jenkins was on one or other governing body.

Over dinner, Paul's father related anecdotes and vignettes of some well-known trade union leaders. He was shortish in stature, powerfully built, and had smooth silver hair cut closely to his head. It was easy to see how, once he started to speak, he would command attention. His speech, with its sense of timing, pause for affect, and accompanied by the slightest of impediments, was that of an actor. He was by turns charming, amusing and indiscreet, as only someone of his age and achievement can afford to be. Yet he in no way dominated the table, and clearly was respectful of other, younger views. Paul brought in the food wearing an apron, and his father teasingly referred to him as the waiter. It was quite clear that there was an excellent relationship between father and son.

Burren was keen to ask Paul's father about his involvement in the Spanish Civil War, but there was not a sufficient gap in the conversation for him to do this. In any case, Mr Jenkins seemed reluctant, or less interested, to talk politics. Rather, it was the arts that he wished to talk about, and especially literature. He was fascinated to learn of Jane's studies and whenever he turned to her it was to enquire about one or other modern writer. When Paul and Burren were talking together Burren overheard Mr Jenkins telling Jane how much he enjoyed talking about books with Jasmine.

Paul teased his father about some of the cases he had lost and this had led his father to recall some of the cases himself. The success that he had achieved was however apparent in his manner. There was that indefinable element that makes for self-assurance, which Burren had recognised in Paul too when they had first met.

The evening broke up with Mr Jenkins saying to Burren and Jane that he had enjoyed their company and that they were always welcome to come and stay at his home.

As they were going to their rooms Paul said to his friend, 'Be sure and let me know what you decide. If you choose LSE you are most welcome to come and stay here. I've talked with my father and he agrees.' He laughed. 'You take your turn with the cooking of course.'

Burren laughed and said that he was a good cook, going back to his navy days.

'Ugh,' Jane groaned. But she was pleased to see the two men together.

On their way back from London on the train, Jane said, 'I think you should try for LSE.'

The Morton years were moving inexorably to a close. For Burren and his contemporaries most of the examinations were now completed and the results were eagerly awaited. Some were confident that they had done well, whilst others expressed much the same doubt that had dogged them all the way through. There was no denying that it had been an uphill struggle for some. Unused to education at this level, there had been too little time to catch up with the years of neglect. Nevertheless, successful or not in conventional terms, almost without exception the Morton students would say that they had enjoyed the experience beyond measure.

That experience, Burren reflected, had consisted not only in having access to the best that Morton with the university had to offer, but also in the myriad activities that were at hand. It resided too in the enrichment of endless discussions on current topics, lasting at times well into the early hours, when deeply held views were exposed and scrutinised, with emotions left in tatters as personal opinion gave way in the face of unremitting sorties. It witnessed as well the guile of egos competing for influence and preferment. But friendships too were forged and would last beyond the moment. Whatever awaited them in the future, Morton would mark a deeply ingrained reference point in their lives.

Now there was nothing more to be done but wait and be judged. Some of them were staying on, Burren included, to find out their examination results before returning home to renew links with the past – or to start afresh. Others were already leaving; bags were packed and trains dispatched them to all parts of the country. Burren said goodbye to Frank Bainwell and they vowed to keep in touch with each other in the future. He asked Frank to give his good wishes to Maureen Styles if he met her again at some Labour Party meeting. Maureen had written to the three men of her post-lunch tea gatherings and wished each of them well. She told of how much she had initially missed being at Morton but was now well settled into her social work.

Chris Megson and Burren made a farewell visit to the Rose & Crown and took a long backward look over the past two years. Their thoughts drifted back to the first evening they had met, and though not openly acknowledged, they both knew they had been competing with each other. Burren told Chris that he had now decided to go to university, and Chris said he hoped Burren would choose the same one as himself.

The muscular figure of Bill Williams had stopped by on his way out. 'So this is your eyrie,' exclaimed Bill. 'I wondered where you went to think those higher thoughts. I enjoyed your company at meal times, John. Helped my digestion. And the intellectual bit was quite stimulating.' The smile was mischievous.

Burren roared with laughter. 'I enjoyed your company too, Bill. I especially enjoyed being witness to your patriarchal control of the table, and the way in which you determinedly ploughed on with unquestioning loyalty to the Labour Party when weaker souls failed.'

One by one they left. Burren was sure that he was now the only one left in the building. He passed by Jasmine's office and looked in. She was seated behind her desk, looking much the same as when he first saw her there.

She looked up. 'Hello. Are you leaving now?'

'Not quite,' he said. 'I'm going to wait for my results and I need to see Sean Halloran again.' He smiled and gave a dismissive sweep of his hand. 'And then I shall be gone.' He could not resist adding, 'No more obeisance to the rules. Free to disclose all!'

She looked at him with a sly smile. 'You do not change.'

He detected affection in her voice.

'I believe you may be going to London,' she said.

'Maybe, and if I do we may continue to meet from time to time as I shall be staying with Paul Jenkins and his father, whom I believe you know rather well. And you will see Jane too from time to time.'

'That will be nice,' said Jasmine.

He left Morton and stepped out on to the street. It was still and deserted; neither traffic nor pedestrians trespassed on the stillness. Even the leaves on the trees lining each side of the road were still – it was a stillness that did not judge or counsel.

Each individual life could be lived anew. Nature, itself remorseless, invited change. He reached the spot where Jane and her bicycle had fallen at his feet. He stopped for a moment and felt the stillness, then turned and looked back down the road along which he had walked, the past filling his thoughts. He looked ahead and briskly went on his way to meet Jane.